# RICO

# CANDICE WRIGHT

Cover Design by ©RAINY DAY ARTWORK

Editing by: Tanya Oemig & Ms. Correct All

Formatting by: Gina Wynn

*This book is dedicated to coffee. Thank you for staying strong and urging me on, helping me through homeschooling, quarantine and keeping my murder spree record to 0 days.*

Every shot that kills ricochets.

~ GILBERT PARKER

# ASHES TO ASHES

# CHAPTER ONE

L ying in the stillness of the dark room, I stare out into the stormy night sky. It's humid tonight. The open window lets in a balmy breeze that tickles my skin, but it doesn't warm me. Not when I can still feel the icy imprint of his hands on me. I take a deep breath, the scent of rain beckoning me outside with the promise of washing me clean. No more fingerprints or bruises or bite marks, all of them rinsed away by the downpour of crying skies, the heavens weeping for the girl who has no tears of her own left to cry.

I was naïve in thinking I would get a reprieve tonight. How silly to assume that burying my mother would grant me one night to grieve in solitude. I left the wake downstairs, walking up the staircase with heavy steps, hindered by the rustling fabric of the dress Clyde chose for me to wear. A fourteen-year-old walks into a funeral wearing a cocktail dress and a fake smile. It sounds like a bad joke, but this joke is my life.

I could hear the whispers as I sat in the hard-wooden chair, watching as they lowered my mother's white, flower-adorned coffin into the ground. Each shovel of dirt thrown over her casket echoed the mud being thrown over me. Nasty words scoring marks into my skin, made by catty women and perverted men who should have tried to help me. Instead, they cast me in the role of temptress and waited with bated breath for me to take my mother's place.

Not bothering to change after I made my escape, I kicked off my shoes and crawled onto my bed, the stupid dress billowing out around me as I grieved in private while hordes of fake mourners milled around downstairs drinking champagne and eating canapés.

It wasn't until later, when the crowd had thinned out a little and the voices that floated up from downstairs seemed fewer, that I realized my mistake.

Dresses made for easy access. Not that jeans stopped him, but psychologically I felt safer wearing them.

It didn't matter. I didn't fight back, didn't tell him no, or flinch when he told me with whiskey-laced breath how beautiful I was, because I knew it could be worse. He had crossed so many lines, but never the final one, the one I wasn't sure I would survive. So, to keep my virginity intact, I stopped fighting.

Maybe that made me complicit. Perhaps it made me a whore like the catty women below said about me. The ones who passed their judgments as they blew their rich sugar daddies and fucked their gardeners on the side.

But they had no clue what it was like to be me. Clyde had pulled me out of school under the guise of being homeschooled. It was a ruse so there was someone home to take care of Mama and someone around for Clyde to amuse himself with whenever the moment arose. I had lost the few friends I had, my brother was long gone, and now my mother, my last tie to the little girl I once was, is dead.

A bolt of jagged lightning illuminates the night sky just as I hear the telltale creak of someone stepping on the loose floorboard outside my room.

I tense, biting my lip as I hear the door open behind me for the second time tonight. I close my eyes at their approach, feigning sleep, forcing my body not to react to the cold fingers on my arm.

Even with a house full of people, I know it's him, his touch as familiar to me as my own, his icy, frigid skin mirroring the coldness of his heart. Fingertips tuck a strand of hair behind my ear, hovering for a moment before a cough from the doorway draws his attention.

"She's asleep?" the lightly accented voice asks. Italian, perhaps.

"Yes, so keep your voice down," Clyde replies, low and somber.

"And she is untouched?" the man persists, not lowering his voice at all.

I'd laugh at that if I weren't so terrified. I'm many things, but untouched is not one of them.

"I told you she was and she will remain so until I hand her over to you in the morning, but tonight G, she is still mine, so do not overstep," Clyde warns, his voice filled with anger.

"Maybe," the other man concedes, "but I paid for a virgin, and that's what I expect to receive. You can have your last night with her, but after that, forget she ever existed. Unlike you, I don't feel the need to trade in my toys every few years. I like to keep them until I break them."

Clyde sighs, stepping away from the bed, his heavy footsteps moving toward the door.

"Yes, G, I am well aware of the deal we made. Now let's finish our drinks. I'm being rude to my guests," he finishes, closing the door behind him.

I strain to listen over the sound of my wildly beating heart that threatens to crack my ribs.

I guess I know why he never crossed that line when he so happily crossed all the others. I wouldn't have been worth as much if he had broken me in.

The storm is raging now, both outside my window and in the darkest part of my mind. A scream builds within, rivaling any a banshee might make, but I swallow it down and bite my lip until I taste blood. The little girl inside me urges me to run, to push open the window and disappear into the night. But then what will happen to the little girl who comes after me?

Climbing from the bed, I grip my hands into fists. Nobody was there for me. They ignored my cries and turned their backs on me. I won't ever be the person who stands by and lets something like that happen, not if I can stop it.

I rip the dress from my body, tearing the fabric in the process, and dump it in a pile on the bedroom floor. Rummaging through my dresser, I grab the first nightshirt I touch, pulling it over my head before grabbing my backpack from the back of my desk chair. I empty the contents on my desk. A cherry Chapstick makes its bid for freedom by rolling off the edge and landing on the carpet soundlessly. Walking on silent footsteps to the door, I pull it open gently, checking that the coast is clear, then step over the creaky floorboard and tiptoe down the dark hallway to Clyde's office at the end.

Pushing the handle down, I find the door unlocked like I knew I would. Clyde thinks he's untouchable. I'm going to show him how wrong he is.

I don't waste time as I move across the thick carpet beneath my feet, feeling oddly proud of myself for all the times I spied on Clyde. I must have always known deep down this day would come.

Lifting the picture of a forest landscape off the wall, I place it near my feet and focus on the safe hidden behind it.

*0817*, Mom's birthday.

I type it in, tensing when it beeps once, then I swing the door open.

The first thing I take is the money, ten stacks of cash

tightly bundled together with rubber bands and shove them into the backpack. Next, I take the ledger filled with names and numbers. I don't know what any of it means, but something tells me this thing might be valuable. Finally, I take the item I came here for, the gun. It's heavier than I thought it would be, looking large and intimidating in my small hand, and yet, a wave of comfort washes over me. It doesn't matter how small I am, how weak I am; this thing evens the battlefield. I shove it into the backpack and close the safe, placing the picture back over it.

Leaving the room the same way I found it, I close the door behind me as voices saying their goodbyes drift up the stairs.

I head back to my room and remove the gun, shoving it under my pillow before grabbing items I'll need. I only pack the essentials I can carry—underwear, socks, toothbrush, a handful of toiletries, and three changes of clothes. There is no space in the backpack for anything else.

Opening the desk drawer, I lift out the tattered copy of *Chicken Little* and run my fingertips over the cover reverently. How I wished for a different life. Shoving it back in the drawer, I slam it closed.

The temperature had dropped, the howling wind blowing in the window, making the white gauzy curtain flutter as if it's dancing to music only it can hear. I pull the curtain closed before climbing under the comforter, the inky blackness of the night wrapping itself around me like a welcome friend.

And I wait.

It doesn't take long, the lure of spending his last night with me too strong for him to ignore any longer.

This time I don't pretend I'm asleep or ignore his presence like a ghostly specter. I turn to face him, watching as he flicks on the lamp and bathes the room with an eerie glow.

I watch him gaze around, his face sad as he takes in the pink and white polka dot wallpaper, the white gloss furniture, the bed, and the white bedding with tiny pink flowers. It's a bedroom fit for a princess, something I never aspired to be, but then this room isn't about me, it's all about Clyde.

"Hello, pretty girl," he whispers when his lust-filled eyes finally land on mine. "Daddy has a special night planned for us."

I don't answer him. I stare at the handsome face my mother loved. The strong jaw, sharp cheekbones, and twinkling bright blue eyes all add to his appeal, but it's just a mask to hide the monster beneath. But he's not the only one wearing a mask, and tonight he's not the only monster in my bedroom.

He removes his clothes, cufflinks first, popping the silver ovals on my nightstand. His white shirt is next, followed by his suit pants, his shoes, and his socks.

"Clothes off, pretty girl, you know I don't like to wait," he scolds lightly.

I sit up and pull my nightshirt over my head without

protest, leaving me naked, my panties likely still in his jacket pocket where he shoved them after the first time he visited me tonight.

He smiles, a genuine one that lights up his entire face and makes the bile rush up the back of my throat, but I fight it down.

"So beautiful," he murmurs, sliding his boxers down to expose his hard length.

I hold my breath as he reaches out to twist a strand of my hair around his finger, my hand slipping under my pillow, my fingers wrapping around the handle of the gun.

See, Clyde is an evil man in the worst sense of the word. He doesn't just use his body to control mine; he turns my own against me, forcing my pleasure, reveling in my responses to his touch. He doesn't just make me hate him; he makes me hate myself.

For a long time, I thought it was my fault that I must have wanted it because good girls don't come when they are being assaulted. That's what he told me, that it's not rape when you like it. For the longest time, I believed him until I stumbled across a blog online written by a rape survivor. Her words changed something inside me, made me see that Clyde's words were just another way of hurting me, raping my mind right along with my body.

Well, it ends today.

"Lay back on the bed, legs spread," he orders, moving around to the end of the bed.

I do as he asks, moving on autopilot, my hand gripping the gun as he stares at me.

"What's going to happen to me now?" I ask, wanting to know what his lie will be.

"Hush now, that's for tomorrow. Tonight is all about pleasure." He smirks, climbing on the bed, kneeling between my legs.

"I know what you're planning on doing," I whisper, the words slipping out before I can stop them. "You won't get away with it, people will wonder where I am, they'll ask questions," I tell him as his large hand slides up my thigh, but we both know that's not true. Everyone I care about is gone.

"I forget how innocent you are sometimes, especially with a body like this. I'll tell people you ran away, but I doubt anyone will ask. Nobody will remember you, Vida, you're a ghost," he says lightly, as if he's talking about the weather. I think it might be his tone that snaps the last of my restraint.

"Funny you should say that." I pull the gun free from the pillow and point it at his head.

His eyes widen a fraction as his hand pauses on my thigh. I let my hate for this man fuel me and pull the trigger with zero hesitation.

My hand shakes, the noise sounding like a bomb that makes my ears feel like they are bleeding.

"I guess this makes us both ghosts now."

# CHAPTER TWO

*I kick my feet, my toes just skimming over the dusty ground as the swing moves back and forth, the squeak of the rusty chain sounding far louder than usual in the dark, empty park.*

*The distant sounds of a couple arguing from somewhere across the trailer park is joined by the sorrowful howl of a dog chained up in someone's yard, lonely and forgotten about. I might only be eight, but I knew the feeling well. I want to howl at the moon myself, but it wouldn't change anything.*

*A snap of a twig behind me captures my attention, and even though I know it's not safe out in the park alone this late at night, I don't panic.*

*I know it's my brother Drake, he always seems to know where to find me.*

*The swing beside mine creaks as he sits down next to me, his long legs crossed at the ankle. He didn't come here to swing; he came here to talk. But I don't want to hear what he has to say, I already know. I heard Mama crying softly in the kitchen earlier when they were talking.*

*"It won't be so bad, Chicken Little. We can write to each other and I'll be back for a visit before you know it," he whispers, nudging my foot with his.*

*I bite my lip hard to stop myself from crying. I'm a big girl now; crying is for babies.*

*"But it won't be the same. Can't I go with you? I'll be good, I swear." I turn to look at him, but it's too dark to see his face.*

*"You need to stay and look after Mama," he answers, standing up and making the swing creak again. "Come on. Let's get you home."*

*He tugs me off the swing and picks me up, and even though I'm mad, I wrap my arms and legs tightly around him. Burying my head into his neck, I take a deep breath, smelling the shower gel he always uses and the faint hint of cigarettes he smokes when he thinks I'm not around.*

*Maybe if I hold on tight enough, he'll stay with me. He's the only one who makes pancakes the way I like them and catches the cockroaches when they scurry across my bedroom floor. Who will do that when he's gone?*

*He carries me all the way back to our trailer, the voices of Mr. and Mrs. Beckett yelling, getting louder as we pass their place. The sound of something hitting the wall and glass breaking makes me jump, but my brother just holds me tighter.*

*My mom opens the door as soon as we get there and Drake carries me inside, popping me onto the kitchen counter.*

"Vida Roberts! What have I told you about running off like that? Especially when it's dark outside. It's not safe out there," she scolds, but I only have eyes for my brother who stands in front of me with a hand on either side of me, bracketing me in.

"It's okay, Ma," he answers her, but she shakes her head; her red hair that's the same as mine bounces around her shoulders when she throws her hands up in the air.

"It is not okay, Drake. When you're gone, there won't be anyone around to chase after her, because lord knows I won't be. She needs to learn this now before she gets hurt," she snaps.

"I'm sorry, Mama," I tell her before she spends the next ten minutes shouting and crying.

"I just worry about you, Vida, that's all. You're my baby, and with your brother joining the army, you're all I have left." She moves from angry to sad quickly, like always.

"Jesus, Ma, I'm not dying. I'll be back when I can, and I'll send money to help. Especially with Chicken Little here growing like a weed," he teases me, tugging on a lock of my hair.

I huff and cross my arms. "I am not a weed. You're just jealous because you know I'll be taller than you one day."

"Sure, Vida, whatever you say," he laughs, his dark eyes twinkling.

I growl at him, which makes him laugh harder. Brothers are pains in the butt.

"You'll see, Drakey Lakey, one day I'll be so tall I'll be able to touch the ceiling," I inform him as he ruffles my hair and moves over to the fridge that hums too loud and keeps me awake at night. Sometimes I dream it's a robot monster that comes awake when everyone else is asleep and wants to kill me, so I hide in my bed where it's safe. Everyone knows monsters can't hurt you if you hide underneath the covers.

"How about I make us some pancakes, then I'll read to you for a little while, okay?" he offers, smiling.

I pout. "Fine, but I'm still mad. You'd better write to me every day."

"I'll write to you twice a day if you are good while I'm gone. No fighting or sassing Mom, okay? You're my best girls. You have to stick together," he says, grabbing the pan from the cupboard next to the stove.

I look at Mama, who is watching Drake with a soft smile on her face.

"Team Drake." I smile. It's small because I'm sad still, but I want Drake to be proud of me.

"Team Drake, I like that." He grins. "What do you think, Ma?"

Mama steps up beside the counter next to me and runs a hand through my hair. She smiles, and hers is a little sad too, but she nods anyway.

"Team Drake, it is."

We eat the best pancakes in the world and watch SpongeBob before I start struggling to keep my eyes open.

"Time for bed, Chicken Little," Drake whispers to me, flicking the television off. Mama went to bed earlier, tired from working all day in the diner down the road, but she let me sit up with Drake for a little while longer, even though it's already past my bedtime.

"Just five more minutes," I whisper even though I really am tired.

*He chuckles, making my head wobble where it's resting on his shoulder.*

*"Tell me a story." I snuggle closer to him, soaking in his warmth.*

*He sighs, but he doesn't complain. He doesn't ask which story either. It's always Chicken Little, a favorite of mine since I was tiny, and even though I'm a big girl now, I still love the way he does the voices.*

*I lie there with a smile on my face listening to the tale of the chicken who wins everyone over in the end, even though the other animals thought he was weird. It makes me feel better about being the weird kid at school. Not that I needed friends, I had Drake.*

I wake with a start, rolling over with a groan at how stiff I feel. I sit up and try to shrug off the dream that haunts me. After everything I've survived, I have no idea why this one hurts me so much more than the rest. Maybe it's because it wasn't long after that I figured out Drake had been telling me the kid-friendly version of my once favorite story based on the movie instead of the original tale. Perhaps if he had read me the true version, where everyone gets eaten by the manipulative fox, I would have known from the beginning that not every story has a happy ending.

Maybe then I could have prepared myself for the darkness that plagued me. Instead, I found out in the worst way possible that the covers on my bed didn't keep the monsters away and when heroes leave, they never return. I would have known that when the sky falls, sometimes there is no one left to save you. You have to save yourself.

# CHAPTER THREE

You adapt quickly in this life, or you die. It's survival of the fittest. It doesn't matter if it's foraging for discarded food in dumpsters or shooting the big bad wolf dead on the same bed he debased you. Your will to survive has to be stronger than the ever-present fear in your mind and the longing for escape that only death can offer.

That knowledge, that will to survive, is what got me through the first six brutal months on the streets.

I left that house on the hill, still wearing Clyde's blood. I should have showered, that would have been smarter, but in a twisted way, his blood on my skin gave me strength. It made me feel like a warrior who had slain the beast. I earned every smear, every splatter, every drop coating my body, and I wore it proudly like a talisman showing the world that had tried and failed to swallow me whole—I survived.

I moved around the house like the ghost he made me, turning on the gas of the stove as I made sure nobody else was there. Making my way to his wet bar, I took the bottles of his favorite whiskey and doused my room with it, covering Clyde, offering him a farewell drink as his soul made its way back to hell.

Knowing I needed to get out of there, I got dressed, layering up my clothes and pulling a black beanie over my distinctive auburn hair, all while feeling strangely detached from the death scene a few feet from me. I had killed a man and not by accident. I'd collected his gun with one aim; shoot to kill. So why wasn't I feeling something, or anything for that matter? I know I should, at the very least, be freaking out, but I felt calm and in control for perhaps the first time in forever.

I gathered my things, threw a lit match, and after watching the flames engulf the bed and lick their way up the pink and white polka dot wallpaper, I left without looking back.

I'd just made it to the bottom of the hill when an explosion rent the night sky, lighting up the house of horrors as it burned out of control.

That's when I realized the rain had stopped, the chaos of swirling winds and rumbling thunder had disappeared as if someone had pressed pause. There would be no rain to douse the flames and the downed trees would hinder the firetrucks I could hear wailing in the distance.

I felt powerful, vengeful too, but I wasn't ashamed of that.

I had saved myself and protected the girl who would come next. I didn't feel like a murderer even though I undoubtedly was. I felt like a Valkyrie, and that's when I realized that although the storm might have stopped raging around us, it was very much alive inside me.

Wrapping most of the money, a change of clothes, the paperwork, and the gun in a plastic bag, I buried it somewhere I knew it wouldn't be found. I stripped off a couple of layers of clothing and tucked them into my pack, moving one of the knives I had snagged from the kitchen into the pouch pocket of my black hoodie so I was prepared if I needed it. Carrying a murder weapon around with me wasn't an option, but I'd be damned if I left myself unprotected ever again.

That was the day Vida died, and the day Viddy was born.

Now, after a year of being on the streets, I had a sort of routine. I never slept in the same place two nights in a row. I picked sites easy for my slight frame to squeeze into but that would be problematic for others. And I chose places that wouldn't draw attention to me when I had nightmares. The thought of being trapped in my head while someone messed with my body gave me heart palpitations, which is likely why I had adjusted to surviving on around three hours of sleep a night.

During the day, I went to the library and studied. I might not be able to get qualifications, with being a dead girl and all, but I could still learn, and I did. I absorbed the words like a sponge, learning what I could from how to cultivate a garden to building a business. Today, I was a nobody, and that was fine, it suited my needs for now. Until I was eighteen, I needed to skate under the radar, but one day, things would be different. I would be somebody; I just hadn't figured out who yet.

"Ten minutes until closing, dear," the librarian calls, making me look up.

"What are you working on today?" she asks with a smile. I like Mary. I think she might have clued into the fact I live on the streets, despite me keeping myself relatively clean and tidy. There is only so much I could do. I used restrooms to wash up, but it wasn't the same as having a shower, and washing clothes was a nightmare.

Even so, she never treated me differently. She didn't follow me around like I might steal the books, and on Tuesdays and Thursdays when the library hosted coffee mornings, she always snuck me coffee and cake.

"Oh, nothing much, just world domination," I answer with a slight smile.

"That's nice, dear." She chuckles before turning to a young woman with a little kid whose arms are filled with books ready to check out.

I pack up my things, place the books back on the shelves, and head to the restrooms before leaving. I take care of business, then take a quick wash and brush my teeth, changing into the second set of clothes. These are black and thicker, helping me blend into the city once night falls. I studiously avoid my reflection in the little mirror above the sink, knowing what I'll see. Being homeless means being hungry. They go hand in hand, and on my frame it shows on my gaunt face, in the way my cheekbones stand out, and in the dark hollows of my eyes.

I need to eat tonight. There is no way around it. If I don't fuel my body, I'll be too weak to fend off an attack should I need to. Taking a deep breath, I pull my shoulders back and let my fuck you mask slip into place.

Waving goodbye to Mary, I head out onto the street. It's busy at this time of day as commuters head home from work. I pull my jacket tighter around me as the wind picks up and make my way downtown to the market district. It's around now that they pack away, the crowds having finished buying their wares, heading off to collect children, or start dinner.

I move quickly, weaving in and out of people, careful not to draw too much attention to myself. The darkness falls quickly, bringing with it the cold, and when I finally make it, most of the stalls have packed up and left.

I move to the one at the very end and smile when I catch Poppy's eyes.

Poppy is the stallholder of a small booth full of homemade baked goods and jams. At seventy-four, she loves interacting with the busy crowds of people after losing her husband Jack the winter before. Having hands riddled with arthritis meant packing away, folding tables, and loading everything into the back of her van was sometimes too much for her.

"I was wondering if I would see you tonight." She smiles, looking relieved.

"I lost track of time," I reply honestly. It happens when I'm reading although I try to be more conscious of it on Fridays and Saturdays when the market is on.

"That's okay. I was young once too. I remember what it was like," she teases. She has her assumptions about me. Unlike Mary, I think Poppy just thinks I have a tough time at home, not that I don't have a home at all. I don't correct her. People can think what they like.

"How are your hands?" I question, looking over at her as she places leftover sandwiches and cakes in a carrier bag.

"They're fine." She brushes me off with a wave, her long gray hair falling forward as she moves.

"Poppy," I warn, crossing my arms over my chest.

She sighs, her slim shoulders dropping. "They hurt today. It's the cold. It makes everything ten times harder than usual but Viddy, this is my cross to bear. We adjust, it's what we do."

Well, I can't argue with that.

"Sit." I point at the wood stool beside the table. She doesn't argue, which in itself shows me how much today has taxed her.

I set about stacking any leftovers into the large Tupperware tubs, placing them onto the front seat of the van, hoping my mouth will stop watering and my stomach will stop cramping now they're out of sight.

Next, I fold down the tables and slide them in the back

with the large wooden sign and the chalkboard showing the prices of each item. I don't make idle chit chat, and after doing this for the last three months, Poppy doesn't expect it.

"There we go, all done except for the stool," I tell her as she stands so I can grab it.

"You are a godsend, child. Here, these are for you." She hands me the bag of food she made up earlier, and I take it without a second thought. There is no place on the streets for pride. Pride will get you killed.

"Thanks, Poppy. I'll come by early in the morning and help you set up for the day."

"You don't need—"

I cut her off with a scowl. "I'll be here early to help you set up," I repeat.

She stares at me, her eyes dipping to my worn clothes and my thin—*too thin*—frame, and for the first time, I think she sees me.

"Okay, Viddy, see you then." I nod and head away before she can ask me any questions that would require me to lie to her.

# CHAPTER FOUR

I eat the cheese and ham sandwiches as I make my way back across town. Once upon a time, I hated cheese. Now, in a constant state of hunger, nothing ever tasted so good.

My head has been all over the place today, thanks to dreaming about Drake. I don't think about him much anymore, the pain is still very much like a dull ache in my chest, but when he sneaks in and takes over my dreams, I'm helpless to stop the memories from pouring in. And that just pisses me off.

To keep my heart guarded against the onslaught of emotions that particular snapshot in time can invoke, I remind myself of all the letters I sent him that went unanswered.

I remember every word I ever wrote, every plea he

ignored. He broke every promise he ever made and left me to fend for myself against the worst kind of predator. No, there is no room left for him in this battered heart of mine, I just wish my brain would catch up.

Turning the corner, I head toward the park when a muffled cry snags my attention, followed by the sound of scuffling feet. My head snaps in the direction of the alley that separates the laundromat from the Chinese restaurant that closed down last month. I palm the knife in my pocket and listen again, and when I hear a terrified whimper, I run toward it.

"Come on, baby, just a taste. I'll make it good for you," a rough voice coaxes as it tugs at the clothing of a teenage girl around my age.

She must sense me there because she turns her head, her horror-filled eyes begging me to help.

Something in my brain flickers. Her inky hair becomes red, her assailant's jeans and T-shirt morphs into a black suit. The past and present collide, sparking a rage so volatile inside me I feel my blood boiling in my veins.

The next five minutes happen almost in slow motion, with me feeling like a bystander, watching myself shove my knife into the asshole's back before pulling it out and pushing it in a second time.

He howls in agony, the sound soothing something inside me. I watch him drop to the ground with disinterest before turning to the girl. Her face is so white she looks like a corpse. I slide the knife back into my pocket and reach out my hand. She looks at it, taking in the blood covering my fingers and down to the man who has now gone quiet. Slowly, she reaches out a shaky hand of her own and grabs mine tightly.

I don't waste time introducing myself, I pull her behind me and run. I run until my legs hurt and my lungs burn, dragging the girl until we are in the part of town that is being rejuvenated or some crap like that. The children's playground is closed as the area beside it has become a makeshift building site. I pull her around to the section of fencing that's cut and bent at an angle just wide enough for us both to squeeze through and lead us to the massive climbing frame, slipping inside one of the colorful tubes that children crawl through as they chase their friends. For tonight, it's the perfect hiding place.

We sit in silence for a few minutes, both of us trying to catch our breath, our fingers still linked together, neither of us willing to let go.

It's a strange thing being one of the disregarded souls that wander the busy streets. We crave invisibility, and yet the absence of human touch becomes unbearably lonely at times. It always makes me wonder how in a city of thousands a person can go unseen and unheard as if they just up and disappeared. They don't of course, it's just once you become one of the many homeless people struggling to survive out here, people look away and stop listening to your pleas for help. It's 21$^{st}$ Century magic, where a human can stand in a crowd and yet be invisible to everyone around them.

"You okay?" I finally ask her. She doesn't answer me, though.

"What's your name?" When I get no reply, I tug on her hand, making her jump.

"I can't hear you," she mumbles, so quietly I almost miss it.

"I... I'm deaf. I can't hear anything." She sniffs. I squeeze her hand tighter, letting her know I understand, but I don't. These streets will eat you alive on a good day; they don't care who you are or what you did to end up as a throwaway kid, but to try to navigate the dangers without one of your basic senses? God, I can't even imagine.

"Thank you for what you did back there. I can't go through that again." She sobs, so I move closer and tug her until she rests her head on my shoulder, letting her cry herself out.

Letting another person in was something I never planned to do, but feeling her crying against me, I sense a kindred spirit in her. I know she can't be out here without protection; she'll end up pimped out at best or worse, raped and murdered.

No, we'll stick together, even if it's just for a little while.

I don't move other than to pull the foil blanket I lifted from the back of an ambulance from my backpack and wrap it around us. It's not perfect, but it's better than nothing.

I keep guard as she sleeps fitfully beside me. She cries out in her sleep so often that by the time the sun washes the sky with streaks of pink and purple, I have a pretty good idea what happened to her.

Nudging her awake, she jumps, looking around disorientated for a moment before she focuses on me.

"Hi," she offers shyly. She has dirt smeared across one cheek and the beginnings of a black eye, which likely came courtesy of the asshole from last night, but lord, this girl is beautiful.

"Hey," I reply, rolling my eyes when I remember she can't hear me.

"No, it's okay," she grabs my arms in response, "if you speak slowly and clearly, I can read your lips, but God, what I wouldn't do for pen and paper." She sighs.

"I'm Viddy," I tell her, making sure I say the words clearly.

She frowns. "Fiddy? Like 50 Cent says his name? Yo, I'm Fiddy," she imitates with some weird hand gesture, making me snort.

"Viddy," I repeat, fighting a grin.

"Viddy?" she says back. I nod, which makes her smile. "Hey, Viddy, I'm Megan." I grab the plastic bag from my backpack before rolling up the blanket and tucking it inside.

I reach inside the little bag and pull out a muffin and offer it to Megan, whose eyes light up.

"Oh my God." She snatches it from me, taking a huge bite before pausing and flushing with embarrassment.

"I'm so sorry," she says around a mouthful of food before

splitting the rest of the muffin in half and offering me some. I shake my head and point to her to eat it.

She narrows her eyes and practically shoves the damn thing in my mouth before I can protest—stubborn girl.

The smell of blueberries is too much for me to resist, so with a shrug, I snag it from her hands and eat it in three bites.

Once finished, I lead Megan down to the little stream that runs behind the park. The water is freezing, but it will do to wash our hands and faces, making sure any traces of blood from last night's events are gone.

We clean up as best we can before starting the trek back down to the market district. Megan gets more and more tense the closer we get to the alley from last night. I could have taken us another way, but I need to see if anyone is talking down there. I'd rather know right off the bat what I'm dealing with than have it coming back and biting us in the ass later.

Megan tugs on my arm, making me turn to look at her. Her face is pale. One of her hands balls up into a fist and presses against her mouth.

"My bag," she says a little too loud, making the two women standing on the corner chatting turn to look at us. Megan flushes with embarrassment before she lowers her voice and repeats herself.

"My bag. I forgot all about it last night with everything that happened. I must have left it in the alley."

"Fuck!" I run my hands over my face. "Is there anything in your bag that could identify you?"

She nods reluctantly.

"Shit," I curse. This is bad. Very fucking bad.

"Okay, here's what we'll do. The alleyway spills out onto Acorn Drive. It will take us down to the market district, but it will add about fifteen minutes onto our journey, and it passes through a not so nice neighborhood. At this time of the morning, it shouldn't be an issue, but you never know. We'll go see if we can find your bag, but if anything happens, we split. You keep going this way, and I'll take Acorn. I'll meet you down at the market. Find a woman called Poppy; her van has a huge red poppy on the side of it. Tell her I sent you to help her set up. If I don't make it there, for whatever reason, head back to the park we stayed at last night."

It isn't until I finish that I remember she can't hear me, and I was speaking way too fast for her to catch more than a few words. I go over it again, slowly this time adding in some actions when she frowns in confusion. Eventually, she gets the gist of what I'm saying because she straightens her shoulders and nods.

I link arms with her and chatter away, even knowing she can't hear, she doesn't need to. This is all for show, just two immature girls gossiping, likely about boys or school as they take a shortcut. It wouldn't do to tiptoe in like a comedic villain from a Scooby-Doo cartoon after all.

I scan the alley as we make our way down it, looking for the discarded bag, wondering why it seems longer today somehow. Movement catches my eye as a figure moves out of the shadows in front of us, making all my instincts move from red alert to DEFCON one.

Instinctively, I take a step in front of Megan as the shadow steps forward, revealing a man dressed from head to toe in black. He looks like what I'd imagine the devil to look like. Tall, with dark messy hair that's a touch too long and eyes the color of pennies, he has the kind of presence that demands attention. His full sensual lips kick up a little at the edge, a seductive tease that doesn't reach his eyes that says *I will fuck you before I fuck you up*. His face is the face you would expect to see on a movie screen, making women lose their minds and panties, sculpted to perfection with an expression that's as hard as granite.

"Interesting," he murmurs, the sound of his voice making my skin tingle with awareness. This man would not be as easy to take out as the others. I can feel Megan shaking behind me, so I cock my head, straighten my shoulders, and glare at him.

"I wish I could say the same. Who are you, and what do you want?" I cross my arms over my chest and lock my legs so they don't shake.

He lifts his arm. That's when I notice the ratty backpack in his hand.

"It seems you lost something." I don't react, knowing that he won't just hand it over out of the goodness of his heart.

"A funny thing happened here last night. A group of men stabbed someone who was doing a job for my boss. They took his product and left him for dead. Know anything about that?"

"About a group of men attacking someone? Not a damn thing," I reply honestly.

"Hmm...." He licks his lips, drawing my attention to his mouth.

"Care to explain this?" He holds the bag out for me to take, one eyebrow raised in a challenge.

"It's a bag. It holds things. I'm surprised you haven't figured that out for yourself."

He laughs, not a jovial sound though, one that sounds deep and ominous.

"Catch."

He tosses the bag, and it isn't until I reach out to grab it, I realize my mistake. I took my eyes off the threat, a mistake I vow never to make again as he grabs me, spinning me around and pulling me against his chest with his arm around my throat.

# CHAPTER FIVE

I throw the bag at Megan, who watches on with wide terror-filled eyes.

"Go!" I mouth silently to her. She shakes her head adamantly, but I scowl and mouth, "Run, I'll find you!" She must realize she can't help, so she snags the bag from the ground, gives me a tearful stare full of despair and regrets before she turns and runs.

"If you run, I kill her," he calls to her, but she doesn't turn back. For the first time since meeting Megan, I'm so grateful she's deaf.

"Damn, nice friend, you have there." The guy laughs, wrapping a hand in my hair and spinning me to face him.

This is where an average person would beg, body shaking with fear, but whatever made me normal died a long time ago. Now the only thing flooding my system is adrenaline and that familiar spark that wants me to hurt this man like he wants to hurt me.

"She's not my friend. I met her hours ago," I answer, not wanting him to send people out to track her down. Better he thinks she's long gone.

"And yet you stepped in front of her the second you lay eyes on me, why?" He cocks his head, genuinely curious. I stare into his eyes and realize he's not as old as I initially thought. It's just the way he holds himself and the malice that emanates from him. He must be in his early twenties, maybe?

"She has been hurt enough by men like you," I tell him dismissively, rolling my eyes. His grip tightens in my hair as he tilts my head back.

"Men like me? Tell me, sweetheart, what do you know about men like me?" he purrs with an edge of violence in his tone that licks over my skin and makes me tremble, only it's not from fear. There is something inside me that reacts to his dominance on a base level. The thought makes me want to both run and purr against him like a cat in heat.

"Men like you like to play with little girls like they are dolls, and when they break, and they always break, they get thrown aside for men like your friend last night to finish off." Shit, I knew I had said too much the second it was out, but it's too late now. His eyes sharpen at my words, his eyes on my mouth.

"So you do know what happened to Jimmy?"

I don't answer, so he yanks my head back hard.

"I have zero interest in little girls, sweetheart." He grins, pressing himself against me, letting me feel the evidence of his lie against my stomach.

"Yeah? So then tell me why your dick's hard for a fifteen-year-old."

He lets go of me so abruptly, I stumble. Dragging his eyes over me, he assesses me. I know what he sees, even starving to the point of malnutrition I have the body of a woman well beyond my years. Large firm breasts, flared hips, and a curvy ass all packed tightly on a five-foot-four frame.

"There is no way you're fifteen, not with a body like that," he argues. I just stare at him, with my hands on my hips. Which naturally draws his attention to them.

When he realizes I'm serious, he drops the cocky, seductive angle he was working and slips back into cold foot soldier mode.

"The boss wants to talk to you." He crosses his muscular arms over his chest.

"And if I refuse?" But I suspect I know the answer already.

"It's not a request. Besides, if by some sheer luck, you manage to slip away, I'll just hunt down your little *not* friend, and she can take your place," he taunts.

I twist my head, clicking my neck before nodding. "Okay, let's go."

My hands are cold and clammy, I'm still trembling, and I can feel sweat on my top lip, all signs that I'm scared, but it's like my body knows something my brain doesn't. I'm smart enough to know I should be experiencing a wave of terror, but it's as if my mind just can't tune in to that frequency. Maybe Clyde did break me after all, only in a way neither of us could have anticipated.

"I don't know if you're brave or stupid," the guy mutters. I think at this point it's safe to say I'm neither, yet both.

He walks beside me, his arm occasionally brushing against mine as he leads us out of the litter-strewn alley and down Acorn Drive to what looks like a bar of some kind.

There's no sign above the door, just a green-painted banner with a four-leaf clover above the scratched dark wooden door. The windows are frosted, letting me know that the lights are on inside but beyond that nothing.

He pulls the door open and nudges me inside the dimly lit room.

It's empty, which given how early it is, I'm not surprised. It seems strange, to me at least, that the door was unlocked. Unless, of course, someone's expecting us or the person who owns this place is a deterrent all of his own.

We walk around the dark mahogany bar, down a short corridor housing the restrooms, toward what's likely supposed to be a stock room. When the door is pushed open to show a large windowless room with row upon row of shelves filled with bar apparel, I know I had assumed correctly. It's all neat and tidy, the only thing out of place is a massive wooden desk in the back of the room and the people behind it watching us enter.

A large fat man with small beady eyes sits in the chair

behind the desk, which creaks under his weight as he moves. Wearing a green suede jacket and a pair of thick black glasses, he looks like a mean leprechaun, but I keep that information to myself. Flanking him is a tall thin man wearing a poorly fitted tan suit that's too short in the leg and too wide in the shoulders and another man in a navy blue suit who is short and bald with an abundance of muscle, making him look like he has no neck.

"What is this?" the fat guy in the chair asks, waving a hand toward me.

You'd think the boobs would have given him a clue.

"She knows what happened to Jimmy. You know, the guy you swore was as loyal as they come," the devil beside me tells him with a sneer.

*Interesting.* When he spoke about his boss before, there was a tone to his voice that for a second showed respect, but this guy here seems to have nothing but the devil's annoyance and scorn.

"Jimmy is family; he's my sister's boy." Not once does he mention he's trustworthy, though.

I breathe slowly and deeply, keeping my body loose in case I need to strike out or run. I can't afford to overreact, so I stay focused on the three potential targets in front of me, not counting the devil at my side.

"Speak, tell us what you saw," the leprechaun barks at me.

"Not so fast, Jasper," the devil snaps before calling to an unseen person. "Bring him out."

A door on the side of the room opens, spilling a little bright white light before it's snuffed out when the door slams shut.

A man who looks like he lives under a bridge and eats billy goats for breakfast drags out the guy from last night. His head rolls from side to side before he's dumped in the chair that the devil drags over into the center of the room.

"What is the meaning of this?" the Jasper guy roars. I clench my fingers into fists, mentally preparing myself for whatever is coming next.

"I want Jimmy here to retell his story once more. That shouldn't be too difficult to share, should it?"

"I told you what happened," Jimmy, aka the lying bastard, groans from the chair.

"Tell me again," the devil orders, his voice dripping with contempt.

"I was making a drop-off and I got jumped by a group of assholes. I blacked out after that. When I woke up, the product was gone, and I was lying in a pool of my own blood."

"And yet there doesn't seem to be a single bruise on you," the devil muses. He turns to look down at me, his eyes hard and unyielding.

"Now tell me what really happened," he orders.

I have two choices. I could lie and back up this asshole's story by claiming I never saw a thing, or I could tell him the truth.

What's it gonna be, V, brave or stupid?

I close my eyes for a moment and take a deep breath before blowing it out. Stupid it is.

"He was trying to rape a kid. I stopped him," I tell the devil, something he likely already figured out. A flash of approval sparks in his eyes before he hides it and turns to face Jasper.

"Oh, come on, you can't believe this street rat got the jump on Jimmy," Jasper scoffs, making the goon beside him in the ill-fitted suit laugh.

"How did you stop him, Cherry?" the devil asks, surprising me with the name. I look up at him and frown.

"I stabbed him twice, then when he was down, I left." His lips twitch, aware I left out the part of taking Megan with me, but he doesn't call me on it.

"And the product?" he coaxes, but I genuinely don't have the answer to that.

"Oh, come on, you can't actually believe this bullshit?" Jasper roars, quickly shutting up when the devil pulls a gun out of nowhere and aims it at his head.

When he says nothing more, the devil turns his head to face me, but he keeps his gun pointing at Jasper.

I shrug, my breath speeding up as my fight-or-flight response kicks in.

"I don't even know what this product is. I'm assuming it's drugs, but even so, it could be a nuclear weapon for all I know because I didn't take it."

"Show me your arms," he orders.

I bristle at his words, but I do as he asks, showing him my

arms are free from the track marks left by injecting heroin, and whatever the fuck else a lot of transients like me succumb to.

"Now show me yours." He turns to face Jimmy, who is breathing heavily with sweat rolling down his face. Jimmy looks like he might pass out any minute.

"No, how dare you come into my place of business and disrespect me, disrespect my family. And you," Jasper growls, standing and pointing at me, "give me one good reason why I should let you live after attacking my nephew."

Nothing I say will be a good enough reason in his eyes, so I don't bother trying to placate him.

"I don't answer to you, but if I were in your shoes, I'd be smart enough to know that just because someone is family, it doesn't necessarily make them loyal to you," I warn him, feeling the eyes of the devil on me once more.

"Why you little—" Jasper starts.

"Enough!" a voice roars from behind me. I fight the urge to whirl around even though my body is so tense, it practically vibrates.

"You guaranteed his loyalty to me," the voice continues, lower than before but pissed way the fuck off.

As he speaks, he steps around me and over to Jimmy, who is somehow still conscious. I take in the unknown guy and know instantly—he's the man the devil calls boss.

He's shorter than the devil, with once black hair that's now heavily threaded with silver and an air of authority and entitlement about him. He's in an expensive-looking custom-made suit and wearing a Rolex, both items likely costing the same as some peoples' rent for a year, but I know his type. Dripping with cash, sporting a tan he probably got from sunning himself on his yacht, yet I guarantee you he would walk past a dozen homeless people and not offer them a dime.

"He is loyal, and the fact you'll take some cheap, two-bit whore's word over mine is insulting," Jasper remarks, but I can feel the difference in the air and hear the tremble of his voice. Jasper fears this guy.

"Reid, bring her here."

I need not question who Reid is as the devil's hand clamps down on my arm. I bite my lip and slip my free hand into my pocket, gripping the knife that started all this.

*Stupid, stupid, stupid.* Yet, as I picture Megan's terrified face, I know if I were given a do-over, I would do the exact same thing.

He walks me over to his boss and I don't resist, gripping the knife tighter, feeling an odd mix of anger that after everything, this might be the end and relief that... after everything, this might be the end. Being on guard all the time is bone numbingly exhausting. And what's more peaceful than death?

The boss grabs Jimmy and yanks him up as if he weighs nothing, throwing him over the chair so his stomach is pressed flat to the seat and his head hangs low to the ground.

The boss shoves Jimmy's black T-shirt up, revealing two

blood-soaked gauze squares, one just above his right kidney the other just below his shoulder blade.

"Two stab wounds and no bruising anywhere else," he tuts. "I have to say, Jasper, out of the two of them, I'm leaning toward the street rat's version of events."

"Even if what she says is true, it holds no bearing here. In fact, it's likely her fault they took the product. How can a man defend himself from thieves if he is unconscious and bleeding? Or perhaps you took it? It must be easier to spread your legs for your Johns if you're off your face on H." Jasper leers, making my skin feel like it has bugs crawling all over me.

"You're not very smart, are you?" I tilt my head.

"Shoot the bitch," he snaps at the goon to his left, but before he can blink, a shot fires out, the sound muffled by a silencer, and the goon falls to the floor. A second later, the other goon follows.

"One more word and you'll be next. You're giving me a fucking headache," Reid growls at Jasper.

The boss sighs and shakes his head before looking at me. "Jasper is the boss around these parts. Tell me why you, a nothing throwaway, thinks he's stupid?"

His scathing words are designed to cut me, but I don't care what this man thinks of me, or what any of them think. All I care about is getting out of here in one piece, finding Megan, and helping Poppy set up her stall.

"He knows his nephew is a flake, hell I know that from spending five minutes in the room with him, but he took the risk using him and guaranteeing his loyalty. When he realized he fucked up, he could have saved face by eliminating the problem. Instead, he went to bat for the nephew who fucked him over and then switched the blame to me. If the nephew was telling the truth, I can't be held to blame because, in his story, I wasn't there. Blaming me just proves you know which of us is telling the truth. What really gets me, though, is how the only thing he seems pissed about is the missing product and smearing his name, not the fact his nephew is a pedophile. Honestly, the only people I know who aren't disgusted by pedos are pedos themselves." I shrug nonchalantly, but it's fake. I need out of this fucking place before I do something stupid because I can feel that familiar darkness rushing through me, coaxing me to hurt, to maim, to kill.

"And what would you have done?" the boss asks me, his voice cold but curious.

"I'd have killed Jimmy before his ass hit the chair and paid for the missing product," I reply. That's when the boss smiles, and there is nothing pleasant about it. In fact, his smile is the most terrifying thing I've seen all night, making my heart beat double time in my chest. He's looking at me like I've surprised him and I'm guessing that doesn't happen often.

"Reid," he murmurs, his eyes never leaving mine. The sound of a gunshot rings out around the room, followed by a roar and another bang-bang before a body hits the floor with a thud.

I don't look to see what's happening. I don't take my eyes from the boss, knowing he's the most dangerous man in the room, even over the guy at my back with the gun.

"There is still the issue of my missing product," he murmurs, fixing a cufflink on his shirt. "You seem resourceful and I need a new runner while I'm in town."

I shake my head but suck in a sharp breath when he snaps his hand out and grips my jaw.

"I wasn't giving you a choice. You'll do as I ask, and as long as you keep your mouth shut, I let you live." He shoves me away, hard enough for me to lose my balance and fall backward to the floor with a thud, my elbow connecting painfully with the ground. I don't show him he's hurt me; I just grit my teeth and climb to my feet. The boss turns, dismissing me as he walks away, telling Reid to take care of it.

Looking up at Reid, I find his angry eyes blazing into mine.

"You do not want to make yourself appealing to a man like the Zodiac. He wouldn't think twice about selling you to the highest bidder if it suited him."

"Thanks for that. Is this the part where I remind you that you brought me here?" I tap my foot and wait.

His hand cups my jaw. Not to bruise like the boss—or Zodiac, I guess I should refer to him as—but in a caress.

"So fucking fearless," he whispers, taking a step closer. I shrug him off and take a step back. Violence I can handle, but soft touches remind me too much of the hell I escaped from.

He straightens up, his hand falling as the soft look in his eye disappears into a blank one.

"Tonight at 10 pm, meet me in the same spot I found you this morning. Do not make me come look for you, Cherry," he warns.

"Don't worry, running and hiding aren't my style, Reid," I say, his eyes flashing when I use his name. I spin and walk away.

"Oh yeah, and what is your style?" he calls out.

I stop and look over my shoulder at the beautiful but deadly man standing in front of four dead bodies like he doesn't have a care in the world.

"I fight." I grin before making my way outside and throwing up in the rosebush beside the building.

# CHAPTER SIX

I should have known there would be a catch. There always is. Instead of just working off the debt for this missing product, I reluctantly became Zodiac's newest recruit. It kept Megan and me fed, but it meant I wasn't around as much to keep an eye on her, which is why shit like this happened.

"God damn it, Megan, I told you not to go alone when it's dark," I snap at her, making her wince when I touch the cotton ball doused in antiseptic to her lip.

"I know, I'm sorry, okay? But Poppy's hands are so bad she can hardly move them and—" I dab her lip again to shut her up, softening my voice out of habit despite the fact she can't hear me.

"You know I like Poppy, and we help her out as much as we can, but Poppy goes home to a nice warm bed in a nice safe house on a nice quiet street. You don't. Every time you pull shit like this, you risk getting raped or killed. It's fucked up, Megan, but this is our life," I tell her, frustrated.

"And what about you, Viddy? Jesus, you talk like you're an adult and I'm a child, when I'm older than you, for Christ's sake." She huffs. "You're gone most of the night, you come back covered in bruises and blood, and you have the balls to talk to me about taking unnecessary risks."

"You're making it sound as if I have a choice, Megan, when we both know what will happen if I don't turn up when I'm summoned."

The familiar flash of guilt in her eyes makes me sigh.

"I've told you a hundred times over, Megan, this is not your fault. It's been six months. You have got to let this shit go. Four more months and you'll turn eighteen and we'll be able to get you off these streets, but you have to stay safe. Don't let all this be in vain, okay?"

I had been making a little money as a runner and saving it for a deposit and rent money, knowing as soon as Megan turned eighteen, I could finally get her somewhere safer, hopefully as far away from here as possible. It's what we've been counting down to. Nobody would rent to two underage girls. They would call social services and throw us into the system when we are so close to freedom. Or at least Megan is. She deserves a life away from the dirty streets and the corrupt people who live here.

"Why aren't you signing? My hands might be full, but yours aren't," I scold lightly. We had spent as much time as possible at the library, learning everything we could about

ASL. For whatever reason, I'm the only person Megan will talk to verbally, and she needs a way to communicate with people other than pen and paper.

She rolls her eyes and sticks out her tongue, making me snort. Moments like this remind me we're just kids playing dress-up in a grown-up's world, even if somedays I feel ancient.

Tossing the used cotton ball to the ground, I turn to face her when her hands sign, slowly at first but picking up speed as she gains confidence.

I follow along until she hits the part in the story about how she got away from the two drunks that grabbed her.

"Wait, stop! Who the fuck is Wyatt?"

She pauses for a second, so I sign what I just said and wait for her to reply.

"He was asleep beside the dumpster they tried to drag me behind. When I first caught sight of him, I thought he was with them, and I knew I was fucked. This guy is huge, Viddy. I wouldn't be surprised if his mother mated with a giant." She shakes her head with a grin, her ebony curls bouncing around her face.

"Focus, Meg." I sigh, exasperated.

"Right, Wyatt. I think at first he thought I might have been drinking and was messing around, but when I started screaming he stepped in and fucked both guys up before bringing me back here."

I fist my hands so tightly I can feel my nails dig into my

skin. Trying to keep my calm, I grit my teeth. "You led him back here?"

"I was scared, Viddy, really fucking scared, but not of this guy who could snap me like a toothpick. I know bad guys, Viddy. Wyatt's not one of them," she insists, urging me to trust her.

I blow out a breath and look up at the rotting ceiling of the old shack we've been staying in. It's attached to the high school but sits at the far end of the football field and houses old and outdated sports equipment and exercise mats. All the newer stuff is kept in the swanky upgraded storage facility closer to the school itself, in range of the school's security cameras.

Apart from the shelter this place provided, and the somewhat comfortable mats to sleep on, Megan and I were able to sneak into the school when it opened and shower in the locker rooms before everyone arrived. We are, after all, teenage girls, making it easy to blend in.

"Where is he now?" I ask, needing to find out what I can about this guy to see if we need to move somewhere else.

"Erm..." She chews her lip, and I know whatever she's about to say will piss me off.

"He didn't want me to wait here alone. He's, or at least he was, out back by the tree line."

I don't say anything as I climb to my feet and pull the door open.

"Viddy," Megan calls, but I ignore her, marching over to

the copse of oak trees that loom dark and ominous in the distance.

I see him before I even make it halfway there, tall and broad, and every bit as intimidating as Megan says. That doesn't stop me, though, not when it comes to Megan's safety.

He doesn't move an inch, his massive arms hanging loosely at his sides, his long hair and beard hiding most of what I can tell is a handsome face. But it's his eyes that make me pause, stopping me from ripping him to shreds with my razor-sharp tongue.

I've seen that look before, the blank stare of someone who has had their world destroyed. I see it every time I look in a mirror but seeing it on this man feels like a knife cutting my insides to ribbons. His pain is so fresh, I can almost sense it trying to claw its way out from inside him like his suffering is somehow an extension of my own. It's so stark and bleak, I almost take a step back. How is he still functioning? How is he even walking and talking when the black shroud of grief he wears is so heavy I can feel its weight from here, almost bringing me to my knees.

"Who are you?" I ask him softer than I ever imagined I would, but Megan's right. One look at Wyatt and I can see he's no monster. He's a wounded animal and whatever hurt him is festering away inside.

"Wyatt," he grunts, his eyes moving over my face before sucking in a sharp breath.

He sees in me what I see in him, and just like that, a tangible link snaps into place between this stranger and me in the most inconceivable way. I can tell we both have different dark stories. We might not have followed in each other's footsteps, but we stumbled down the same dark path.

He's not bad, but just like me, he isn't good either.

"I think you need her even more than I do," I murmur softly, worried I'll spook him if I talk too loudly.

He cocks his head, unsure what my words mean.

"Megan," I explain. "She's light when everywhere else I look is dark. Of course, she has no idea she radiates this purity, which makes her a beacon for people who want nothing more than to snuff out the light or steal it for themselves."

I wrap my arms around myself, chilled at the thought of a world without Megan in it. She got hurt tonight because I couldn't be with her. I can be the monster who will kill for her, but she needs a savior too.

"Come on, time to step into the light, big guy." I reach out my hand for him, surprising us both.

He looks at my knuckles that are bruised and bloody from the scrap I found myself in earlier, then up to my face. Slowly, he lifts his large hand, with scars on his knuckles, and wraps it around mine, making me smile.

A look passes between us, a knowing that he's not coming just for Megan, but for me. I can feel the odd protectiveness coming from him for two girls he doesn't know, and yet I can feel it as surely as I can feel my heart beat in my chest.

I almost take a step back and sever the connection. The last time someone swore to protect me, they abandoned me when I needed them most. I'm the one who does the protecting now, but I can't deny the comfort it brings the whisper of the lonely girl inside me.

I grip his hand and lead him back to the shack in silence until we reach the door, then I look up at him as he towers over me. "If you hurt her, I will gut you like a fish," I warn him, expecting him to bristle at my words.

Instead, he does something that shocks the shit out of me. He smiles widely, revealing matching dimples, before ruffling my hair like I'm five.

"Good girl." He winks before disappearing inside, leaving me standing there with my mouth open.

# CHAPTER SEVEN

I should have known things would eventually take a nosedive. Six months of being Zodiac's runner turned into six years. It hadn't been too bad, depending on how you look at things. A little bloody and violent, but manageable. Living in a different city that Zodiac only visited on occasion allowed me to stay on the edge of his gang. Do I like working for that psychopath? No, but I'm not dumpster diving for food anymore. I had money; I had Megan and Wyatt. They were safe.

And just when you think you're catching a break, karma comes along and fucks you up the ass without lube—a reminder that, in the grand scheme of this game called life, we're all nothing more than pawns. Apparently, turning twenty-one reminded the powers that be I still existed, and now everything is going to change for the worst.

When I die, God—or whoever is running this shit show —and I are going to have a come to Jesus meeting.

"This is a bad idea, V," Wyatt warns me, his lips pressed in a hard line.

I sigh and rub my hands over my face, then pause to look at my palms. "That's all I have these days, Wyatt. Bad ideas and bloody hands."

"It doesn't have to be this way. Stay with Megan or go back to school. Something. You can be free of this life now." He looks down at me with a sad expression, knowing that's not an option for someone like me.

The weight of his concern has emotions bubbling up to the surface. I snuff them down quickly. "I'm glad Megan's prick of an uncle tracked her down and gave her the inheritance she's entitled to. She has the shop she always dreamed of now and somewhere safe to lay her head down at night. She has you to keep her safe. She's happy, Wyatt. That's all I ever wanted for her. A safe, normal, happy life."

"And what about you, Viddy? Don't you want that for yourself?"

I glance up at the apartment building when the light goes on in Megan's bedroom, and then offer Wyatt a wry smile. "With a white picket fence, kids, and a dog? We both know I'd go fucking insane."

He doesn't crack the slightest smile. Ignoring the thickness in my throat, I continue, "Wyatt, I'm twenty-one tomorrow. Zodiac wants to induct me—officially—into the gang. Refusing isn't an option. If I did, it would only bring trouble to Megan's door. I'll never do that."

"A gang though, V..." His voice trails off and an ice pick chinks a piece of the hardened wall around my heart. I step into him and wrap my arms around his waist. After a beat, his giant arms come around in return and squeeze me until it's difficult to breathe.

"I could kill them all for you," he offers, making me snort.

Once upon a time, Wyatt had a wife and a kid. But they were brutally killed during a gang initiation. Instead of lying down and dying with them, Wyatt tracked down their killers and wiped them out.

The. Entire. Gang.

This situation with me having to be inducted is his worst nightmare playing all over again.

"And spoil my fun? Hush, now. I have a plan, but it will take time. For now, I have to go and play the part. Just promise me, whatever happens, you'll keep Megan safe. And if something happens to me—"

He cuts me off by gripping my face in his hands. "Nothing will happen to you, Viddy, or I'll paint that city red."

I swallow the lump in my throat. "I'll be safe, I promise." I just hope this isn't the one promise I'll have to break.

Wyatt drops his hands from my face and steps back. "At least say goodbye to Megan before you go," he pleads, trying to delay the inevitable a bit longer.

I shake my head. "I can't. If I watch her cry while she begs me to stay, I'll cave and put us all in danger. Even without Zodiac, I've made a lot of enemies of my own doing his dirty work."

He sighs, his shoulders slouching, and nods in understanding.

"I need you to do something for me." I shove a Post-it note in his hand with the information he'll need. "I buried something a long time ago and I need you to move it to a safe deposit box for me."

He stands a little straighter. "Of course, I'll do it tomorrow."

I blow out a relieved breath. "Thank you. I have to go." I lift up on my toes and place a kiss on his stubble-covered cheek.

"Take care of each other. I'll be in touch." I pull away, or try to, but find myself yanked back against his hard chest. I try to hold it together, but I die a little on the inside as I break off the tiny part of my heart that's still capable of love, leaving it with the only two people in the world who mean anything to me.

Steeling my spine, I pull away and toss my hair over my shoulder, offering Wyatt a reassuring wink before turning and walking away.

I keep my head held high and my emotions locked down tight as I walk through the town that was never really my home, to the bus station near the market district.

With my bag tossed over my shoulder, I climb aboard the quiet Greyhound and make my way to the seat at the back. I slide the bag between my feet and place my forehead against the cold glass as the twilight sky darkens to indigo blue and let the tears fall for the first time since my mother's funeral.

As the bus pulls away, I say a silent goodbye to the concrete streets of purgatory and prepare myself for the next step. One that brings me closer to the devil and his wicked smile. One step closer toward a new kind of hell.

I DOZE LIGHTLY as the world passes by outside the window. At least this time, I will be off the streets. The money I had saved for Megan wasn't needed after she received her inheritance, which meant I now had the funds to keep myself afloat for a while. I was used to living frugally and that wouldn't change. If I was going to survive here, I was going to need money.

I never touched a cent of the money I took from Clyde's safe. I never went back there at all to avoid temptation. I knew even back then I would need it in the future. I went hungry more nights than I can count, knowing I had a stash of cash I could use anytime I wanted, but a sixth sense always held me back. Now that cash and the gun still buried beside it would be safe in a safe deposit box where I could access it when I needed to.

The money in my bag would be plenty for now. I'll get a hotel room until I can find a cheap apartment and take it from there.

Gazing outside, I notice the mishmash of old and new

buildings morphing into tall skyscrapers and massive, imposing towers of steel and glass reaching up into the dark sky.

I imagine this is what Dorothy felt like when she landed in Oz, small and very alone. I spot a man in threadbare clothes pushing a shopping cart stuffed with empty cans, and I realize the landscape might have changed, but the dirty pavements are still the same.

The lost and forgotten people still fall through the cracks, no matter what the zip code is.

The farther into the city we move, the more gaunt faces and rail-thin bodies I see bundled up in shop doorways and peeking out from cardboard box houses that offer them little protection from the elements.

A man across the aisle and two seats over from me looks at the same scene with disgust written on every line of his face before he tuts and turns away.

Out of sight, out of mind.

I've lost count how many times I have seen people react the same way over the years.

But what he finds so distasteful, I find comfort in. How can I not find comradery in these people? Their ailing bodies and damaged minds keep them in some kind of limbo, not quite ready to die but not really living either, as they hide from whatever traumas made this transient life a better option than the one they ran from.

If I had made different choices, I would be sitting there right beside them still, waiting for the restaurants to throw away leftovers so I could battle with the rats for the scraps of food others discarded without thought.

Working for Zodiac means that part of my life is in the past now. The future, however uncertain, will buy me warm food, clean sheets, and hot water. Even if that hot water is used to wash the blood from my skin and the stain from my soul.

# CHAPTER EIGHT

The hours tick by as the low murmur of voices dim to whispered snores before finally, as the sun bathes the sky in a warm orange glow, the bus pulls into the city station. Sensing we've arrived, people begin to wake, bleary-eyed as their internal alarm clocks go off. I stay seated and take in the colossal station as people rise from their seats and stretch out the kinks in their backs or necks before grabbing their bags and standing in the aisle, waiting for the doors to open.

I wait, not in any particular hurry, until everyone else disembarks before making my way off the bus and into the station that is a riot of noise and motion, even at this early hour.

I hold on tightly to my bag, bypassing the swell of people ebbing and flowing around me like an ocean of chaos, and slip outside through the emergency exit.

Taking a deep breath, I'm assaulted by the smell of diesel fumes and garbage, but just beyond that, I smell the subtle, yet enticing, hint of coffee.

Figuring coffee is as good a place to start as any, I follow my nose like a bloodhound until the bus fumes dissipate. The coffee aroma is accompanied by the tantalizing scent of pancakes and syrup.

The coffee shop I end up at is quiet, thankfully, so I don't have to wait long before a perky blonde waitress with a big smile and even bigger hair wanders over to the table I'm sitting at watching the city wake up around me.

"Hey, sugar, what can I get you?" She has a Texan accent, telling me she's even farther from home than I am.

"Pancakes and coffee, please."

She scribbles my order onto her pad, ripping off one end and placing it on the table. "Won't be long." She turns at the sound of the door opening, smiling at me before she heads over to an older couple walking through. They look to be in their late seventies, early eighties. They sit in a booth on the other side of the room on opposite sides of the table, but what makes it difficult to pull my eyes away from them is the moment they sit down, they reach across the table and link fingers.

Watching them feels intrusive somehow, but I can't seem to look away either. A love that spans a lifetime, weathers every storm, and still holds strong when it's withered with age is proof that magic does exist in the world. At least for some.

I don't know how long I zone out watching the couple laugh and smile at each other, but it's long enough for the waitress to return with my coffee and a stack of pancakes that make my mouth instantly water.

"There you go, enjoy. If you need anything else, just give us a holler. My name's Carol, by the way."

I offer her a small grin, but I can't tear my eyes away from the food. I wait until she walks away before diving in. I groan when the taste explodes on my tongue, and I have to forcefully remind myself to take my time. I don't need to shovel it in so nobody comes along and takes it from me. Heck, I don't even have to share it with anyone. For the first time in forever, I can simply sit and eat. So that's what I do, whiling away the morning until the urge to find accommodation forces me to move.

"Hey, Carol?" I call when she walks past my table. The small coffee shop has filled up now, but Carol is still the only waitress working, so I don't want to hold her up too long.

"More coffee?" she asks, holding up the coffee pot.

I shake my head and place my money with a nice tip on the table for her.

"No, thanks. I have to get going but I was hoping you could point me in the direction of a cheap motel. I'm new in town and haven't had a chance to check anywhere out yet."

"Oh, I can do one better. I have a list somewhere. Trust me, you're not the first person to head on over from the station looking for somewhere to stay. Give me two shakes and I'll be right back." She doesn't wait for my response before she turns on her heel and hurries over to the man in the suit three tables over, pouring him a fresh coffee before snatching up his empty plate and taking it to the counter.

Reaching over, she grabs something before walking back to me.

"Here we go. This is a list of all the places to stay in the city, starting from the most expensive at the top to the cheapest at the bottom. You might want to avoid most of those. A pretty, young girl like you will draw a lot of attention and not the good kind," she warns.

"Thank you, I'll be careful," I answer. Those places don't scare me, not after some of the places I've slept, but even if I were terrified, it's not like a girl like me has many options.

She shakes her head, a small frown on her face, but she holds back whatever she wants to say. Giving her a little wave, I make my way outside and scan the list in my hand, moving right to the bottom.

Pulling out the basic cell Zodiac insists I carry, I fire off a text to the devil, or Diablo, as I had started calling him. I hadn't seen him, or Zodiac for that matter, since that day in the pub, which seemed like a lifetime ago now. I wasn't far enough up the leadership totem pole for that thankfully, at least until now. This phone was our sole means of communicating, even when they sent a guy over to drop off or pick up the product or cash.

**Me:** I'm here.

His reply is instant.

**Diablo:** Tell me where. I'll pick you up.

**Me:** Negative Ghost rider. I have to find somewhere to live first.

I move to slip the phone back in my pocket, but it vibrates again.

**Diablo:** Tell me where you are, accommodation has already been arranged for you.

Fuck. I didn't want them to know where I was staying, though it wouldn't take much to find me if they wanted to. Still, these aren't people you fuck around with.

Shit. I shove the list in my bag before texting him the name of the coffee shop.

Frustrated, I slump down on the wooden bench next to an enormous planter filled with pink and white flowers. Staring down at the phone in my hand, I resist the urge to call Wyatt and Megan and let them know I arrived safely. I don't trust that my calls and texts aren't being monitored, and the last thing I want is to lead anyone in their direction.

With a defeated sigh, I slip the phone into the side pocket of my bag and wait.

An old gray-haired woman sits on the other end of the bench, using her cane to carefully lower herself down. She rummages around inside a plastic bag and pulls out a half-eaten loaf of bread.

I watch in fascination as she rips off small pieces and tosses them to the birds, who are now crowding around her feet, pecking each other out of the way to get to the prize.

It seems like a waste of perfectly good food to me, but what the fuck do I know?

I'm so distracted watching her that I don't know anyone else is here until a shadow falls over me.

*Dammit, Viddy, you know better than to let your guard down like that.*

Glancing up, I see the devil smirking at me as a halo of light illuminates him from behind, acting as a reminder that even the devil was an angel once.

"Hello, Cherry."

# CHAPTER NINE

I t's been six years since I've seen him, and the memory of the man hasn't done him justice. He is still too handsome, still too dominating, and yet my body responds to him like my adolescent one had. And it pisses me off something fierce.

"Diablo," I answer without thinking.

He pauses before throwing his head back and laughing. The sound does funny things to my insides. I ignore it and stand up so he isn't looming over me anymore.

He takes a step back so he can take me in, eyes staring at my black shitkickers before slowly working their way up my denim-covered legs, the oversized black hoodie that hides my figure underneath, to my face.

He might not have changed much over the years, but I have. Having money meant having more food, and with

Megan having an apartment, it meant clean clothes and showers when I needed them. I might have refused to put her at risk by moving in with her, but I wasn't crazy enough to pass on the essentials.

"You look good," he finally says. I shrug even though his words warm something inside me.

Jesus, woman, get a grip.

"So, where are we heading?" I question, letting a little of my impatience sound in my voice.

He laughs again, clearly not bothered by my prickly tone. He presses a hand against my lower back, moving me in the direction of a sleek black car. I move to shake him off, but he slips his hand around my hip and grips me hard, taking the bag from my hand and tossing it over his shoulder.

"Hmm...still as feisty as ever I see. Good, you'll need that here," he murmurs, opening the passenger side door of the car and waiting for me to climb inside so he can slam it closed.

The smell of leather is foreign to me as I close my eyes and grip the seat to stop myself from jumping out and demanding he give me my bag. I know the harder I push for something, the more forcefully he'll push back.

The trunk slams a few moments later before he climbs into the driver's seat and grins at me. "Hold tight."

It's the only warning I get as he pulls away and speeds down the road, weaving in and out of traffic like a stunt driver on a movie set. Maybe I don't need to worry about my future after all because if Diablo gets his way, I'll likely die in a car wreck.

I glance over at him and see the small grin on his lips and know he's doing this just to get a rise out of me, but I refuse to give him the satisfaction.

I take in the expensive black suit he's wearing and the pressed white shirt with cufflinks at the wrists that catch the light as he shifts gear. He wouldn't look out of place in one of these shiny buildings, brokering deals for some billion-dollar corporation, but I know the deals he brokers are far more nefarious.

"Nice car," I comment, turning to look out the window, even though at this speed everything is just a blur.

"Wait until you see my apartment," he answers off the cuff.

I whip my head around to face him, expecting his stupid grin, but he looks deadly serious.

"Why the fuck would I want to see your apartment?" I snap, really wishing I had my bag now and the blade tucked inside.

"Because you need to get ready for the initiation. If you pass, you'll get your own swanky apartment."

"Explain," I order, knowing I'm skating on thin ice, but initiation? Apartment? What the fuck?

He looks at me sharply, his brow creased in confusion.

"You don't know about the initiation? Then what the fuck are you doing here?" he barks.

"Are you kidding me? You think Zodiac gave me a choice?" My eyes widen incredulously.

"Fuck." He slams his hand into the steering wheel twice in anger.

"Why are you so pissed? You were fine when you thought I was here by choice, so what's the big deal?" I'm not sure it matters either way.

"It matters because he wants something from you if he made it so you couldn't refuse. Your debt has long been paid and you've earned him more money than most runners. Plus, you're a hell of a lot more reliable."

"Men always want something from me. I've known this since I was 12 years old. And rich, entitled assholes with money are the worst." I sigh.

Out of the frying pan into the fire. Flames, here we come.

"That might be true, but initiates are given time to prep so they know what the fuck they are getting into. Don't let the riches fool you. Beneath the suits and Rolexes, Zodiac and his disciples are still just a gang. It's blood in and blood out. There is no walking away from this once you're a part of it," he warns me, every inch of his body coiled tight.

"He was never going to let me walk away. It's like you said. He wants something from me so he moved the players around the board, safe in the knowledge that the pawn would end up exactly where he needs her to be."

"What the hell is he playing at? You're just a kid," he grumbles, still pissed.

I roll my eyes. "It's been years since you've seen me, Reid,

I'm not a child anymore. Actually, today's my twenty-first birthday." I shrug, I'd almost forgotten myself.

The car squeals and pulls to the right as Reid swings the car to the side of the street and parks, leaving the engine running.

"What the fuck? Are you trying to kill—" My words are cut off by a hand in my hair and hard, unyielding lips on mine.

My heart accelerates faster than the damn car as I freeze in utter shock. When he teases the seam of my lips with the tip of his tongue, I open to him on reflex, allowing him to slip inside. Slowly, my frozen mind starts to thaw as he teases and coaxes me to respond. I grip his arms where he holds me in place and let the unfamiliar sensation wash over me. Want and need war with logic and fear, but passion wins out in the end as I melt into him.

When he pulls away, his hands still holding my hair tightly, he stares into my eyes with a look that should terrify me. The man looks starving. That's the only way to describe it. Starving and like I'm the only thing on the menu he wants to devour.

"Happy Birthday, Cherry," he whispers, his hot breath skating over my lips.

"What the?" I mumble, my brain still short-circuiting.

"Consider it a gift. I wanted to do that since the first time I laid eyes on you, but you were far too young for a man like me."

"I'm still far too young for a man like you," I answer, hating that my voice sounds a little breathless.

"Maybe," he concedes, "but you're old enough now that I won't feel bad about taking what I want." He smirks, his words acting as if he has poured iced water over my head.

He sits back up, adjusts his dick unashamedly, and winks at me before pulling back out into the flow of traffic as if he didn't just rock my world.

"I might be young, Diablo, but I'm smart. Don't sit there thinking I'll be an easy lay. That's not me. You can take your fancy car and your thousand-dollar suit and shove them where the sun doesn't shine. I'm not for sale and if you try to take me, as you so eloquently put it, I'll cut off your dick and feed it to the birds like day-old bread, and I'll do it all with a fucking smile on my face."

# CHAPTER TEN

R eid's apartment is the stuff of dreams. It's on the top floor of a swanky tower block right in the heart of the bustling city.

High ceilings and light wooden floors teamed with floor to ceiling windows give the space a light and airy feel. The corner apartment has an open plan concept, where the kitchen, sitting room, and dining area blend into one another seamlessly.

The kitchen boasts oak cabinets, granite countertops, and stainless-steel appliances that don't look like they get used much.

The sitting area has a large, light gray, corner sofa with a handful of cream cushions tossed haphazardly upon it and just in front of that is a large well-crafted dark wood coffee table sitting on top of a gray and black checkered rug. The table and chairs in the dining area match the colors of the sitting room with a dark wooden table that sits four and gray high back chairs surrounding it.

With lamps in each corner and a ridiculously large television mounted on the wall, I can imagine spending evenings snuggled up on the sofa, watching movies to the pretty backdrop of the city below.

"I'll show you where everything is in a minute. Let me take you to your bedroom first."

I tense beside him, which he doesn't miss.

"Relax, Cherry, you'll be in the room beside mine, but if you change your mind, you'll know where to find me."

I follow him to the bedrooms, tapping my fingers lightly against my leg as my nerves begin to get to me.

"This is yours for however long you need it." Reid pushes the door open and steps to the side for me to take it all in.

The high ceilings and light stone tile floors complement the warm cream-colored walls. One wall, however, is a deep navy blue, acting as an accent color, drawing the eye toward the huge bed that sits against it. I stare at the monstrosity in shock, taking in the cream linens and navy throw pillows, wondering why on earth someone would need a bed that size. Either side of the cream leather headboard are simple black bedside tables with glass-bottomed lamps on top of them. Across from the bed is a large, whitewashed dresser with another lamp on one side of it and three tall candles on the other. Hung on the wall above it is a huge ornate oval mirror, which I quickly turn away from when I catch a glimpse of my pale face.

"I'm pretty sure this room is bigger than the entire trailer I grew up in," I admit.

"I imagine it is. That door leads to a walk-in closet. It's full of the crap I can't fit in my room, but I can make space if you need it." He points to one of two doors on the left, before stepping forward and pushing the remaining door open.

"And this is your bathroom."

I step up beside him, all thoughts of keeping my distance disappearing when I spot the tub.

I vaguely take in the limestone floors and countertop and the double-wide sink. My focus is all for the sunken bathtub in the corner. It's crazy to admit that at twenty-one I've never had a bath before, but it's true. Our trailer only had a shower, and although Clyde's house on the hill had one, I was never stupid enough to leave myself vulnerable for an extended length of time, so soaking in the tub wasn't an option. Showers meant I could get in and out but soaking in a bath would have offered Clyde a temptation he would have found impossible to refuse.

"You know most women who make it as far as the bedroom only have eyes for me," Reid comments drolly.

I tear my eyes away from the bath and look up at Reid's amused face.

"Only one thing in this room will be making me wet, Reid, and it's not you. The sooner you come to terms with that, the better," I snap, frustrated that his words have an effect on me.

Spinning me around, he has me pinned against the door with my wrists trapped in one of his strong hands above my head.

"Challenge accepted, Cherry. You really should be more careful when you throw down the gauntlet like that," he murmurs against my ear.

My body is strung tight, my chest heaving as he places a kiss against the side of my neck before pulling away.

"Get some rest. You have a rough night ahead of you," he warns before storming out of the room and slamming the door without looking back.

"Fuck, I'm in so much trouble," I curse, moving over to the window and looking down at the street below.

Something tells me I might have been safer down there in the gutters than in the devil's penthouse.

One thing is for sure, I need to learn to hide my body's reaction to Reid better because I know damn well he picks up on everything. If I want the upper hand, I need to keep my cards close to my chest.

Hearing the sound of a door slamming, I make my way back into the living area and find it empty. Did he leave me here? A quick search shows me I am indeed alone, so I take advantage of the fact and raid the fridge, helping myself to leftover Chinese food and a can of Coke.

I sit alone at the table. The silence starts grating on my nerves, so I turn on the TV and flick to the news station. I half listen to the pretty reporter drone on about the latest crime wave in the city.

Finishing up, I place my plate and glass in the sink before grabbing my backpack from beside the door where Reid put it earlier and make my way back to the room that's temporarily mine.

There's no lock on the door, so I shove the dresser in front of it before stripping off my clothes and taking a hot shower. As much as the bath calls to me, I don't know how long I have until Reid comes back, and I don't trust him to stay out.

I stay under the water longer than necessary, unable to make myself get out. I swear, I will never take the luxury of having a shower for granted ever again.

Eventually, when my skin resembles a prune, I shut off the water and climb out, drying off with a towel so soft I'm sure it's made from clouds.

I plait my hair into two Viking braids, slip on black ripped jeans and a black tank top before sliding my shit kickers back on.

Rummaging around in my bag, I grab a flip knife and slide it into my jeans pocket before grabbing my hoodie. A quick whiff tells me it needs washing, so I toss it on the floor, eyeing the closet.

Chewing my lip, I decide, what the hell, he's letting me borrow a room in his swanky pad; I'm sure he won't care if I borrow a sweatshirt.

Pulling the door open, I pause, my mouth dropping open.

This is a closet? It's bigger than most people's bedrooms. Most of the stuff that's hung up looks to be suits and shirts, so I slide open the drawers beneath the rails and find what I'm looking for. I pick a black hoodie with a gold star on the left side of the chest. It's nothing fancy, although I'm not even going to think about how much this thing might have cost. For tonight, it's just what I need.

Slipping it over my head, I chuckle when it reaches to just above my knee. I could wear this thing as a dress and nobody would bat an eye. I take a deep breath, comforted by the smell of laundry detergent and the faint hit of sandalwood.

Nothing smells better than clean clothes, I don't care what they look like. Some days, when things were at their worst, I smelled as bad as I looked, and I hated it.

Figuring a nap may be in my best interest since I have no idea what tonight might have in store, I make my way over to the bed but pause before turning back to the closet.

"Fuck it." I don't care how stupid it makes me, but sleeping out here makes me feel vulnerable, and I'm already struggling without Wyatt and Megan by my side.

Snagging the pillows and the large thick comforter from the bed, I drag them into the closet and close the door. I make a little nest in the far corner and climb in, pulling the blanket tightly around me. Closing my eyes, I pull the collar of the hoodie over my mouth and nose and breath deep, letting the comforting smell relax me until I drift off into a deep sleep.

# CHAPTER ELEVEN

A thumping noise penetrates my sleep, but it isn't enough to pull me out of the dream I'm having involving a certain sexy dark-haired dickhead.

It isn't until there is a massive crash that I'm startled awake and alert just as the door to the closet flies open.

Reid freezes, seeing me, his chest heaving before he stalks toward me.

"What's wrong?" I quickly scramble to my feet, imagining there's a fire or something when he picks me up, stomps into the bedroom, and tosses me unceremoniously on to the bed.

Before I have time to react, he's over me, pinning my hands, like he did earlier against the bathroom door, as he glares down at me, making every survival instinct I have scream.

"What's wrong is that I couldn't fucking find you," he barks.

"I'm exactly where you left me! Now get the fuck off me," I grunt, trying to buck him off, but he just presses me harder into the mattress, his face serious.

"Stop squirming for a fucking minute and listen to me or I'll forget all about the initiation and fuck you until you can't breathe, let alone move."

I freeze solid beneath him. The only thing moving is the rapid rise and fall of my chest as my heart tries to beat its way out from inside me. My mind starts to glitch, one minute I'm here and the next I'm back in that damned house I escaped from.

"Touch me and I'll kill you," I snap, but there's no heat behind my words. All the heat has drifted far lower, coiling like a snake in my stomach. I can't figure out what I'm supposed to be feeling. Loathing, lust, and shame war within me while the only thing stopping me from spiraling is the knowledge that I'm not that little girl anymore. I'm stronger now and I know how to fight back.

"Oh, Cherry," he purrs, leaning in and nipping my ear with his teeth, "I'm not afraid of something as trivial as death."

His words are spoken with a casualness that only the devil would use, but before I can say anything, his smirk slips, and that seriousness replaces it once more.

"I have enemies, as I'm sure you do. When I couldn't find you..."

I'm torn between the warmth of knowing he would care if something happened to me and the coldness of knowing he left me here unprotected, regardless of the dangers.

"Well, I'm here, safe and sound, at least for now. So how about you get off me and tell me what to expect tonight?"

He doesn't climb off me, though, because the ass seems to continually need to do the opposite of what I want him to.

Instead, he releases my hands and cups my face with his large ones, his eyes filled with warning and a hint of regret.

I brace myself, slipping my imaginary armor over my heart before he can shred it. I'm prepared for anything, my death included, but Megan and Wyatt are my weakness. I hope I've done a good enough job hiding the tracks that lead me back to them. Not that they'll find an easy target in Wyatt. He'll rip them apart with his bare hands before he lets anyone lay a finger on Megan. Or me. I swallow, shaking off the memories of my little makeshift family. Now is not the time or place.

"There are currently ten division heads working for Zodiac. There should be twelve, but we recently lost two, which is where the initiates come in. There will be five of you, the best from the rest, so to speak. We don't have as significant a foothold outside of this city as within, but we do have you guys. Two of you will step in to fill the last two spots, but you'll have to prove that you are worthy of the task."

"Of course I will," I sigh, not expecting anything less. He grits his teeth before looking away.

"What aren't you telling me, Diablo?" I whisper. He turns back to face me, his warm breath washing over me as he drops his head far enough that when he speaks, his lips graze mine in a barely-there touch.

"Only two of the initiates will walk away from this. The others can't live once they've seen inside the inner sanctum."

I squeeze my eyes shut, not surprised in the least. Isn't this the way it always goes for me? I open them back up and stare at him, locking down my emotions tight so he can't read me.

"Anything else I should know before you lead me to my potential death?"

He sighs, crawling off me before reaching down and yanking me to my feet.

"Reid," I prompt when he doesn't say anything else, but I can see the tension in his shoulders.

"There has never been a female division head," he admits, making me laugh.

"Fucking peachy."

"SERIOUSLY?" I gaze up at Reid, who grins down at me.

"Pretty cool, huh? Zodiac has a hard-on for anything space related. His grandfather was apparently some famous Russian cosmonaut, but who knows for sure."

I stare up at the enormous domed building before me and shake my head.

"Can't really say I gave much thought to what an evil lair looks like, but I wouldn't have guessed a planetarium in a million years," I confess.

"That's the beauty of it, Cherry. Everything's subjective. People see what they want. Driving home at night, they pass this place with a smile, thinking about being a kid looking up at the stars. They never consider the possibility that the stars are just a distraction from the dark deeds occurring below them," he muses, leading me toward the hidden doorway at the back of the building.

"Maybe," I concede, "or maybe people are all too aware of the horrors real life has to offer and thinking of stars and making wishes is symbolic. A way to keep the faith and remember that this shit will one day pass." I shrug.

"I never took you for a dreamer, Cherry," he teases, closing the iron door behind us and leading me down a dimly lit hallway.

"Dreams are free and accessible in the darkest hours. They offer you an escape, they give you hope, and for those brief moments in time, you are free to be whoever you want. The best thing, though, is that nobody can steal them away, because they are yours and yours alone. When you live among thieves and pickpockets, you learn to appreciate the priceless treasures that are so easily deemed worthless to others." I walk ahead of him, feeling his eyes on me, judging me. Most people think I must be dumb. I mean, how can a street kid who didn't go to school be anything other than stupid?

But people's underestimation of me says more about them than me. I've been out to prove something to not just myself, but everyone around me since I was a kid. Street smarts aside, the library became, in its own way, my home. I devoured everything I could get my hands on, soaking everything up like a sponge, thirsty for knowledge in the way only someone who had been deprived of it could appreciate.

I'd been kept in a bubble at the house on the hill. I didn't see or speak to anyone unless I was paraded around like a pretty doll before being returned to her box. Even the internet access I had was heavily restricted and monitored. But once I was free, I felt liberated in a way, gorging myself on anything and everything until my eyes would blur, and my head felt like it would explode.

I don't share this though, because playing dumb right now can only work in my favor.

As the hallway opens up, it becomes light enough to see we're not alone.

As much as I would love to look up and gaze at the stars, I keep my eyes on the players in the room, each person a potential victim or victor and all of them stand between me getting to hug Wyatt and Megan again or my blood spilling out on the floor.

I wonder if once upon a time, this place was filled with seats where children sat gazing at the stars in rapture. Now the only seat I see is the one at the head of the room where Zodiac sits watching everyone with his cold, calculating stare. I feel Reid step around me, and without a word, he takes a spot near Zodiac with his hands clasped behind his back, and his head bowed. The others dressed in the same black suits and white shirts follow and form a sort of oval shape, leaving me on the fringe and four others dressed in street clothes similar to mine.

"Welcome initiates." Zodiac's voice echoes around the dim room. "For those of you who don't know me, I am Zodiac, and these are the ten heads of the divisions within this city," he announces.

I look around the other division heads and see them all standing in a similar pose to Reid, hands clasped behind their backs, heads bowed. I can't guesstimate their ages without looking at their faces, but I can see they are all fit and muscular like Reid is, and none of them look shorter than six feet tall.

I look like the token virgin sacrifice compared to these lot; even the other initiates tower over my short frame.

I narrow my eyes, wondering if that's precisely what I'm here for. Some kind of gang initiation where I end up raped and with my throat slit.

Slipping my hand into my pocket I grip my knife, running my eyes over who I think is the biggest threat, but I know the only way to cause any kind of chaos will be to cut off the head of the snake. Without taking my eyes from Zodiac, I move into the center on the oval. The four other initiates eye me shrewdly before following me until we're all grouped together in our own circle within the division head's oval.

"Two of you will become division heads. You'll have your own sectors to run, and you'll answer to me directly. You'll be paid to live like kings and queens," he says with a dip of his head acknowledging me, which of course, draws everyone else's eyes to me too.

Asshole.

"Let's begin, shall we? You might want to fan out a little," he laughs, obviously knowing what's coming. I've never been more grateful than I am right now that fear doesn't affect me like it does others, at least not in the same way it used to. I'd have likely puked everywhere by now or passed out, so thank God for small blessings.

Feeling more eyes on me, I look around and see the division heads watching me too. Some with curiosity, some with lust, and a couple look like they would love nothing more than to run me through with a knife. I ignore them all, glancing at Reid, who offers me a small discreet nod, which I guess means I've got this. Fuck, I hope he's right.

The smell of sweat, fear, and anticipation taints the room, so I fill my lungs with it and use it to fuel me. I know what's at stake here and what's that saying? I didn't come this far, just to come this far. I twist my neck, feeling it crack and make my body loose and ready.

"When I tell you to fight, you'll fight each other," Zodiac announces.

I blow out a breath. Great, just great. It's like David and Goliath.

"You'll fight until only one remains standing. One

initiate, however, will be given immunity from the test. They will automatically move on to the next round, along with the last person standing." The others whisper to each other before turning to me.

Great, it looks like I'm going to be everyone's first target. One on one, I might have stood a chance but four on one? Not gonna happen. I need that immunity.

I ignore the bloodthirsty assholes around me, deciding I don't like them on principle, and focus once more on Zodiac.

"The first initiate to draw initiate blood will be given immunity."

I pull the knife from my pocket and flip it open, keeping it close to my leg. There is no way none of the division heads haven't seen it, but they don't say anything. That's when I notice other initiates have knives and brass knuckles and other weapons of their own.

They are all watching me avidly now, waiting for Zodiac to give the green light to start, so ready and willing to take me out first and spill my blood because I'm the easy target. Wait, that's it!

"Fight!" Zodiac roars.

As predicted, the others move toward me almost as one, but I lift my knife and drag it across the palm of my hand and hold it up high in the air and yell at the top of my lungs, "Initiate blood has been spilled!" Everyone freezes as the blood starts running over my hand and down my arm.

"You dumb bitch, he said you had to draw our blood, not your own," one of the initiates snorts.

"Actually, Zodiac's exact words were—the first initiate to draw initiate blood will be given immunity. I'm an initiate, and I am, in fact, bleeding," I point out.

"Clever girl," Zodiac calls out, again drawing attention to my sexuality. I know it's on purpose, I just don't understand why he's doing it or what it will mean for me.

"Being smart will always be your greatest strength. Think first, fight second. Well done." He nods to me and indicates for me to step out of the circle, so I do, with zero hesitation, and take my first deep breath since walking in here.

I move to stand behind two unfamiliar division heads. They don't speak to me and I return the favor by standing by silently, watching and waiting for Zodiac to resume things.

"Fight," he yells once more. I watch each of the remaining initiates as they attack each other with rage and frustration. It's every inch as brutal and as bloody as I knew it would be, but I don't look away. I need to know precisely what my opponents are capable of.

It takes me less than five minutes to realize there won't be any more tests because there won't be any more initiates. One of the guys isn't knocking these guys out to make sure they stay down; he's slitting their throats so they never get back up again.

And not a single person steps in and stops him.

I don't know whether to be thankful that I won't have to compete in any more tasks or horrified at this guy's lack of empathy for human life. In the end, I settle somewhere in the middle.

It's just another day I survived. I cling to that knowledge above everything else.

When the last guy remains, Zodiac and the other division leaders' clap. The loud noise reverberates around the room, their praise unwarranted and unnecessary. Even the guy standing in the center of the chaos, covered in blood, looks disgusted. I push through and make my way to the center, the dark-haired, blood-soaked guy looking toward me with tense muscles ready to pounce once more. He relaxes when he notices it's me. He takes a step toward me and holds out his hand. I stare at it for a second as the clapping dies down around us before looking into his cool blue eyes, where he tries to communicate with me.

I imagine if he were speaking out loud, he would say, *we're in this together.*

I cock my brow in reply, a smirk saying *for now perhaps.* He throws his head back and laughs.

I slip my hand in his and use him for balance to step over someone whose face is now a bloody pulp and stand next to him, shoulder to, well, face. The guy is freaking tall.

"Division heads, may I present our newest members. Leo." Zodiac indicates the guy beside me before staring down at me with a calculating look on his face.

"And Gemini."

# CHAPTER TWELVE

The other division heads offer us both congratulations before dragging the dead initiates off somewhere, as they laugh among themselves. Their blatant disregard for human life is unbelievable.

"Well done, Gemini. I have to say, I wasn't expecting much," Zodiac offers as he approaches, with Reid just behind him acting as his guard and reminding me of the night we met.

"People rarely do, but strength is more than just being able to use your fists, like you said," I tell him, pinching the skin on my thighs, using the bite of pain to keep me grounded.

"True," Zodiac agrees before lifting a strand of my hair and inspecting it. "But beware of wolves with sharp teeth, little Red. Not everyone fights fairly."

I don't know if he's warning me about him or the others, but he needn't have bothered. Nobody here knows that better than me.

I smile up at him, a sweet smile which Wyatt finds hilarious because I'm anything but, then let it morph into the grin I use when I mean business.

"Some people see Red skipping through the woods without a care in the world, but that's their mistake. If they looked closer, they would see her red cape is wolf fur coated in blood."

He takes a step back, letting go of my hair, and just like me, he can't tell if I'm threatening him or just making an off the cuff comment.

"Touché." He dips his head before calling for Reid. "Take her to her new apartment," Zodiac orders before walking over to Leo.

"Christ, woman, you had me worried for a second," Reid curses, leading me across the room and down the hallway we entered through.

"Yes, I could tell how worried you were when you jumped in to save me." I roll my eyes. I've spent far too much time with liars. Words mean nothing to me. Actions are everything and Reid proved that the only person who has my back is me.

"That's not how it works here and you know it. We all went through it, Cherry, and if I jumped in, it would have made you look weak. Zodiac would have had us both killed on the spot."

I shrug my shoulders. He's probably right. Doesn't make it sting any less though.

"Maybe, maybe not. You're right with what you said before, Zodiac wants something from me specifically. I just don't know what. You notice how many times he mentioned I was a woman? He set me up with a big bullseye on my forehead. The question is, why? If I hadn't pulled that stunt with the knife, I'd be dead. If he wants something from me, my death puts a kink in the plan. Unless—"

I stop in my tracks just outside the door, making Reid bump into me. He grips my arms to prevent me from falling but lets go once he's sure I'm stable.

"What? What is it?" he questions, looking around sharply.

"Not here. I'll tell you in the car."

He doesn't say another word, and neither do I as we walk over to Reid's sleek black sports car and climb in. I yank the seatbelt over me and hiss when I catch my hand.

Leaning over me, he pops open the glove box and pulls out a bandage roll before taking my hand carefully in his.

"This might need stitches," he murmurs, gazing down at the cut that's still bleeding, although it's more of an ooze than a gush, so that's something at least.

"You have superglue back at your place?" I ask, pulling my hand back. Having him touching me messes with my brain and right now, I need my wits about me.

"Yeah, sure." He nods, strapping himself in and starting up the car.

"Then you can glue it together for me and I'll be fine."

"You don't like hospitals?" he guesses, looking at me with surprise before pulling away from the planetarium, heading in the direction of his penthouse.

"Hospitals ask too many questions," I answer. I don't have anything against them besides that.

"You're not a minor anymore, Cherry," he reminds me. "I don't know your story, but it doesn't matter now. They can't send you home now that you're an adult."

"There is no home for me to get sent back to and I don't want to talk about it. What I want to talk about is the fact I don't think that test back there was about me, I think it was about you and possibly the other division heads."

He frowns, his hands gripping the steering wheel hard.

"How so?" he rasps.

I like that he doesn't dismiss my suspicions. I doubt it's because he trusts me. Maybe he has been questioning Zodiac himself.

"The fact that he kept pointing out I'm a woman bugged me. Like I said, if he specifically needed something from me, then he wouldn't have set up my murder scene like that because that's what it was. We both know there was no way I should have survived. I think Zodiac was testing to see which of his division heads are still unwaveringly loyal to him. He wanted to see if someone would step in."

"Well, if that's true then we all passed with flying colors." His shrug is blasé, making me want to elbow him in the face.

"At least until he realizes his mistake," I murmur, looking

out the window as the rain lightly starts to fall. The neon lights outside appear to blur and distort, making the world around us look as if it's melting.

"And what mistake might that be?" he questions quietly, his tone even so he doesn't give away his emotions.

"That he chose the wrong bait. Nobody there gave a fuck about some random street girl. Maybe if it was their sister or daughter or something, then Zodiac might have gotten the reaction he was seeking. But even that depends on these men having any kind of empathy left in their black souls. He might have been better off placing a big old pile of money in the center. Money is likely the only thing that still motivates most of them."

"Still as jaded as ever I see," he jokes.

"Perhaps I am, but it doesn't make it any less true. Regardless of all that, the biggest mistake Zodiac made was making me a focal point. He accidentally showed each and every one there that women are smart. He reminded himself of the very reason he forced my hand all those years ago. He's just now figuring out that the test to see if his crown was safe from his dark princes was never in jeopardy. In playing his games and being so deceitful, he gave a pawn the potential to become the queen."

"Talk like that will get you killed, Cherry," Reid warns, pulling into his parking space underneath the apartment building.

"Are you gonna tattle on me, Reid?" I tease, climbing from the car and making my way inside.

Reid follows behind me, mulling over my words.

"You want Zodiac's position," he surmises, looking both impressed and appalled. "You want him gone so you can rule?" He barks out a laugh that grates over my skin and has me itching to reach for my blade once more.

"I want my freedom back and if that means staging a coup, so be it."

"He'll kill you, or worse." I don't ask him what could be worse than death. I'm all too aware of the things that go bump in the night.

"He'll have to catch me first, Reid. Besides, if he leaves me alone to do my job and doesn't pull shit like that again, I'm sure our paths will rarely cross. I might kill to protect myself, but do I really look like a murderer to you?" I shake my head, looking away with a small grin.

He laughs, silly boy. Didn't I already warn him tonight about underestimating me? Oh well, it's best to let him think I'm all talk. He made it clear tonight where his loyalties lie. And that's with himself.

"Come on, let's sort your hand out and you can take a bath in that big old tub that you orgasmed over earlier," he offers, changing the subject.

I wait as he ushers me inside his apartment, flicking on the lights before moving over to the windows and drawing the blinds to hide us from spying eyes, and knowing Diablo, sniper rifles.

"Sit at the table and I'll go grab my supplies," he orders.

With my hand throbbing like a motherfucker, I see no need to argue.

He slips off his jacket and hangs it on the back of one of the chairs before rolling the arms of his shirt up to his elbows. I have to look away so he doesn't see the flush spreading across my face. What is it about his forearms and rolled up sleeves that turn me into a simpering ninny?

I wait for him to walk away before reaching down and pulling off my boots, wiggling my sock-covered toes into the thick carpet beneath the table.

I keep the hoodie on, needing it as a shield, hiding behind the protection it offers. Being here alone with Diablo feels far too intimate and far more dangerous than it did in the room full of men at the planetarium.

"Okay, I have everything we should need." He tosses the first aid box onto the table and pulls out a chair and turns it to face me before sitting on it. He maneuvers my legs so they're trapped between his, and before I can protest, he lifts my hand from the table and inspects it.

"Hmm... okay, this might sting a little," he warns before ripping out an antiseptic wipe and cleaning the wound. He's gentle, but it doesn't stop the hiss from escaping between my gritted teeth.

"Motherfucker," I grunt.

"Such a potty mouth. I hope you don't kiss your mother with that—" I cut him off before he can go there.

"My mother is dead. I have no family. End of conversation. Unless, of course, you want to spill your guts about all the weird and wonderful things that made you the cunning sociopath I know and loathe today," I snark.

He presses hard on my cut, this time on purpose.

"Asshole," I spit, trying to pull my hand away, but he holds firm.

"What's the matter, little girl? You can dish it out, but you can't take it, huh?" he taunts.

"I can take whatever you throw at me, Reid," I sass back, knowing I'm playing with fire. You don't issue challenges like that to men like Reid. He'll eat me for breakfast, and not in the way that leaves me spread out naked across the kitchen countertop.

"Is that so?" he purrs, grabbing the superglue and holding my hand up closer to the light. I watch as he deftly applies a thin strip of glue along the seam of the cut and pinches the edges together. I wince, but I know the shallow cut is so much better than what the alternative could have been.

"Now," he leans forward so his face is mere inches from mine, "where were we?"

Before I can say or do anything, his phone rings, making him curse. He reaches into his back pocket, pulling his phone out and looking down at the screen. He glances up at me quickly before shifting my legs out of the way and moving over to the far side of the room. His voice is low so I can't hear what he's saying, but he seems agitated. I clean up the mess, toss the wipes in the trash and shove everything back into the first aid kit before heading back to the room he told me I could use earlier.

As I push the door open, a hand on my shoulder makes me jump. I spin and only just stop myself from throwing a punch because I know it can only be Reid. He has his phone pressed to his chest while he scans my face.

"This isn't over, Cherry, but I have business to attend to. I'll show you to your new place tomorrow. For tonight, just crash here. I likely won't be back until the morning."

He turns and walks away before I can answer him.

Sighing, I shove the door the rest of the way open and close it behind me, shoving the dresser in front of it like earlier. It won't keep anyone out for long, but it will buy me time to wake up and arm myself.

Hearing the door to the apartment slam shut, I move over to the window and peer down onto the surprisingly quiet street below. When I see Reid's fancy black car pull out and disappear downtown, I take a deep breath and feel my muscles start to relax.

I look over at the bathroom, not even trying to stop the grin from spreading over my face.

I have a date with a bubble bath and I've never been more excited in my life.

# CHAPTER THIRTEEN

The rumble of my stomach rouses me from my sleep. My eyes spring open, my body wired and alert in a nanosecond when I notice how quiet it is, but then I see the suit jackets hanging above me and relax.

Sleeping on the streets makes you conscious of every noise. The sound of someone's breath as they veer too close to you can buy you valuable seconds to escape pawing hands, but it's more than just that. The scurry of clawed feet as the rats scavenge for food and the wail of police sirens became the soundtrack of my youth, and I had no idea how loud the sound of silence could truly be until I came here. Curled up under the thousand-dollar suits in Reid's quiet closet gave me ample time to overthink things, and when I had finished that, I overthought some more.

Crawling to my knees, I stretch and work out the kinks

before climbing to my feet and heading out into the bedroom. I didn't bother closing the blinds last night, so the early morning sun streams in through the window, bathing everything in a golden hue.

I quickly use the bathroom, brushing my teeth with one of the spare brushes I found under the sink, and stare at myself in the mirror. It's not something I do very often— the face staring back always reveals the image of that haunted little girl I've tried to leave behind.

Now though, I notice the subtle differences I missed before. My cheeks are a little rounder, softening my appearance a touch, making a nice change from all the sharp angles my face and body usually sported. I know I have Megan to thank for that. Since getting her own place, she had made it her aim to fatten the three of us up, and she turned out to be surprisingly talented in the kitchen. My skills never moved beyond heating shit up in the microwave, but Megan was good at a lot of shit she put her mind to.

I shake off thoughts of her and focus on me. My hair is long, too long really, sitting just above my ass. More often than not, it was mistaken for brown unless it caught the light just right. Now that it has been washed and brushed more frequently, it's easier to pick up the deep mahogany-red tones.

Stepping back, I lift the T-shirt of Reid's I snagged after my bath and check out my body again, marveling at the changes. My figure stopped being childlike the day I hit puberty, giving me the body of an underwear model overnight even though I was still an immature girl with no idea that men had stopped looking at me as sweet and innocent. Their feeble minds were unable to comprehend that just because my body had changed, my age hadn't. Mother Nature made me a target for the worst humanity had to offer and I was too young to understand the repercussions until it was too late.

When I was on the streets, though, the weight fell from my frame at an alarming rate. My curvaceous physique was replaced with a gaunt one. At the time, I was happy about it. I hated how I looked, it made me feel exposed and vulnerable. Now, I realize I have the power to take back my body as my own. If I want to walk down the street naked, I should be able to do it without the threat of wandering hands.

It's time I stopped blaming myself for shit that was beyond my control.

I stare at my curves, my high breasts with rosy nipples hidden beneath a grubby sports bra, my flat and still a little too thin stomach, and the flair of my hips. I wasn't a little girl anymore. And I was done hiding.

I pull the T-shirt back over my head, deciding food should be my first stop. Then I could figure out this clothing situation.

The plain white T-shirt hits me mid-thigh, covering everything. Even so, as I shove the dresser aside, I grab my flip knife and tuck it into my bra. There is no such thing as being too careful.

I pad down the hallway, passing Reid's closed door. I

press my ear against it, but I don't hear anything, so I carry on to the kitchen.

I pause in the center of the room when I find him sprawled out on the sofa. He's dressed all in black: black jeans, black T-shirt, black boots. He must have come back at some point and changed, unless he keeps spare clothes in his car, which I suppose is likely given his line of work.

Creeping over to the kitchen, I fumble around until I have the coffee machine working and a bowl of Froot Loops in my hand. Despite the noise, Reid hasn't moved, so I eat my food and contemplate my next step. Apparently, I'm getting a new apartment today, so the sooner Reid takes me, the sooner I'll be out of his hair.

After I've finished eating, I place my bowl in the sink and pour a cup of coffee for myself and one for Reid. I add a little creamer and sugar to mine but leave Reid's black, unsure how he drinks it. I walk over and set his on the coffee table before nudging Reid in the arm with my foot.

Taking a sip of my coffee, I wait for him to move. Nothing. A frisson of apprehension runs through me.

Placing my cup on the table beside Reid's, I move closer until I'm practically leaning over him. I slip my hand over his shoulder and press two fingers to his neck, looking for a pulse, when I'm yanked off my feet and pinned beneath Reid's hard body.

I open my mouth to shout when I spot all the blood.

"What the fuck? Reid, look at me." Sliding a hand under his chin, I tilt his head up, making him moan in the process. When I get a good look at his battered face, I curse.

"Jesus, what happened?" I graze my thumb gently over his cheekbone. His breathing speeds up as his eyes snap to my mouth before he dips his head and presses his lips to mine.

He swallows down my protests, his tongue demanding entrance, and in my confusion over just what the fuck is happening, I give it to him.

He tastes of beer and blood, not an appealing flavor in theory, and yet, I can't seem to break away. I slide my hands up over the corded muscles of his back and moan into his mouth before he abruptly snatches his mouth from mine.

He stares at me like he's not seeing me for a moment. That's when I notice the gash he has on his forehead and the jagged split through his left eyebrow.

"Reid, you're hurt. Let me clean you up, okay," I coax as soothingly as I can. He seems disorientated as fuck. I don't know what the gash on his head is from, but head injuries can be tricky things even if they seem innocent on the outside.

"Hey, look at me. You're okay now. You're at home. I'm going to get the first aid kit and patch you up, all right?"

He continues to stare at me before nodding jerkily and rolling over enough for me to slide out from under him.

The first aid kit is on the table where he left it last night, so I grab it and place it on the floor next to the sofa before moving quickly down the hall to the bathroom. I rummage through the bathroom cabinet and find a prescription for some pain meds for Kai Reid. Interesting. I just assumed his name was Reid. I store that information away for later and collect a couple of clean towels. I soak one and wring it out as tightly as I can so I don't drip water all through the apartment and make my way back to Reid, who hasn't moved from his spot.

"Here, I found these." I hand him the pain meds and sit on the end of the sofa beside him, watching as he pops the lid and swallows a couple of pills down dry.

"What happened?" I ask softly as he sits forward and twists to face me.

I lift the wet towel and use it to clean the blood from his face.

"Some assholes thinking they had strength in numbers. They learned a lesson about knowing their enemies." He shrugs, grunting with the movement.

I toss the bloody towel on the floor before leaning over and inspecting the cuts on his face.

"The one on your head doesn't look too bad now that I've cleaned it up, but I'll need to glue the one on your eyebrow closed," I warn him. He nods, so I open up the kit and play doctor for him as he did for me the night before.

He sits quietly, not making a sound or even flinching as I work. Once I've applied the glue, I purse my lips and blow softly over it, which causes him to groan. I stop and bite my lip, feeling kind of awkward. This feels intimate, a thought that is quickly confirmed when he leans over and lifts me onto his lap so my thighs straddle his, and he pulls me in tightly for a hug.

Unsure what to do, it takes me a while to reciprocate, wrapping my arms around him and resting my head on his shoulder. I run my fingers through his hair in a soothing motion until he relaxes under me completely.

"I know you are supposed to be showing me my new apartment today, but you need some rest first. Let's get you into bed for a few hours and take things from there?" He pulls back and looks at me, studying my face intently.

"You are even more beautiful than I dreamed you'd be," he declares, making me blush. I laugh awkwardly, not sure how to respond.

"You're acting weird and no lie, it's freaking me out," I tell him the truth, seriously wondering if he should go to the hospital and get checked out.

He stands with me in his arms, forcing me to wrap my legs around his waist as he moves across the room to the bedrooms. He bypasses his and shoves the door to my temporary one open before lowering me to the floor near the bed.

I open my mouth to ask what the heck he wants but snap it shut when he strips off his T-shirt to reveal *holy mother of abs*. Reid is the very definition of the word ripped, and when he pops the button on his jeans, showing the dark happy trail leading down to the holy grail of dicks, a whimper escapes before I can stop it. His eyes snap to mine, flashing for a moment before a grin spreads over his face, making the cut on his lip start bleeding once more.

He either doesn't feel it or just doesn't care. Instead, he stalks toward me until I'm backed up against the bed with nowhere to go but down.

"Kai," I warn. He freezes and visibly shivers.

"Say it again," he orders, one large hand cupping my jaw, the other gripping my hip, keeping me in place.

"Say what?"

"My name, say my name, Red," he urges with a murmur, rubbing his nose from my chin up the side of my face to just behind my ear.

Red? Great now I'm just collecting nicknames left and right.

"Kai," I whisper, feeling oddly compelled to please him.

He groans, placing a soft kiss on my neck before trailing kisses along my jaw until his lips meet mine once more.

This time his kiss is a tease, a hint of what he has to offer, with a softness to counteract the hardness pushing against my stomach.

Pulling away from me a little, he shoves his jeans down his legs, showing off the deep V that girls must go gaga over. I'm not immune—I have the strongest urge to reach out and touch it—but I know I'm playing with fire, so I squeeze my hands into fists to stop myself from getting burned.

He sits on the edge of the bed and pulls off his jeans and boots before kicking them aside and reaching up for my hand. He tugs me onto the bed, making me squeak in surprise before he rolls us both onto our sides, my back to his front, with his arm banded tightly around my waist.

"Erm, Kai." I squirm, but he just grips me tighter. I can feel the evidence of his arousal pressed against the globes of my ass, which, of course, just makes me squirm even more.

"Jesus fucking Christ, Red. Either stay still or spread your legs wide and prepare yourself for my cock because if you keep rubbing that ass of yours against me, I'm going to forget what's right and wrong and fuck you so hard you'll feel me inside you for days."

I freeze at his words. Hell, I'm not even sure I'm breathing. I wait for the cold unrelenting fear to wash over me with its memories of icy fingers, and yet I don't feel cold at all. No, all I feel is hot and very freaking wet.

I've never wanted a man before, never felt the raw sexual need to feel rough hands on my body or thick fingers pushing inside me. But Reid makes me feel things that are so alien to me, solidifying the knowledge that if I let him, this man could truly be my downfall.

# CHAPTER FOURTEEN

My eyes snap open at the sound of ringing. The room is dark now—we must have slept the entire day away. I feel Reid move behind me as he sits up and looks for his phone. I hear the rustle of clothes as he searches through his pockets before the ringing stops.

"What?" his voice asks behind me. I almost answer until I realize he's not talking to me.

"No, she's asleep, hang on."

I close my eyes and keep my breathing even, trying to ignore the encroaching memories of the last time I played possum like this and why.

"Red, you awake?"

I don't answer, keeping my body loose and relaxed even as he runs his fingers up my leg and over my exposed thigh.

"Nah, she's dead to the world, I must have tired her out,"

he laughs. He climbs off the bed, which is just as well because his words are making it hard for me to stay relaxed.

I hear the snick of the door opening before Reid's voice gets farther away.

I don't waste time second-guessing myself. I climb to my feet and follow quietly, keeping myself hidden in the hallway as he moves around the kitchen, making coffee. Thankfully, he starts talking louder now, likely feeling safe in the knowledge that I can't hear him.

"Not my fault you're acting like a pussy," he teases with a laugh.

He's quiet for a minute while he listens to the other person before snorting. "You're just jealous you won't get her cherry." He's quiet again as his words beat at my skin, leaving me feeling like a fool. I knew I had to be careful, but even so, I've struggled to keep myself from falling for his charms. Finding out he's just another lying asshole is precisely what I need to fortify the walls around my heart.

I don't know who he's talking to, but it can only really be one of the other sector heads or Zodiac, and I can't see him talking to the boss man like that.

I think back to what I told him last night, about my suspicions about Zodiac, and wonder if he'll go running to him, selling me out, but it doesn't seem his style. I'll just have to be sure to keep my cards close to my chest. Wyatt and Megan have softened me, but I need to be on my A-game if I'm to survive swimming in these shark-infested waters.

"Yeah, lay low for a bit. I'll call when I'm healed up. Nothing we can do about it now, Jude."

I file the name Jude away for later and slip back the way I came, climbing onto the bed before lying in the position I was in before. I hear his footsteps approaching so I close my eyes and wait for his next move.

He climbs on the bed behind me, tucking us back into the spoons position. I tense before I can stop myself and know he felt it too when he freezes.

"You awake, Red?"

"Hmm..." I mumble, pulling away when he tries to tug me closer.

"I need the bathroom," I tell him quietly, climbing from the bed and locking myself inside the bathroom. I take care of business and use the reprieve to come up with a viable plan.

When I open the door, I find him standing right outside it, watching me with barely concealed hunger. It doesn't matter that I'm mad, pissed, and disappointed in the man, my body still responds to his like we are connected with an invisible tether that sends a pulse of lust from his smirk to my pussy.

It's official. I hate Kai Reid.

"You feeling better?" I ask, not giving anything away. If he wants to play games, so be it.

"Turns out a beautiful nurse is enough to heal most wounds." He grins, slipping my hair off my shoulder.

"Imagine that." I roll my eyes. "Well, since you're feeling

better, you won't mind showing me my new pad. That way, I can get out of your hair."

I try to push past him, but he blocks the way with his body, halting my movements.

With a huff, I look up at him and see his grin grow wider.

"Something wrong, Red?" he goads me.

"Nothing some food and some coffee won't fix, especially seeing as my last one went cold while I was playing nursemaid to you."

I cross my arms and wait for him to move. He takes in my defensive posture and steps back with his hands up in capitulation.

"Okay, you get showered and ready, and I'll whip us up some scrambled eggs, sound good?"

"That would be great, thank you." I offer him a small smile of my own. I might have to lock up my wayward libido, but there is no point in being a bitch unnecessarily. I'm going to be working with him in some capacity or another after all.

He leaves me to it, so I take the quickest shower in the history of showers and get dressed in my jeans, tank top, and the hoodie I've now claimed.

I make sure everything of mine is shoved into my backpack and then after a moment's hesitation, I shove in the T-shirt I slept in last night too.

Reid is just plating up the food when I set my bag down next to the sofa.

He carries both plates to the table and indicates for me to sit. I do, choosing the seat that gives me an unobstructed view of the city at night now that the blinds have been opened.

I take a bite of the eggs and moan. "Wow, these are good."

"Why, thank you. The secret is the cheese," he reveals.

I file that away for later. Surely even I can't mess up scrambled eggs and cheese, right?

"So, after you take me to my new place, can you take me to the division that's now apparently mine?" I need to find my footing around here and the sooner I do that, the better.

He pauses with his fork halfway to his mouth. "What?"

"I'm a division head now, right? That means I have shit to do. I have never been the kind of girl to sit around and do nothing, so I want to get started as soon as possible."

He doesn't look thrilled at the prospect, but that's not my problem.

"If that's what you want, I'll need to make some calls, but I can do that while you're checking out your new pad."

"Sounds good." I nod and continue to eat, finishing off my eggs and toast way before Reid does.

He laughs when he takes in my plate before staring at his own.

"Jesus, you must have been hungry." He shakes his head, finishing up his food as I take my plate to the sink.

"Sorry, it's a habit. You learn to eat what you can when you can and as quickly as possible on the streets so nobody can swipe it from you."

I turn to face him when I hear his fork clank loudly on his plate.

"You don't have to worry about that here. You're hungry, you eat. If you find it in the fridge or cupboards and you want it, eat it. Nobody is going to take it away from you anymore."

I try not to let his words warm me, but even knowing he's a two-faced asshole doesn't make this mask of duplicity he wears any less appealing.

I offer him a nod and turn back to the sink before swallowing. I make quick work of the breakfast dishes and the ones left over from last night while I wait for Kai to finish.

"I'm just going to jump in the shower, and then I'm all yours." He speaks from right behind me, making me tense.

"Okay, I'm ready when you are."

He presses a kiss to the side of my head in a bizarrely soft gesture before heading back to the bedrooms.

I turn to watch him go and frown when he uses the room he loaned to me. Why isn't he using his own room? Unless that is his room? Fuck me, I'm such an idiot.

I creep down the hallway and wait for the sound of the shower before dipping inside the room Kai said was his.

I pause in the doorway. It's an exact duplicate of the other room only flipped. Everything is the opposite way round, and instead of being decorated in navy and cream, this one is tastefully done in a soft green and white.

Nothing looks out of place. There certainly isn't any handy clue lying haphazardly on the bed waiting to be found. A peek in the closet shows the same as the next room —rows of suits with shelves of jeans and T-shirts and footwear stacked neatly underneath.

Not a thing appears to be out of place, and I don't have time to start rummaging through shit without getting caught, so I pull the door closed behind me and return to the bedroom. The room reveals nothing, so I move to check out the bathroom, but a groan has me freezing.

Shit, has he hurt himself? I make my way to the door but pause when I hear my name being moaned. I flush when I realize he's not hurting, well other than his dick taking a beating.

My head spins at the knowledge that he's making himself come thinking of me.

I have to fight back the urge to slip my fingers inside my panties and return the favor, but lusting after the devil will only lead me to hell.

The water shuts off and I know I'm out of time, so I pull the door shut behind me and head back to the kitchen area to wait.

I tidy around a little until he reappears wearing a grin and just his jeans and boots, a white T-shirt gripped in his hand. His golden skin is still damp, so I shut my eyes to stop my wayward thoughts. Kai Reid makes me forget I'm a smart girl. The second I stepped inside his apartment, I've felt a reckless need to let down my guard and be the twenty-one-year-old I could have been. I have to stop thinking like that. Reckless and wild sound fun, but I'm still wise enough to know the consequences could be catastrophic.

"Can you put some of this on my back? It will help with the bruising." He tosses me a tube of ointment.

I catch it and point to the sofa. "Lay down there for me."

He does as I ask, walking to the sofa with the kind of swagger only a man completely comfortable in himself can have.

And why shouldn't he be comfortable? He looks like the incarnation of every teenage girl's wet dream and every cougar's leading man in their late-night spank bank movie reel.

I wish I could say I'm unaffected, but the dampness between my legs begs to differ and I know the cocky asshole knows it too.

His back is toned and I want to scratch my nails down it. A little blood and pain would do him good. Leaning down, I see the purplish hue on his skin, the telltale signs that he will look and feel awful tomorrow.

"They got you good, huh?"

He makes a noncommittal sound, so I squirt some of the cream in my hand and smooth it over his heated skin. He moans.

"Sorry, I'm trying to be as gentle as possible, but there is not much here that isn't going to hurt. It looks like you've been kicked, repeatedly."

He doesn't answer, but I never expected him to. He's been quite tight-lipped about the whole situation.

I rub the foul-smelling cream over his back, smoothing it over his hard muscle and down to the waistband of his jeans. The more I touch him, the harder I find it to breathe.

"Okay, you're done. I don't know what this shit is, but it smells like dead fish."

He laughs and climbs up from the sofa, reaching out to the coffee table for the T-shirt.

I avert my eyes when I notice he's hard as a rock. Jesus, didn't he just rub one out in the shower?

"I'm just going to wash my hands," I mumble, heading over to the sink while he finishes getting dressed.

Snagging a set of keys from a little hook near the door, he slips them into his pocket before shrugging on a leather jacket from the larger coat rail beside it.

He takes in my hoodie and jeans, and the backpack I now have gripped tightly in my hands, before grabbing a helmet and another jacket like the one he's wearing.

"Put these on. I want to take the bike." He shoves the helmet in my hands and tosses me the jacket, heading out into the corridor as I drop my bag to my feet and slip the buttery soft leather jacket and the helmet on.

"Come on, Red, times a-wastin'!" he yells.

I shake my head, not bothering to protest that it's me that's been waiting for him and pull the door shut tightly behind me

# CHAPTER FIFTEEN

Thinking better of it, I asked Kai to show me the division first, knowing it would mean he would need to stick around with me for a bit.

This was not because I wanted to spend the evening in his presence. The sooner I could put some distance between us and the crackling spark of electricity, the better. No, I planned to use him right now for appearance's sake. I wanted the people of my new district to see their new leader and assume I'm in allegiance of some kind with at least one of the other division heads.

I think back to Leo, covered in blood when he offered me his hand in an unlikely truce, and wonder if that might be the way to go. Having others at my back will mean I'm not the easy target people will be expecting. I just need to figure out what they'll want in return and whether I'm willing to give it.

"So this area here, all the way down to the docks, across the bay and over to the corner of 5th is your territory. The only person the people here will answer to is you, and the only person you'll answer to is Zodiac, so you'll pretty much have free rein. Eighty percent of all earnings made selling his product go straight back to Zodiac. But you are free to set up other side earners. Anything you earn from that is all yours. If you need Zodiac to provide you with anything beyond the product that needs moving, like girls or weapons, he'll source them and take additional cuts. Otherwise, like I said, anything you do outside of him, as long as it doesn't interfere with your division duties, is yours."

"Like what?" I question, wanting to soak up any information he can give me.

"Well, in my division, for instance, I have runners flooding the streets with Zodiac's product, and I make a good income from it even after Zodiac takes his eighty percent. But my main source of income comes from offering protection," he admits, making me frown.

"What kind of protection?" Because I doubt it's quite as noble as it sounds.

"Businesses pay us to keep trouble from their door, whether that's homegrown trouble or from farther afield. It's up to me and the guys I use to keep people safe."

"And if people don't pay you for protection?" I question, looking up at him from under my lashes.

"Oh, they all pay eventually, especially when they find trouble consistently darkening their doorstep."

"Right, that's what I figured," I mutter, turning to look around the darkened street he's parked us on.

"Bad guy, remember? I run drugs for fuck's sake. What did you think my side job would be, knitting?" he snaps, almost as if I've offended him. I can't help but snort.

"You really shouldn't jump to conclusions. You don't know me well enough to anticipate what I'm thinking. I don't care how you make your money. Am I a fan of innocent people getting hurt? Nope, but I know it happens. Sometimes accidentally, sometimes through direct exploitation. Who the fuck am I to tell you how to run your division?" I wave my hand over his body before pointing at his sleek bike parked just behind us.

"You dress in designer duds, live in a penthouse apartment, and have a fancy bike and car at your disposal. It's obviously working for you." I turn and walk down the quiet street, slowing my steps as he falls in beside me.

"So you don't judge, fine. I guess that's my issue, not yours. Saying that, I don't really think the protection route will work for you anyway. You're not exactly intimidating." He smirks, but I just roll my eyes.

"Tell me that again when I'm pointing a gun at your head," I huff.

"Touché."

I hear faint music playing and follow the sound to what looks to be some kind of jazz bar on the corner—a warm yellow glow spills out when the door swings wide, illuminating the cobbles of the street outside.

"I like this place, it's like a mix of old and new. Reminds me of home. They were doing this big regeneration thing. I can imagine it looking just like this street."

"Yeah, well don't get too excited, most of this division is a shithole. Some of the small businesses like this one are struggling to stay afloat with the newer big corporate companies opening downtown."

I shrug. I get that, but I'm hoping there can be space for both.

"Is there a home base or office or some shit down here that the district head works out of?"

"More often than not, most business is done over the phone as it's safer, but if meetings do need to happen, they usually take place down by the docks where there are less prying eyes."

"Makes sense. Okay, what about minions?" I look up at him when he barks out a laugh.

"Minions? Fuck, are you serious? Jesus Christ, you are." He runs his hand through his hair before looking back at me.

"Okay, look, there are a few men that ran for the guy before you, but the fact that he's dead should show that maybe they're not the kind of guys you want watching your back."

"You're probably right, but I need to start somewhere. At the very least, I need to have people running Zodiac's product while I get my shit in order. Just because I'm coming into the game late doesn't mean Zodiac will do me any favors. In fact, the last thing I want is a favor being owed to Zodiac."

"You're not wrong there," he grumbles, looking away, his shoulders dropping.

"Do you know a way to contact these guys?"

He shakes his head before pausing like something just occurred to him.

"The previous Gemini kept a ledger with the names of the guys that worked for him and other shit like that in a safe down at the docks."

My eyes widen incredulously at that, making him laugh. "Don't look at me like that. The whole thing is coded. If it was stolen, it would be worthless. Besides, who would be crazy enough to steal from a division head?"

"I don't know, maybe the same person who decided to kill a division head?" I throw out. "So this code? I don't suppose you happen to know said code now, do you?"

His lips twitch at my words. "Maybe. What's in it for me?" He turns and stops me from walking with a hand on my hip.

"Well, I promise not to stab or shoot you for the next twenty-four hours no matter how strong the urge might be," I graciously offer.

His eyes widen before he laughs.

I stand there watching him, silently threatening to pull the wings off each and every butterfly taking flight in my stomach.

"Okay, fine. I'll help, but you'll owe me a favor," he concedes.

"That, my friend, will depend on the favor. If you can deal with that, then fine."

He stares at me for a moment, before nodding. "Deal." He winks before walking back over to his bike and climbing on.

I walk toward him, reaching for the hand he holds out to me, scolding myself for remembering too late that you should never make a deal with the devil because he's a tricky fucker who will try to outmaneuver you at every turn.

I'm just going to have to make sure I remain one step ahead.

Climbing up behind him, I wrap my arms tightly around his torso once more and hold on tight as he roars down the street. It only takes about fifteen minutes to get to the docks and much like the street earlier, it seems far too quiet for a city this size.

"It's not as busy here in division twelve as I assumed it would be," I tell him when the bike stops.

He flicks the kickstand down with his foot and plants his feet to steady his bike as I swing my leg over and climb off.

I pull the helmet from my head and shake out my hair as he climbs off and takes the helmet from me.

"People are being cautious as they wait for the new head to be instated. There's been some unrest—gangs turning on each other—and it's spilled onto the streets more than once."

His answer has me frowning as I ask the next question. "What exactly happened to the last Gemini?"

"He was shot dead in his office right here at the docks."

"Of course, he was. Let me guess. It was a gang-style execution shot. In the head, right?"

He nods, a look of surprise on his face.

"You know, every time you look surprised, it makes me want to punch you in that pretty little face of yours," I growl.

He steps closer to me. "You think I'm pretty?"

I shove him away. "That's what you got from that? I don't even know why I bother." I sigh.

"It's just hard sometimes to remember that you're not just some girl, especially when you start spouting off shit about gang-style executions." He shakes his head.

I don't know why, but him calling me some girl makes my temper flare.

"You do know that this shit is my life, right? This might be me turning up for my first day at work, but I've been in the game since you dragged me into it. Fuck, I've been dealing with shit on Zodiac's behalf for the last, however freaking long it's been. It feels like forever, a monotonous cycle of fucking people up before they could do it to me first."

He scowls at me, mulling over my words before crossing his arms over his broad chest.

"I thought you had people working for you?" he spits out as I stare at him in disbelief.

"What, a teenage throwaway street thug? Oh yeah, I had droves of people willing to watch my back," I sass, not mentioning Wyatt or Megan at all.

"Then how the fuck did you manage to end up here? Only the best of the rest get picked by Zodiac for this shit."

"There you go assuming again. Just because I didn't have anyone at my back doesn't mean I wasn't capable of handling my own dirty work."

He stares at me for the longest time, likely trying to bridge together how I look with the pieces of information he knows about me. I can be ruthless when needed, but it doesn't change the fact I look like a high school cheerleader. He knew I was one of Zodiac's top earners, I just didn't realize he thought it was because someone else was doing the heavy lifting. Honestly, it wasn't often I had to result in using brute force or bullets, most people gave me respect because I returned it. It really is as simple as that. Well, that and the knowledge that if anyone crosses me, I deal with them immediately and brutally, with no excuses.

"You know, you have the face of an angel, Red, but I have the strangest urge to go home and salt my windows," he admits, making me laugh in surprise.

"Come on, let's get this ledger and then I'll show you to your new place." He reaches over and takes my hand, tugging me down to the building at the far end of the docks.

The lack of streetlights here has me palming my trusty knife and gripping the hilt tightly.

A beeping brings my attention to a keypad that's illuminated green in the dark night sky. Reid types in a number too quickly for me to catch it, but the whole thing sets off another red flag.

Why exactly does he have the code to get in here? And why on God's green earth would the previous Gemini be stupid enough to share information about a ledger with someone from another division? I understand the concept of loyalty, even among the criminal underbelly, but this just seems like asking for trouble. Plus, if Reid knows the encryption code the ledger is written in, then it stands to reason the other division heads do too. When Kai said the information inside the ledger would be worthless to anyone who took it, he clearly wasn't including the other division heads.

Nothing about this scenario makes sense to me, including Gemini's apparent gang-style killing. This screams setup, which makes me very freaking anxious.

I push those thoughts away for later as the door swings wide. Reid fumbles around for a second before a dim light flicks on and I'm pulled inside.

The fluorescent strip lighting makes an annoying humming sound that would leave me shooting it within minutes if I were forced to work here day in day out.

"The safe's over here." He lets go of my hand and moves over to the cheap scratched desk in the middle of the room. Dipping down, he fiddles with what I'm guessing is the safe before standing back up with a notebook in his hand.

"Here it is." He holds it out to me, so I take it, shoving it into the front pocket of my backpack while he does something else, hidden by the desk.

"Something else in there I might need?" I question lightly, but he stands abruptly and pulls me back to the door.

"Nah, I was just changing the code to something more memorable for you. It's now your birthday. I'll change the one on the door too," he offers, pulling it closed behind us.

"So were you and the other Gemini friends?" I question quietly as he changes the code. He needn't bother, I'd change it in a heartbeat if I planned on making this place the base of my operations.

"Johnny? Fuck no. The guy was a conceited tool," he spits, grabbing my hand and leading me back toward his bike.

"You don't get to where we are by having friends," he warns me, but he needn't have bothered. I'm not the naïve girl he seems to think I am.

Coming here tonight with him was exactly what I needed to remind me of the kind of man he is. He wants something from me, just like Zodiac does. It might be the same thing or something else entirely, but whatever it is left the last Gemini dead. Let's hope history doesn't repeat itself.

# CHAPTER SIXTEEN

I cling to Reid as he maneuvers his bike along the roads toward what will be my new home.

I breathe in the leather of his jacket and close my eyes, enjoying one of the rare peaceful moments of just being free. When I was a little girl, if someone had told me my life would turn out like this, I would have thought they were crazy. Now, at twenty-one, and with the crushing weight of the world on my shoulders, I wish things could have been different. I wish I had appreciated the little I had instead of wanting to grow up as fast as I could. I wanted to escape that trailer park so bad I could taste it, but now, I'd sell my soul to go back.

The ride takes far less time than I would have hoped, but it's just as well. Looking up, I realize I'm standing next to an apartment building similar to Reid's. Another monstrosity of chrome and glass, but I guess I can see the appeal. It's not that I'm ungrateful. Living on dusty pavements and dirty doorways meant I spent many a night looking up at the towering buildings with their twinkling lights, imagining people snuggled up watching television or families eating around a large table, laughing and joking with each other. Now though, it seems the reality is colder than I thought it would be. There is no coziness to the sleek lines and sharp edges, no warmth in the cool glass and dark corners. I guess it's the family that makes a place a home, whether that be a hovel or a mansion, and without one, maybe I would always feel adrift. This time when I look over the city, it will be from the other side, looking down from my tower, wishing I were back with the only two people on this planet who give a shit about me.

The bike stops and I climb off this time, not waiting for Reid to help, needing a second to wipe away the feeling of melancholy.

I pull the helmet from my head and hand it back to Reid, who hangs it on the edge of the bike's handlebars before he climbs off himself.

The graceful way he moves captures my attention. His footsteps as he approaches are so sure and purposeful, making his movements seem almost fluid somehow. If the guy wasn't the devil incarnate, I'm sure he would be able to walk on water and make it look easy.

"What's that face for?" he asks, cocking his head to the side.

"I'm wondering if you ever did ballet?" I ask, making him frown.

"What the fuck?" he asks, looking confused.

I can't help but laugh. "Yeah, you have the perfect figure to pull off a leotard and a pretty pink tutu," I tease, laughing when he slings his arm over my shoulder and starts poking me in the ribs.

"Hey," I gasp, pulling out of his hold, still chuckling.

"I'm all man, baby, but I can't deny I like that you think about me." He smirks, making me roll my eyes.

"Okay, big strong man, show me where to go." I grin, shaking my head. I can't help it, he's so ridiculous.

He pulls me close, then tucks my hand in the crook of his elbow.

"I would say such a gentleman, but we both know that's not true."

"Yeah, I can't argue with that. Doesn't mean I don't have manners, though. I know how to open doors and shit, I just usually prefer to kick them in," he admits, making me chuckle. Well, at least he's honest.

Entering the elevator, I lean over to the bank of buttons and look up at Reid in question. "Which floor?"

And now it's his turn to roll his eyes at me. The whole thing is so out of place, making him look younger and softer underneath the hardened exterior.

"Penthouse, obviously. Only the best will do." He smirks.

We stand in relative silence as the elevator ascends before a thought occurs to me.

"Don't these kinds of places usually have doormen or something? Come to think of it, I don't remember seeing one at your place either."

"Fewer people around who are unconnected to this life, the better. Too many prying eyes mean too many questions, and then you have to consider the possibility of eliminating someone just because they accidentally saw something they shouldn't have," he answers with a shrug. It makes sense, though I figured Zodiac would be all about the bells and whistles as he's definitely the type to lord his riches over others. Or even entice them with a golden carrot, but I can see the logic in having fewer eyes around.

The doors open, revealing a short hallway with two doors at the end facing each other. Seems I might have a neighbor. I'm not sure how I feel about that. I kind of liked the idea of being up here alone. I'm a private person and would rather not have to deal with everyone else's bullshit, but beggars can't be choosers.

"Who else lives in the building? Are they all connected to Zodiac in some way, or are they just regular residents?" I ask, stopping when he does outside the door on the left.

He looks at me oddly for a minute, so I explain what I mean.

"Is this place the kind of place where flying bullets are a rare occurrence or a likely probability?"

"Ah, no, most of the apartments are empty right now. The

building itself belongs to Zodiac, as you know, but most division heads are given the option to move their own teams into the other apartments at their discretion. It's entirely your call, of course, but soldiers are a lot more loyal when they have an incentive like a swanky apartment," he tells me, swiping a keycard through the lock before swinging the door wide.

I think about what he says and realize he might be right. It's at least something I need to think about when I'm recruiting.

Walking down the short hallway, I find myself in the entrance to the central hub of the living area.

As Reid places the keycard on the kitchen counter and flicks the lights on, I take note of the floor to ceiling windows, the fancy kitchen, and the wooden floors and turn to Reid with a question on the tip of my tongue but he must anticipate what I was going to say.

"Yes, it's all pretty much the same as my place—everything from the kitchen to the bedrooms. The same designer did all the penthouses in all the divisions. The only differences you'll find are the structural ones. Zodiac didn't want it to seem like he was playing favorites."

I nod, moving past the kitchen area on my left, to the living area on my right. It's as big as Reid's place, if not a touch bigger, the layout is just different. The living area has a sunken floor, meaning I have to step down into it. I move quietly across the room, passing the large sofa, the same color and style as Reid's, but a huge oversized three-seater instead of a corner piece. The table and rugs, the cushions, and lighting are all the same. It's flipping weird, but I bite my tongue not wanting to sound ungrateful. The dining table in the far corner near the window is a circular one, seating four people but feeling cozier somehow with its rounded shape, making me picture intimate dinners. I shake it off and move to the bank of windows and look out.

Bright city lights illuminate the inky sky as far as the eye can see, looking like a blanket of neon fireflies. I stare for a moment, picturing Megan and Wyatt staring out at the same sky, and perhaps for a second, I imagine Drake gazing up at the moon too. Feeling nostalgic, I allow myself a brief moment to dwell before I lock everything away in the box. I try not to open it very often, especially around others.

"So what do you think? There is one other place I can show you, but I'm not gonna lie, it looks just like this one. It's the one the previous Gemini lived in so you would be living in his old apartment, and something tells me that would annoy you."

"No, you're right, this place is fine. Trust me, I'm not picky. This is all a little overkill for just me, but I get it, appearances and all that."

"Yeah, Zodiac's big on showing off his wealth. He cares what others think, so he wants his team to look the part."

I nod, having already figured that out for myself. "This place is good, I swear. I just wish I had some coffee and stuff, toothpaste, and the essentials, but tomorrow will be fine." I shrug. He glances down at his watch before shaking his head.

"Give me an hour, and I'll be back. There is a twenty-four-hour store not far from here. I'll pick up some stuff for you while you settle in."

"You don't have to do that," I protest, but he holds up his hand to stop me.

"Call it a housewarming gift from me to you." He smiles.

"Well, in that case, thank you." I smile in return, lifting up on my tiptoes to press a kiss to his cheek.

He gazes down at me, a warmth filling his eyes before he blanks his face and nods.

"Lock up. The key is on the kitchen counter. I'll buzz when I'm back. If you think of anything specific you might need while I'm gone, just text me."

"Will do, and thank you again."

He waves me off and heads out. I stare out the window a little longer, absorbing the quiet until I see Reid climb on his bike and pull away. I don't waste another second. I grab the keycard and head out the door, slamming it behind me.

I head to the elevator and hit the button for the ground floor, tapping my foot impatiently while I wait. When I finally make it to the ground floor, I jog across the lobby and push my way through the glass doors into the cool night air and head across the road to the all-night cafe I saw as we pulled up. It's a known fact that luck is never really on my side but seeing this place when we got here had me feeling like maybe, just for once, my luck would change.

I pull open the door and head over to the counter, where

a lone girl with rainbow-colored hair sits flicking through a magazine.

At my approach, she lifts her head and adopts a fake smile.

"Welcome to Beans & Co, what can I get you?"

I look around the row of computers at the far end of the cafe by the windows and nod in the direction.

"I need to use one of those and I'll take a large latte, please."

"The computers are all shut down now—" she starts, but I stop her, leaning over the counter with my hand on her wrist.

"The new Gemini has been appointed and I have been tasked with a few jobs. I don't want him to get mad at me, and I really don't want them to be mad at you when I know you're just doing your job," I whisper, glazing over the threat by adding a little sweetness to my voice. Her face pales at the name *Gemini*. She lifts a set of keys and practically shoves them at me.

"Sorry, of course, you can use them anytime. This key opens the cafe, it's the spare. You can come here whenever," she offers.

*Jesus girl, you wouldn't survive a second on the streets.* I want to snap at her for giving in so quickly but shut the thought down. She doesn't need me to be a bitch to her when she is only doing her job.

I place the keys on the counter before looking back up at her. "Thank you, but that's not necessary. I just want to use one of the computers, that's all. I'll be ten minutes, tops," I promise her.

"Yes, no problem." She turns as I make my way over to the first computer and turn it on. I wait for it to boot up and decide to text Reid in the hope of distracting him so he doesn't hurry back.

**Me**: *Hey, can you grab me some tampons, some Twix, and some Coke?*

I press send before placing my phone on the table and concentrating on the whole reason I came here to begin with.

I slip the memory stick I stole from Reid's jacket pocket and slide it into the computer and wait for it to reveal whatever Reid is trying to keep hidden from me. As the data appears on the screen, I hear footsteps approach. Looking up, I see the girl with my coffee in her shaking hands.

"Here you go," she offers.

"Thanks, how much do I owe you?"

"It's on the house." She smiles timidly.

"Wow. That is so nice of you. I won't forget this kindness, Shelly," I tell her, glancing at the name badge on her left pocket.

Her smile grows bigger now and she starts to relax a little.

"Hey, I don't suppose you have a spare memory stick I could use, do you?" I ask her softly, not wanting to spook her any more than I already have tonight.

"Oh, um, yes, actually. We have a box of spares. People forget them all the time, so we keep them for a month then toss them in the spares box if they go unclaimed," she rambles.

"That's perfect."

She scuffles off to fetch one as my phone chimes with an incoming message.

**Reid**: *Tampons? Seriously? Can I just kill someone for you instead?*

**Me**: *Funny, but unless you are sacrificing someone to the period gods, that won't help.*

I scan over the information on the computer screen, only understanding parts of it because I have no clue who a lot of these people are, but that will come. What I don't understand is why Reid would take this, it's just— and then I see it.

I sit for a moment, just staring at the screen until the words blur.

"Balls," I mutter as Shelly comes back with the memory stick.

I thank her and download everything from one stick to the other before wiping the computer, shoving the memory sticks into separate pockets, and sipping my hot coffee. Once I'm finished, I head to the door and call out a goodbye to Shelly before hurrying across the road. I head straight up to the penthouse, my mind swirling around with the information I just found and what I'm going to do with it. By the time I'm in my apartment, the coffee feels like a lead weight in my stomach. The only conclusion I've come to is that I have to keep this information quiet. There is a reason it has been kept quiet for this long, and I suspect it's why the previous Gemini was killed.

So I'll lock it away until the day comes that I need to use it. And the day will come.

Until then, I'll keep Reid at a distance because once he knows I've figured out who Jude is, all bets will be off.

# CHAPTER SEVENTEEN

"Y ou didn't tell me which ones to get, so I got a mix. You owe me for this," he growls, making me smile as he tips up the bag on the counter where multiple boxes of tampons spill over the edge and onto the floor.

I palm the memory stick and laugh at him, moving in for a hug. I place a chaste kiss on his lips.

Of course, that's not enough for Reid. He grips me tightly and takes our kiss from sweet to blistering in a nanosecond. I just about manage to keep my head clear enough to slip the memory stick back into his jacket pocket before I pull away to keep this from leading somewhere I'm not ready to take it.

"Fuck it. If that's how you say thank you, I'll buy you all the tampons you need," he offers with a grin.

Stepping back, desperately needing to put some distance between us, I ignore the scattered boxes and grab one of the bags from the counter. I take note of everything as I unload it, mentally tallying up the amount as he watches me quietly. I swallow down the lump in my throat at his thoughtfulness. Things like this make it impossible to hate the man.

"I'll pay you back tomorrow, once I hit up an ATM," I promise, smiling when I see the pancake mix and package of mixed berries.

"Nope. It's my gift, remember? Now, I have to go. I have something I need to do. You gonna be okay?" he asks, scanning my face. I wonder how much is sincere concern and how much is an act. He's so damn hard to read.

"I'm good, thank you. I'll message you tomorrow. I'll likely have a thousand things to ask you."

He chuckles before rapping his knuckles on the countertop and heading for the door. "Fine by me, just don't make it too early. A face this handsome needs its beauty sleep." He winks, pulling the door open and stepping out into the deserted hallway, then closing it behind him.

The smile slips from my face now that I'm alone. I carry on with putting the groceries away on autopilot as I focus on formulating a plan of what to do now.

Being forced into submission as a kid and made to follow a strict and restrictive set of rules means I'm loath to start following someone else's rules again. I can act the part for a while, but becoming someone's lapdog once more is not an option. When Zodiac figures that out, I'll become a liability. The only way to stop myself from becoming a casualty like the Gemini before me is to change up the game.

Or perhaps to play a different game altogether.

A smile spreads wide as I finally figure out what I'm gonna do.

AFTER A RESTLESS NIGHT of sleep and a breakfast of pancakes and coffee, I head over to the bank before making my way to one of the fancy boutiques I passed on my way here. Knowing I'm going to get one shot at making a first impression, I spend the next few hours looking for the perfect outfit. I settle on a dove gray fitted dress with capped sleeves and a thin black belt that shows off my small waist. I pair it with high black peep-toe shoes and pay for it in cash, trying not to swallow my tongue at the price tag. Next up is a makeover at a salon across from the boutique that manages to squeeze me in. That's where I spend the next four hours getting crimped and primped until finally, I emerge feeling like a new woman.

I always thought this whole kind of thing was a frivolous luxury only rich bitches could afford, but even I can't deny the results as I look in the mirror at the glossy and classy reflection staring back at me. I can barely recognize myself.

I stare at the image for so long it starts to blur, but I just can't connect the street rat I still feel like on the inside to the sophisticated woman staring back.

After returning to the penthouse to change into my new

clothes, I splurge on a cab to the next place that's on today's agenda—Echo's.

Echo's is the blues bar that caught my attention last night. Even now, standing in front of it with the lights off, I can feel myself relaxing. It makes no sense being drawn to a place I've never stepped foot inside of, but there is something about it that feels comfortable and inviting. I learned early on to trust my instincts and this place is luring me in like a beacon.

Even though the sign beside the doors states that they don't open for another hour, I can see a few people milling about inside, so I knock loudly and wait.

"We're closed," a voice yells from inside, dismissing me.

I knock again, this time with more force because I'm obnoxious like that. I hear someone complaining before the sound of locks being opened.

When the door swings open, a tall man with a gray beard narrows his eyes at me and snaps, "What the hell, lady? Can't you read?"

"I can read just fine thanks; I just can't wait until opening. I want to talk to the owner, please."

He crosses his arms over his chest, standing to his full height, trying to intimidate me, but I'm shorter than everyone and have had far scarier men try that tactic on me.

"I don't have the time to deal with whatever shit you want to gab about." He turns to leave so I play my ace card.

"Fine. I'll be sure to relay that information back to Gemini."

He freezes like I thought he might. I stand with my arms

crossed against my chest, fighting back a grin. Just like last night, I pretend I'm Gemini's assistant. I don't know when I decided to keep up with the ruse, but after saying it to the girl at the coffee shop, who I suspected would have fainted if she found out who I really was, I realized that anonymity could work in my favor.

For a start, it removes the target from my back. People knowing that the new Gemini is a woman will have every gangster wannabe trying to either put me in my place or take it. Pretending I'm just the assistant leaves me with enough power to be obeyed but without the headache of watching over my shoulder every second of the day. At least until people start asking questions.

I know it won't last forever. There are eleven other division heads out there who know exactly who I am, but for now, until I have myself established, it will work.

"Gemini is dead," he remarks warily, turning to face me once more, his aging face looking worn and tired now.

"The old one is, yes, but a new one was appointed yesterday. You must have known it would happen," I say softly.

He nods, his shoulders dropping. "So, who are you, and what do you want me to do? I don't have much money for protection fees, but I can give you a cut of the profits until this place sells, then you'll have to take this up with the new owner."

I don't like the defeated look about this guy, but hopefully, I can change that. His words let me know that just like Reid, the previous Gemini was into the protection business. I guess it's an easy side business without the added stress of worrying about overheads.

"I'm not here about that. May I come in and talk to you somewhere more private?"

He stares at me for a moment before sighing and pulling the door wider, indicating for me to come in.

As he locks the door behind us, I look around, taking in the cozy booths with small circular tables scattered around the room, all facing a small stage on the far left. The stage is empty right now, but with its tall retro-looking microphone and the elegant black piano, I can easily picture someone standing there belting out words about lost loves and broken hearts as an audience listens raptly.

"This way." The man grabs my attention again, leading me across the room to the bar on the right.

Lifting the portion of the bar that opens, he waits for me to walk through before pushing open the door marked *Staff Only*.

I smile at the two men cleaning glasses behind the bar and eyeing me curiously, before following the owner through the door and down a dimly lit hallway.

Multiple doors line either side, but we carry on past them until we reach the stairs at the far end. There's a fire exit propped open beside them as a delivery guy stumbles inside with a crate of bottles that clink loudly against each other.

I make my way up the stairs and see there is only one room up here and the door has been left open. I take that as an invite and stroll inside just as the owner collapses with a groan into a chair behind a large maple wood desk.

"I don't have long before opening, so what can I help you with?" He leans back, his tone not precisely hostile, but it's not inviting either.

"I came here with a business proposition, but now that I know you're planning on selling, I have another idea in mind. Do you own this place outright?" I question, sitting in the chair in front of the desk and crossing my legs.

"No, there is still around eighty thousand to be paid, not including interest," he answers with a frown.

"How about I pay off the outstanding loan and interest and give you fifty grand in cash if you agree to keep your name on the deed."

"What? I don't understand. You want to buy it, but not buy it?" He shakes his head in confusion.

"I want to use this place as a base of operations, at least for a while. 50k is a nice chunk of change to have in your pocket. You could go on an extended vacation."

"But why would you want to use this place when Gemini has spaces down at the docks?"

"You mean the place where the previous Gemini was killed? Do you really think that's a safe space for a woman to be? Not to mention the whole place stinks of fish and is fucking depressing."

His lips twitch when I drop the f-bomb.

"I can't see business booming if people find out Gemini is going to be here. The name alone will draw all kinds of unwanted attention," he warns me, tapping his fingers on his desk.

"You leave that to me to worry about. Besides, this will be *my* home base. Gemini is kind of a recluse, so it will be me holding down the fort."

He's quiet for a moment while he considers my offer.

"What about the staff? I don't want them being left in the lurch," he asks quietly, making my respect for him go up a notch.

"Barring any unforeseen issues, I don't plan on getting rid of anyone. However, if someone chooses to leave, I'll respect their wishes. Nobody is going to be forced to do anything they don't want to. Do you mind me asking why you're selling?" I cock my head to the side in question.

"Money is tight. I've plowed every penny I have into this place, but with the gangs causing trouble, more and more people are staying home where it's safe rather than going out. I barely break even some days. I just figure there has to be more to life than this and honestly, I'm just fucking tired."

He rubs a hand over his face before focusing back on me. He doesn't speak for a minute until he seems to come to some kind of decision.

"If you're serious about this, then yes, I'd like to take you up on your offer," he agrees with a small, relieved smile.

"Excellent. I'll come by tomorrow with the cash and contracts, but for now, how about you show me around and tell me all I need to know about this place?"

# CHAPTER EIGHTEEN

A week later, I find myself sitting back at that desk, but on the opposite side, in the office that's now mine. I take a deep breath before slowly letting it out, happy everything had been signed and paid for. Echo's is now officially mine.

A knock at the door has me lifting my head and sitting up, removing my feet from the edge of the desk.

"Yes," I call out and wait as the door opens to reveal a pretty, young girl carrying a plate holding a croissant in one hand and a cup of what I'm hoping is coffee in the other.

"Gary sent me up with these, ma'am. He said you haven't eaten yet."

I startle at the fact that someone has been paying enough attention to know that. I've only met Gary twice, but as far as men go, I like him. No creepy vibes or worries that he'll shoot me in the back when I turn around, but that doesn't mean I'll let my guard down just yet.

"Thank you. What's your name?" I stand and walk over to take the plate from her.

"Clara, ma'am," she replies, and I swear she curtseys. I have to hold back a snort.

"It's Viddy, Clara, and thank you. I love pastries of every kind. It looks delicious."

She lifts her head and blushes before mumbling a goodbye and scurrying outside, pulling the door closed behind her.

I move back to my desk and kick off my heels, still unaccustomed to wearing the torture devices for long periods of time, but the blood-red heels and matching skin-tight dress make a statement that jeans and a T-shirt just can't do. They say *I'm here, and I mean business.*

Lifting my phone, I dial the man I've been avoiding and wait for him to pick up. I lift the cup of hot coffee and take a cautious sip, trying to avoid third-degree burns, but needing the hit of caffeine. I'm running on nothing but fumes after a chaotic week.

"Cherry, this is a pleasant surprise," he answers, his voice making my nipples pebble in response as per flipping usual.

"Reid, I have a favor to ask of you. Are you free at all tonight?"

"Mmm... I can only pray this is the kind of favor I hope it is," he teases.

I roll my eyes. "Get your mind out of the gutter. I need

something and you are the only person I know in the city right now."

"Okay, that's fine. Come by the apartment tonight at about eight o'clock and we can talk then."

"I'll be there," I reply before hanging up.

I sit quietly, listening to the low hum of music playing below as I eat the delicious flakey pastry.

The mental list I had started for myself the night Reid dropped me off at my apartment has grown, even as I check things off it. It seems for every job I do, three more appear.

Now, a little over a week after I arrived in tattered jeans with a backpack and not much else, I have a penthouse apartment, a closet full of clothes, and a business to operate out of. The next part of my plan, though, requires me to start collecting allies because something tells me I'm going to need them. Unfortunately, building alliances will take time, which is why I can't cut Reid out completely. As pathetic as it is, he's all I've got.

Hitting the button on my desk phone, I wait for Gary to pick up.

"Yes?" He answers gruffly.

"Gary, could you come upstairs for me for a moment, please?"

"I'll be right there." He hangs up, so I sit and wait until I hear a loud knock at the door and invite him in.

"Ma'am?" he questions, sitting in the seat in front of the desk when I point to it.

"Please, call me Viddy. I need your help. I need someone

who knows people. The previous owner told me you've lived here since you were a kid, so I'm guessing not much happens in division twelve that you don't know about," I state, watching him.

He shrugs casually, but he doesn't deny it. "What do you need?" he asks, looking wary, as if I might want one of his kidneys.

"Truthfully? I need people I can trust. I want every single person in this building safe at all times, but while I'm here, I might attract an... unsavory element," I hedge, making him snort.

"What would you like for me to do?"

"I'm going to need a security team for myself, but before that, I want a team of men and women on the doors and inside the club whose sole duties are to protect its customers and the staff."

He looks at me thoughtfully before smiling. "I know a group of people who might be able to help with that, actually. They are veterans, all of them highly trained, but for one reason or another find themselves back as civilians, and the adjustment has been difficult for them. They're a little rough around the edges, but they are good guys, and I trust them with my life," he adds.

I study him for a minute, taking in his close-cropped silvering hair and weathered face.

"Did you serve with them?" I ask him softly.

"Some of them. The others I know from the veterans

center down near the park," he replies, looking at me as if his answer will make me change my mind somehow.

"I'm going to take a chance on you, Gary. I don't trust easily and with good reason, but when I look in your eyes, I see nothing but honesty. Bring in your team, I'd like to meet them. Also, I want you to take over as the manager here. You are more than capable. I don't have time to do the day to day running. I'll double whatever you're earning now."

He stares at me with his mouth open in shock.

"Are you interested?" I prompt with a smirk when he doesn't say anything.

"Hell yeah, you sure about this? I mean, you don't know me, you should probably give me a trial run."

I stand and walk over to the window, looking out into the dark night before answering. "The fact that you even said that at all just tells me I picked exactly the right person. There are two things you should know, though."

He looks up expectantly as I turn back to face him.

"I'm not Gemini's PA or assistant. I *am* Gemini. I'd like to keep my identity under wraps for now until people can learn to see past my boobs. The second is, if you betray me, I'll carve out your heart with a spoon and feed it to you, showing you exactly why I was made Gemini above all other initiates," I warn him, making myself seem far more scary than I am.

"Well, fuck, I knew there was something about you the second you stepped inside the bar. You have this air of confidence about you, which most people your age don't have. It's the kind of confidence that can't be faked with clothes or makeup or any of that superficial shit. It's the confidence you can only get from living a lifetime of experiences. Something tells me you might have lived more than most."

He stands and offers me his hand. I reach over and slip my smaller one into his far larger one.

"I think I'd be honored to work for you, boss lady," he adds with a wink, making me laugh.

"Well, that's good to hear. I'll leave everything in your capable hands, but please don't hesitate to yell if you have any issues, okay? I won't be here tonight as I have some business to attend to, so you'll be in charge. I'll text you my number so you can get ahold of me if you need to, but otherwise, congrats."

"Thank you. Don't worry, I'll hold down the fort until you return." He heads to the door with a jaunty wave and smile on his face making him look younger than his early forties.

Once he's gone, I turn back to the window and watch the people mill by below, a small smile of my own on my lips. For the first time since I got here, I feel like everything is falling into place.

# CHAPTER NINETEEN

The cab drops me off at Reid's a little after eight thirty, thanks to the crazy traffic downtown. The lobby is deserted as I make my way to the elevators and head up to the penthouse. I'm frowning by the time the doors open at how surprisingly easy it was to get this far. I could pull out a gun now, and when Reid opens his door, I could shoot him in the head. I understand why Zodiac thinks doormen are an unnecessary risk, but that doesn't change that there should be some kind of security in place.

I tap the door and wait, but when I don't hear anything, I knock louder. Just when I'm about to pull out my phone and call him, he answers, wearing nothing more than a towel around his waist.

*Holy fucking fuck.*

"Shit. Sorry, Cherry, I lost track of time," he mutters, his eyes roving hungrily over my body. Cursing, he turns and walks back inside, but I'm frozen on the spot. My brain misfires as it struggles to process all that is Reid, every hard, wet inch of him.

"You coming?" He winks and I don't miss the innuendo, or the tenting at the front of his towel. He's not far from the truth with the coming comment, but even a nun would be hard-pressed not to get wet panties with that kind of view.

"Go and get dressed and I'll make us some coffee," I mutter, studiously ignoring his dick. He chuckles as I feel my cheeks heat.

He laughs. "You sure? I'm more than happy to stay like this. I wouldn't want to deprive you."

"I honestly don't know how I haven't killed you yet," I groan as he walks away, and I take in his tight ass in the white towel hanging dangerously low on his hips.

"You won't kill me yet, at least not until you've had your fill of me. Mark my words, Cherry, one day there will be nothing, not even a towel, between us," he yells over his shoulder, thankfully disappearing and giving me a reprieve. The sad thing is, I think he might be right.

I set about making coffee, grabbing the cups before moving over to the fridge to snag the creamer.

Large hands grip my hips from behind, making me jump. He doesn't grind into me like I was half expecting, saving me from having to elbow him in the throat. Instead, he dips his head and inhales deeply.

"Are you sniffing me?" I spin in his arms, looking up at him.

"I can't help it. You smell like strawberries and vanilla. It makes me want to eat you." He presses me against the counter, letting me feel the hard length of his dick between us.

"Reid," I warn him. Every time he pushes the issue, it gets harder to refuse him.

It pisses me off that I feel anything at all. Reid is dangerous with a capital D, and I take too many risks already with this crazy life of mine to justify taking any more. Especially when I know all it will buy me is pain.

I shove him back and step around him, snagging my coffee and making my way over to the sofa.

"What are you wearing? You look like a sex kitten. I can't think with you looking like that," he grumbles, still shirtless but at least he has jeans covering his dick now.

"I came straight from my office and I'm here for a reason, remember? And before you open your mouth to speak, it's not to suck your dick. You have plenty of women to do that for you," I gripe, sitting down on the edge of the sofa.

"Fine, you're safe for now, but I'll wear you down eventually, Cherry, you can bet on it." He grins, sitting beside me.

That's what I'm afraid of, but I'm hoping if we keep our distance from each other, whatever this thing is between us will fade.

"I need weapons," I tell him without preamble, turning the subject to the reason I came here.

He pauses with his coffee to his lips, looking at me with a frown.

"What kinds of weapons?" he asks cautiously.

"Just a couple of handguns. I'm a young single girl with a lot of enemies now that I'm the new Gemini. I need to be able to protect myself," I admit.

"Why not go to Zodiac? I told you he'd help source all that for you."

"I don't need a crate of guns. I need maybe four guns max, small enough for me to shoot and carry comfortably, and plenty of ammunition to go with them."

"Do you even know how to shoot? It's a little more complicated than aim and shoot."

Actually, it's not. That was good enough against Clyde.

"I know that. I've spent plenty of time at the gun range. I might be Gemini now, but I was a runner before that. I both carried and shot a gun before, many times, but I want something clean that's untraceable if possible."

He sighs. "Yes, I can get you a few guns, no problem. I actually have one you can have now until I get them. It's a spare I have, but I never use it. It gets cleaned regularly, but then it goes back in its case. If you want it, it's yours," he offers.

"That would be awesome, thank you."

He nods his head and disappears down the hallway,

giving me some time to sit quietly and drink my coffee before he returns.

It's tidy in here, and knowing Reid, somehow I can't picture him polishing or vacuuming, so I wonder if he gets someone in to clean for him. The man must be nuts. It would take a lot for me to let a random stranger into my inner sanctum like that.

"Here we go, a Sig Sauer P365. Should be a good size for you. You got a permit?"

I snort at him. "No, I don't have a permit. I've only just gotten a permanent address, but it's next on my list." I know it sounds silly, criminals worried about permits, but it's a way to keep the cops off your back. He hands me the gun and a box of ammo. I grab my bag from the floor and slip them both inside.

"Thanks, Reid, I appreciate it. Let me know if you need a favor," I hold my hand up when he grins, "that doesn't involve your dick, and I'll see what I can do." I place the coffee cup on the table before climbing to my feet and sliding my bag over my shoulder.

"You're no fun," he complains, "but don't sweat it. I'd rather know you have something for protection. You get ahold of the previous Gemini's guys?" he asks curiously.

"A couple." It's not a lie, but I won't be using them for anything other than as runners. I sure as shit won't be using them as security, but I don't share that with him.

"Okay, good, there must be a few who would make good

guards. A security detail would make people less inclined to mess with you," he urges.

"I'm working on it. Don't worry Reid, I'm a big girl, I can take care of myself. I've been doing it for a long time."

"This is a big city, babe, the scale of debauchery is off the charts. Whatever it is you think you know, you don't. I don't want to see this pretty face on the front page of the newspaper because they found you floating face down in the bay." He huffs.

"Reid, I get it, and I'm touched by your care, but I'm meaner than I look. You have to trust me when I tell you this. I spent too long climbing my way out of hell to ever go back there."

"Okay, I'm gonna hold you to that, Cherry."

"You do that, Diablo," I sass, making him laugh. Which, of course, makes my pulse speed up.

Yeah, I need to leave before I strip us both naked and forget the world around us exists.

# CHAPTER TWENTY

"Y ou sure you guys are okay with this? I know Gary told you that you'd be acting as protection for the bar, so if you don't want to do this, then I won't force you." I stare at the two men in front of me, Danny and Baker. Danny is the taller of the two. He has auburn hair a few shades lighter than mine and aqua color eyes that make me want to dive in and swim. Baker is a touch shorter, perhaps 5'11 to Danny's 6'1. His hair is such a pale blond, it almost looks white, and his eyes are a stone gray. He gives off an outwardly cold untouchable vibe because of it, but then he smiles, revealing twin dimples, and it softens his features completely. Both of them were recommended by Gary, who told me they are ex-military and highly skilled.

They are a part of the crew brought in to coordinate security for the bar, but I'm about to do something slightly insane tonight and I could use some backup. Not that I won't go alone if I have to.

"So, you want us to act as protection for you tonight?" Danny asks, looking me over. I know what he sees—a short ass at 5'1 now that I've kicked my damn heels off, wearing black skin-tight jeans and an off the shoulder lemon sweater, with my hair loose and crazy. I look every inch the twenty-one-year-old I am. I'm playing to my strengths today, and with where I'm heading, the less I look like a threat, the better.

"Tonight? Yes, but honestly, I'm looking for more than that if you guys feel like a good fit. I need a full-time security team; one I can trust to have my back a hundred percent."

"Can I ask a question?" Baker crosses his arms across his broad chest, his cold eyes focused on mine.

"Sure. I might not be able to answer, but I won't lie to you," I reply, perching my ass on the edge of my desk.

"What's your story? How did you get tangled up with this Gemini and do you need us to get you out, because we can do that? We can hide you somewhere no one would find you," he offers. Danny nods beside him in agreement.

That's sweet. It's a shame I'm the big bad wolf and little red all rolled into one in this story.

I sigh, knowing this might not go down well, but if I don't gain their trust from the beginning, then it's game over before we've even started.

"What I tell you stays in this room," I order, and despite being fifteen and twenty years younger respectively, the soldier in them recognizes a command when given, making them stand a little straighter.

"You have our word," Danny vows, and for whatever reason, I believe him. Even if they turn down my offer and walk away, I don't think they'll repeat anything I'm about to say.

"I don't work for the new Gemini. I *am* the new Gemini," I tell them softly and hold back the smirk when both of them look at me in shock.

"What? How? Why?" they manage to blurt out between them. I take a risk and give them my story, glossing over Megan and Wyatt as much as I can, and finish up with my plan.

"Holy fuck! I don't know if I'm impressed or just plain horrified," Baker blurts out.

"It's okay to be both. It's not the life I envisioned for myself, but it's the one I've found myself tangled up in. I'm not gonna lie, it's gonna get bloody, and I can't guarantee everyone will come out the other side—" This time it's Danny who holds up his hand.

"We get it. This city has been under the control of that fucking tyrant as long as I've lived here. You're either with him or against him, and if it's the latter, he will wipe you and your whole bloodline from the planet as a punishment and a lesson to the next person who dares to defy him. If you think you can topple him from his throne, I say fuck yeah, I'm in. I have enough blood on my hands to pave my way to hell already, what's little more?"

He looks at Baker, who is watching me avidly.

"Why were you on the streets?" he asks me softly, but I don't miss the way his jaw clenches.

I don't answer, there was a reason I left that part out.

"Someone hurt you?" he asks, not giving me a chance to avoid answering.

I nod once, not giving him the details, those are mine and nobody needs the ability to track me back to Clyde. Plus, if I don't mention it, it's far harder to slip up and say something I shouldn't.

"Fuck, you were just a kid," Baker growls. I don't say anything, letting him work through his anger, knowing it isn't directed at me.

"The things I saw when I was a soldier were fucked up. We were in the middle of a war zone, but even so, I wasn't prepared for the things I saw—the women, the children..." He swallows hard before looking away for a minute. When he turns back, his eyes are blazing.

"When I came home, I thought I had left the dregs of society behind. Instead, what I found was worse. We don't have war and poverty as an excuse, we are just natural-born monsters with an appetite for greed so profound that it's impossible to sate. I'll help you, I'll be at your back, your side, and right in front of you if that's what you need. I'll be damned if I came home from war just to live in a new type of warzone."

I swallow down a lump in my throat and fight back the shimmer of tears I can feel pressing in on me.

"Thank you. I'll try to rein in my crazy when I'm around you, but things are going to get worse before they get better and I need to prepare for that."

"Girl, let your freak flag fly, we won't judge. Now tell us what you need from us today and we'll get loaded up." Danny grins, which lights up his whole face. It's infectious, and I can't help but smile back and fuck, it feels good.

"Are you guys armed?"

They look at me as if to say *what do you think*?

I roll my eyes. "Right, stupid question. Okay, I need to visit one of the division heads. I'm gonna call him up first. He slipped me his number the night of the initiation. I need allies, and the more division heads I have on my side, the better."

"So is the guy replacing Leo?" Danny questions, tilting his head.

"Yep. I don't know the story behind the old Leo passing though, do you?"

Danny shakes his head, but Baker looks at me thoughtfully.

"Don't hold me to this, but I heard that there was a disagreement between Zodiac and Leo. Then the next thing I know, Leo, who was my age, had a surprise heart attack."

"That seems a little convenient," I hedge.

"Yeah, that was my thought too, but like I said, it's just a hunch. I didn't know the old Leo, so it's possible he had an underlying condition or something." He shrugs, but I file the information away for later. I'm all too aware of what a prick Zodiac can be.

"Well, regardless, Leo is new to the game like me. As neither of us has tight alliances with the other divisions, I thought it would be smart to reach out to him. We have a tentative truce going on, so I'd like to cash in on it while I can."

"What kind of truce?" Danny frowns.

"The kind made over dead bodies," I deadpan and watch as he shakes his head with a grin. Yeah, I think we are going to all get along just fine.

PULLING up outside Leo's apartment, I wait for Baker to park before climbing out.

I stand and take in the building, noticing its similarities to mine as Baker and Danny flank me.

"Cozy," Baker drawls, making me snort.

"They all look like this. Trust me, it's not any cozier inside, but it's better than the streets."

"Can't argue with that. Come on." He indicates for me to follow, so I do, with Danny bringing up the rear.

The lobby is empty as I figured it would be, so we walk over to the bank of elevators without anyone stopping us.

I hit the button for the top floor and stand in the back, making room for the guys' large frames.

Nobody speaks, all of us on guard, especially when the doors slide open, revealing two armed men.

"This way," the thinner of the two says, indicating for us to follow him to the end of the hallway.

"You two, wait out here with us," he tells Danny and Baker, who begin to protest. I place my arm on Danny's and shake my head.

"It's fine. I'll scream like a girl if I need you," I tease.

"No guns," the larger of the two guys grunts, holding out his hand for me. I slip my gun from the back of my jeans, check that the safety is still on, even though I know it is, and hand it over to him.

"Viddy, I'm not happy about you going in there unarmed without us," Baker complains.

"I'll be fine, I promise. Leo isn't going to hurt me. We are just going to chat."

He scowls but seeing I'm not going to relent, he sighs, his shoulders dropping as I move to knock.

A moment later, the door swings open, showing a smiling Leo wearing dark blue jeans and a faded ACDC concert T-shirt. I never really paid much attention to him physically when we were at the planetarium before, far too focused on the carnage and hyperaware of what Zodiac's next move might be. Now seeing the messy blood-free hair, silvery-blue eyes, and slightly wonky smile, I can appreciate that this guy is seriously good looking.

"Gemini, come in." He looks at my guys behind me with a small but sincere smile.

"No harm will come to her while she's inside, I swear."

He closes the door behind us before they can say anything and places his hand on the small of my back as he leads me to the kitchen.

"I was just making some coffee; you want a mug?"

"Please." I nod, sitting on one of the barstools next to the counter.

I look around the apartment and again, everything is eerily similar to mine and Reid's except that there is no dining area, which I guess is why there are stools at the counter.

"So what brings you out to my neck of the woods?" Leo asks, pouring coffee into a white mug and handing it to me with the creamer from the fridge.

"Sugar?" I think for a minute that's what he's calling me, but then I realize he's pointing at the sugar bowl and I nod.

I reach over to grab it as I begin. "I want to—" I stop talking when I knock the spoon off the counter with my elbow, making it clatter to the floor.

"Sorry." I hop off the stool and bend down to pick it up, spotting something else on the black tiles, mostly hidden behind the stool leg next to mine.

I pick it up with a frown but shove it in my pocket quickly when I realize what it is and why it might be here. I'm about to say something when something else catches my eyes.

From down here, I can see underneath the kitchen cupboards, and the one on the far right seems to have a blinking red light underneath it. I'm assuming it's not a bomb, which means it can only be one thing. A fucking camera.

"Hey, you okay?" Leo steps around the counter toward me. He holds out his hand, so I slip mine inside his and let him pull me up.

Instead of finding my balance, I fall against his chest, lifting up and whispering against his ear.

"Please follow my lead. Trust me," I implore before moving my head and tugging him down until I can press my lips to his.

He freezes for a minute, and just when I think he's going to push me away and demand to know what the fuck is going on, he starts responding. His hands slip to my hips before dropping to my ass.

Before I can catch my breath, I find myself hoisted up, my legs circling his hips as I wrap my arms around his neck and whisper in his ear, "Bedroom." He doesn't need telling twice, moving across the room at a rapid pace, shoving a door open with his hip before I find myself in his bedroom.

"Closet," I mutter, feeling him thicken against me. I can't lie, the effect his kiss is having on me is making everything else fuzzy.

"Closet? Okay." He chuckles, likely thinking I'm just a little odd. I mean, he's not wrong, but if he thinks I'm bringing him in here to be fucked, he's sadly mistaken.

He pulls open his closet door, and as soon as we're inside, I wriggle until he places me on my feet.

I push the door closed and turn to face him, my chest heaving.

"Babe, are you sure about this?" he asks, confused, but his eyes are filled with lust.

I step forward until my front is against his and place my fingers over his mouth.

"I found a camera in your kitchen, so unless you put it there, someone is watching. If there are cameras, I'd imagine there might be listening devices too."

He pulls back, looking down at me with anger this time, all signs of lust disappearing.

"Are you fucking serious?" he growls.

I nod. "It's under the kitchen cupboards. If I hadn't dropped the spoon, I wouldn't have even noticed it. But that's not all." I chew my lip as I dig inside my pocket and pull out the item I found near the stool earlier—a bright pink pacifier.

His eyes widen for a second before I find myself pinned to the door with his hands wrapped around my neck.

"Whatever the fuck you think you know, you don't," he snaps, his hands tightening a little in warning.

I don't fight him. I'm not sure I could if I tried. Even though I have my knife in my bra, I'd rather not use it when I can see fear guiding his actions.

"Let me go and I'll make you a deal," I choke out.

He releases me abruptly, making me stumble a little. Running his hands through his hair, he looks at me warily before a flash of regret crosses his face. I have a sinking feeling it's not because of what he's done but what he's about to do to keep his secret.

I talk quickly. "Listen to me, I'm guessing you have a daughter?" He doesn't answer, but I can see a twitch in his cheek.

"Do not bring her here under any circumstances. Whatever has been seen can't be changed, but it can be underplayed. It could be your girlfriend's kid. You can claim you've broken up and she has taken off, taking the kid with her."

"Why the fuck should I trust you?" he spits.

"Because right now, I'm all you've got. You're in this up to your neck, and it's not just your life on the line. It's your little girl's. I can't do much to help you, and after seeing you fight I doubt you'll need it, but I can help with your kiddo. I'll make you a deal. Form an allegiance with me, not division twelve and ten or Gemini and Leo, but as you and me, the kids from the gutter. We can have each other's backs, and I swear on all that's holy that if anything happens to you, I will protect your daughter as if she were mine."

His chest is heaving now, his breath rushing in and out as he processes my words, his eyes flicking around the closet before returning to me.

"Why?" he grunts out, but I don't miss the flash of relief in his eyes.

"Because I can, because it's the right thing to do, and because I'll be damned if I let Zodiac ruin her life like he has ours," I snap impatiently.

He slides his hand around my hip, and the other cups my jaw as he uses his body to press mine against the door.

"I don't trust anyone, not with Lily. I wouldn't hesitate to throw you to the wolves if it meant protecting her, so no matter what deal you think I'll strike up with you, it will always be her."

"And it should be, it just makes you a good father. You don't have to decide if you want this right now. I'll never speak a word about Lily outside this room, but please, please hear me when I say, if Zodiac knows about Lily, it's only a matter of time before he comes for her."

"If that's true, then what does an allegiance with you even matter?" he curses.

"Because if enough of us band together, we can overthrow him. Then we can all finally find some fucking peace."

"Even if what you're saying is true, if you cut off the head of the snake, there will be chaos. What you're talking about will spark an all-out war as people vie for the top spot. That's going to put my daughter in more danger than she is now."

"Not if there is someone ready to step into his shoes."

"And you think that person should be you?" he scoffs, making my hackles rise.

"Careful, Leo, that sounds an awful lot like disbelief. I have surprised bigger men than you and lived to tell the tale, but by all means, try me."

He turns and stomps farther into his closet, agitated, before spinning to face me once more.

"What guarantee can you give me?"

"None for you. You are too heavily involved. I can't guarantee your safety any more than mine, but I can guarantee your daughter's. If something happens to you, you can either trust me to raise her or I can set her up far removed from this life where she can play in a yard, not worry about getting fucking snatched by the bogeyman and being used as a weapon in a vendetta she is too young to understand."

"If I'm supposed to trust you with the most important thing in my life, I need something of yours that makes you vulnerable too. I can't risk it otherwise," he tells me without an inch of remorse, and I get it.

Hell, I even respect him for it. How many other people can say that their father would burn the world to rubble and ash just to protect their kid? Hell, mine bailed the second he found out my mother was pregnant.

I won't give him Megan and Wyatt because, as far as I'm concerned, they aren't in this anymore. I came here so they could be free from me and my bullshit, but I can give him info that could hurt me.

"This goes no further. I'm counting on you to keep your word."

He nods. "As long as you keep yours, your secret is safe with me."

"When I was fifteen, I murdered my stepfather in cold blood, then I blew up the only home I had and walked away. There is an open investigation with regards to his death and my disappearance. As of right now, the consensus is that a business deal went wrong and I was taken as collateral before a hit was ordered on him."

"Why would they think that? Who the fuck was your stepfather?"

"His name was Clyde Mandel."

I'm quiet for a minute, feeling sick at speaking his name out loud as it makes me feel dirty all over again.

"Wasn't he that rich real estate mogul that had a penchant for—" His mouth snaps shut as he looks at me. It feels like he's stripping back the layers of my skin and exposing a wound that never healed.

"Good for you." He nods before stepping forward and pulling me in for a surprising hug. My arms hang loosely at my sides for a minute before I slowly lift them and grip his waist.

"He's the kind of man I'd sell my soul to keep my daughter away from."

"Yeah, well, not everyone has someone who will go to bat for them like you would. Sometimes, you have to just burn shit down yourself."

# CHAPTER TWENTY-ONE

S itting across from a young couple who look like they're still in high school, l watch the way they interact with each other as I wait for the computer to boot up. Why I come here when I could take my new laptop to the office, I don't know, but sometimes I don't want to be Gemini. Sometimes I just want to be Viddy, whoever that may be.

"Your coffee, Miss, can I get you anything else?" I'm startled out of my thoughts as the young waiter places my coffee in front of me in a cup that's so big I'll need both hands to hold it.

"No, thank you. I think I'm good." I smile at him, making him flush, his pimple-riddled face taking on a rosy hue. He dips his head, embarrassed, before walking back over to the counter, leaving me to my thoughts.

I type in my password as the young couple climb to their

feet and make their way outside, hand in hand, before turning my attention back to work.

I have been doing my research, trying to figure out all of the players and what their roles are before making my next move. I had studied the information I had copied from the ledger and from the memory stick Reid had taken.

A shipment is coming into the docks tomorrow and I need reliable runners. Looking over the records made by the last Gemini, I'm relieved to find he was a meticulous fucker. I can already tell who the runners are I'm likely to use, which is why I have meetings set up to deal with them all evening.

I take a sip of my coffee, feeling jittery. It's not from the caffeine, but from knowing I'm going to have to make a statement tonight to get people to follow me. I need blind obedience right now, and with everything balanced so precariously, I have to set the precedent.

Leaving thoughts of runners for a second, I look over at the other three names I've highlighted on my list. Chewing my lip, I try to decide which contact to reach out to that will hopefully not involve me dying.

Milo Bellingham, Kristoff Libernesh, and Ronald Harris are the three key players in the import-export business. Of course, there are others, lots in fact, that deal with Zodiac directly, but I want to work with people that have no allegiance to him. I want to make sure that if called upon, it will be me they stand beside, for the right price of course. That's why these three stand out for a multitude of reasons. Ronald Harris owns a manufacturing company that makes military-grade weaponry, and although they have a major contract with the US government, it is known on the black market that they sell arms to the highest bidder.

Ronald himself isn't the guy I'm after though, it's William, his son. William, if rumors are to be believed, is chomping at the bit to take over and move the company in a slightly different direction. At the moment, their weapons are making them money, but they are also making them vulnerable. There is no policing who is buying them, and finding fingers pointed at you when your guns turn up at multiple crime scenes is taking its toll on the company's stock. If I can get William to stop moving stuff through the black market and get him to sell only to me, then I can redistribute them. Yes, the weapons will still end up in the hands of criminals, but I'm talking about criminals who know how to hide their tracks, not everyday kids shooting up their fucking high school.

A horn sounds from outside, followed by squealing tires. I lift my head before yelling pulls my attention to the window.

I frown when I see a young boy running from a police officer, who looks like he should have laid off the donuts if he's planning to catch the kid anytime soon.

I would generally dismiss the whole thing, but something about the kid tugs at me. Maybe I can convince the police officer to give him a break. I shove the laptop in my bag, toss a twenty on the table for the still full mug of coffee, and head outside in the direction the boy and officer ran off too.

It's dark out; the winter months' long nights can sometimes feel never-ending. A glance at my watch tells me it's only 9:30, but in this city, it doesn't matter what time it is. Once the sun sets, the monsters come out to play, which is why I make sure I have my gun handy.

A scuffle followed by a muffled yell has my head turning toward the alleyway leading to the back of the warehouse district. Nobody comes this way after dark willingly. If gunshots or screams are heard coming from this area, people just ignore it and scurry on their way pretending otherwise. I move silently toward the alley, finding it littered with trash, the dumpsters at its entrance completely overflowing with discarded food and waste, the rancid smell making me grimace.

I pull out my gun from the back of my jeans and grip it tightly as I make my way toward a shuffling noise. A sense of foreboding washes over me like a sixth sense, taking me back to another time and another alleyway. As I come closer to the end, flickering light from one of the streetlamps above illuminates a scene that turns my stomach.

The cop is there, his chest rising and falling rapidly as he tries to catch his breath. Whether that's from the running or the actions of the boy knelt in front of him with the cop's tiny dick in his mouth and tears running down his face, remains to be seen.

Evil doesn't surprise me. It's what I know, what I see every day, but for me, the people who take a position of trust and use it as a power play to manipulate those weaker than them are the worst of the worst.

I don't bother asking questions. I don't even stop to think about how this poor kid might react to what I'm about to do. All I see is red. It colors everything as I walk up silently to the cop who has his head thrown back and his eyes closed in ecstasy. He doesn't hear me, doesn't see me, too caught up in his moment of debauchery. The boy sees me though and that damn haunted look in his eyes is one I'm all too familiar with. I keep my eyes on him and lift my gun. He doesn't flinch, fuck he doesn't even stop sucking the acrid little dick until I place my gun against the cop's head and pull the trigger.

The cop's body falls back into a crate behind him, making a loud clattering sound, but neither I nor the boy stops looking at each other. He remains on his knees as I shove my gun in my bag.

"I'm Viddy." Even after the loud bang of the gun firing, my voice still seems deafeningly loud, breaking the strange moment between us.

He stands and moves back away from me, his hands out in front of him as if to warn me away.

"Wait."

He freezes at my words, the terror on his pale face making me soften my voice further.

"I'm not gonna hurt you. I know you have no reason to trust me, and that's okay, I'm not expecting you to. Do you know who Gemini is?" I ask him softly.

He stares at me before his eyes dart around the alley as if waiting for someone else to jump out of the shadows. Eventually, he nods, so I continue, taking one step closer to him. He backs up until he is pressed against the wall with nowhere to go.

"You know the old Gemini is dead?"

Again a nod, this one fast as if answering me quickly will mean he can leave faster.

"I'm the new Gemini," I admit, making his eyes widen before his shoulders fall in defeat.

"I live in a fancy penthouse in the heart of the city, but before that, I lived on the streets and had done so since I was fifteen years old."

He looks up at me sharply, his head tilting to the side as if in question.

"Someone hurt me. The streets were a better option than the house that was supposed to be my home," I divulge, stepping closer once more. "Do you have a home you want to go back to?" I ask quietly.

He violently shakes his head no.

"The person that hurt you," he whispers, surprising me, "what happened to them? Are they still looking for you?"

"I shot and killed him. He was going to sell me and get a new girl, a younger one. I couldn't let that happen." I answer him truthfully, reaching out a hand slowly as if approaching a rabid dog ready to chew my arm off at any second

"You shot him?" he asks reverently as my hand slides over his hair.

I tug him toward me and he puts up zero resistance when I pull him to my chest. He doesn't hug me, and I don't expect him to. We stand there in silence, him with his head against my shoulder and me stroking my fingers through his dirty hair.

"Yeah, I did," I reply with zero regrets.

"Can you... would you show me how to shoot?" He pulls his head back to look at me.

I should tell him no. I could help him escape this life, and at his age, he should be holding a baseball bat or a hockey stick, not a gun. But looking beneath his bravado, the kid's not much different than me. I know that even if I gave him everything his heart desired, it would never erase his memories. He might physically be a kid, but on the inside, he likely feels a hundred years old.

Instead, I give him the only thing that might fuse together some of the jagged cracks in his heart. I give him his power back.

"Yeah, I can do that, and when you're ready, I'll stand beside you and watch you show whoever hurt you that they can't hurt you anymore, even if I have to hold them down myself," I promise him.

He looks shocked that I agreed so readily, but then he snorts, surprising us both. "You know that's fucked up, right? We're standing in the dark after you shot the cop who was making me..." His voice drifts off for a second as he sniffs and swallows.

"Everyone's fucked up, some of us just hide it better than

others. Now, I don't know about you, but I'm sick to death of hiding."

He nods slowly in agreement, his eyes shimmering with unshed tears. "Me too," he whispers.

"What's your name?" I ask him, pulling my phone from my pocket and texting Danny.

"I'm DJ," he offers hesitantly. No last name, but I don't push him.

"Hey, DJ, I'm Viddy. It's really nice to meet you." I grin at him, and that's when he does something that steals a little piece of my heart. Standing there in shock, both of us covered in blood splatter, he smiles.

# CHAPTER TWENTY-TWO

I observe DJ from the kitchen area of Baker's apartment as the kid sits on the living room floor watching cartoons.

"I'm not sure what's going on here, Viddy, but you can't just collect kids," Baker grunts from beside me.

"Not to mention, you killed a fucking cop," Danny hisses. "People will search for him."

I sigh and take my eyes from DJ and turn to face them both.

"Do you know that DJ is thirteen years old?" I ask them quietly.

"Even more reason you can't keep him, V. He will have people at home worried sick about him."

I look at him with pity, bursting his bubble with the truth. "I found him on his knees with tears running down his face while that dirty fat fucking cop shoved his dick down his throat. And you know what? DJ would choose to do that every single day if it meant social services can't find him and send him home. What does that tell you?"

Danny looks like he's going to be sick and Baker has gone an alarming shade of green.

"Guys, it's handled. You can bet your fucking asses there will come a time we'll be dealing with DJ's family, but that's for another day," I reassure them. "Right now, we have other shit to deal with. I picked up the keys for my new place today. I want you to take the cop's body there and dispose of it."

Turning to Baker, I sigh. "I'm sorry we invaded your space, but I can't take him back to the penthouse. After you found those cameras, I can't risk exposing him to Zodiac. The truth is, he's no safer with me than he is out there, but I couldn't just leave him."

"I still don't understand why you won't let us get rid of the cameras, or at least loop some footage so it looks like they're still recording," Baker grumbles.

"You know why. I can't let Zodiac realize I'm on to him, and if his tech guy is half as good as you, he'll know in a heartbeat if you tamper with the footage."

"Is this why you got a new place?" Danny asks.

"Yeah, that and it's mine so no fucker can take it from me. Plus, I got it for a steal." I grin.

Danny and Baker look at me before looking at each other then back to me again.

"Okay, spill. What aren't you telling us?" Baker asks with a frown.

"My new place is Shadow Falls," I tell them, biting my lip.

"Shadow Falls? Why does that sound familiar?" Danny says, frowning.

"Holy fuck, you have got to be kidding me," Baker shouts. We all turn to look at DJ, but he's still watching TV.

"What the fuck is Shadow Falls?" Danny's eyes dart between us both.

Baker rubs a hand over his face before glaring at Danny. "Legend has it, it was once a second home to British royalty, but regardless of what its origins are, it became a mental institution in the fifties. I believe it closed down for a while after a fire gutted it. It then got a facelift and became a small private hospital until it attracted a serial killer. The angel of death, if I remember correctly. She killed thirty-four—"

I interrupt him, "Thirty-six—"

He glares at me before continuing, "People while she worked there. There was no saving the hospital after that. It's been empty ever since as far as I know, which is about fifteen years ago."

Danny looks at me like I've lost my mind.

I huff, "I get it, it's weird. Deal with it and look at the damn pros of this property. It's out of the way, sitting on fifty acres, and the whole thing is enclosed by eight-foot-high fencing. There is a small chapel on-site and a cemetery."

If anything, he looks even more disgusted.

"Oh, for goodness sake, the graves are empty. After the angel of death debacle, they cleared the area and had the bodies buried elsewhere. According to the schematics, there are tunnels running underneath the place that lead in and out of the property. If I fill coffins with my cargo," I use the keyword, not wanting DJ to overhear, "then nobody will suspect anything. It will simply seem as if the cemetery is open once more. Also, and this is my favorite part, there is a mortuary with an incinerator." I clap my hands and grin but rein it in when I realize I'm the only one excited.

Baker catches on. "That's why you want the cop taken there."

"Well, I'm not really looking at taking up taxidermy."

"Okay, I can see the merit, I guess. I'm just glad it's you sleeping there and not me." Baker shivers, making me chuckle.

"Some tough guy you are. Please tell me you're not afraid of ghosts."

He huffs and turns away, making me laugh out loud.

"Well, I'm glad I amuse you." He sniffs, fighting back a smile. "What about the boy? Are you gonna eventually move him in with you?"

"No. I don't want him caught up in this, and keeping him away will keep him safer, at least for now."

"So where are you going to put him because I know you're not going to return him to the streets," Danny comments.

"No, of course not. I'll figure something out but for now, would you mind if he crashed here?"

Baker shrugs. "The kid can stay here as long as you want. I'm never here."

"He's been taking care of himself on the streets for a long time. I think he can manage here just fine for a few days. Don't worry. I'll make sure he has a cell phone with each of our numbers, just in case." I chew my lips because I'd rather have someone with him.

"I can call Chris to come over and watch him for a while. Her arm is still in a sling, so she's taking it easy for now," Danny offers.

I hadn't yet met Chris, the lone female on their team. She had torn the ligaments in her shoulder, so she had been resting up.

"That's a good idea. Thanks, Danny." He nods and turns to make the call while I wander over to DJ.

He looks at me as I sit cross-legged beside him.

"I have to go soon. I'm going to need the clothes you have on, so Baker here is going to lend you some sweats while one of his team is fetching you some new stuff."

"For me to keep?" he asks, confused.

"What, the clothes? Yeah, bud, those are all yours." I smile, but he frowns.

"Do I just have to do the one or both of them as payment?" he whispers, fiddling with the hem of his T-shirt.

I reach over to grip his hand, probably a touch too tightly, and use my other to cup his jaw so he has no choice but to look at me. "Never again will someone put their hands on you when you don't want them to. You will not now, nor later be obligated to pay me back for these things, and even if you were, it would not be with your body. You are not paying for services rendered. Your body is yours alone, do you understand me?" I keep my voice low but firm. His lip wobbles, but he nods.

"Okay, but what about when you send me back?" he chokes out.

I lean forward and press my forehead against his. "I'm not sending you back. You deserve a better life than the one you've been given, and if I can help you get that, then I will. I can't take you home with me, even though I'd love to have you. It's too dangerous right now, and some of the people I will be dealing with would use you to hurt me. Now, is there anyone else you'd feel comfortable staying with?"

He shakes his head before frowning. "The only people who care about me are Ben and Kevin."

"And where can I find Ben and Kevin?"

"Usually on the corner of Wilson. There is an abandoned warehouse there," he admits, fiddling with his hem once more.

"They're homeless too?" I prompt, wanting to clarify.

He nods before looking down.

"Okay, DJ, I'll find them for you and let them know you're safe. For the next few days, you'll stay here until I can find a better alternative for you. I know this is all new and scary, but if you can just trust me, I promise I won't let you down. I won't walk away from you when you need me and I will never forget you," I vow.

I'm not sure I would believe him if the tables were turned, but I'll just prove myself to him. It's not even so much of not believing in people, it's being too scared to have hope because when that gets stripped away, it leaves you with nothing. When you've been let down time and time again, you learn to stop hoping—that way, people can't disappoint you.

"When it's safe, I'll come pick you up and we can start your shooting lessons," I offer, ruffling his hair.

"Okay, Viddy." He sniffs.

I can hear the tears in his voice, so I pull him to my chest and let him cry against my shoulder. His soft sobs are silent even though he's trembling so much he's making me shake too.

I look over his head and see Danny approaching with a box of tissues in his hand, his eyes filled with sadness as he takes in DJ wrapped tightly in my arms. He hands the box to me and sits on the sofa beside us.

Sensing movement, DJ pulls back and looks up, jolting when he sees Danny sitting and looking down at him. His cheeks flush with embarrassment, but he doesn't look away from him.

"Viddy has your back, kid. I don't know if you understand what a big deal that is, but if she says she will keep you safe, she'll move heaven and earth to do so." Danny looks at me for a second before continuing. "Here are my ten cents worth. What you've been through, what you've endured, would have brought stronger men to their knees. You, DJ, are a fucking warrior and don't you forget it. And with Viddy, you also get me and Baker and Chris, who you'll

185

meet in a little while, and a bunch of other people who will literally kill for you."

DJ looks shocked for a minute, swallowing hard before turning to look at me. I nod, and with that, he turns back to Danny, straightening his spine and lifting his head proudly.

"Thank you." DJ's voice is still quiet, but there is a thread of pride in it now.

"Don't mention it. Now how about you jump in the shower? I'll order you a pizza and Baker will sort you out some clothes and give you a cell phone with all our numbers in it. You can call or text us whenever you want and we'll reply as soon as we can."

"A shower? Yes, please, I'd really like that." DJ nods vigorously.

Baker, who had disappeared momentarily, returns with an armful of clothes.

"Hey, DJ, these are for you. I'll set them on the bed in the spare room which is at the end of the hallway. I'll show you if you like. Not gonna lie, these will swamp you, but they have a drawstring waist and they're clean, so they'll do for now. Take as long as you need. Me casa is su casa."

He moves back and waits for DJ, who stands slowly. Again, DJ looks at me, so I nod, letting him know it's gonna be okay. He walks over to Baker, who is smart enough not to crowd him and indicates for him to follow.

They disappear down the hallway, which is when Danny lets out a loud sigh.

"Poor kid. Most other kids his age would have been

thrilled about getting a phone, all he cared about was the shower." He shakes his head, but I'm not surprised. It was the same for me.

"Cell phones mean nothing if you have nobody to call," I remind him.

"Well, he has us now," he adds, making me smile.

"Very true. Now you might want to get ordering that pizza. Food will be the next thing he wants, then sleep. That's all that will really matter. Is Chris on her way?"

I accept his hand when he stands and let him pull me to my feet.

"Yeah, said she'll be about ten minutes, which was about ten minutes ago—" His words cut off when there is a knock at the door.

"And there she is." He chuckles, moving to the door, checking the spyhole first.

As he swings the door open, I see a tall blonde walk in. Her sleek platinum hair is cut into a bob that skims her jaw, and when she looks toward me, I see she has the palest blue eyes I've ever seen.

"Hey, I'm Chris. You must be Viddy. I've heard a lot about you," she greets me with a smile as Danny takes the bag she is carrying from her. I look at her other arm and the sling.

"I am indeed. It's nice to meet you. You sure you're up for it?" I nod to her sling, but she shakes her head.

"It's no problem and to be honest, you're doing me a favor. I've been going stir crazy sitting at home."

"Hey, Chris," Baker calls, making us turn when he heads toward the kitchen.

"He okay?" I ask him quietly.

"Yeah, I had to show him how to work the shower and where everything is, but he's doing okay. He's a tough kid," he replies, grabbing a roll of black garbage bags from under the kitchen sink.

"I'll wait until he's done to bag up his clothes. I don't want to freak him out any more than he already is, but you lady, need to strip."

I roll my eyes at him. "I know the drill, but I'd really like something other than my underwear to wear home."

"Oh, I brought you some things," Chris interjects. "Danny said you were tiny, and well, I'm not, so I went for cropped leggings and a hoodie. It's not much, but it should do until you get home."

"Oh, thank you. That's perfect, actually."

I strip off the top I have on and shove it in the bag Baker is holding open, as well as the tank top beneath it before pulling on the soft gray hoodie Chris holds out for me.

"It's only splatter. Think the sports bra will be okay, or do you want that too?" I ask, knowing the blood likely never even made it to the tank top, but it's better to be cautious.

"Nah, you'll be fine. Same with your underwear, but I'll need your jeans, and I'll take your shoes too. They are in a bag in the car with DJ's, right?"

I nod while popping open the button on my jeans and lowering the zipper, shoving the jeans down my legs. The hoodie hits me mid-thigh and hides everything, but even if it didn't, I know none of the people here are checking me out. Baker is just doing his job. I pull them off and slip on the black leggings and roll the waist over once. They are not cropped on me; they look like regular leggings.

"I have flip flops for you too, for when you're ready to go."

"Thanks. I'll get everything cleaned and couriered back over to you."

She waves me off as Danny hangs up his phone and steps closer.

"Okay, pizza is ordered. It'll be here in twenty. We can leave as soon as DJ is out. I don't want to bail on the kid while he's in the shower," Danny adds. I squeeze his arm in agreement.

"Okay, is there anything I need to know or tread carefully with? I don't want to trigger something because I'm ignorant," Chris asks, tucking her hair behind her ear.

"Just keep it light. No offense, but he won't tell you shit anyway. He won't trust easily, so don't feel bad if he doesn't say much," I warn her.

She shrugs, not fazed. "It's all good. I brought my Kindle and Xbox. I figured I could hook that up for him and read while he plays so he doesn't think I'm hovering."

"Sounds good."

The pizza arrives just as DJ reappears, looking like a different kid now. He stays across the other side of the room until I spot him and beckon him over.

"DJ, this is Chris. She's gonna be staying with you for a

little while. She brought her Xbox for you to play, and the pizza is here, so help yourself to whatever."

I give him the cell phone Danny passes to me. "This cell is yours. It has all our numbers in it, so use them whenever you need to. I'm not gonna lie, I'm not sure when I'll be back. It might be a few days, but you'll be safe here, I promise."

"Will you get in trouble?" he asks me quietly, everyone else in the room going silent at his words.

I move slowly toward him, feeling a pang in my chest as he moves into me. I wrap my arm loosely around his shoulder.

Being starved of human contact makes you crave it and fear it in equal measure, especially when you've been hurt. This simple move shows me that he's beginning to trust me. Even if it's just a little, it's a start. Nobody should have to navigate this world alone, least not a kid who needs nurturing. Fuck, even I have people in my corner, and I'm so far past redemption it's ridiculous.

When I die, I might very well leave behind a legacy of darkness, but the people I love will survive because I was willing to risk everything for them, and DJ has somehow made his way onto my list without even trying.

"No, DJ, I'm not going to get into trouble, and neither will you. I'll take care of everything."

I shot a cop and feel zero remorse for it. Even if it comes back to haunt me, I'll never regret it, and I'll make sure DJ doesn't either.

I look around at the people watching us and feel a

stirring inside me, a coil of power as something shifts and changes. I might not have grown up to be the woman I thought I would, but that's okay. Plans change, people do too. If you get burned by fire, forge yourself into someone new, someone stronger.

I was pure Gemini today when I killed that cop and instead of feeling like I might have just fucked everything up, I feel like I've gained control, and this right here is just the beginning.

# CHAPTER TWENTY-THREE

I close the laptop and rub the back of my neck to work out the kinks. A quick look around my dimly lit office reminds me I've been here longer than I planned. Thank God I messaged DJ earlier before I lost myself in work.

My guys had managed to track down the Ben and Kevin that DJ had mentioned. I had been surprised to find out Ben was in his thirties and Kevin was his son, and they had been frantic to find out if DJ was okay. I had taken a chance and pulled them off the streets and put them in a two-bedroom apartment. DJ considered them family and I wanted him to have that. But even so, I would be keeping my eye on them before I let DJ move in with them as he wanted. Another couple of weeks at Baker's wouldn't hurt him and he had been adjusting well. Of course, it might have something to do with the little crush he had on

Chris. Turns out kicking his ass on the Xbox has given her a god-like status. I can't help but smile, thinking about how relaxed he seemed when he FaceTimed me yesterday.

The phone on my desk rings, jarring me out of my thoughts and making me sigh. No rest for the wicked.

I pick it up without thinking. "Yep," I answer, spinning in my chair as I cradle the phone between my neck and shoulder.

"Um...there is a guy here, looks like he's been in a fight. He's calling himself Aries," one of my guards mumbles, sounding unimpressed with the name. I hold back a grin so he can't hear the smile in my voice.

"It's fine. Let him up." I hang up. Kicking off my shoes, I make my way over to the attached bathroom, snagging the first aid kit from beneath the counter, pausing to check my reflection in the mirror.

The woman staring back at me is far removed from the girl I was when I arrived in the city. Dressed to make a statement rather than to blend in, today's outfit is a simple sleeveless black shift dress that hits the top of my knee and has a split in the back that reaches high enough to tease but not enough to flash the tops of my thigh highs.

The dress itself molds to my body like a second skin, showing exactly what lies beneath the layers of expensive material without revealing an inch of skin.

My dark red hair spills over my shoulders, tousled and wavy as usual, but thick and shiny and, most importantly, clean. It started up in a neat chignon, but my hair does what it wants, always escaping its confines by afternoon.

I keep my makeup light and natural all except the pop of color from whichever lipstick I choose for the day. Today's is a vivid pink aptly named Bubblegum Grenade. Kind of reminded me of myself. A little sweet, a little deadly.

A tap at the door has me pulling away from my reflection back into my office, where I dump the first aid kit on the oxblood leather Chesterfield sofa in the corner before pulling the door open.

"Aries is here, ma'am," Thomas, one of tonight's two guards, informs me.

"Send him in, please, and tell the rest of the guys they can go home."

He nods and I close the door and return to my chair.

The door opens once more, and Diablo walks in missing his usual smirk and swagger, before collapsing on the sofa clutching his ribs.

I take a moment to study him, picking up which version of him I'll be getting tonight, as he returns the favor.

"Well, I guess someone just couldn't handle you being so pretty." I sigh, standing up and rounding the desk.

He laughs before groaning. "Don't make me laugh. I think I've cracked a few ribs," he admits.

"Okay, let me take a look. I've had a really long day and I'd rather not have to deal with you dying on my office floor because a rib punctured your lung."

"I can feel the love from here." He grimaces, gripping the hand I offer him and using it to help himself up.

I wait until he's standing directly in front of me before closing the distance between us. Looking up at him, I scan his face, taking in the tightness around his mouth and the shadows under his eyes.

"What happened?" I ask, knowing he won't answer, but something in me feels compelled to ask.

He stares down at me for a moment before dipping his head and brushing his lips over mine.

He uses his mouth as a distraction, and I let him for a moment before I slip my hands to his waist and grip the hem of his shirt. Pulling my lips free from his, I slowly inch his black T-shirt up over his lickable body.

I wince for him when I see his ribs are already a deep purple color.

"Jesus, Reid, you need a better security team. Either that or you should find a new profession because one of these days, you won't get back up again," I warn him, a sickening feeling washing away the traces of lust between us.

"It's just some bruising, Cherry. Patch me up like a good little nurse and I'll be as good as new."

"You know I look at you sometimes and am completely dazed by how fucking gorgeous you are," I tell him, taking him by surprise, judging by the look on his face.

"I think to myself, how the hell is he single? He's powerful, loaded, and kisses like he's going for the gold medal at the kissing Olympics." His face takes on that lazy, smug look of his, making me shake my head with a small smirk of my own.

"But then you open your mouth, and I have the overwhelming urge to cut out your tongue, and then everything makes sense." I laugh, shoving his T-shirt up as far as I can before he dips and helps me pull it over his head.

"No tongue means no oral and, babe, you'll do the world an injustice if that happens."

"How you fit that head of yours through the door is beyond me."

"It does seem to grow around you," he muses, making me snort.

"I mean the other head, the one with the very lonely brain cell. Now stand still for a minute while I check you over."

He shuts up, and I trail my hands over his hot skin, gently probing his ribs before sliding my hands around to his back. I smile when I feel him shiver, loving that I have as much of an effect on him as he does me, even if we never take it further than the strange relationship we have with each other now.

I circle him slowly, my breathing speeding up along with his as I end up back in front of him, looking up at his too handsome face.

"You'll live this time but take it easy for a little while, and if you start having issues breathing, get your ass to the hospital. You have someone who can stay with you tonight?"

He looks away for a second before shaking his head. "No, but if you're offering..."

I open my mouth to shoot him down, but his next words stop me.

"Please," he whispers, with nothing but sincerity on his face.

"Fine, but you owe me and no funny business. I'm so tired I could fall asleep standing up."

"Scouts honor." He lifts his fingers in the Vulcan sign, making me laugh.

"You were never a boy scout." I chuckle moving to the top drawer of my desk and finding the painkillers I keep there to stave off migraines.

"Maybe not, but you should see how good I am at tying knots." He winks.

Ignoring him, I toss him the painkillers, which he catches one-handed before I shove my laptop in my bag and slip my heels back on. Snagging my black peacoat from the hook near the window, I beckon him over.

"Come on, the sooner we leave, the sooner I can get some shut-eye."

Grabbing his T-shirt from the sofa where I tossed it, he slips it back on before following me to the door.

I say goodnight to Thomas, who protests at leaving me unguarded, but he relents when he realizes I won't give in. We make our way outside and over to Reid's car, which is parked at the end of the street.

"You okay to drive?" I ask over my shoulder, looking up at

him. He nods, which is just as well as I don't have a license yet.

I wait for him to beep the locks before opening the passenger side door and climb in as he gets in beside me with a groan.

"So how's business over on the other side of the city?" I ask casually.

"Same as usual. Nothing worth mentioning. Same shit different day." He shrugs, driving through the dark city toward his apartment.

"We could just go to your place, it's closer," he offers, changing the subject, but I shake my head.

"It doesn't feel like home yet. I like your place better." It's not a complete lie; it's just not the whole truth. I'm not ready to show Reid my actual home, and I don't want to take him to the penthouse now I know it's fitted with Zodiac's cameras. I can only assume that Reid's place is camera free. If it wasn't, his little secret wouldn't be a secret anymore.

I wait for him to climb out and walk around to open my door, holding out his hand for me to grasp. I reach for it and sling my bag over my shoulder.

Like usual, his hand doesn't let go. He holds on tight as he maneuvers me up to his apartment, flicking the lights on once we are safely locked inside.

"I'm surprised you didn't bring security with you tonight," he says, breaking the silence between us.

"There is no point when I'm here with you. I know you'll protect me." I shrug, moving through the living area to the room I used when I was here last. Before I can open the door, Reid's hand on my hip stops me.

"Stay in my room with me tonight? I won't try anything. I just want to hold you for a little while." I turn to look up at him and see something lurking in his eyes that I can't quite put my finger on, and at this point, I'm too tired to analyze.

"Okay, Reid, if that's what you want, you got it." I move to his room and head straight for the bathroom, wanting to wash the grime from the day away.

I turn on the shower before twisting to find Reid in the doorway.

"Can I borrow a T-shirt and some boxers?" I ask softly.

He nods and disappears, reappearing moments later with a plain white T-shirt and black boxers in his hand.

"Here." He places them on the counter before moving back to his spot in the doorway.

I stand there and cross my arms, waiting for him to leave, but he isn't taking the hint.

"Reid," I warn. He steps forward until he's pressed against me, slinging one hand around my back and the other into my hair, keeping me in place as he gazes down at me.

"I won't touch you unless you beg me to, Cherry," he whispers against my lips.

"You're in for a long wait then because I won't beg. Ever."

"I want to see you," he urges, his lust riding him hard, and I'd be a fucking hypocrite if the thought didn't leave me dripping.

I frown at him, ready to shut this shit down, but there is

something about him, something in his tone making me pause, an almost desperation. What the fuck happened to him tonight?

"You don't touch me while I'm naked. The second you break that rule, I will walk out of this apartment and I won't look back." My heart beats in a rapid staccato, trying to deal with the shock I just gave it agreeing to this.

It's not so much him seeing me naked; it's him being so close to me when I'm vulnerable—that's not something I ever do.

Pulling away, I turn my back on him, lowering the zipper at the side of my dress. When the fabric loosens, I slip my arms free and slide the material down over my hips, revealing what I'm wearing underneath—black lace bra with matching panties and lace-top thigh highs.

"Holy fucking shit," he hisses.

Kicking my shoes into the corner, I let the dress fall the rest of the way to the floor before kicking it over to my shoes. I sit on the edge of the toilet seat and begin the slowly seductive task of rolling down my thigh highs.

He doesn't move, doesn't make a single sound until the stockings are off, leaving me in the black lace underwear set.

"I'm a stupid fuck," he mumbles to himself, and in this regard, he's correct. It's like being an alcoholic with a glass of whiskey in front of you, oh so very tempting but not worth the headache it will leave in its wake if we succumb to the lure of temptation. I don't know what Reid is to me. I'm not brave enough to admit I feel more for him than I should, but to him, I'm just an addiction that will either burn out or blow up in our faces.

"You can always walk away," I whisper, giving him an out, but we both know he won't take it. He can't break this never-ending cycle of want and need any more than I can.

"Take them off," he growls.

I don't object to his words, finding I quite like the idea of doing his bidding, in the bedroom at least. Being in control all the time can be exhausting. Sometimes it would be nice to hand the reins over to someone else for a little while. Right here, right now, I'm not Gemini and he's not Aries. We're just two people who want what we can't have, which makes this all the more illicit.

I slip the straps of my bra down my arms before reaching back to undo it, tossing it toward my dress. Hooking my fingers in the edge of my panties, I slide those down my legs.

Stepping out of them, I leave my panties on the floor before climbing into the warm shower.

I feign indifference and dip under the warm water, pretending I can't feel his eyes on me, but I freeze briefly when I see Reid out of the corner of my eye bend down and snag my panties off the floor. Bringing the lace to his nose, he inhales deeply. As if sensing my gaze on him, his eyes snap to mine.

The raw, unfiltered need in them makes my legs tremble so much I have to reach out and use the wall to steady myself.

I stand completely unable to move as he pulls his T-shirt

over his head in that one-handed way guys do, without even flinching when I know his ribs must be screaming at him.

"Reid," I warn, tensing to see what his next move is.

"Not gonna touch you, Cherry, but that doesn't mean we can't touch ourselves," he growls, popping open the button of his fly and slowly lowering the zipper.

I step back from the spray and watch him through the clear glass as he reaches inside his jeans and pulls out his erect cock.

Lifting his other hand to his face, I notice he still has my discarded panties in his grip. He inhales deeply once more before slowly stroking his cock up and down, his eyes never leaving mine.

"The smell of you drives me crazy. I have to fight every instinct I have to stop myself from pinning you down and devouring you until my face is dripping with your juices, and you're begging me to fuck you."

I whimper at his words, pressing one hand against the cool glass as the other one lifts of its own accord to play with my very erect nipple.

"Fuck yes, babe, touch yourself. Show me what I do to you."

I pinch my nipple harder, gasping and pressing more of myself against the glass.

"Fuck, so goddamn sexy. After I finished eating you out," he continues his fantasy as I trail my hand slowly down my ribs, "then I'd shove my cock so deep inside you, you'll never want me to leave."

Slowly at first, I circle my clit with my fingertips, watching as his eyes fix on the movement of my hand.

"I bet you're fucking tight. You'd squeeze my dick so hard I'd shoot ropes of cum inside you like a teenage boy because that's what you do to me, Cherry. You make me feel wild and out of control, and I'm not sure I like it." He punctuates his words by pumping his cock hard before stepping closer to me. I can't take my eyes away from the erotic taboo in front of me even as he eradicates the distance between us until the glass door is the only thing keeping him away.

"Slide two fingers inside yourself for me, Cherry, and pump them in and out. I want you to imagine it's my cock." He looks down at his dick before looking up at me with a grin on his face. "Maybe you should make that three fingers, babe, I want you to feel that stretch. Imagine it, the feel of my hard cock slipping inside you. You can feel it right?"

"Yeah, feels good," I whisper, finally finding my voice.

"The real thing will feel even better. One day, Cherry, you'll let me inside you, and this thing that sparks between us will explode. But I won't stop even as the world burns around us."

I let his words wash over me, thrusting my fingers into myself harder and harder as his eyes track my movements. I lift my free hand and tease my nipple as I keep pumping my other hand, imagining it's him taking me hard and fast. This might be all there will ever be between us, but fuck it. If this is all I'll get, I'll take it. It will be a memory I relive when I'm alone at night with nothing but my fingers for company.

"I'm close, Cherry, tell me you're close too. I don't want to come without you."

I mew at his words, circling my clit with my wet fingers, harder and faster to the point of pain, racing to the edge, wanting nothing more than to free fall into the abyss with him.

"Yes, yes," I cry out as he starts cursing. I can't hold back anymore, screaming out my release as I detonate. I vaguely hear him following me over, but my focus is on trying to stop my legs from collapsing beneath me.

When the door is abruptly yanked open, I squeal, cursing myself for trusting him, but he just lifts me onto the counter before grabbing a large fluffy towel and wrapping it tightly around me.

"I don't want you to fall and hurt yourself," he answers my unvoiced question.

I stare at him, my heart still beating like crazy, the warm glow of my orgasm making me feel languid and loose, but the wariness is still ever-present.

I lift my hand and touch his cheek, "Who are you?" I whisper, dangerously close to crossing a line. He tenses before he turns his head and grabs my hand, sucking two of my fingers into his mouth.

"Delicious, just like I knew you would be."

I blush. Jesus, the things I've seen and done, and this guy can still make me feel like a teenage girl. Maybe that's what I like about him, his crazy ability to make me feel like I'm getting a do-over—a way to experience all my firsts again without the darkness and icy fingerprints that haunt me.

He lifts me from the counter, leaving me to dry myself as he strips off the rest of his clothes and climbs into the shower.

I dry off as quickly as I can and get dressed in the clothes he left out for me, deliberately not watching Reid even though I can't think of a single thing I want more. I don't trust myself and I know if I let my heart overrule my mind, I'll regret it in the morning.

Reid is the man who makes my skin hum and my blood sizzle, but he would take me out on Zodiac's order, and that means there can never be a future for us. Nothing is more important to me than loyalty, and Reid is loyal, just sadly not to me.

I make my way into the bedroom and pull back the thick comforter and climb underneath it, so beyond tired that I'm almost asleep by the time Reid joins me.

He tucks me up against him, my back to his chest, and wraps his arms around me, holding on tight. And that's where I stay for the rest of the night, safely in the arms of a killer whose loyalty is to my enemy.

# CHAPTER TWENTY-FOUR

"Hey, we've been waiting for you. Come on in." I follow Leo in through the front door of his large townhouse and into a brightly lit kitchen where a little girl who can't be any older than eighteen months is strapped into a highchair bashing a spoon against the tray in front of her.

"Gem—" I cut him off with a shake of my head.

"It's Viddy," I offer with a smile.

"Viddy, I like it. Well, Viddy, you can call me Cash, and this little princess is Lily." He indicates his daughter, who turns to look at me and offers me a grin that shows more gum than tooth. I can't help but smile back.

"Well, aren't you just the cutest thing in the world," I coo, laughing as she claps her hands. I lift my head when an older woman walks into the room with her silver hair pulled back into a tight bun. She has on a simple black dress and a towel with a picture of a large yellow rubber duck printed on it thrown over her shoulder. She pauses when she realizes Cash has company.

"I'm so sorry. I just came down to give Lily her bath."

"It's fine, Jen, you can take her up. I'm pretty sure she has more pureed carrots in her ears then she managed to get in her mouth." He laughs, making her smile.

"She'll get the hang of it eventually. It's all part of the fun. I'll get her all cleaned up and bring her down unless you want me to keep her for a little while?"

"No, I want to spend some time with her."

She nods, bending down and unclipping the squirming girl who reaches her arms up for her.

I wait until they've both disappeared before turning to look at Cash, who is much closer to me than I realized. "She's adorable, Cash," I tell him.

He doesn't answer, crowding me instead as he backs me into the counter.

"A part of me wants to rip your eyes out just for seeing her, but I can't deny the relief I feel at the thought of having someone else to watch over her if something happens to me," he admits, his face showing just how conflicted he feels.

"I won't hurt her, and I won't ever knowingly put her in danger. I know you have no reason to trust me, Cash, but I'm asking you to anyway."

He sighs and steps back with a nod, moving to grab two bottles of water from the fridge. "Come on, let's go sit."

I follow behind him, down a short hallway into a large

sitting area. A cream leather sectional sofa takes up most of the room, with a large television on the wall facing it and in the corner three huge colorful buckets filled with toys. Otherwise, the place is pretty sparse.

"Take a seat. Jen will bring Lily down in a bit. She'll play then snuggle up for a while before bed. You okay with that? If you want to talk business, it will have to wait until after that."

"No, that's fine. I have to say, I didn't picture you in a townhouse." I kick off my shoes and tuck my legs up underneath me.

"Yeah, well, the penthouse is out now." He scowls, likely thinking about the cameras I found.

"So, what were you expecting?" He sits close to me, turning toward me so his knee brushes mine.

"I don't know, maybe a castle with a shark-infested moat and a dungeon underneath it." I smirk.

"Ah, that's the holiday home." He winks, offering me one of the bottles of water.

I take a sip while he watches me.

"Have you decided what you're going to do with your division?" He leans back, taking a mouthful of his drink.

I shrug. "I have an idea, but that's all it is at the moment. If it comes to fruition, I'll let you know. What about you?"

He blows out a breath and looks at me. "From what I can tell, the guy before me ran a pretty tight ship. He has a large scale car ring going on the side, which makes a pretty penny, but it's not exactly inconspicuous. With Lily, I want something that will skate under the radar, not attract cops from far and wide."

"From what Aries says, most other divisions run protection as a side business. You could always do that, or maybe a loan shark. You do seem pretty good at the whole breaking kneecaps kind of thing," I tease.

He contemplates my words before nodding. "Actually, that's not a bad idea."

"You could sell the car ring and your contacts to another division head or just have someone else run the business and you could be a silent partner. Maybe use it as a dummy corp to take a percentage of the profits or something."

"How old are you again?" he asks, looking at me with wide eyes.

"Twenty-one?" It comes out more as a question than an answer, making him laugh.

"Jesus." He swipes his hand over his face before focusing on me once more. "Okay, tell me what you need from me to get us out from under Zodiac's thumb, and I'll get the ball rolling. I have Jenny here as a full-time nanny, but I want to spend time with my kid outside of this place and not worry about being seen."

I sigh and shake my head. "At the minute, neither of us is powerful enough or have enough resources to take him on. It's going to take time. I'm sorry." And I am.

"I get it, and it's my own fault. We all make choices. I fucked up and have nobody else to blame but myself. How long do you think this will take?"

"It will depend on the other players. A year, maybe two. We need to put a contingency plan in place for Lily in case something happens to both of us. I also want Jenny to know how to get to my place and be able to get Lily inside to one of the panic rooms I'm having installed. She'll need to come by so my security team can get her sorted out. I also want her to know where my secondary safe house is located should we need it."

He reaches over and snags my bottle before tossing it on the floor along with his.

"What the—" I don't finish because I find myself yanked across the sofa and pulled on top of his lap. I'm forced to straddle him, which in this outfit means my tight dress has no choice but to ride up my thighs.

"Cash?" I question quietly, unsure how I'm supposed to react here.

"You know there is nothing sexier in the world to me than someone who cares about my kid's safety as much as I do," he growls.

"Wait, is this your way of trying to tell me you find Jen attractive because I don't want to step on any toes," I tease, laughing lightly until he presses his mouth against mine. His kiss is softer than I expected, especially after the last time, making it easy to melt into.

"I haven't been with a woman since Lily was born. She has been my sole focus since then. But watching you take that blade to your hand at the planetarium that day while your red hair gleamed like blood under the lights, well, it made me fucking hungry for something other than violence. You stood your ground in a circle of wolves ready to pounce and made us all look like chumps, and damn if that didn't make me harder."

He tugs me closer, letting me feel the hard length of him pressing against my core.

"Now the wolves are dead, yet your blood still calls to me, drawing me in, and I have no idea why. What makes you so special, Viddy?"

"I'm nothing special, Cash, and the truth is, for every wolf slain, there are dozens more waiting in the wings to strike. That's how pack mentality works."

"You should move in here with us so we can pool our resources," he suggests, but I shake my head even knowing how hard that must have been for him to offer.

"I'm too much of a liability and I'd never risk Lily like that, but thank you." I press a soft kiss to his lips before pulling away.

"The thought of you out there alone—"

I cut him off. "Don't start doubting me now." I start to climb off his lap, but he grips me tightly.

"I'm not ready to let you go," he admits quietly as he presses his face into the crook of my neck and breathes me in.

"I'm not yours to hold onto, Cash, and truthfully, your lips are not the only ones I've kissed lately," I warn him.

He tenses underneath me for a second before he sighs and his whole body relaxes. "I'm not jealous, I have no right to be. You're not mine, even though I'd have been honored if you wanted to be. But having allies in your corner is smart."

I shove him in the chest and growl. "I'm not fucking for favors. I won't be using my pussy as a bargaining tool," I snap, moving to climb off him again, but this fucking dress makes it impossible. He circles my wrists with his hands and pulls them behind my back, gripping them tightly as he tugs me so close his lips are a hairbreadth from mine.

"I was talking about your heart, Viddy, so retract your claws. I see what you try to hide, smartly too because you're right; nothing is a bigger liability than the ones you love. Most people in our situations choose to avoid attachments for this reason, but there is something about you that makes grown men, dangerous men, gangsters, and murders, lose their fucking minds around you."

My breath comes out in quick, rapid pants at his words, but he's not done.

"I should have snapped your pretty little neck the second you found out about Lily and yet here you are. Your hot little pussy, inches above my cock and all I can think about is fucking you, possessing you, owning you. It's like you weave magic wherever you go."

I laugh, my breath blowing against his face.

"I've seen what I look like, I know the effect this face has on men. It's not my fault people are too fucking shallow to look beneath the pretty to see the dark and ugly that swirls beneath it. It's what makes me a good predator. I don't have to chase my prey if they seek me out themselves now, do I?

It's always the same, this body, this face, I might look like I'm made to sin, demanding attention whenever I go." I lean back a touch, and when he lets go of my wrists, I lift my hands to cup my breasts. His eyes zero in on the movement, his tongue trailing over his bottom lip.

"But years ago, before these came in, I was the prey. I've been torn apart in more ways than you can count. I put myself back together piece by bloody piece, and I decided this body that men so desperately coveted, the one they turned into a weapon they used against me, should be used to bring them down. Seems kind of poetic, don't you think?"

"You could leave, run far away, hide—" I press my fingers over his lips.

"I spent most of my life in the shadows with the bogeyman nipping at my heels. I deserve more than that. I'm not running anymore, Cash, it's my turn to hunt." I finally break free and slide off his lap, pulling my dress down and sitting beside him with my legs crossed as if the last five minutes didn't just happen.

"Look—" Whatever he was about to say is cut off by the reappearance of Jen and Lily.

"Sorry, she wants her daddy," Jen apologizes as she walks over to Cash and hands Lily to him.

"It's fine, Jen. You're off duty now unless I get called out for something, but it should be fine."

"Okay, thanks. It was nice to meet you," she tells me softly before turning and leaving.

"She seems nice," I point out, watching Cash make faces at Lily, smiling when she giggles loudly.

"She's great with Lil, been with us since the beginning. I'd be lost without her to be honest. I had interviewed a hundred nannies before she turned up, and Lily just took to her straight away."

"Where's Lily's mom?" I ask, knowing it's none of my business, but unable to stop the words from spilling out.

"She OD'd two weeks after Lily was born." He looks at me then, his eyes darkening with regret and grief.

"I'm sorry, Cash," I whisper, knowing what it's like to lose someone you care about.

"Caroline and I met in high school. We had similar backgrounds, disinterested parents, and no bright prospects beyond minimum wage jobs. It was the only life we knew. We ran with the wrong crowd, we were all so fucking misunderstood, or at least we thought we were." He sighs, looking away for a moment before continuing.

"We got into drugs. It let us forget the shit we had to go home to. When Caroline found out she was pregnant with Lily here, she entered a drug rehab program at the hospital and got clean. I went cold turkey too, although I was never as far gone as Caroline. I never injected like she did, hadn't crossed the line from want to need but it was the right thing to do for my girl and our baby. I wanted to give Caroline the family we never had."

He runs his fingers over Lily's head absently while he speaks. "By this time, I was working as a runner for Zodiac, so I buckled down and got the job done, saving the money I made for a nice place for us, away from the rundown one-bedroom apartment we had moved into when Caroline's parents kicked her out."

He smiles at Lily as she starts babbling incoherently.

"Lily came into the world, kicking and screaming at 12:31 a.m., in the middle of a thunderstorm and I fell in love the second I laid eyes on her."

He turns his eyes to me, his smile fading as pain washes over his features.

"I thought we had beat the odds, but two weeks later, I came home to find Caroline dead in a pool of vomit with a needle still in her arm. Lily had been fast asleep in her crib while her mom died a few feet from her." He shakes his head, and I move closer, leaning my head on his shoulder, smiling at Lily when she reaches out and touches my hair.

"She was a good person, but she wasn't strong, not like you," he whispers.

"She was strong enough to save her little girl from becoming an addict too. That takes more strength than you can imagine."

He's quiet for a moment, reflecting on my words as Lily decides to crawl toward me. I catch her as she makes a lunge then pause as she snuggles up on my lap. She tucks her head under my chin, grabs a handful of my hair, and promptly falls asleep.

I look at Cash, who has a soft smile on his face.

"I think I'm in love," I whisper, wrapping my arms around

his precious bundle, breathing in the faint scent of baby powder.

"She has that effect on people. It's something you both seem to have in common."

I ignore that comment and snuggle back against the sofa and close my eyes, allowing myself to relax, trusting that Cash will watch over us while we sleep.

# CHAPTER TWENTY-FIVE

I wave to Thomas, who waits with his arms crossed as he leans against the side of the car. I know he'll stay there until I disappear inside, so I hurry through the glass doors so he can get home. After falling asleep at Cash's, I was out cold until Lily started to stir.

Cash offered for me to stay, but watching him with Lily in his arms, looking adorably sleep ruffled, I knew I had to get out before the lure of domesticity pulled me in.

Making connections is fine, necessary even, but my heart needs to remain out of the firing line. I already have Reid to contend with, blurring the line between us over and over, I can't afford to add Cash to the equation too.

I hit the button for the elevator and wait in the dimly lit foyer as the glass doors open behind me.

I turn with a smile, expecting Thomas to tell me I forgot

something. After all, most people are already in bed at three in the morning, but the smile drops from my face when I see Zodiac heading my way.

"Ah, Gemini, I was wondering when I might run into you." His eyes trail over my body, his gaze feeling malevolent, but I manage to resist the urge to shudder.

"Zodiac, sir," I greet him quietly, turning to face forward once more. The elevator doors slide open. As I move to step inside, Zodiac's hand presses against the small of my back and my step falters for a second. I walk inside and turn, moving away from him as I press the button for my floor.

"Which floor?" I ask politely when all I want to do is drink a bottle of holy water before beating him to death with the bottle.

"Same as yours. It seems we'll be neighbors for a while," he purrs.

Mother fucker.

"Oh? And what does division twelve have that the other divisions don't?" I ask innocently, already knowing the freaking answer.

The doors slide open. This time, when his hand pushes against my lower back, I brace, ready for it.

"Why, you dear, of course. I thought having me next door would serve as an extra layer of protection, no? This city can be a dangerous place for a woman alone."

"I'm stronger than I look, sir, but I appreciate the concern," I grit out, walking toward my door, palming the keycard in my pocket.

"Yes, well, only time will tell. Just remember, I'm right next door," he adds, delivering his threat exactly as he intended to. I wait for him to move to the other side of the hallway before slipping the card into the lock. As soon as it beeps, I push it open and step inside, closing the door behind me. I don't care if I'm being rude, and I'm sure he'll make me pay for the disrespect later, but I can't spend a single second more in that man's presence.

I kick off my shoes and head to the kitchen, grabbing a glass from the drainer, and pour myself some OJ from the fridge, the sharp syrupy sweetness washing away the acrid taste of nausea.

I wander over to the sofa, not bothering to close the blinds, and look out at the night sky.

I hate this apartment, more so now that Zodiac is next door. I can't wait for Shadow Falls to be ready for me to move into. Even then, I'll still have to pop back in and out of here to keep up the pretenses because if Zodiac thinks I'm living elsewhere, he will likely have me tailed.

I don't move as I sip my juice, acutely aware that Zodiac is likely watching me on camera next door. As much as I'd like to strip off and take a shower, I can't risk it. Just the thought of his eyes on me makes me want to hurl.

Instead, I force myself to lie down on the sofa and close my eyes, tucking one of the cushions under my head. I drift in and out of sleep restlessly, my dreams filled with faceless men and eyes watching from the shadows and making my skin crawl.

When I wake up later, I feel even more tired than I did before I went to sleep, especially with the growing weight of expectations weighing down on me.

It isn't until I sit up and the blanket slides from my shoulders that I realize something's wrong. I barely make it to the sink before I empty my stomach contents, over and over until there is nothing left inside.

Conscious of the camera on me, I grab a glass and fill it with cold water, chugging it back before wiping my mouth with the back of my hand.

I make my way to the bedroom on shaky legs and shut myself in the closet while I grab clean clothes and toss them in a bag.

I brush my teeth in the bathroom, ignoring my pale reflection in the mirror, before I grab my laptop bag from under the sofa and head out, texting Ben, who I had hired to be my driver, for an immediate pickup.

Blowing out a deep breath, I just make it into the elevator when Zodiac's door opens. He catches sight of me and smiles that creepy as fuck smile of his before the elevator doors close, shutting him out.

I let out a shaky breath and press my head to the cool metal of the door, trying to swallow the bile in my throat.

I think back to when I woke up and noticed the blanket over me, a blanket that came from my bed. Knowing that someone, and it doesn't take a genius to figure out who, was in my apartment while I slept, is almost enough to send me spiraling into a panic attack. It's only by sheer stubbornness of refusing to let Zodiac see what he's done to me that I manage to hold it together.

Somehow I make it outside before turning and puking into the bushes that line the edge of the building. Fortunately, there is nothing in my stomach but water, so I wipe my mouth with the back of my hand and rummage in my bag for a stick of gum as a now worried-looking Thomas climbs out of the car.

"Jesus, Viddy, are you okay? You're as white as a sheet. Do you need to go to the doctor?" I wave him off. Finding the gum, I slip a piece in my mouth.

"I'm okay, just get me out of here please."

He must hear the slight edge of desperation in my voice because he gently takes my elbow and walks me over to the car before helping me inside.

I buckle up and lean back, concentrating on my breathing so I don't puke again. My heartbeat starts to return to normal the farther we get from the building, but instead of feeling calm, I'm furious.

That fucking asshole. I cannot wait until the day I bring him down. I want him to stare into my eyes as I pull the fucking trigger.

# CHAPTER TWENTY-SIX

"Mr. Harris will see you now," a tall thin impeccably dressed man tells me, indicating for me to follow.

I've never stepped foot on a boat before, and I sure as shit didn't expect to have a business meeting on one, but if that's what the guy wants, then so be it.

The tall man knocks on the door, swinging it open when a voice from inside calls to enter.

"Gemini is here to see you, sir," he announces as William Harris looks up from his paperwork.

*Fuck me.* This guy is hot as sin and looks nothing like his beady-eyed father. Is there something in the freaking water around here?

"Well, you're certainly easier on the eye than your predecessor," he tells me with a warm smile, standing to shake my hand.

I move closer to him and let his large hand engulf mine.

"Funny, I was just thinking you're far more attractive than the pictures I've seen of your father."

He grins. "That will be all, John, thank you." William nods to the tall guy who leaves and pulls the door closed behind him.

"Here, take a seat." He pulls out the chair facing his desk for me to sit in, so I do, crossing my legs at the ankle.

I take in his dark messy hair, strong jaw, and light green eyes and think he would be classically handsome if not for his slightly crooked nose and the thin white scar on his forehead that disappears into his hairline. These little imperfections, though, give me a glimpse of the kind of man he is beneath the polished veneer. He might have been born with a silver spoon in his mouth and pockets full of money, but William Harris is every bit the fighter I am. And it can't be easy walking in his father's shoes.

"I'll admit, I was surprised you wanted to meet with me, and now seeing you, well, it seems you surprised me all over again. If you knew me, you'd know that doesn't happen very often," he admits with a rueful shake of his head.

"Yes, I seem to be having that effect on people lately. I'll admit, I'm not exactly advertising the fact that the new Gemini is a woman, but I didn't want to start the first of what I'm hoping is many meetings with you based on a lie."

"I respect that. I'm unsure though, what it is you'd like to discuss." Straight to the point. I like that.

"What do you know about Zodiac and the operation he

runs?" I ask, perhaps showing more of my hand than I wanted to, but I have a feeling William is too perceptive for me to use vague half-truths.

He picks up his pen and spins it on the table absentmindedly while answering. "Zodiac runs this city. A city he has divided into twelve sectors and has a minion running each piece, no offense, so he can reap the benefits without really getting his hands dirty. He makes most of his money from his drug trade, although I have heard he has his fingers in many pies. I have to be honest, Gemini, I have no intention of working with the guy. I'm sorry if that means you've wasted your time," he says politely.

"I don't want you to work with Zodiac. I want you to work with me," I tell him truthfully, watching as the pen stops moving as he stares at me.

"If you work for Zodiac, I'm not sure how there can be a separation of the two. Besides, Zodiac and my father have a long and unpleasant history. My father would sooner set him on fire than assist him in any way. It's why he stopped trading with the previous Gemini before his death."

"Good. I don't want anyone who has any kind of loyalty to Zodiac. I'm only interested in making a deal with someone who I trust to have my back and vice versa."

"And you think my father might be able to help you with that?" He quirks an eyebrow at that.

"No, I think you might. Harris Holdings and Conglomerate are one of the world's biggest arms dealers," I hold my hand up when he appears about to interrupt, "sourcing their supplies almost exclusively to the government. But we all know the government are cheap bastards, which is why I'm sure your military-grade weapons tend to end up on the black market. I know the previous Gemini bought a bulk of these and sold them to motorcycle clubs down the West Coast. Now normally, having stuff end up on the black market wouldn't be a major issue for a company your size, it happens. Everything can be bought and sold for the right price. However, with gun crime at an all-time high, with mass shootings taking place in schools and malls being splashed across the news every day, your company is seeing a stark decline in its shares."

He sits forward now, that relaxed attitude of his completely gone, revealing the sharp and shrewd businessman instead.

"You seem to know an awful lot about me, and yet, I know nothing about you. Tell me, Gemini, are you here perhaps as a Trojan horse? Did Zodiac decide to send in a pretty face before his army strikes?"

"I'm a street kid, Mr. Harris, who has honestly been chewed up and spat out more times than I care to admit. Zodiac wants me to be his puppet, pulling my strings while I do his bidding. Unfortunately for him, he chose the wrong girl. What I want is to be free, and to do that, I need more power than he has. That's where you come in. I want to broker a deal where instead of selling your shit on the black market, you sell it to me lock, stock, and barrel. I have a dummy corp set up that for all intents and purposes is a gun supplier. I just won't have the government breathing down my neck like you do. The company will be legal and will have legitimate business deals running through it, but it will also act as a front for some, shall we say, less than stellar buyers I may have interested. The benefit for you is that you'll still get paid, but any of the bad press and publicity will be traced back to my company, not yours."

He leans back in his chair, considering my offer. "My father would likely be more than happy to strike that kind of deal with you, as long as you have the revenue to put your money where your mouth is."

"I don't want to make a deal with a man who will likely be dead in a year. Sorry if that seems harsh, but his health problems are well-publicized. Of course, so are his somewhat less than pleasant opinions on the opposite sex. It's you or not at all. I have two others lined up to speak to after this meeting, should you decide to decline." I shrug, lying my ass off. I mean, I do have a plan B, but it will take me far longer to bring Zodiac down.

"How do I know this is a legitimate offer and not some scam?"

"You don't, but I have more to lose here than you, and despite what some people might think, I don't actually have a death wish."

"Maybe not, but you sure do have some brass balls." He shakes his head. "You know Zodiac will kill you if you cross him. He won't care that you're a woman."

"Trust me, you aren't telling me anything I don't already know."

His eyes narrow at my words, but before he can say anything, I hurry on.

"What do you say, Mr. Harris? Want to break out from Daddy's shadow?"

He growls and stands up, stalking toward me. I don't cower from him, even as he leans down over me. "Just because I'm not the same particular brand of evil as Zodiac doesn't mean I'm a good man. If you push me, I'll push back, and I'm not sure you'll like the consequences."

"Hmm... is this the part where I cower in fear?"

He looks frustrated but steps back and runs a hand through his hair. "Jesus, are you always this infuriating?"

"Why, yes. Yes, I am, but I'm also loyal to a fault, smart, and willing to do anything to bring Zodiac to his knees."

He stares at me long and hard before whispering, "Jesus, what did he do to you?"

I ignore his question and ask one of my own. "Deal or no deal, Mr. Harris? I have other people to meet with."

"I'm going to regret this, but I see something in you that makes me think if anyone can take Zodiac out, it's you. Fine, deal. And please, for the love of God, call me Will," he replies with a small smile.

My returning smile is far bigger, but I keep my composure, not wanting to give away my relief. "Will it is."

I WASN'T LYING to Will about the other meetings, but the nature of them was vastly different than the deal I struck with him. For starters, I didn't once picture Milo or Kristoff naked, although the same couldn't be said for how they looked at me.

Milo, although on the pervy side, seemed harmless enough. Well, as harmless as the second-largest drug dealer in the area could be. He and Zodiac are archnemeses so naturally he was my next point of contact.

This time I went heavily guarded, unsure of the welcome I would be receiving, and I went under the guise of the reclusive Gemini's secretary. I don't know if he bought it, but his suspicious mind wasn't strong enough to stop him from striking up a deal, especially when it would mean getting access to Zodiac's supply.

I don't want drugs flooding the streets of division twelve, so instead, I'm going to sell the whole stock to Milo for a discounted price and give him safe passage to use the docks to move his product.

Kristoff, on the other hand, made my skin crawl. I wanted no part in anything he had to offer, and I made sure to let him know it. Whatever deals he has with Zodiac or any of the other eleven divisions was between him and them, but I refused to allow a skin peddler to set foot in my division. Meeting him was for only two reasons, one—to let the dirty fucker know he was unwelcome and any business he might have had with the previous Gemini stopped the second he died and two—to plant a couple of bugs Baker got for me.

And now, sitting back in my office, I realize I've done everything I can to level the playing field. Now I just have to let the game play out and hope I survive.

A knock at the door has me looking up just as Gary pokes his head around.

"Hey, V, you hungry? I come bearing gifts." He pushes the door open at my smile and carries a tray over to me, placing it down on my desk.

The smell alone makes my mouth water.

"Beef Stew and fresh bread, comfort food in a bowl."

"I think I might love you, Gary," I admit, grabbing the spoon from the tray while he laughs heartily.

"I thought food was a way to a man's heart?"

"Well, whoever said that shit clearly never met a hungry woman. We can get real bitchy, real fast," I confess, moaning in delight when the beefy goodness explodes on my tongue.

"Aye, I think my wife might agree with you there, lass."

"I didn't realize you were married, Gary," I mutter, taking a bite of the bread.

"Yep, going on twenty years now. Best woman I know. She has to be to have put up with my sorry ass after all."

"I think you're more of a catch than you realize." I smile, watching as his face turns serious.

"I know it's a lot to ask, but if war comes, or should I say when, can you give me a heads up? I want to get Flo as far from here as possible until it all blows over."

I pause with the bread halfway to my mouth. "War doesn't always come with a warning. Sometimes you don't know it's coming until you find yourself standing in the middle of it covered in blood. But I promise, if I sense things going south, I'll get your wife out of the city and somewhere safe. You have my word."

He nods, his shoulders relaxing.

"You don't have to be here either. I can do this alone. I don't want to put anyone in any unnecessary danger, but I can't guarantee there won't be casualties," I warn him.

"I'm not leaving. I want Zodiac gone as much as you do. Besides, who will keep you fed if I leave?" He huffs, making me laugh.

"Well, you're not wrong there. Thank you, Gary, for everything. Taking care of this place for me, for hooking me up with Danny and Baker and the rest of the guys. I don't know what I would have done without you."

"Oh, hush, woman. We both know you would have figured it out. I don't think you know how to fail, but I'm glad you're here. Flo and I were never fortunate enough to have kids, and after seeing what you're like at twenty-one, I'm kind of glad," he teases as I throw my spoon at him.

He laughs, bending to pick it up, placing it on the edge of the desk. "Seriously, though, I feel kind of protective of you. I know you're all hard outside, but you're all soft inside. I don't want you to lose that."

"You make me sound like an M&M." I smile, touched by his words.

"Yeah, well, your secret is safe with me." He winks before turning to leave.

"I'll come up in an hour to collect the dishes and bring you a slice of cheesecake." He disappears before I can thank him again, which is just as well. He has me choked up enough that I'm not sure I could get the words out past the lump in my throat.

So much has changed in such a short space of time and yet I know this is just the start.

I've taken chances, reached out and made connections and begun to pave my own way.

All that's left to do now, is wait.

# WE ALL FALL DOWN

## ONE YEAR LATER

# CHAPTER TWENTY-SEVEN

"This place is nice..." Baker laughs, dragging his finger over the edge of the desk.

"Yeah, I love what you've done here." Danny chuckles, taking in the mounted deer head staring down at us.

I look up at it and turn away. I'll never admit it out loud, but the damn thing gives me the creeps. I swear its eyes follow you when you move.

"It was the previous Gemini's hunting cabin, which is fucking ridiculous because there is nothing around here to hunt." Turning, I look around at the sparsely decorated room with its walls covered in dark wood paneling. There is a twin bed in the far back corner with a bedside table and a lamp beside it. Next to that is a small table only big enough to seat two people, with mismatched chairs, then the desk that Baker is now perched on, and a small kitchen area with a sink, fridge, and a stovetop. A single door to the right leads to a bathroom and a single door on the left leads down to the cellar beneath the property.

"Well, that was until I figured out exactly what he used this place for," I tell them, turning toward Danny, who looks out the window at the sound of gravel crunching under tires of an approaching truck.

"And what is it you figured out?" Danny asks absent-mindedly as another truck trundles along the dusty track toward the cabin.

"That he wasn't using this place to hunt down the weakest animals but the weakest humans. It's a kill cabin."

"The fuck?" Baker curses, looking down at his feet, making me laugh.

"You're thinking about the bodies that are likely buried beneath you right now, aren't you?" I tease.

He lifts his head and glares at me, making me laugh even harder.

"Laugh it up, but don't come crying to me when you have a ghost haunting your cute ass."

"Stop checking out my ass," I yell with a shake of my head as I make my way over to the door that leads down to the soundproof cellar.

"I'm gonna assume if you're worried about ghosts that you really won't want to come down here now, will you?" I grin over my shoulder at him.

"Fuck no. I'll switch on the camera feed while you're

down there so I'll know if you need me, but otherwise, I'm going to sit here in a circle of salt where it's safe."

I chuckle all the way down the steps, making my way to the lone chair in the far corner. The room is nothing but a large concrete space, void of anything but the chair.

Danny follows me down, looking around the room for threats, but we both know it's empty as the only way in is the door we just walked through.

"You sure you want to stay for this? It's gonna get bloody," I warn him for the second time today.

"There is always a little blood involved with you, Viddy. I don't know why you keep asking me. You'd think after almost a year you'd know by now that I'll be at your side every damn time. I knew what I was getting myself into when I agreed to work for you."

I grin at him. "I just don't want you to feel like I'm taking advantage of you."

He rolls his eyes and crosses his arms over his chest. "You know, it baffles me how someone so ruthless and bloodthirsty can be sweet enough to give me a toothache."

"Hey now, let's not get carried away." I huff as I sit on the chair and cross my legs, letting my fitted black dress rise up my legs a touch to flash a little skin.

I've kept it simple today, teaming the figure-hugging dress with high heeled black Jimmy Choos. My outfit is elegant, classy, and dark enough to hide the impending bloodstains.

The door opens, and a few guys walk down, chatting

together amicably as they make their way down the rickety steps that groan with protest.

They don't even look up and acknowledge us as we observe them from the dark corner. I can identify each one on sight, Freddie, Boise, and David. Three of the last Gemini's most respected men.

My problem is, over the time they've worked for me, they haven't been pulling in any more money than others, and yet the suits they wear are handmade Italian and the watches on their wrists cost the same as a small car.

The door opens once more, letting more men through as Danny and I stay quiet and watch them. I spot the ones who see us straight away and make a note of who they are until finally, everyone is accounted for.

I wait for Baker to slide the lock into place and for the lights to flick on before engaging them.

"Hello, boys." Some startle at my words, some don't react at all, but all of them look a little freaked out at being locked down here.

"What's going on, why are you here?" the guy called Freddie asks, all bluster and bravado.

See, Freddie here still thinks I'm Gemini's secretary, which is fucking stupid after all this time. If it were me, I'd be curious about the man behind the curtain, but not these guys, and as of yesterday, I know why.

"Well, hello, Freddie. I was wondering if you were finally going to acknowledge my existence."

"Lady, I don't know what you think you're doing but when I tell Gem—"

I pull my gun from the holster behind my back, my silencer already fitted, and shoot him in the head. He crumples to the ground as everyone stands around, staring at him in shock before turning to look at me warily.

"Perhaps we should start this again."

Nobody says anything, but I'm betting if Baker hadn't frisked them and removed their weapons, a few would have their guns pointing in my direction right now.

"I don't know what the previous Gemini was like. Frankly, I don't care, but things have changed now. You've been given time to adjust but if I can't guarantee your loyalty by now, I never will. Not much has been asked of you, and yet some of you greedy fuckers still want more. If you're curious to know what happens to people that betray me or mine in any way, look at Freddie over there. Now, does anyone else have anything they would like to admit to me?"

Nobody says anything, but I don't miss the way Boise shuffles a little.

"Hmm... You see, I had an interesting call from a dear friend of mine. He seems to think a few of my men are working on a deal with Kristoff Libernesh, offering him safe passage at the harbor in exchange for cash. Cash I'm clearly not getting a cut in."

I pace backward and forward slowly, the loud clicking of my heels against the concrete the only sound.

"Now, it's not the lost revenue that bothers me you see, but the blatant disregard for my rules. I know, I know," I look at them and shake my head ruefully, "rules can be tedious. We are criminals, after all, we're expected to break the rules, right?"

I lift my gun and fire a round into Boise's head this time before continuing to pace.

"The problem is, without rules, there is chaos. In those situations, someone, namely me, is left cleaning up the mess. Now, does that seem fair when I'm not getting anything in return for my troubles?" I ask, turning to glare at David.

"I...I—" he babbles, but I lift my free hand to cut him off.

"It doesn't matter now. What's done is done and your money means nothing to me. Your accounts have already been emptied along with Curly's and Moe's and redistributed to a more worthy cause," I answer vaguely, letting them make of it what they will. What they don't know is that I sent the money to the victims so they can escape from their current lives and make new ones.

"You," I point at the tall dark-haired guy in the corner. Mike is one of my newer recruits, but so far, I like what I've seen.

"Ma'am?" he asks respectfully with his hands held loosely at his side.

"Do you remember what my number one rule is?"

I know he does, and when he nods, I indicate for him to say it out loud for the rest of the crowd.

"You don't peddle in flesh and you don't make deals with people who do," he answers succinctly.

"Thank you, that is correct. So tell me, David," I turn to glare at him once more, "why did you and your boys here decide to ignore that?"

"Libernesh approached us on Zodiac's orders. He didn't want anything from us but safe passage," he mumbles, tripping over his words, but everything out of his mouth infuriates me.

Motherfucking Zodiac.

"And do you answer to Zodiac?"

"Erm...well...he's Zodiac," he answers, making me shake my head.

"Mike tell me, what would you do in the same situation?" I question, not taking my eyes from David.

"Report everything back to you, ma'am," he answers with zero hesitation.

"Imagine that, David. Did the thought even cross your mind?"

He looks like a deer caught in headlights.

"Of course, you didn't, which tells me whatever loyalty you have, isn't for me." I lift my gun and shoot him too, tired of listening to his excuses.

I turn to the rest of the guys and study them.

"If you don't trust me to deal with this shit, then how am I supposed to trust you? This is the only time I will have this conversation with you all. If you cross me, I will eliminate you and send you back to your families in pieces."

"Yes, ma'am," rings out around the room, so I nod in acknowledgment.

"Send these guys to Libernash. He wanted them; he can have them. Dismissed." I wave them off and move back over to Danny, who is still standing where I left him with his arms crossed over his chest, looking dark and formidable.

I stand beside him as the locks disengage loudly and watch as the remaining guys wait for their cue.

When Baker swings the door open, I walk through the room without looking back, knowing Danny is bringing up my rear.

"Get it done and clean this place up, and there will be a hefty bonus in each of your accounts by midnight tonight," I call over my shoulder before making my way up the steps into the dingy cabin.

I feel the watchful eyes of the deer on me and stick my tongue out at it.

"Judgy asshole," I mutter, making Baker snort.

"You get all that? Anyone look extra twitchy?" I ask, perching on the edge of the desk for a minute.

"Of course, I got it all. Apart from the three you shot, everyone else seemed unfazed."

I nod, thankful. I had the same vibe, but it's easy to miss shit when you're in the thick of things, which is why I always insist on extra eyes and a second opinion. I might find myself in the role of executioner more often than I like, but it doesn't mean I thrive on it. I might not like playing God, but sometimes death is the only option.

I send a message to Ben, who lets me know he's outside already.

"Ben's here, so I'm gonna go. Make sure they clean this place up. I'll see you guys later tonight," I call out, making my way over to the door.

"Who's on protection detail?" Danny asks before I leave.

"James is with Ben, don't worry. I told him to wait in the car. You guys are more than enough protection for just little old me." I flutter my lashes at him, knowing how pissed he gets if I leave without taking any of my guards. It's not intentional, but when you've spent a lifetime having nobody to look out for you other than yourself, it takes time to break the habit.

"Good. I'll call when we've finished up here." He nods

"All right, laters." I step out into the afternoon sun when the SUV swings around the corner from the back of the cabin.

I wait for James to climb out and smile when he holds the door open for me.

"Miss," he greets me politely, holding out his hand as he assists me into the car.

"Hey, James, Ben. Sorry for the wait."

I move to the far side and strap myself in as James climbs into the passenger seat beside Ben.

"It's fine. Where to, Viddy?" Ben calls, looking at me in the rearview mirror.

"Home, please. I need to shower and change before my meeting later."

"Okay. Oh, and Chris messaged me to tell you she took DJ and Kevin to a theme park today. She says you owe her big time as she hasn't stopped throwing up. Apparently, rollercoasters and hot dogs don't mix. Who knew?"

He shakes his head while I grin.

I might have been the one to take DJ under my wing, but every single one of my team pulled him into the fold and treated him as family and it's because of DJ I even met Ben and his son Kevin in the first place.

Ben and Kevin had been on the streets for six months after Ben's wife died, and his ex-father-in-law tried to file for custody of Kevin. Ben had heard firsthand about the abuse the man had bestowed upon his daughter; there wasn't a chance in hell he was risking his boy falling into his clutches, so he ran.

They stayed mostly in shelters, and when DJ had come for food, he and Kevin had struck up a friendship, even in the most unlikely of circumstances, hell maybe because of them. DJ insisted I find Ben and Kevin and let them know he was safe. I just went one better and offered them the safety and protection they so desperately needed.

I took the life of a dirty cop that night and saved the lives of three people who deserved it. I might not be a good person, but I like to think I can still balance the scale of morality in my favor a little.

# CHAPTER TWENTY-EIGHT

I sip coffee and watch as William, or Will as he insists I call him, skims over the report I just gave him.

"And this is next year's projections?" he asks, looking up at me. The guy might have nearly twenty years on me, but you'd have to be dead not to find him attractive. Today his dark chocolate hair is neat and slicked back at the sides, the top a little longer showing a touch of rebellion. His dark blue suit and gold tie would look ridiculous on most of the population, but on him, it seems effortlessly classy and attention-grabbing without being tacky.

"No, that's this year's gross earnings. Next year's projections are almost triple," I reply, crossing my legs, feeling my body heat when his eyes trail their way up my bare skin.

"My father used to say never get into bed with a woman

unless it's to fuck her, but getting into bed with you, even if it's only for business, was by far the smartest thing I ever did." He grins, making my stomach clench with need.

You'd think I would have built up some kind of resistance to hot men by now with the amount I'm exposed to them on a daily basis, but apparently, the more I see, the more I want. My pussy is a gluttonous bitch who is sick of being denied.

"Mixing business with pleasure is never a wise choice, Mr. Harris." I wink, standing on shaky legs. It's the same spiel I always give him. Heck, it's the same spiel I give to Cash and Reid, too. It just doesn't change my body's reactions to any of them.

We've been playing this game now for a year, two magnets trying to push the other away, and yet the attraction is still there.

"That's true," he agrees before standing and walking around his desk toward me, "but fuck if I don't want to make you the exception."

He stands in front of me, too close to be described as anything other than intimate. I look up at him under my lashes, willing myself to step back, but my feet are frozen to the floor, refusing to move.

"Fuck it," he growls a second before his hands are in my hair and his mouth is on mine, firm and unyielding, melting away any resistance I had. I grip the lapels of his suit and return his kiss with the same feverous hunger. It's like a beast has awoken inside me and she's been starved of affection for so long she's ravenous.

His tongue slides against mine as his grip tightens, leaving me unable to move and entirely at his mercy. Where there should be panic, there is only white-hot need rushing through me, a hunger that wants to be sated and refuses to be denied.

It takes everything I have not to mewl in protest when he rips his lips away from mine, both of us breathing so heavy you'd think we had run a marathon.

"You come alive like that for everyone? Jesus fuck, babe, it's like you caught fire underneath my fingertips."

"I don't have much to compare it to," I answer without thought, biting my lip when he freezes.

"Are you..." His words trail off as he takes a step back and drags his eyes over my body up to my face.

"How the fuck you look like that and manage to remain pure will baffle me to the day I die," he stutters out in shock.

I laugh then, loud with a hint of something darker threaded through it. Not anger but sorrow, and I know he picks up on it when his eyes flash with anger.

"I'm anything but pure, Will. Don't try to put me on a pedestal, I'll only dirty it up with bloody footprints."

He cups my jaw, tilting my head back so I'm forced to look at him.

"Warriors always wear the blood of the people who tried to make them fall. Don't be ashamed of what you did to survive or of who you had to become."

"A killer?" I ask, my eyes staring into his, feeling myself getting lost in them once more.

"A queen."

I blink at his words and the hint of pride behind them. Stepping back, he puts some space between us. The electricity that previously crackled, fizzles out as he steps back around his desk and puts more distance between us.

"Whoever ends up with you better appreciate the priceless gem he's getting." He rubs a hand down his face.

"And if they don't?" I mean, it's kind of a moot point because I'll never be the kind of woman who puts up with shit. I'm not saying I need sunshine and roses; it sounds kind of boring if I'm completely honest. What I want is someone who makes me laugh more than he makes me cry, but that would mean letting someone close enough to scale my walls, and I don't know if I'm emotionally equipped to deal with that shit, not right now at least.

"Then I'll cut off their hands. If they can't handle you with care, then they don't get to touch you at all," he answers in the same tone he might use to ask someone to pass the salt.

"I'm gonna go before I take my panties off and throw them at you," I tease, well I think it's a tease, but if he asked me, I don't think I'd put up much resistance.

"Wise idea. I'm two seconds away from spreading you out over my desk and eating you for dinner. If I wasn't caught up in all this shit my father left me to clean up, I'd say fuck it, but I fear I would end up making you an even bigger target, which is saying something when you walk around like a neon sign saying *try me*. And yes, I mean that in every conceivable way."

I laugh, moving toward the door. "I never did have any patience, Will. If someone wants to come and take my crown, at least they know where to find me. They see the tits and ass and think I'll be an easy target. It's not my fault few tend to look close enough to see the monster inside. Let them come for me, I'll be ready."

"Everyone's a monster these days, V, it's the world we live in. It's eat or be eaten." He grins.

"Well, now I know what you can do with that tongue, Will, maybe I'll be back sooner rather than later." I pull the door open and see James waiting for me.

"Viddy?" Will calls from behind me, making me turn to look over my shoulder at him. "Be careful, and call me if you need me."

I nod, even though we both know I won't. "Bye Will."

"Until next time, Viddy."

And damn if his words don't feel like a promise. Fuck, I need to get laid. A vibrator is just not cutting it anymore.

# CHAPTER TWENTY-NINE

The soft strains of a saxophone playing a melancholy tune float up the stairs from the bar below.

I toss the pen onto the desk and push my chair back before standing and stretching. Twisting my neck from side to side, I wince as the movement sends a sharp stabbing pain into my overly tired brain.

Hitting redial on the phone before switching it to loudspeaker, I walk over to the window and peer through the venetian blinds to the cobbled streets below.

The view is the same as it was the first time I saw it, but now it's bustling with life. Couples making out, groping each other with heavy hands and barely contained lust as they wait for cabs home. Alcohol has lowered their inhibitions, making the thought of people watching them more of a turn-on than a deterrent.

Drunken revelers spill out of the various clubs and bars, singing out of tune songs about love and heartbreak, as the still sober people maneuver around them with small knowing smiles and shakes of their heads.

I had brought division twelve back to life and I felt a strange amount of pride in not only the division, but the people's resilience to bounce back. It hadn't been easy, but then nothing worth having ever is.

"Yo, boss lady, what can I get you?" the voice calls over the phone.

I roll my eyes at the moniker given to me by a man old enough to be my father.

"I need coffee, Gary, lots and lots of strong coffee before I slip into a coma. I don't know why I hired all this security when the only thing guaranteed to kill me off is paperwork," I complain, making him snort.

"Ah, feeling sorry for your bitchy self now, are we?" He chuckles as I watch a young girl turn an alarming shade of green before she bends at the waist and pukes all over her shoes.

*Classy.* I grimace in distaste but keep an eye on her until I see two other girls approach. One takes her shoes from her hand, the other holds her hair back. Friends, I surmise. All of them seem a little wobbly on their feet, but only the one girl looks to have overdone it.

Walking back to the desk, I realize I didn't answer Gary. "Shit, sorry, Gary, I spaced out. This is exactly why I need coffee, and I'm not bitchy, I'm tired and hungry," I pout.

"You need more than a few hours of sleep at night, that's what you need," he gripes.

"And how do you know how many hours I sleep, Gary? Have you been spying on me?" I tease.

"No ma'am. I like my balls right where they are, thank you very much."

I smile even though he can't see it.

"I'll make you some coffee and I'll find you some of those pastries you like. Beth made a fresh batch that will blow your mind."

He hangs up before I can thank him, but then two seconds later, the phone rings again, so I answer it with a grin. "Ready to blow my mind already?" I laugh, but the voice that answers back definitely doesn't belong to Gary.

"Name the time and place and I'll be there. Better yet, let me up and I'll fuck you over that desk of yours," Reid growls.

I shake my head, the smile falling from my face. "What do you want Diablo?"

He laughs before it turns into a hiss, making me frown.

"Buzz me up, Cherry," he orders, making me bristle. The last thing I want is to deal with him when I'm tired, horny, and my defenses are lower, but that hiss sounded like he's in pain, and as per usual, it's me he comes to for patching up.

*It's always been me.*

"Fine but behave. I'm not in the mood for your particular brand of drama."

"You wound me, woman," he jokes before hanging up.

I make my way over to the attached bathroom, snagging

the first aid kit from beneath the counter, pausing to check my reflection in the mirror.

I look like a siren today in my scarlet wrap dress that hits mid-thigh and dips in the front to give a hint of cleavage. My hair escaped its confines earlier, and after spending the last few hours running my fingers through it, it looks like it's been gripped tight while I've been fucked hard.

Running my tongue over my glossy red lips, I smirk knowing the second Reid sees them, he'll be picturing me on my knees with them wrapped around his dick.

I really am evil sometimes.

I stroll back into my office, dump the first aid kit on my desk, and pull the door open.

"Aries is here. Can you let him up please, Thomas?"

My guard nods at me as I turn to leave.

"Oh, and could you let Gary know I have a guest and to send up extra coffee?" He nods as I close the door.

I move back to the window, watching the last of the partygoers make their way home when the door opens and Reid walks in.

He freezes when he catches sight of me, his eyes traveling slowly from my bare feet, up my body until they reach my face.

He groans. "I'm just gonna start calling you Captain because I swear every time I see you, my dick stands up and salutes you."

"In that case, I'm going to start calling you Picasso

because whenever I see you, your face is a mangled mess," I return.

He laughs before wincing. "Shit, it hurts my head to laugh," he admits.

"Okay, sit in the chair and let me look."

I move over to the desk and wait for him to sit before running my fingers lightly through his hair. "You have a large egg back here. Looks like someone tried to crack open your head like a piñata, but at least it isn't bleeding."

"Then it looks like it feels." He hisses when I touch a particularly sensitive spot.

"What happened?" I ask like I do every fucking time. It's getting old, and yet, we both know I won't turn him away.

He's quiet, but he always is. The man has a way with words until you ask him a simple question, then he shuts up tighter than a hooker's legs in church.

"Some asshole jumped me from behind, fucking coward," he spits out, but I just stare at him in shock before feeling his forehead. "What? What is it?"

"I'm just checking for a temperature. You must be sick. I mean you just gave me a straight answer so either you're ill, or it's the end of the world—*eek*!" I squeal when he yanks me down onto his lap, wrapping one of his arms around my neck and pulling me close.

When he speaks, his lips brush my ear. "I've missed your sassy mouth, Cherry."

I sigh and snuggle in closer, pressing my head against his chest. "I missed you too."

We sit quietly for a minute before he reaches up and tilts my head back with his hand on my jaw. Then ever so softly, he places a chaste kiss on my mouth before swiping his tongue over my bottom lip.

A groan rips free from his chest and the next thing I know, I'm straddling his lap, my dress riding up over my hips, and his hot hands are gripping the bare skin of my ass. The crackle of electricity races through me, heating my blood and dampening my core. It's always this way between us.

We've never taken things further than that night in his shower, both of us smart enough to know falling for each other would be our downfall. Maybe it's just as well if this is how potent things are between us when we do nothing more than kiss. Sex would probably incinerate us both.

"Stay with me tonight," he whispers, making me groan, unconsciously grinding down on his rock hard cock.

"It's not a good idea, Reid. If we keep playing with fire, one of us will get burned," I warn him, feeling heat spiral through me as he grips my ass harder, rubbing my sex over his cock.

"I know, but right now, I don't give one single fuck about doing the right thing."

"Fuck," I groan, pulling free from him before standing on wobbly legs, and shimmying my dress back into place.

Walking around my desk, I sit in my chair and try to look as unaffected as possible, but with wet panties and flushed skin, I fear it's unlikely I'm pulling it off. Ignoring him for a moment while I gain some composure, I open the first aid kit and shuffle around until I find the painkillers and toss them to him.

"Take a couple of these. It will take the edge off. Gary's bringing up some—" I shut up when there's a knock at the door.

"That will be him now. Come in," I yell, knowing security wouldn't let anyone else up without calling me first. I'm grateful for the reprieve. Gary might be the only thing that stops Reid and me from ripping each other's clothes off.

"I come bearing gifts," Gary announces as he steps through with a tray in his hand, nodding in thanks to Thomas for opening the door for him.

"Gary, you are a god. Place it on the desk for me."

He does as I ask as I stand and move around the desk toward him. Lifting up on my tiptoes, I place a kiss on his weathered cheek.

"Thank you. Can you rustle up a couple of coffees for my guys outside too, pretty please? I've kept them here far longer than I planned tonight," I admit.

He laughs, shaking his head. "They know what you're like, we all do. I'll fetch them a drink, don't worry. You about done?" he asks, looking over to Reid quickly before looking away.

"Twenty minutes and I'll be out of here, I swear." I wink, letting him know I'm good. He squeezes my arm before nodding his head toward Reid in respect and leaving, pulling the door tightly behind him.

I feel Reid's eyes on me, but I don't look up, as I sit back down and sip my coffee.

"That one's for you." I point at the second cup. "I'm almost done here, then I'll take you home," I tell him as he leans forward, making my body tingle with awareness.

"You've done well for yourself," he says quietly, reaching for the remaining cup.

"I'm just doing my job," I answer vaguely, entering the final figures I was finishing up with into the laptop before shutting it down.

"It's more than that. I've been to all the divisions now, seen most of the division heads in action. All of them are given respect as is their due, but with you, it's different. I can tell it's because they truly do respect you, not because it's expected or forced."

"Well, yeah. It's because I show them respect back. It really is as simple as that. You forget I've seen some of the other division heads in action too, and most of them have forgotten how they got where they are and look down on the people running for them. Beats me why when it's where we all started."

"Money corrupts, it's an age-old story," he points out, lifting one of the flakey pastries from the plate and taking a large bite. His eyes flutter closed for a moment before he wolfs down the rest of it in three bites.

"Money only corrupts if you let it. Honestly, it's just a fucking excuse to be a dick if you ask me." I reach out and snag the other pastry before Reid can take it.

"Zodiac says you're doing well, better than he thought you would. In fact, he wants to call a meeting at the planetarium to discuss it with the others so they might implement whatever it is you're doing."

I pause, looking up at him sharply. "Excuse me?"

He looks at me with a peculiar look on his face. "What?"

"If you think for one second I'm going to tell a bunch of asshats how I'm making money so they can turn around, stab me in the back, and take it from me you're out of your damn mind," I snap.

"Cherry, if Zodiac wants you there, you'll be there," he warns, his voice hard.

"I never said I wouldn't be, but if he's expecting a step by step guide on how to sell more product, he'll be bang out of luck. I sell his shit, I make him more money than he dreamed I would, and it's still not enough. No, that's not what he wants, Reid, he wants to know what other pies I have my fingers in, and that won't happen."

He opens his mouth to argue with me, but I hold up my hand to get him to shut up.

"Just leave it, Reid, I'll deal with it when and if I need to."

He sighs but drops it.

I shove my laptop in my bag and slip my feet into my heels.

"Come on, the sooner we leave, the sooner you can get some rest."

"So you're staying with me?" he asks, standing up and towering over me.

"Yes, I'll stay, but Reid, we can't keep doing this. You and I both know there is no future for you and me."

"Maybe not, but then there is no future guaranteed for any of us. All I care about is being with you in the here and now. I'm so fucking tired of existing, Cherry. Sometimes I actually want to live a little," he says softly.

My shoulders slump, my resistance draining out of me. I grab his hand and tug him to the door. Saying goodnight to my guys, we head down to Reid's car.

"My place or yours?" He winks after we both climb in and the engine begins to purr.

"Yours," I answer like I always do.

"You know I'm starting to get a complex. You never take me home with you. You're making me feel like a dirty little secret." He turns to look at me, his words light, but there is a dark undertone to his voice.

"You saw it the day you showed me around. It's nothing special, it looks exactly like your apartment. It's just a place I lay my head, Reid, but it's cold. I felt more at home on the streets," I tell him as he grips the steering wheel a little tighter than before.

"An apartment is an apartment. I'm hardly ever there, that's all." I try to soothe him. I don't want to piss him off, but I'm not taking him back to an apartment full of cameras that Zodiac can enter whenever he likes.

"I know you're never there—"

I cut him off. "You know? You watching me, Reid?" I tease, but there is no hiding how sharp my voice is.

"I mean, you're always at that bar. I'm just making an observation."

Observation, my ass.

"Did you know Zodiac lives in my complex?" I question lightly. He whips his head around to glare at me.

"Zodiac has a house on the outskirts of town. A massive place that looks more like a fucking hotel than a home," he replies.

I don't answer him because Zodiac having a house does not change the fact he has an apartment too.

"Does he have a wife?"

Again, I've done my digging, but it's always nice to know if Reid will tell me the truth or start in with the bullshit.

"Yeah, but don't ever mention Estelle to him. He will skin you alive if you so much as breathe her name."

I wave him off. "It never crossed my mind. I have zero interest in her. Her life must already suck donkey balls being married to him. No, what I'm saying is, he might have a home and a wife to go back to, but that doesn't change the fact he has an apartment, or perhaps a fuckpad, right next door to my apartment. So, as I'm sure you can imagine, being at home for me is about as relaxing as swimming with sharks."

"Fuck," he curses before switching on the radio, effectively shutting down any more conversation.

Warmth fills my chest when I realize he genuinely didn't know and that he seems pissed about it. I turn to look out the window, biting the smile playing on the edge of my lips. Yeah, it's not nice being the last person to know shit.

Still, I can't help the spike of apprehension that makes the hair on the back of my neck stand up because I can't figure out what Zodiac's end game is and just what it has to do with me.

I close my eyes and think about how much has changed in the last year, some of it good, some of it not so much, but all of it an inevitable step in the right direction. And that direction is freedom from Zodiac.

Reid sits slap bam in the middle of everything at the moment. I think if push came to shove, he would still side with Zodiac. His loyalty to him has always been unwavering, despite how he might feel about me. But even knowing all this, I can't stay away from the man any more than he can stay away from me.

Pulling up at Reid's apartment, I'm filled with a sense of déjà vu like every time I come here. Granted it isn't often. Only on the nights he comes to my office with a bloody face and a bleeding heart. But being here always takes me back to that first night. It feels like a lifetime ago now, where a different girl merged from this same car with a knife in her pocket and tape covering the hole in her shoe.

Now my shoes have blood-red soles, and my knife is sheathed beside my gun.

I wait for Reid to climb out and walk around to open my door for me, holding out his hand for me to grasp. We walk silently, hand in hand until we reach the elevator.

"You really shouldn't keep coming here without security."

He sighs, breaking the silence between us as the doors slide open and we head toward his apartment.

"Nobody is going to try and hurt me when I have the devil standing beside me," I point out, stepping inside when he opens his door. I make my way through the living area and leave my bag on the floor by the sofa and my gun and holster on the coffee table. I pause before continuing toward the bedrooms and look over my shoulder to find him watching me.

"Which room do you want me in?" We both know the answer, but it's a game we keep playing, nonetheless.

Reid stalks toward me, not stopping until his hands are on my hips and his head is dipped low beside my ear.

"Where I always want you, Cherry, in my bed beside me," he murmurs, walking me backward to his room. He lifts his hand and shoves the door open, walking us inside and over to the foot of the bed.

One of his hands leaves my hips and drifts up to the little belt cinching my dress together at my waist.

His dark gaze sears into me, daring me to stop him, but as I stare into those hypnotic eyes of his, I realize I don't want to. I like Reid's hands on me. He makes me feel alive.

I don't move as he slowly unties the belt, making the fabric around my bust loosen. Peeling the dress slowly apart, he reveals my red lace bra and panties underneath.

"Jesus, Cherry, the things I want to do to you," he mutters more to himself than me.

I pull my arms free and let gravity take over. The dress drops to the floor, pooling around my heels.

He takes a step back, raking his eyes up my legs, pausing on my lace panties for a moment before gliding up my stomach over my breasts to my face.

We stare at each other, fire licking up my skin as his fingertips scorch wherever they touch.

I don't know who moves first, but his mouth is on mine before I can speak, a hand-wound tightly in my hair to keep me in place.

I taste blood on my tongue, knowing his lip must have split again, but instead of pulling back, I kiss him harder. I paw at his shirt, breaking the kiss only so he can pull it over his head, then I'm down on the bed with him looming over me.

His lips move over my chin, down my neck, sucking on my pulse point. I swear it must have a direct connection to my pussy because I'm so close to coming just from that alone.

He moves again, sucking one of my nipples through the lace of my bra. I surge up, scoring my nails down his back hard enough to draw blood. A growl rips from his throat before he drifts lower, kissing his way down my body, dipping his tongue in my belly button, making me squirm before his hot breath hits me where I need it most.

"Fuck me, you're soaked," his voice groans out. I'm too far gone to be embarrassed. I thread my fingers through his hair and tug hard.

"The bra and panties stay on, Cherry. Otherwise, I don't

trust myself to be able to stop," he whispers. I'm just about to scream at him for being a tease when he dips his head and sucks my clit hard through the lace barrier.

"Holy fucking shit," I gasp in response. He grips my hips hard to anchor me in place while he sucks and nibbles away at me as if he has all the time in the world. He doesn't relent until I'm a quivering mass of need, two seconds away from screaming for him to just fuck me already when he bites down on my clit unexpectedly. The sharp bite of pain is more than I can handle, pushing me over the edge into a freefall of sensation, leaving me a babbling mess.

He lifts his head, a devious smirk on his bruised face, looking entirely too happy with himself, all while I struggle to catch my breath.

"My turn." I move to sit up, but he pins me down.

"No, Cherry, this was just for you."

I protest, but his lips swallow it down. He kisses me softly and slowly, drinking me in until I'm boneless, and all the fight has gone. Only then does he roll us both over, wrap his arm tightly around me and hold me as we both fall asleep.

# CHAPTER THIRTY

When I wake up, I'm not surprised to find myself alone. I am, however, shocked to see the apartment completely empty.

Usually, on the rare nights Reid gets me to stay over, I'll find him in the kitchen making coffee or bacon, but today he's gone.

I shrug it off and have a shower, washing my hair before climbing out, drying off, and helping myself to his wardrobe. I braid my hair and slip into a pair of his sweats, rolling them over at the waist a few times to get them to stay up before pulling on a large gray hoodie.

I'll need to go home and change before heading back to Echo's, but it will do for now.

I text Ben and grab my discarded clothes and shoes before moving into the sitting area. I wander over to the window to wait for Ben to arrive, wincing at the bright morning light. When I look down to the street below, I spot a black Lincoln pull up and see Zodiac step out with Reid right behind him.

Ice floods my veins. I have no reason for this reaction, and yet every instinct I have tells me to get the fuck out of here. I've learned the hard way to trust my gut and I'm not about to change that now.

Grabbing my bag, I shove my dirty clothes inside it with my gun holster and hook my shoes over my fingers before heading out, closing the door quietly behind me. I forgo the elevators and head to the stairwell, shooting off a text to tell Ben I'll meet him around the corner near the park. I'd rather Reid thought I left earlier, that way I can play dumb about him bringing Zodiac and see if he'll bring it up. If he doesn't, then I'll know this was an ambush of some kind.

This is the problem with Reid. The further I fall for the enigma of him, the more I realize he's not worthy of my love or trust no matter how much I want him to be that person for me.

I head out through the underground garage, noticing that Reid's bike is missing, but his car is still here. I cut through the back entrance and out into the park just in time to see Ben pull up in the black SUV.

I wince when a stone slices the heel of my foot, making me curse myself for not sticking the torture devices back on, no matter how ridiculous they would look with borrowed sweats.

Ben spots me and slows, so I wait before pulling the rear door open and climbing inside.

"Hey, Ben, thanks for coming to grab me."

He looks at me in the rearview mirror, shaking his head. He has this big brother routine down pat.

"And what time do you call this young lady?" he teases, making me snort.

"Shut your pie hole and take me home. I look worse than I did when I was homeless." He shakes his head at me with a big grin on his face before doing as I ask.

I lie back and close my eyes, letting last night's events and this morning play over and over in my brain while I analyze everything.

Was it all an act to get me to lower my defenses and catch me off guard, or was Reid simply taking advantage of the situation he created? Either way, one thing is glaringly apparent, I can't keep putting myself out there if Reid is going to continue playing Zodiac's lapdog.

I've spent the last year putting things in place, changing the players around the board, but it looks like I might need to up my timeline a little because it seems Zodiac is getting antsy.

"Which home do you want to go to?" Ben calls back, making my eyes open.

"Better just go to the penthouse. It's closer and something tells me there will be eyes on me today."

"Everything okay?" he asks sharply.

"Yes, I'm likely paranoid, but paranoid is better than

dead, right? Call Baker and Danny. They're on rotation for today, but they aren't due in for another hour. See if they can come in early and I'll pay them a bonus."

"They'll do it without the bonus, you know that, but I'll call them once you're inside," he agrees.

"Thank you, Ben."

The rest of the drive is silent as I watch the city whirl by until we arrive in the center of my division, back to the penthouse I despise. I wait while Ben parks and smile when he insists on walking me up, not that I mind indulging him. It's nice to feel like I matter, even if it's in a boss-employee kind of way.

"Bullshit," he spits, making me frown as he offers me his hand and helps me from the car.

"What's bullshit?"

"That you seem to think we all only care for you in an employee-employer capacity. We care about you because you care about us. Jesus, you literally plucked me off the streets. Who even does that?"

Shit, I didn't realize I said all that out loud.


"You took a chance on me when nobody else did, you think I'll ever forget that?" He shakes his head, answering his own question.

"Working for you has given DJ, Kevin, and me a roof over our heads and enough money for me to send both boys to college. You took a bunch of has-beens, jaded soldiers, a homeless man, and a brutalized child, and you made us into more. You breathed life back into a group of people so ready to lay down and die, and you did it with soft smiles and kind hands. You gave us hope where there wasn't any to be found. You made us a family, Viddy. Jesus, you have changed the lives of everyone you touch. How do you not see that?"

I blink rapidly to fight back the tears, choked up by his words. *How can I not be?*

Ben's protective instincts were evident when I first met him. I originally planned to offer him a place on my security team, but he suffered from terrible PTSD and thought it would act as a deterrent. He was upfront about it from the start, refusing to be the weak link in my team. He insisted that I couldn't have a guard who can't bear the sound of gunfire without curling up in the fetal position. I didn't push him, offering him instead the role of my driver, which he readily snapped up. When DJ moved into Ben's place, he and Kevin had each other for company, especially on the nights I called Ben out.

It all worked out in the end. DJ and Kevin are thriving, and they had an unbreakable bond I knew would last a lifetime.

"Family, huh? I like that," I tell him with a smile. "But if you make me cry, I'll kick your ass."

"Noted." His lips twitch as we enter the elevator. He hits the button for the top floor and we make idle chit chat about the boys as the elevator ascends.

When the doors open, he takes a protective step in front

of me, one born of instinct, and it's that move that saves my life because when a gun fires, the bullet rips through Ben's shoulder, instead of my head.

He falls back and I hit the button to close the doors before covering Ben's body with mine.

Bullets fire in quick succession but they miss me as the doors close. I listen for a minute to the *clink, clink, clink* they make hitting the thick steel door, sounding almost harmless now.

I lift up and look down at Ben's pale face. His skin is clammy and his top lip is dotted with sweat.

"Ben, talk to me." I slap his face, but Ben has left the building, mentally at least, as shock sets in.

This is what he was talking about. The bullet isn't life-threatening, but Ben's mind can't separate the past from the present, and likely thinks he's back in the sandy desert as opposed to the floor of the elevator.

Climbing off him, I whip out my phone and dial Danny, who picks up after the second ring.

"Hey, Viddy, we were just—" he answers, but I cut him off as I pull my gun from my bag.

"I need you to get to the penthouse. Ben's been shot. We are in the elevator right now, but I have no idea where the shooter is. I need the team here, and I need you to get Baker to hack into the camera feed so I know where this asshole is and if he's alone," I bark, my mind focused and ready for what I'm about to do. There is no fear, just pure unfiltered rage.

"Fuck, we're on our way. Stay put—"

I cut him off again, pulling the boss card. "Danny, I want to know where they are."

"Dammit, fuck, hold on, he's doing his thing right now. Okay, there are two that we can see. One is standing near the elevator on the penthouse floor and the other is in the lobby. The other floors look clear, but the second the elevator moves, I have a feeling they will both descend on you. We are ten minutes out, Viddy," he warns because he knows exactly what I'm about to do.

"Well, then you'd better put your foot down, Danny," I answer before hanging up. The phone rings immediately again, but I ignore it. I'm about to shove it back in my bag when I see who's calling.

Fuck. I don't have time for this.

I answer but don't get to speak before Reid growls down the phone at me. "Where the fuck did you disappear to?" Is his way of greeting me, his tone arctic cold compared to his usual honey-laced voice.

"I had shit to do. Besides, you disappeared first. I didn't know how long you were going to be or if you were even going to come back at all. Now if you're done bitching, I'm kinda busy."

Ben chooses that moment to groan loudly. Reid is deadly quiet for a moment before his voice turns lethal. "Who is that?" he snaps.

My, my, my, does someone sound jealous? If I wasn't so pissed that I was being shot at, I would have laughed.

"That would be Ben, my driver. He just took a bullet meant for me. Now, if you'll excuse me, I'd like to send one back."

"What? Where the fuck are you?" he roars down my ear, loud enough for me to pull the phone away with a frown.

"Jesus, Reid, I'm at my apartment," I answer, then hang up and toss the phone back in my bag.

I take a deep breath and focus. Instead of getting the elevator to switch floors giving both guys a chance to corner me, I decide to stay where I am and deal with the one asshole first.

So that's what I do, dragging Ben's heavy body into the corner so he has some protection against stray bullets. He groans again, his eyes snapping open and landing on mine as he reaches out and grips my arms hard enough to leave bruises.

"Who the fuck?" His words are slurred for a second as his brain starts to clear.

"It's Viddy. You were shot. I need you to focus for a moment, Ben. In two minutes, I'm going to open these doors and start firing. You need to take cover. I hate that you're caught up in this, but until I can take them out, we're stuck here. The guys are on their way, but I want to know who sent these assholes and why."

His pale face looks at me with a grimace as his shoulder wound makes itself known. "Okay, don't worry about me, just do what you have to. But for fuck's sake, be careful."

I nod and move to the other side of the elevator, using the

panel next to the door for cover, knowing this guy will be ready for me. It's just going to be a case of who shoots first. The only difference is, I have a small amount of cover, whereas the shooter will be completely exposed in the wide-open hallway.

I hit the button to open the doors and drop to the floor with my gun raised. As soon as feet come into view, I fire, aiming to cause damage, not to kill. I have questions that need answering.

He stumbles back onto the now bloodstained light gray carpet, but he still has his gun, so I fire again, hitting him in the shoulder. The gun falls to the ground beside him, and before he can reach for it, I'm on him, straddling his chest with my gun pointed at his head. He freezes, looking up at me as I reach for his gun and toss it away.

"Hi," I say cordially, as if we were bumping into each other in a coffee shop. "Can I help you with something?"

He swallows hard before looking toward the stairwell door.

Yes, mister, I'm well aware of your friend, but I also know the door squeaks, so I'll hear it if anyone tries to push through it.

"You're making a mistake," he warns me, making me laugh out loud at his audacity.

"You came to my home and shot at me, and you have the balls to tell me I'm making a mistake."

"I wasn't shooting at you, I was aiming for Jude," he cries out when I press my fingers into his shoulder wound.

"Well, the guy lying in a pool of his own blood isn't Jude, it's Ben, and Ben's my family. Do you know what I do to people who hurt my family?" I ask him with an evil grin. "Now, who sent you to kill me?"

"No, I'm telling you I was sent here for Jude. I was told he would be here with you. My orders were to take him out."

"Well, you were fed bogus intel." I shrug as if to say *it happens*. "Now tell me, who sent you?"

He shakes his head, so I press my gun harder against his temple.

"He'll kill me," he grits out.

"And just what do you think I'll do?" I shake my head with a snort.

"I can't go against an order when it comes from Zodiac, you have to believe me. I didn't want to do this. I was just doing what he told me to," he pleads, finally cluing into the fact that I'm serious. People always seem to think I'll be more forgiving because I'm a woman, but my boobs are not magical stress balls that keep me calm.

"Zodiac ordered a hit on Jude?" I ask, surprised. This is the confirmation I needed. Up until now, I couldn't prove one way or another if he knew about him.

He nods against the gun.

"Anything else?" I ask, waiting to see if he spills any other secret, but he shakes his head. Just as well, really, I'm running out of time here.

"Thanks," I offer before firing the gun and shooting a bullet into his brain.

Climbing off him, I stand and move over to pick up the gun. I check it out, feel the weight of it in my hand, and nod. I can add this one to my growing collection. I'm still admiring it when the stairwell door flies open. I don't think. I just lift the gun and fire. The bullet hits its target, right in the center of his forehead.

Wyatt would be so proud.

The body collapses to the ground like its strings have been cut, severing it from its puppet master, and in a way, I guess it has been.

I look at the man and recognize him as Cancer.

Fuck, I just shot a division head.

Looking at the smoking gun in my hand, I groan. I wanted to keep this one. Quickly, I wipe it down, removing my prints from it, and take it over to the other guy I shot and place it in his hand. It's unlikely to hold much water if truly investigated, but if someone stumbles across the scene before my guys get here, it will give me a cover story.

I make my way back to the elevator and find Ben sitting up with his head buried in his hands, shaking a little.

"Hey, it's okay. No more gunfire for now. They're both dead," I comfort him.

He looks up at me with bloodshot eyes, looking both angry and defeated.

"I'm sorry, I'm fucking useless," he bites out.

"Hey, shut the fuck up. I'm fine, you're fine, if perhaps a little bloody. I don't need a big strong man to take care of me," I snap, making him sigh.

"Clearly," he huffs before looking at me. "You okay?"

I sit down beside him and lean my head against his good shoulder.

"Things are about to get bad, Ben. We need to be prepared. If you need to leave, you say the word, and I'll get you and the boys out of here and set up at the safe house outside the city."

"I've already told you I'm not leaving you, don't say that shit to me again," he growls. "When the time is right, we will send the boys off with Chris, but I'm staying," he says adamantly.

I lift my head and tell him what just happened, leaving out the part about the first shooter looking for Jude instead of me.

"So one of the division heads is dead? As callous as it sounds, it's happened before. That's how you came to be here after all. I can't see why this would be any different."

"It's different because Zodiac ordered the hit, and he just sacrificed one of his star players to take out another."

Ben whistles, likely realizing, as I have, that something far more significant is going on here. This is about to become a clusterfuck of epic proportions.

# CHAPTER THIRTY-ONE

Danny and Baker flank me as Thomas drives Ben to Shadow Falls, where my personal doctor is on his way over to fix him up.

"You wipe the cameras?" I ask Baker, my arms crossed over my chest.

"Yeah, it's done. I've downloaded the footage for you to go over later and I'll call the cleanup crew whenever you're ready. I can't believe the fucking nerve of this guy," Baker grouses, kicking the first shooter in the head, tutting in annoyance when he gets blood on his shoe.

"I'll get you to call them soon, I'm just waiting for—" My words cut off when a pissed off Reid strolls through the stairwell doorway, looking down at the body he's stepping over, pausing for a minute as he registers who it is before turning to look at me with questions in his eyes.

"What the fuck is going on?" he asks calmly. Too calmly. I can see how angry he is by the way his whole body practically vibrates.

"Take some pictures, then call in the cleanup team. I want this whole place spick-and-span when I return," I instruct Danny and Baker, before walking over to Reid.

"Let's take a walk," I suggest to him quietly.

"We'll talk in your apartment," he snaps.

I stand tall and toss my hair behind my shoulder, glad I had taken the few minutes to get rid of my bloody clothes, shower, and throw on jeans with a long-sleeved deep purple Henley. I'd opted for black ballet flats, the whole outfit making me look like a young girl, giving me an innocent vibe, which is the look I'm going for right now in case anyone is watching.

"I don't take orders from you. Now, let's take a walk," I repeat. He grits his teeth, looking at Danny and Baker before back to me.

"Fuck it, fine." He grabs my hand before tugging me past Cancer's body, down the stairs, and out into the warm sunny morning air.

He doesn't say another word as he leads me over to his car, nudging me inside before reaching over and strapping me in. I look up at him, surprised, but he just glares, letting me know there will be no talking just yet.

He drives us to the huge local park, which is a relief as I was thinking he might insist on taking me back to his place.

With emotions running high right now, somewhere public is the safer option.

He parks and practically drags me out, gripping my hand tightly as if I might disappear if he lets go even for a second.

The central part of the park is bustling with families taking full advantage of the sunshine. Children play on the swings while their parents talk among themselves from the benches outlining the play area. Their gaze drifts up occasionally to keep a watchful eye on their charges, making sure they are safe and where they are supposed to be.

Reid leads us down the jogging path that loops the play area in a wide arc, disappearing into the shaded wooded area. Once we are far enough away from prying eyes, he spins me to face him, scanning my body, taking me in, inch by inch.

"I'm okay, Reid, I promise," I reassure him, but he doesn't answer, just grinds his teeth together.

"Are you planning on killing me and dumping my body, Reid?" I ask half teasing, half serious.

"Do you have any idea how worried I was? I didn't know if I would find you dead or alive!" he roars, not liking my joke one little bit.

"Look at me, Reid, really look at me. I'm here, I'm okay. I don't have a single mark on me."

"Someone tried to kill you." He seethes, pausing only when I shake my head with sad eyes.

"No, Reid, someone tried to kill you," I whisper, making

him freeze solid, his hand grabbing hold of my hip, anchoring me to him.

"What?" he asks, wanting me to be wrong.

"Do you trust me, Reid?" I ask softly, tipping my head up to look in his eyes.

He grits his teeth, his jaw clenched so hard, I'm surprised it doesn't crack.

He doesn't answer me with words. He dips his head and slants his mouth over mine, his tongue seeking entrance, so I let him in. He presses me against the tree and kisses me with everything he has, using his body to tell me all the things he can't say out loud.

I break the kiss, needing him to hear what I have to say, no matter what it will do to the fragile state of our relationship.

"Zodiac sent them," I warn him.

He shakes his head, but he doesn't shout his denial like I thought he might. Instead, he rests his forehead against mine. "You sure?" he asks, making me tense, not because I think he doesn't believe me, but because he doesn't sound surprised at all.

"I'm sure," I whisper.

"I'll take care of it," he tells me, starting to pull away, but I grip him tightly.

"Tell me, Jude, is he just after you, or is he after Kai too?" I ask him the question that I know will change everything.

He locks down tight, his grip becoming painful, but I don't pull away. His hand lifts and wraps around my throat as he takes a step back. He keeps me pinned against the tree as he puts distance between us, his face carefully blank.

"You know." It's a statement, not a question so I don't answer.

"How long?" he grits out, his grip tightening a fraction. It doesn't hurt yet, but it's a reminder of how close I am to a man who could snap my neck without breaking a sweat.

"The first night, at your apartment. You went out, but Kai returned sporting bruises and needing to be patched up. He called me Red, you always call me Cherry. I brushed it off until you took me to division twelve for the first time."

He loosens his grip a little, so I carry on.

"I knew there was no way you should have known the combination to the safe. Anything else I could have justified, but not that. That night Kai gave me a ledger and pocketed a flash drive."

His eyes flair at that.

"I took it from his pocket while he drove me to my new apartment. I looked and found out everything that was in that file about the Reid brothers. Identical twins, but Jude Reid has a death certificate with his name on it. Apparently, you died in a car crash with your mother after she took you and ran from your father. That's when I realized the spare room in the apartment isn't really spare at all. The closet is full because you use it, don't you?

"So you looked into me?" He rages.

"Not to begin with. I looked at the flash drive while Kai went to the store for me. When he got back, I slipped it into his pocket before he even knew it was missing. I call you both Reid, not because I can't tell you apart but because I didn't want to slip up."

"Does Kai know? Has he been keeping—" I cut him off with a shake of my head.

"He doesn't know I know anything either, at least he hasn't let on if he suspects anything."

He stares at me, his breath sawing in and out of his chest as his thoughts race behind his eyes.

"You can tell the difference between us?" he asks curiously, his hold loosening further.

"You mean apart from the bruises you collected last night that I'm guessing Kai doesn't have? I can now, but before it was only when you guys would call me with different names, Cherry and Red. Now it's second nature. It was you with me last night, your arms I fell asleep wrapped up in, but it was Kai who came back with Zodiac after you left. So I guess my question is, where did you go, and how does Zodiac know you're alive?"

His eyes widen before he lets go of me completely.

"I went to get coffee and some of those damn pastries you like so much," he spits out, gripping his hair.

"So how did Kai know he was in the clear to turn up? If you guys don't think Zodiac knows about you, then you turning back up with coffee and a smile would have been a bit of a giveaway," I drawl.

"I texted Kai, let him know I was okay and that I was

going to drop you off," he admits, but his words make me frown.

"Wait, did you tell him you were getting coffee first?"

He looks at me and shakes his head. "No, why does that matter?"

"Because the way you worded it sounds like you were taking me home as you replied. Not that you would be taking me home after coffee and pastries."

"And?" he snaps impatiently.

"And that would mean Kai brought Zodiac to your apartment, thinking it was empty. He wasn't trying to catch me out," I reply, relieved. I didn't realize how much that had been weighing on me until it just lifted.

"Neither of us are out to get you. Jesus fucking Christ, is that what you think? How can the woman who sees everything be so fucking blind?" he whispers, stalking forward once more, this time lifting me off my feet so I'm forced to wrap my legs around his waist.

"I've wanted you way before I should have. I despised myself back then, yearning for a girl who was far too young for me, but then—"

"Then?" I prompt when he stops talking.

"But then you turned twenty-one and I ran out of excuses why I needed to stay away."

"And yet you still held back," I remind him.

He presses me against the tree, kissing me softly before answering.

"Because it wasn't just me anymore and the closer we got

to you, the more we wanted. But how the fuck could we ask the girl we both want to choose between the two of us, especially when we've done nothing but lie to you."

And just like that, everything stops. I've spent so long playing the part of pretending that Kai and Jude are the same person that I forgot when the truth came out, I might be forced to choose between them.

I unwrap my legs from around his waist and let him place me back on my feet, feeling strangely bereft when he steps back.

"I need to call Kai," he tells me softly.

I nod before sliding down to sit at the base of the tree while he makes the call. He steps away, just far enough that I can't hear what he's saying, but I can tell the conversation is less than pleasant by how animated he is when he talks.

Hanging up, he stalks back to me, scrubbing a hand over his face before sitting next to me.

"He wants me to drop you off at the apartment. I need to go and check out Cancer's division before people get wind of his demise and start destroying shit. I'll meet you both after I'm finished, okay?"

I nod, continuing to face forward for a moment as I brace myself for what I'm about to say. "I've never asked you for a damn thing, but I'm asking for something now."

He reaches out his hand, so I place mine in his and let him pull me up. I stare up at him as he dips his head, our faces now only inches apart.

"Tell me the truth, just this once, don't lie to me." I take a deep breath and blow it out.

He licks his lips as my warm breath skates over his skin.

"Are either of you going to try to kill me?" I ask the question I've held back since I found out about their duplicity.

He looks shocked for a moment before the shutters fall over his eyes. "That's what you think, that I'd hurt you?"

I shrug, ignoring the anger in his voice. "I'd be stupid to deny the possibility, wouldn't I? After all, how well do I really know you, Jude? Or Kai, for that matter? I'm trying to separate what I feel for you from the likelihood that you've killed before to keep this secret. So why not now? Why not me?" I ask him, searching his eyes for answers he will never give me.

"You really have no clue how I feel, do you? Fuck! Okay, one thing at a time. Let's go back to the apartment and talk. I'll answer everything I can when I get back, I swear."

It's a risk, taking him at his word like this. He's a skilled liar and a master manipulator. But my want to believe in him outweighs the logical side of my brain that tells me to remain cautious, so I just nod and watch him visibly relax.

He pulls me in for a hug and stands there, holding me tight.

The world around us fades away as a sad kind of calmness washes over me. Everything is about to change. I can feel it as surely as I can feel the cooling wind against my skin. The winds of change have always been unkind to me.

Every major event in my life is marred by its cold indifference. I've learned to expect it.

People are flawed, and we strive to find that one perfect person who is destined to complete us in some way? I call bullshit. There is no such thing as perfect, not for people like us. And as for love? Well, that's a commodity none of us are willing to pay the price of having. The only thing that matters is loyalty.

I know all this, believe it wholeheartedly, so why does the thought of losing either of the Reid brothers make me feel like someone has taken a hammer to my heart?

We don't have a label. I'm not theirs and they aren't mine, and yet we gravitate toward each other as if guided by something otherworldly. We can't work, there won't be books written about our story. Who the fuck would want to read something so tragic that was destined to fail from the start?

And yet, it's always been the Reid brothers for me. My very own kryptonite. They make me weak, make me feel, make me want things I have no right to want, and they offer me nothing in return but pretty little false hopes wrapped up in blood-red bows.

"Hey." His hand at my jaw snaps me out of my thoughts. I look up at him and memorize his face. Each bruise, scratch, and blemish upon his skin that does nothing to hide the handsomeness beneath it.

"Why are the wolves always so pretty and the sheep so bland?" I muse to myself.

"You ready?" His voice rumbles over me.

"No, but we still need to go," I answer, but I don't move, staring my fill. I memorize the slope of his nose, the curve of his jaw, the intensity ever-present in his eyes, in case this is the last time. I'll hold these moments and a dozen others so tightly inside me that the winds of change can't blow them away.

Only time will tell if this will be the beginning of something new for us or the unraveling of what we already have. If it's the end, I'll want these memories, no matter how painful, to torture myself with, like I do when I drag out the ones related to my brother.

"Come on," he murmurs, his voice low as if the heaviness of the moment weighs upon his shoulders. He slides his hand over mine, holding me to him as we walk slowly back toward where he parked earlier.

I feel his eyes on me as he climbs into the driver's seat, but I turn away from him and look out the passenger side window. I watch the families in the park as we pull away, wondering how they sleep at night, knowing some monsters lurk in the dark like Zodiac, like Kai and Jude, and like me. Or perhaps they sleep at night because there are monsters out there like us, willing to do the things most people can't stomach.

Some people have a strong moral compass, a rigid definition of what's right and wrong, black and white, good and evil. They see the world in balance like some kind of living and breathing yin and yang, but it's all about perception. People choose to see what they want, inserting their version of what makes things black and white. It's like looking at the world through rose-tinted glasses when really everything is just shades of gray.

Good and evil are subjective. Good people can do bad things and bad people can be useful. Like the yin and yang, there can be no light without darkness, but the idea that it's a fair balance is a fucking joke.

My moral compasses were smashed years ago underneath the size eleven Italian loafers that crept into my room in the dead of night.

Do I consider myself bad? No, I don't go around preying on the weak and vulnerable. I have no interest in sullying the innocent. If anything, innocence is something I like to preserve, knowing how fleeting it can be. But I have zero problem invoking my fury on those I deem deserve it. Does that mean I'm playing god? Perhaps, but someone has to. Where the fuck was my god when I prayed on my knees with blood slicked thighs?

No, I make the rules in my life, and if that means playing judge, jury, and executioner, then so be it.

"I'm not used to you being so quiet, it's kind of unnerving," Jude teases, but his tone is off, letting me know that he's telling the truth. My silence worries him.

"Sorry, lost in thought." I smile, hoping it doesn't look as forced as it feels.

My phone rings at that point, so I reach behind me to slide it from my pocket, answering it when I see its Danny.

"Hey, D, what's up?" I ask, keeping my tone neutral.

He'll know from me calling him D, that I'm not alone. This isn't our first rodeo, working out a system where I could inform them in seconds if it was safe to talk or not was paramount.

"Just wanted to let you know the Doc patched Ben up and he is now sleeping it off with a fancy cocktail of pain meds. He woke up just long enough to ask how you were. I told him you were fine and that you're with Aries now, figuring shit out," he adds at the end, making me grin. That's Danny's way of telling me he knows who I'm with, and he'll track my phone if I'm not back or if I don't report in within the designated six hours I set out.

"Did Chris go on her date?" I ask, needing to know if she has the boys.

"Yeah, she's going to be busy for a few days but said to call anytime if you needed her." I let my body relax, knowing she'll guard Kevin and DJ with her life.

"Good, I'm happy for her. She doesn't need to worry about things here, tell her to have fun in Safe Harbor."

He's quiet for a moment as he takes in my words. Safe Harbor is our code for our safe house. Knowing how dangerous our lives are daily, he must have figured out for me to mention it that shit is about to hit the fan.

"I'll pass the message along."

"Thanks, D, you call the cleanup crew yet?"

"Yeah, they are here working on it now as we speak. I'll leave you to it and call later if we find out anything else."

"Sounds good. Stay vigilant and nobody on the teams

goes anywhere alone," I order, not willing to risk any of my men.

"You got it," he agrees before hanging up.

"Another man you have wrapped around your finger?" Jude snaps, his hands squeezing the wheel tightly.

"Not your business now, is it, Jude? I don't belong to you or your brother, so who I let between my legs is entirely up to me," I snap back, pissed that he thinks he has the right to be jealous.

I'm not dumb enough to think either of the Reid boys is living a life of celibacy, so if they think for one second I'm going to, they are in for a big surprise. I mean sure, I might not be fucking anyone right now, but that doesn't mean I won't ever. I think of Will and Cash, knowing either of them would take me up on the offer, if only for a night. Something has held me back from taking it further than kissing. Why? I don't know, because I sure as shit don't plan on waiting around for the Reid boys forever.

"Don't go there, Viddy, not on this," he growls at me, but I don't heed his warning. If anything, it's like pouring gasoline on a flame.

"Are you fucking kidding me?" I curse, gripping the car door as he takes the turn to the underground parking facility too fast.

The car screeches to a halt in its usual spot, next to the bike Kai always drives.

Jude turns off the engine, his eyes flaring as he turns to face me.

"I don't want to hear about you with other men any more than you want to hear about me with other women. You push this and I'll push back, so be very fucking careful, Viddy. You're playing with the big boys now, not some small-town playground bullshit."

Oh no, he fucking didn't.

I undo my seatbelt, so livid my vision blurs for a minute with white-hot fury. I bank it, letting it turn my words into a weapon, melding them until they are sharp enough to draw blood.

Leaning toward him, I grab the collar of his T-shirt and pull him closer, placing my lips against the shell of his ear. "If the thought of another man's tongue licking over the folds of my slick pussy pisses you off so much, perhaps you should have been man enough to do something about it sooner. Poor baby, did you really think I was going to wait for you to man up? You didn't want to fuck me when I was just a girl, but you sure as shit can't handle me as a woman," I purr, shoving him hard enough that his head cracks against the window behind him.

I climb out of the car and slam the door closed, making my way to the elevators.

I don't stop to see if he's okay, my body is too charged with rage. I need an outlet and if I stay here that outlet will involve my fist and Jude's face.

As the elevator slides open, an arm wraps itself around my waist and one hand goes over my mouth to prevent me from screaming. He needn't have bothered. I don't scream, and if I did, it wouldn't be here and now like this.

He picks me up off my feet, using his height advantage against me, but I don't put up a fight, knowing to wait and play to my strengths.

He loosens the hold he has around my waist and hits the button for the penthouse before spinning me around and pinning me to the wall.

With his hand still over my mouth, he presses his body against mine and brings his face closer, his temper making him seem larger somehow, like a barely contained storm in a port threatening to destroy everything around him, namely me right now.

"I told you that mouth was going to get you into trouble one day, didn't I? The thing is, Cherry," he spits out, using his nickname for me, but said with so much hostility if I were less angry myself I would have felt his words pierce what's left of my heart. As it is, it bounces off me like everything he says. All his outrage does is fuel mine until there is no room left inside me to contain it, and when there is no space inside, it leaves only one place for it to go. Outward.

I bite his hand, making him curse before I growl in fury, like some wild untamed creature.

He silences me with his mouth, his kiss, wild and filled with dark promises. There's no turning back from this. Once you have been this deep, there is no going back to the shallows. It's sink or swim, but right now, I'm drowning in all that is him.

I don't know who moves next, but the next conscious thought I have is when the red haze starts to pull back, I'm bleeding from a split lip where he bit me, and he has a scratch on his face from the top of his cheekbone down to his jaw.

The elevator pings open, but neither of us pulls apart, both breathing heavily as we stare at each other with equal parts lust and hate.

I wipe the blood from my lip with the back of my hand and step out of the elevator backward, unable to sever the connection between us.

He doesn't follow me out, doesn't speak, doesn't even blink. He just hits the button and waits for the doors to slide shut, finally freeing us both from the blazing heat tethering us together.

I move on autopilot to the apartment in a haze. Perhaps if my head had been clear, I would have heard the warning bells clanging in my head. But when I knock on the door, all I feel is restless and agitated.

"Hello, Red," Kai greets as he swings the door open. I lift my head at the sound of Kai's voice and freeze solid, as I stare over his shoulder at Zodiac standing just behind him. His eyes rake hungrily over my body as I turn my gaze up to Kai's carefully blank one. The staggering weight of their betrayal, although expected, hangs heavily between us. His face shows no remorse, so I do the only thing I can—I shut down everything that makes me Viddy and become the Gemini they made me.

"Sweet words, pretty faces, dirty fucking liars. It's a tale as old as time." I laugh, a hollow sound that makes Kai wince. I don't say anything after that because Kai steps forward and presses something to my arm, making my body convulse as volts of fire wash over me and then blissfully everything goes black.

# CHAPTER THIRTY-TWO

I don't wake slowly, hazy, and confused about what happened. I wake with the taste of betrayal on my tongue and the clarity that all my suspicions were true. Just this once though, I desperately wanted to be wrong.

I'm tied at the wrist and ankles to a wooden chair, with ropes as opposed to cuffs, judging by the fibers I feel cutting into my arms as I pull against the restraints.

There's a bag or sack of some kind over my head, but it's thin enough that I can see faintly through it. If I had to guess, I would say I'm in either some kind of warehouse or basement. There are no windows and the only door I can see is across the room from where I'm sitting, up three wooden steps. The rest of the room is concrete and completely barren, bar me and the chair I'm sitting on. It reminds me of the basement in the kill cabin, suggesting it's unlikely I'll be walking out of here alive. I guess I should be happy there is no table of torture tools, but I'm smart enough to know they can do more than enough damage to me with their bodies and hands, particularly while I'm restrained.

A noise at the door has me dropping my head loosely to my chest. I make my body go lax and take myself away to another time and place. I think of Megan's laughing face and Wyatt's hugs. My family is my happy place, my home. I can take whatever these guys throw at me as long as my family is safe. Once I'm free, I'll kill them all.

The door swings open and footsteps make their way down the steps with a grace that tells me it's Kai. Zodiac's footsteps are much heavier, as if he feels the need to announce his presence before he even enters the room. The twins, however, move with graceful stealth.

The hood is pulled off, so I lift my head and glare at my kidnapper. Faking sleep won't work with these guys, they aren't rank amateurs and I refuse to ever be someone's victim again.

"Hey, Red," Kai grins at me like I'm sitting across a table from him at a coffee shop, not strapped to a chair after he tased me.

"Hey, asshat, to what do I owe the pleasure?" I ask, sarcasm rife in my voice, making him grin.

"I thought we could have a little chat, just the two of us," he says casually before sitting on the floor in front of me. I swear if my legs weren't strapped to the legs of the chair, I would have kicked the asshole in his face.

"Sure, what would you like to talk about, Kai?" I ask sweetly.

He looks at me with a grin, likely knowing, if given a chance, I'd drown him in a vat of honey. How's that for sweet?

"How long have you known Jude and I were twins?" he asks casually.

"Like I told Jude, since the first night you came back to the apartment bloody and bruised. Well, no, that's not entirely true, I had my suspicions then, but I couldn't put my finger on what was wrong until you took me to the docks."

He nods like he expected that answer. I'm sure Jude filled him in on everything I said already.

"And who have you told?" he questions, his tone still light and even.

I snort at that. "The way I see it, anything I say right now is all just going to go in one ear and out the other. You won't believe a damn thing I say, so what's the point? I should have just left things alone, huh? I shouldn't have said a damn word to Jude because my bid to save his life just cost me mine and at his own brother's hands. Nice."

I turn away, not wanting him to know how much that hurts.

He stands and cups my jaw, turning my face back to his. His poker face is far better than Jude's, or maybe it's that Jude might have some kind of feeling toward me and Kai couldn't care less.

"Tell me who you told," he repeats his words softly.

"I didn't say a single word to anyone—nobody on my team, not another division head and not Zodiac. I didn't say a single thing to anyone. Hell, I never even deviated from calling you both Reid, so I didn't slip up. Not sure why I even bothered now. Neither of you gives a shit about me. I realize now this was all just a game to you two. Maybe you're both right and I'm just a little girl in way over my head." I laugh antagonistically. "But then if I'm just a little girl, what does it say about you and Jude?"

He doesn't rise to the bait, just slips his hand around my throat and uses his thumb to stroke my pulse point.

"You told someone. Nobody but Jude and I know about his existence. Everyone who knew is dead," he warns, his grip becoming a little tighter.

"Now that's not true, is it, Kai? Zodiac knows about you both. It was Zodiac's name the first shooter threw out, and the second shooter was Cancer. What the hell kind of sway do you think I have over a guy I've never even spoken to?"

"You're a very resourceful girl," he adds, letting his eyes travel to my chest, telling me exactly what he thinks my *resources* might be.

"Yeah, so resourceful I hired someone to shoot at me." I roll my eyes.

He frowns, tipping my head back, exposing my throat. Perhaps he plans on tearing it open with his teeth like the monster he is.

"I thought you said they were shooting at Jude?"

"According to the shooter, sure, but I didn't know that when the elevator doors opened, and the bullet came racing toward us. It was only because Ben stepped in front of me that I'm even here. The bullet hit his shoulder, which just happened to be head high for me. So maybe Jude was the target, and I was collateral damage, or maybe, despite what the shooter said, I was the target all along. I only have the words of a dead guy to go off." I sniff, looking at a spot over his shoulder. "Think about this, though, I've known about you and Jude for a year. I've never used it against you or treated you differently because of it, so what would I have to gain, barring these fancy rope accessories, by telling you now?"

He continues to stare at me, his hand at my throat, tightening enough that I can feel the pressure pounding in my head. Dipping his face closer, he presses a gentle kiss on my lips, making me jump in surprise. Out of everything he could have done, I didn't expect that.

He lets go abruptly, and I suck in a lungful of air as he circles around me.

"Why should I trust you? You've been bouncing between us, playing brother off brother. Maybe you decided it would be easier to get rid of one than have to choose?" he murmurs darkly.

I can't help it, I laugh. Even when he grips my hair and yanks my head back painfully, I can't help but chuckle.

"And you assume I'd pick you?" I choke out.

His eyes flare at my words. *Oh, he doesn't like that.*

"Tell me, Kai, did Jude tell you what I taste like when I come?" I taunt.

He releases me as if I burned him, but only for a moment. He bends and grabs my Henley at the three little buttons at the collar. Before I can say anything else, he rips the material down the middle, exposing my stomach and purple lace bra.

"Temper, temper. Are you mad because your brother went there or because I let him? I have to say, the things he can do with his tongue had me almost begging him to fuck me."

I watch as his chest heaves up and down, his fist clenched tightly at his side as he stares at my chest.

"You chose him?" he growls, his anger leashed only by the weakest of threads.

"Up until an hour ago, I would have begged, borrowed, and stolen for a chance to have you both, but now you can both go to hell. I'd rather fuck Zodiac than let either of you touch me again."

"Oh, see now that's just not going to work for me," he mocks as he kneels in front of me.

He slides his hand up my calf and over my thigh, gripping me tightly before he leans forward and sucks one of my nipples through the lace of my bra. As much as I want to throat punch him, I can't deny the fission of heat that wraps itself around me, slicking my core.

I wait for the familiar feeling of shame to wash over me, but when it doesn't, I figure I might be just as messed up as he is.

"Move your hand, Kai, or I'll remove every single offending digit even if I have to use my teeth to do it."

"Kinky. But don't worry, babe, your pussy is safe for now."

I growl as he stands and moves behind me. A second later, I hear the snick of a knife, the sound amplified by the quiet. I feel the ropes go lax and then my arms are free.

"You can take your *for now* and shove it. You won't be getting anywhere near my pussy. I'd suffer the agony of barbed wire panties if it means keeping you out." I pull my arms free and rub my wrists as he kneels again in front of me to cut my feet free. The urge to kick him is overwhelming.

As if sensing where my mind has gone, he closes the distance between us once more, gripping me by my neck and yanking me toward him, his mouth at my throat.

"You say that, but we both know if I slipped my fingers inside you right now, I'd find you dripping. You might not want to want me, but it doesn't change the fact you do."

Fuck him. His words hurt more than they should, likely because everything he's saying is the truth, but if he wants to throw stones, fine. Let's throw fucking stones.

"Maybe I am wet, Kai, maybe all I truly want is for a hard cock to slide deep inside me and fuck me hard, but nobody said it's your cock I'm thinking about. You blew any chance you had when you tasered me. Now the closest you'll get to tasting my pussy is by kissing your brother," I purr maliciously. I might not have my knife, but I'll still use my tongue to flay him alive.

"You think I care that my brother got in there first, Red?"

His free hand slides over my ribs, cupping my breast before he rubs his knuckles over my nipple, making it harden under his touch.

"We're twins, Red, we know how to share our toys." His voice rumbles out, making my stomach clench tightly. His words should infuriate me. I'm nobody's toy, not anymore, but I can't deny the effect it has on my body or the riot of images flashing through my mind of me pinned between the two men who would take everything from me if I let them and leave me decimated when they tossed me aside.

"I thought you chose Jude, but now I know you want both of us—"

I cut him off. "Maybe in another life, Kai, but in this one, you'll always just be men who fucked me over. It's not an exclusive club." I snort, yanking myself free.

"I have the footage from the security cameras. I can prove everything I said is true," I tell him, needing to get away from him before we either fuck or kill each other. Maybe both.

"Zodiac already pulled the cameras, there was a fault. None of the cameras were on when the shooting happened." He stands back, crossing his arms over his chest.

I laugh. "Shockingly convenient, huh? Good thing I had my own security system installed." I add drolly.

"Despite what you think, Zodiac isn't involved in this shit. He doesn't know about Jude, and you can't believe shit from a dead man who was likely sent by someone to cause a divide within the divisions."

I huff at him. "Like I didn't know about Jude?" I ask

sarcastically, shaking my head. "Believe what you want, Kai, I'm past caring. Even if Zodiac was being set up, which I don't believe for a single second, then Cancer was playing for the other side. From what I can remember, except for you, he was Zodiac's most loyal supporter."

"I want that video footage, Red," he orders, making me bristle.

"I'll have it sent over to you as soon as you let me go."

"If you're lying..." His voice trails off, not needing to say anymore. He'll kill me. I wouldn't expect anything less.

"I'm not. Now can I get the fuck out of here so I can get away from you?"

He steps away, letting me finally take a breath that isn't filled with his intoxicating cologne.

"I need that footage and for you to keep your mouth shut about Jude. I don't care who says shit, you play dumb, got it?"

I nod my head and twirl a piece of hair between my fingers. "Yes, sir," I say in a high-pitched voice before heading toward the door.

I stop for a second when a thought occurs to me. "If your story is still that Zodiac doesn't know about Jude, then why did he let you tase me and bring me here, wherever the fuck here is?"

"He's here because he wants to know why you killed Cancer. Killing another division head, unless it's in self-defense, is punishable by death. You better hope he believes you're telling the truth because Zodiac will be after your blood."

"And I know just the soldier he'll send to get it." I tap his face and roll my eyes when he pulls the sack from where it's hooked in his back pocket.

"Is that really necessary?"

He doesn't answer me. He just pulls it down over my head before grabbing my hand.

"It's either this or I tase you again and carry you out," he whispers.

He opens the door and picks me up, bridal style, and carries me up a flight of stairs before unlocking and opening another door that leads to another flight of stairs.

When we reach the top, it's to find ourselves in a brightly lit hallway, making it easier to see through the hood. He places me on the floor and grabs my hand, walking me down the hall and into a large kitchen area. I guess this means I'm not in a warehouse then.

I don't speak and don't move my head in any direction, not wanting the other occupants of the room to figure out I can see.

Zodiac is sitting at the end of a large country style table with a cup of coffee in front of him. Over near the sink is a woman who turns at the sound of our approach. She frowns for a minute before turning back to the sink, effectively dismissing me.

Well, okay then, no sister solidarity there. I could brush it off as her being scared, but the look in her eye wasn't fear but indifference. She doesn't particularly want me here, but it has little to do with me being held captive and more to do with me invading her territory.

"Let's go," Kai orders, jerking me forward as Zodiac stands.

I watch as Zodiac walks over to the woman and pulls her into his arms, kissing her with far more heat than warranted given the company. I assume this is the mysterious Estelle, but then nothing in the rule books says Zodiac can't be a jealous, possessive bastard as well as a cheater.

Nobody makes a single sound or says a single word, which I figure is for my benefit. They don't want me to know where I am or who I'm with.

Kai guides me outside and I follow along, pretending to stumble, keeping the fact I can see undercover as long as I can.

We stop for a minute. Out of the corner of my eye, I see Zodiac climb into a black Range Rover, closing the door quietly behind him.

I lift my hand to pull the hood free, but Kai catches it.

"Leave it on until we get there."

"What, you think a woman with a mask over her head isn't going to draw some attention?" I snap.

"Nobody fucking cares. Now let's go," he mutters, taking my elbow in his hand and guiding me to the black Lincoln parked beside the car Zodiac just got into.

He helps me climb in, strapping the seatbelt across my body before gripping my face hard in warning. "Do not remove the mask," he orders. As much as my natural-born defiance wars within me, I chose to pick my battles and nod.

Plus, having an armed Zodiac this close to me makes me antsy. I know he wouldn't think twice about putting a bullet in my head, especially if he's as protective of Estelle as I've been led to believe. There is no way he would leave her open as a possible target to be used as retaliation. If I had to guess, I would say the hood is less about knowing Zodiac is here and more about keeping our location a secret from me

I memorize the journey, knowing now that this will be the first place Zodiac will go when the shit hits the fan. I don't speak, listening to the soft strains of some love song playing on the radio.

"Where to? Office or apartment," Kai asks when we've been driving for about ten minutes.

"My apartment is fine," I reply quietly.

"You don't need to go to your office for the footage?"

I smile under the hood. If he thinks I'm leading Zodiac to Echo's, he's sadly mistaken.

"Nope." I pop the p, before leaning my head against the window.

"You know, if you have truly nothing to do with this, then everything will go back to normal. This is just business, you know that, Viddy," Kai adds, so fucking blasé about the whole thing. I guess he must do this shit a lot to become so desensitized to it.

"Right, normal. Where I pretend there is only one Reid, and you guys pass me back and forth between you until I cross some arbitrary line and Zodiac orders you to put a bullet in my brain?"

"Red—"

I cut him off, closing my eyes once I recognize which part of the city I'm in.

"Don't call me that." I sigh. "I'll give you the footage, then what? I know what it will show you, I had a front-row seat after all. I'll send you the version with audio and Zodiac the one without sound because I'm nice like that, but then that's it between us. I don't want your apologies, fuck, I don't want anything from you. No more calls, no more late-night visits where you or your brother need patching up. I don't have it in me to *play pretend* anymore while waiting for one of you to shove a knife in my back. I know your secret. You already eliminated the original Gemini when he found out, why would I be any different? You go back to your division, I'll stay in mine, and we can hate each other from afar until you're ready to finish me off."

"I don't hate you," he grunts without thinking, but he doesn't say he won't kill me.

"That's okay, Kai, I hate me enough for the both of us," I tell him softly, because it's the truth.

The rest of the journey passes by in silence, thankfully, and when we pull up at the apartment a little while later, I wait for further instruction.

Kai turns the radio off, leaving us sitting in silence for a moment, the only sound is our breathing. He pulls the hood from my head, the sudden bright light making me blink rapidly as he smooths the hair from my face and tucks it behind my ear.

"Don't hate me, Red," he whispers, reaching over to unclip the seatbelt. "You have no idea what you stepped into," he adds, a tiny hint of panic in his voice, but when I look up at him sharply all I see is his cool calm facade

"Maybe not, but that won't stop you guys from using me as a scapegoat now, will it?" I mutter, before climbing out and slamming the door.

He's at my side in an instant, leaning close.

"Remember to keep your mouth shut about Jude to Zodiac. Regardless of what you think, he doesn't know about him."

"And what makes you so damn sure?" I snap, wondering why he can't see what's right in front of his face.

"Because if he knew, we'd both be dead."

# CHAPTER THIRTY-THREE

I spot Zodiac walking toward us as if exiting the building, which of course, is bullshit.

"Viddy," Zodiac greats me cordially as if I didn't see him standing behind Kai when he tased me.

"Zodiac," I reply before Kai steps up beside me. I hate being in close proximately to Zodiac, especially alone, and it's not because he's a bad guy, fuck at this point, all I know is bad guys. No, it's because Zodiac sets off a warning bell in me of a different kind. The way he looks at me makes my skin crawl. I feel dirty, as if my skin is layered in a slick oily film whenever his eyes are on me.

"I'd apologize if my actions today seem...extreme, but I lost a man today. Although I must say, you look remarkably well given Reid's usual brand of torture." He quirks an eyebrow as Kai grows tenser and tenser beside me.

"Oh, don't worry, Kai hasn't lost his touch. Let's just say his methods are a little...different when trying to get information out of a woman. Of course, it would have been so much easier on everyone if someone had simply just asked me what happened."

"With the cameras not working, I needed to be sure," Zodiac explains, looking at Kai before facing me again.

His voice turns icy. "Kai here tells me you're innocent, but if I find out you planned this all, a taser will be the least of your worries."

"Good job I didn't do anything except protect myself," I grit through my teeth, thankful for once I don't have my gun on me as there are too many witnesses here for me to shoot him in broad daylight.

I turn and walk toward the building before entering and making my way over to the bank of elevators. I step inside and scan the floor, not a drop of blood in sight. Damn, my boys are good.

I wait for Zodiac and Kai to enter before pressing for the doors to close.

"My apartment or yours?" I ask Zodiac casually, not missing the way Kai's head jerks around to face mine. I guess Jude didn't pass on that tidbit of information.

"Yours is fine," he replies calmly, but a tiny hint of an undefinable accent peeks through, letting me know he's pissed.

I hit the button to my floor and stand silently, taking more pleasure than I should from the tick in Zodiac's jaw. I know better than to poke the tiger, but today, I can't find the energy to rein it in.

When the doors open, I step out into the hallway and see it's free of corpses. The carpet has been ripped up and taken away, and a new one is in the process of being laid.

"Excuse me," I murmur, making the guy fitting the carpet look up at me. I don't acknowledge I know him, and he returns the favor by scooting out of my way so we can get past.

They follow behind without giving the carpet fitter the time of day as I stand and wait for them to let me in.

"Well," Zodiac snaps when I don't immediately move.

I lift my hands to show they're empty. "You guys took my stuff. If you give it back, I'll let you in." Zodiac looks as if he wants to rip my head off my shoulders, but before he can do or say anything, Kai reaches into his pocket, pulls out my keycard, and leans over to open the door. His arm brushes against my breast, so I step back and keep my face blank. He's trying to get a reaction out of me, heating my body to melt the ice around my heart, but he's not going to win.

I don't react to him at all. I don't need to. I've moved past the betrayal I feel from him, now I'm just angry at myself when I damn well knew better.

"Here, Red," he passes me the key and hands me my phone from his back pocket too.

I reach out to take them from him. He holds on for a moment, refusing to let go until I look up at him. Whatever he sees makes him flinch slightly. He releases my stuff, so I shoulder my way past him into the apartment, heading straight to the kitchen and grabbing a bottle of water from the fridge, about the only thing I have in there, and a couple of painkillers from one of the kitchen drawers. I need something to ward off the headache pounding at my temples.

Sending out a text for Danny, I wait for him to reply as the two unwelcome assholes take a seat on my sofa.

I watch Kai take everything in. He hasn't been here since the night he showed this place to me. And nothing much has changed. Zodiac, however, just watches me with his icy gaze. I stare at him for a second before turning away, in case I turn to stone. He doesn't bother looking around because he knows exactly what it looks like in here with his cameras and a nasty habit of coming and going whenever he chooses. The dickhead hasn't figured out that I have my own cameras in here now, allowing me to watch him watching me.

I resist the urge to shiver at the thought. Thank Christ this isn't the place I lay my head at night, or I'd never sleep.

"No personal touches, no throws or throw pillows or scented candles? No woman's touch at all. It doesn't feel much like a home, does it?" Zodiac says, drawing the attention of Kai.

"It's no more impersonal than his place. I'm never here, so what does it matter?"

"I gave you a perfectly good apartment building—" I cut him off, making his eyes flare at my blatant disrespect.

"But you didn't give me a curfew, and if I'm here, I'm not

out there making you money," I add, knowing I need to back off before things escalate any further.

"So the security footage?" Kai prompts, looking between Zodiac and me.

My phone chooses that moment to ding with the needed files. Not taking any chances, I forward copies with audio to Kai, and by default, Jude, having figured out early on they must have cloned phones. I send the one without sound to Zodiac before placing my phone back on the counter with a *c u l8ter xx* text. Anyone looking would assume I was likely banging my head of security on the side, but the actual message is a code we use. The c u l8ter means the phone is compromised, and the kisses represent how many potential threats I'm with.

"Now, I haven't had a chance to debrief Kai here, but it's safe to assume since you're not bleeding that he's pretty confident this footage will clear your name. I'd still like to hear your version of events before I watch it," Zodiac tells me, almost daring me to argue.

"My driver, Ben, and I were exiting the elevator when bullets started flying. Ben took one in the shoulder. I closed the doors, checked to make sure my man was okay, and grabbed my gun. After making sure Ben was still alive, I opened the doors and fired back. When the shooter was down, I tried to get him to tell me why he was there, but all he kept saying was pussy has no place in the division, and said one of the heads had hired him to take me out," I lie smoothly, feeling Kai's intense stare on me. Even with how pissed I am, I'm still protecting him. Why? I have no fucking clue.

"And you believed him?" Zodiac laughs incredulously.

"He was pretty convincing with the whole gun thing, but what sealed the deal was when Cancer appeared with a gun aimed at me."

"He could have been here for any reason," he snaps, but I shake my head.

"You don't go into another division head's sector without permission, and you don't under any circumstances go to their apartment building unannounced, brandishing a gun. If he wasn't guilty of betraying the division, he was at least guilty of stupidity."

"I want all copies of the footage sent to me," he grits out, his anger palpable.

"There is only the digital copy I just sent you. I don't keep hard copies of anything. It's too easy for people to find," I lie again.

"You'd better hope that's true. I'd like to know why you deemed it your business to fit security cameras in my building without consulting me first." He stands and walks toward me with the grace of a panther.

"I didn't know I had to. It was a standard safety precaution, and in my defense, I didn't know you had your own cameras installed, or I wouldn't have bothered. Lucky for us, I did, huh, as Reid said yours had unexpectedly been switched off," I point out. His eyes drift to the cupboard in the kitchen briefly, where I know one of his planted cameras is, before skirting away.

"And where exactly are these cameras of yours? It's not fair to other residents for you to assume they would be happy about such an invasion of privacy without being consulted about it."

I have to swallow down a chuckle at his fucking hypocrisy.

"Only the entry and exit points of the buildings and the stairwells."

His shoulders relax for a moment before I add, "Oh, and outside my front door."

His whole body goes wired then because he knows I know he's been inside here. He doesn't know I know about the cameras he has in here, but there is no way the camera at my door would miss his large frame.

"I want that footage too, for the entire time they've been installed," he snaps, making Kai step forward, looking even more confused.

"That will take time, but I'm sure my men can do it. I'll forward it to Reid."

Zodiac reaches out and cups my jaw, his grip a touch too tight for comfort, but I don't wince. "Send it directly to me."

"If that's what you want," I reply evenly.

"I expect you to be at the planetarium on Saturday, no excuses."

I nod my head, willing myself to keep my mouth shut, but I just can't. "So that's it? You have me tasered and tied up and then you just let me go? You haven't even watched the clip yet. What if I'm lying?" I ask as he grips my face harder. This time he'll leave fingerprint bruises, but I don't care.

"I think you're forgetting who the boss is. I made you, I can break you. You have no power here." He seethes, his mouth against my cheek.

I don't answer, letting him say his piece even though my heart is beating a mile a minute. It's not with fear, though, but with anticipation.

"So fucking defiant," he growls, licking the side of my face. I fist my hands hard so I don't reach up and rip his face off. I see Kai out of the corner of my eye tense and step forward, but I don't move.

Zodiac lowers his voice so only I can hear him. "It would be a shame to have to get rid of you. You might make me a decent chunk of change, but nobody is irreplaceable, and I could fetch a pretty fucking penny for you."

"I gave you what you wanted, so if there is nothing else, I'd like to get some sleep," I reply in a monotone voice as he loosens his hold on me and takes a step back.

He moves so fast I don't have time to react as the back of his hand collides with the side of my face, making my head whip around so hard my neck cracks painfully. I bite my lip hard enough to draw blood, but I refuse to let this asshole know he caused me a second of pain.

Straightening the lapels of his suit before checking that his cufflinks are still in; he moves toward the door before throwing a reminder over his shoulder to be at the planetarium.

As soon as he is out the door, Kai is in front of me, reaching out, but I lift my hand to stop him.

"Leave now," I order, my voice sounding surprisingly strong.

"No, fuck that, you're hurt," he spits out like I'm unaware of the throbbing around my eye socket. His eyes are full of anger, but more than that, I see them swirling with questions. Seems Zodiac might have made a bigger mistake here than he realizes.

"My pain is of no concern to you. Now get the fuck out of my apartment."

"Red," Kai starts but I snarl at him.

"Get the fuck out. This, whatever this is, whatever it could have been between us is over. I don't want to see you anymore. Don't call, don't text, and don't come by. Find a new nurse to use as an emotional punching bag and doctor your wounds. I'm so fucking done."

I move to step around him, but he pins me against the counter.

"You need to listen to me, there is more going on here—" I need to shut him up before he gives himself away on camera so I do the only thing I can, I reach up and kiss him.

I pour everything into it, taking him off guard for a minute before he wraps his arms around me and kisses me back with as much vigor. All the hurt and pain, the want, and yearning for this man and his brother goes into it until I feel completely empty inside.

I rip my lips from his, both of us breathing heavy.

He lifts his hand and lightly skims his fingers over my cheekbone, making me hiss.

"You need ice," he curses, moving to grab some, but I stop him. I lean up and place my lips against his ear so that the cameras won't pick up my whispered words.

"If you don't leave, I'll spill your secret to anyone who will listen. I hid it for a year, because even though I knew better than to trust you, I fucking cared about you, about both of you. Now though, the sight of you makes me sick. Just go." When he hesitates again, I pull back and shout at him, "*Just fucking go!*"

He drops his head to his chest for a moment before lifting his stormy eyes to mine and nodding. "I'll go, but this isn't over between us," he warns me as he opens the door.

"We never even began. Goodbye, Reid."

I wait for him to step out and as soon as he looks about to speak, I slam the door shut and deadbolt it. I lean against the door for a moment and take a deep breath, but my insides feel like they've been carved out with a spoon.

Heading back to the kitchen, I grab my phone and pull it apart. Sure enough, there is a small round green disk inside it. I knew the second my phone was taken they would bug it.

Turning my back to the room, I take the bug from my phone and turn on the faucet and let the water run. I make it look as if I'm bending over to sip the water when in fact, I slip the bug down the drain and let the water run over it.

Drying my hands, I grab the ice from my freezer and place a handful in a clean towel and press it against my eye before moving over and collapsing on the sofa with my eyes closed. I fidget around so it looks like I'm trying to get comfortable and pretend to nap for thirty minutes. In actuality, I use the time to plan my next move. I still have a few loose ends I wanted to tie up, but I've got no choice but to move up my timeline.

Climbing to my feet, I sway unsteadily, knowing I need real rest and food so my overtaxed body can heal, but it's going to have to wait.

Moving down the hallway to the bedroom, I head straight to the closet. I only keep the bare minimum here for appearance's sake.

I grab a clean set of jeans and a hoodie, sticking with the pumps, and pull my hair into a ponytail. The other items in the closet are strategically placed clothes, pantsuits with jackets and feminine looking blazers, but they are just there to hide what I needed them to. I slip a burner phone out of the pocket of a plain black blazer and slide it into the hoodie pocket before slipping a small handgun from another. I check the chamber, then flick the safety on and shove it in my pocket too.

Making my way into the bathroom, I check out my face in the mirror and see my eye is already puffy and turning purple at the edge.

I let my eyes drift lower, taking in the ripped jeans and baggy hoodie and shake my head ruefully. Seems you can take the girl out of the gutters, but you can't keep her away from trouble.

I sigh and shake it off. There will be time later for a pity party.

Moving back to the kitchen, I pop two more pain pills to help numb the throbbing in my face before I spot my gun and knife on the counter. Kai must have placed them there before he left. I was so mad at him I never even noticed.

Picking up the knife, I check it over and slide it into my back pocket before picking up the gun and dropping it inside a food bag I find in the bottom drawer.

I shove that into the wide pocket of my hoodie too and head out the door.

The new carpet is down now, and the guy who is finishing up stands at my approach, his eyes widening when he takes in my face. Walking past him without a word, I head to the elevator just as he hurries to catch up, a bag of tools in his hands.

"Wait," he yells out, so I hold the doors open as he almost plows into me in his hurry to catch up.

I slip the gun from my pocket into his bag as he moves to stand beside me and offer him a tiny nod.

"I'm so sorry. I have an emergency call. I'll be back to finish the job tomorrow," he says loudly, making sure any listening devices pick up his voice loud and clear.

"No worries." I offer him a small smile before turning

away, making it seem like he is just another regular everyday guy. Only in my world, there is no such thing.

Trevor here is the guy in charge of my cleanup crew. I knew he would stick around until I returned because he always does, never leaving a scene until I've spoken to him and let him know every single place I've been and every little thing could have possibly come into contact with. There is a reason his cleaning company is one of the most expensive crews in the country, and it sure as shit isn't because of his ability to dust and vacuum. If you have a crime scene that needs cleaning, you call Trevor, it's as simple as that.

He'll get rid of the gun for me because I can't take the risk that Zodiac or Kai hasn't used it to set me up. After all, it's what I'd do.

Stepping out of the elevator, I walk toward the main entrance, finding Danny and Baker waiting just outside the door for me.

Danny takes a look at my face and growls, but he doesn't speak, just flanks one side of me as Baker does the other, making sure I'm protected as I climb in the car that's waiting.

As soon as I'm inside, I release a deep, relieved breath.

"I really hate this shithole," I grumble. Ironic how I prefer the streets to a penthouse.

"What the fuck happened?" Danny asks quietly, looking like he's trying to rein his temper in.

"Not here. Take me home."

"On it," Baker answers from the driver's seat as he pulls out into the busy flow of traffic. I lie back and close my eyes.

# CHAPTER THIRTY-FOUR

I wake with a gasp, sitting up too quickly, which makes the world spin a little. It isn't until I realize I'm home and in my bed that I relax and my breathing evens out.

Pulling back the deep purple comforter, I see I'm still wearing the hoodie and jeans from earlier, but my feet are now bare. A glance at the glass bedside table shows my gun and knife, so I swing my feet over and stand, cracking my back as I stretch out the kinks. My thick plum curtains are drawn, but the absence of light peeking in around the edges where they've been closed haphazardly tell me it's dark out.

I wiggle my toes on the fluffy white rug beneath my feet and take stock of how my body feels. There is some bruising around my wrists where I struggled against the ropes, and my face feels tender like the skin is pulled too tight. Thanks to Zodiac's handiwork, I'll likely be sporting a shiner for a few days.

Everything else feels surprisingly okay—other than I'm so exhausted I feel as if I could sleep for a year.

I straighten the bed, arranging the silver and white throw pillows over the top and smile to myself. Zodiac would have a field day if he saw this room. With the pillows, the scented candles on the dresser at the foot of the bed, and the soft chenille blanket thrown over the reading chair in the corner, this room is the epitome of homely. It's the one place I feel I can let my guard down and just be me.

I head into the adjoining bathroom, flicking on the light and wincing a little as the brightness of it bounces off the white and gold tiles.

Grabbing my toothbrush, I brush my teeth, checking out my reflection as I do. My hair is a crazy mess, no surprise there, but my eye looks better than I thought it would. If I ice it for a while, I should be able to cover most of the bruising with some makeup.

I finish up and toss the toothbrush in the holder, not bothering to shower and change yet. I need to report in with my team and get our plan set in motion.

I make my way down the wide staircase, the bottom step creaking when I reach it, and head left toward the kitchen area. Shadow Falls is far bigger than I need, which is why I've only bothered to have the west wing remodeled so far. Well that and the underground tunnels, but it is more than enough for my team and me.

I hear the light chatter of voices before stepping into the room and find Danny and Baker sitting at the counter, looking at something on an iPad. Thomas is in the corner quietly talking to Ben while Cash and Will are staring at each other like they each want to shoot the other in the face.

"Ah, lass, you're awake." I turn and see Gary heading toward me from the walk-in freezer with a bag of ice in one hand and a tub of ice cream in the other. "I was just coming to wake you. I thought ice cream might stop you from shooting me."

I laugh lightly at that. I have a trigger reflex, so anyone brave enough to wake me knows better than to stand too close.

"Hey, guys. Ben, it's good to see you up. How you feeling?" I ask, snagging the ice cream and spoon from Gary before kissing his cheek and heading over to Ben.

Once I'm close, he pulls me in for a hug, and I let him, needing the comfort tonight.

"I'm feeling much better, thanks." I pull back and find myself in Will's arms for a minute.

He looks me over, his face going hard as he takes in my eye.

"Hey, I'm okay. Promise."

He snags my ice cream and pulls off the lid, tossing it on the counter before handing it back.

I beam at him and take a large spoonful.

"All right, move." Cash shoves him aside and presses a

kiss to my forehead before wrapping his lips around my spoon and stealing my mouthful of ice cream.

"Hey," I complain. He just laughs at me, asshole.

"Where's Lily?" I look around for her.

"I sent her with two of my men and Jen down to the safe house with Kevin and DJ. I know Chris will keep her safe and my guys can back her up if needed."

I don't ask them if his men are trustworthy. I've met a few and liked them all and there is no chance he would risk his little girl's safety.

"Sounds good. I know I have the panic room set up here for them, but I think they should be as far away from the city as we can get them right now."

"I think you're right. What I want to know is, what the fuck happened and what do you need from me?"

I place the ice cream on the counter and turn back to Cash, lifting up and wrapping my arms around him. He holds me for a minute as the room goes quiet around us.

"Zodiac has called a meeting for all the division heads on Saturday. You'll be the only one in that room with me that I know is one hundred percent on my side, but if it comes down to you having to take me out, don't hesitate. Lily needs you, Cash, don't be a hero. He will have you killed on the spot for disobedience."

"No, fuck that, and fuck you for thinking I could do that, V," he snaps, shaking me before pulling me tighter.

"You have to, for Lily. Promise me, Cash." I look up at him.

His jaw is rigid. He nods once, a short jerky movement, before he steps back and turns, stalking out of the room. I move to go after him, but Will stops me.

"Just give him a minute, love. He understands what you're saying, and he'll do it if necessary, but you are asking him to choose between the two people he loves," he tells me softly.

I freeze at his words, looking up at him in confusion. "What?" I gasp.

"You didn't know? Hell, Viddy, how is that possible? I'm pretty sure all of the men in this room are a little bit in love with you."

"What?" I choke out again, turning to look at the others who all look at me with soft smiles, except Gary, who has a beaming one.

"My wife says you can be my hall pass girl if you're interested." He wiggles his eyebrows, making me burst out laughing.

Once I get myself under control, I look at them all again and see what Will's talking about.

"I...I love you guys too but..."

"You're in love with someone else," Will answers for me. I look over my shoulder at him and see his eyes soften.

"We know. It's why Cash and I never took things further with you even though I'd give my left nut to have you. You're just not mine to keep. Besides, my desires run a little darker than I think you could handle."

I tilt my head, curious at that, but Baker speaks before I can say anything.

"Okay, before this turns into a mass orgy, I think I've found something, V."

"Oh, gross. I love you guys, but sorry to say, in a brotherly way. I don't want to be thinking about your dicks, at all."

"You'd let your brother grab your ass and tongue fuck you? Kinky," Cash says as he re-enters the room. I reach for the ice cream spoon and lob it as his head, but of course, he catches it.

"Fine. You and Will are the exceptions to the rule. I can't help it; you have that whole murdery vibe going on that I seem to be attracted to. It's just..." I bite my lip, trying to figure out how to soften the blow.

"Your body wants us, but your heart belongs to another. I know, but if you ever need to fuck him out your system, I'm available," he adds to a chorus of *me too*.

I grumble under my breath and move to sit next to Baker at the counter. "Everyone has gone crazy."

Baker smiles at me but spins the iPad around to show me what he's found.

"I sent DNA samples off from the two shooters to the guy we have down at the precinct. I wanted to see if there were any hits and the results are in. The first guy is a gun for hire. His name is John Eccles, and he was just starting out for all intents and purposes. He has a few kill claims under his belt, but there was never enough evidence to pull him in. The second guy, Cancer. He's not in the system, but his DNA had enough familial markers with another sample for a hit to pop up." He taps something on the screen before showing it to me.

"Gianni Romano, AKA—"

"Zodiac," I finish for him. "Holy fuck."

"That's not all. We ran with what we had and found the same familial markers in the previous Gemini, and three other division heads. We can't run the other heads because they aren't in the system, but if we can get samples, I bet there are more."

"But even if he is the father to some of the others, Viddy isn't his kid, and neither am I. What the fuck are we doing here, unless he just ran out of offspring," Cash adds, looking as incredulous as I do.

"I've run Viddy's DNA before destroying it, no match. I'd like to run yours too Cash, just to be sure."

Cash nods absently. "That's fine, man, whatever."

I scrub a hand over my face and try to figure out what the hell is going on.

"Do you think these guys know they're all brothers?" Cash asks me.

I think back to the times I've interacted with any of them and pause.

"Is it possible they all individually know that Zodiac is their father, but don't know they are not the lone child?" I think about how they all look at Zodiac reverently, not hesitating to do his bidding.

"I can see that. Especially if he told them to keep it hush-hush so it didn't show favoritism. It would make them feel special and somehow safer from Zodiac's ministrations to find out they were blood-related," Will adds from behind me.

"They clearly don't know Zodiac well if they think family means anything to him."

The tablet beeps, making me stop as Baker pulls in a sharp breath.

"There was one more hit."

He spins it around, showing a picture of Reid. I swallow around a knot in my throat as I stare at the picture, wondering why my brain didn't make the connection straight away. It would explain why Kai's so fucking loyal to him.

"Fuck, is that Aries?" Cash snaps.

"No, that's not Kai." I run my finger over his smiling face and feel my heart crack at the handsome man decked out in a full police uniform.

"That's his brother, Jude."

# CHAPTER THIRTY-FIVE

"Viddy, we have a huge fucking problem," Will says when I answer my phone.

"Tell me." I stand up and grab my jacket from the back of my chair. We've been working flat out to get all our ducks in a row, and with Saturday only four days away, time is fast running out.

"My guys just intercepted a cargo ship coming into the dock space you lease me. It's full of people, and that's not all. There is a guy here asking to see you, won't give me his name, but he's adamant you'll want to see him."

"I'm on my way, thanks, Will." I hang up and head for the door finding Thomas outside.

"Hey, Thomas, I have to go out. Can you call Danny and Baker and get them to meet me at the docks? Ben's downstairs, but I can't wait as something urgent has popped up."

"Want me to come with you, ma'am?"

"I need you to stay here and guard Echo's. This could just be some kind of ploy to get me away from here. Lock shit down if you need to. I'll leave everything up to you and Gary. If something feels off, clear everyone out, okay?"

"Yes, ma'am, and I'll call the guys right now."

I nod and make my way downstairs and out the fire exit where Ben is waiting. Thankfully, he decided to stay, knowing I wasn't planning on being here long tonight.

I climb in the passenger seat beside him, which surprises him as I usually get in the back, but I want to be extra vigilant.

"Everything okay, V?"

"No. Will called so we need to head to the docks now. He intercepted a cargo ship coming in filled with people. Now I know it could very well be one of Kristoff's deliveries getting waylaid and turned around or the prick thinks he can sneak in under the radar using Will's dock space. He might know Will and I have some kind of deal, but he would have no idea we're actually friends."

"Okay, I'll get us there. Where is your team?"

"Danny and Baker have guys spread out everywhere trying to get what they need. I was supposed to stay at Echo's with Thomas, but this takes precedence, and I need him to watch over the place."

He whistles. "Those boys will be pissed." He's not wrong,

they take my safety very seriously, especially since what went down with Zodiac.

"I know, but my hands were tied. I'm going to call Cash in and see if he'll come help out."

He nods, knowing I trust the guy.

I dial his number and wait for him to pick up. "Hey gorgeous, I'm just in the middle of something."

"Shit, never mind."

"Wait, what's wrong?"

"I need back up until my boys can get to me, but it's fine. Don't worry, I'll figure something else out."

"What? Hold on." He mutters something to whoever he's with before I hear movement, and he's back. "Where are you?"

"Heading to the docks."

"I'll be there in twenty," he replies, hanging up.

"He's on his way," I tell Ben, who laughs.

"Of course, he is."

It's quiet in the car as we drive to the outskirts of the city before Ben speaks again.

"Have you decided what to do about the Reid brothers?"

"No fucking clue. I'm supposed to be done with them, but even though I've cauterized the wound, it's still bleeding. I don't know if Kai knows Jude is a cop or if Jude is playing Kai as well as Zodiac, and I can't ask while I have all this hanging over us."

"I'm sorry, V, I know you care about them."

"I don't just care about them, Ben, I'm in love with them

both. How fucking pathetic am I? I turned into my mom, loving someone, or in my case, *someones*, who are the kind of people who will never return it. I'll never get my happy-ever-after with them because I'll always have to worry about one of them slitting my throat in my sleep."

"I don't know everything that happened, V, and I don't need to, but I have eyes. I've seen them, and yes, I have no clue right now when it was one or the other, but they care for you. It was in every look they gave you. Oh, they might fight it, but the heart is fickle and wants what it wants, and those boys want you."

"I don't trust them, Ben, and worse, I don't trust myself when I'm with them."

"Then just let the dust settle where it may. If it's meant to be. it will figure itself out."

I look at him and feel my lips twitch. "You're awfully philosophical tonight."

He groans before looking briefly at me. "It's Chris's fault. She watches all those Hallmark movies when she comes around. It's been so quiet without the boys that I've had that channel on for some familiarity, and I swear those movies are addicting. I've lost hours, V, because I had to find out if the small-town lumberjack really could win over the big city girl who was just returning home for Christmas."

He looks at me again with such a look of distaste on his face that I can't help it, I laugh and keep laughing until we pull up at the docks.

"I'm never telling you anything again." He huffs as I finally get myself under control.

"Oh come on, if the shoe were on the other foot, you'd be the same way."

"Maybe," he replies, trying to hide his grin before sighing. "Okay, let's get this over with."

We make our way down to where Will told me he would be and see him standing there waiting.

"Hey, Viddy, thanks for getting here so fast. You armed? "

"Always."

He nods and with a hand at the small of my back, he ushers me onboard with Ben following up the rear.

"Anyone need any medical attention?" I ask him quietly.

"Some have a few minor scrapes and bruises but nothing major. They are just through here." He takes me down the steps and opens a small wooden door, revealing a dozen people. I nod to Will's guys guarding them, guns in hand but not aimed at anyone.

Scanning the room, the first thing I notice is these are not Kristoff's usual fare. He has his girls snatched to order, but they all have beauty and youth in common. These people look like ordinary everyday people picked up from a shopping mall or something. There is a young girl or two sure, but also a couple of middle-aged women, a few men in their 30-40s, and a couple of men who must be in their late 60s.

"What the heck is this?" I mutter to myself.

"That's what we want to know," Will says.

"Who's the guy that wants to speak to me?"

"He's next door. Come."

I take the hand he offers and follow him out and down the short hallway to the second door. When it swings open, I gasp before I'm running and hitting the man with my body hard enough to almost knock us both back a step.

"Viddy." His deep voice washes over me, making tears spring to my eyes.

"I guess she knows him then," Will comments before stepping closer.

I lift my head and stare into Wyatt's pretty eyes. "Fuck, Wyatt, I missed you."

He lifts his hands and shows me they are cuffed. "Think you can get these off?"

I turn to Will and he steps forward with a key. "Sorry, man, we had to be sure you didn't mean her any harm," Will tells him as he opens the cuffs.

"Wyatt, what's going on? Why are you here? Where is Megan?" I fire off as my brain recovers from the shock of seeing him.

"Calm down, Viddy, Megan is fine. Well, now she is anyway, but that's a story for another day. All you need to know is she's protected and not in danger."

I trust him, so I know he wouldn't lie about something like this, but it doesn't answer the other stuff.

"Why are you here, Wyatt, and how the fuck did you end up on this ship?"

"Well, from what I was able to pick up when the assholes

taking us thought we were all out cold from the spiked water they gave us, we are supposed to be some kind of sacrificial offering for Saturday. I don't have much more than that." He shrugs.

I turn to look at Will and see Ben walk up behind him with Cash in tow.

"Viddy, looks like you started the party without me."

"Sorry, Cash, guys, this is Wyatt, one of my best friends in the whole world."

"Viddy, he looks like he eats small children for breakfast."

"Only on Tuesdays and Thursdays," Wyatt rumbles from behind me.

"Zodiac is up to something. He had Wyatt snatched with another bunch of people for a sacrifice," I say, scrunching up my face until a light bulb goes off.

"The planetarium. With Cancer dead, Zodiac will want a replacement, and this must be the new recruits challenge." I shove my way past them and move back into the room, scanning the people who look terrified out of their minds. It doesn't improve any when the guys step in behind me.

"Joan?" Cash's voice chokes out, shocked, from next to me. I see an older woman with red hair threaded with silver look up sharply at the sound of her name being called.

"Cash?" she says, confused.

"Who is she, Cash?" I ask him, watching her climb to her feet and wrap an arm protectively around her waist.

"She was Caroline's mom. I haven't seen her though, since the funeral."

"But I thought you said they didn't get on, that they kicked her out when she was pregnant."

"She did, so if they brought Joan here as a weapon to be used against me, they chose badly."

"He didn't bring me here because I matter to you, he brought me here because of my connection to Lily and to him," she says with a sniff.

"What the fuck are you talking about?" Cash steps forward, but I hold him back.

"My sister can't have kids, but I didn't know that at the time. I was fourteen and never really paid much attention to my older sister's life. That was until her husband raped me and got me pregnant."

"With Caroline," Cash's shoulders slump. "No wonder you hated her."

"I didn't hate her, Cash, I just didn't know how to love her. Every time I looked at her, I saw the man who held me down as my sister cooed softly in my ear that everything would be okay. The fucked up thing is, they didn't want to raise the baby they forced on me, but they refused to let me get rid of her or give her up for adoption. I felt like I was being tortured day in and day out in a nightmare I couldn't escape from. When Caroline died, I felt relieved," she admits with tears streaming down her face.

I feel bile rushing up the back of my throat. "Joan, what's your sister's name?"

"Her name is Estelle, and her husband is Gianni."

I look up at Cash and see him figure it out the same time I do.

"Lily is Zodiac's granddaughter."

"Wait." A young girl of maybe twelve steps forward, her big green eyes brimming with tears. "My brother works for Zodiac," she admits as all the pieces start to drop into place.

"Who's, your brother, sweetheart?" Will asks her softly.

"J...Joey, but most people call him Taurus."

I look out over the people here and do a headcount, there is enough for a single sacrifice per division head, bar one. Kai.

"Zodiac is going to make his initiates sacrifice everyone here to prove their loyalty and to remind the division heads who is in charge. I can't send these people to their deaths, but Zodiac will be on to us when they don't arrive."

"We were supposed to be held here until Saturday and then taken straight to the drop off, wearing some kind of ceremonial robes and hoods, so I doubt he'll know we're missing until then," Wyatt adds, but on the back of it an idea forms.

"Will, Cash, I need you to round up some people for me. I'll text you the names. Ben, I need you to take me somewhere. Wyatt, can you watch these guys for me? I want them safe and unharmed, but if they try to leave or signal anyone, incapacitate them. I know you have a million questions, and I will answer them all, but right now, I have someone I need to talk to."

# CHAPTER THIRTY-SIX

I sit in the dark room listening to the rain fall softly outside before a beep at the door snags my attention.

I don't move from the spot, I just continue to sit and watch the raindrops hit the windows before they slowly drip down the glass like tiny tears.

"Hello, Red."

"Kai," I greet him, never looking away from the glass until he sits beside me.

"What, pray tell, has you breaking and entering my humble abode?"

"I'm not sure myself."

We sit quietly side by side for what feels like forever before I finally look up at him.

"There is a strong possibility I might not live to see Sunday."

"Red, you have more lives than a cat." He grins.

"I know things, things that I came here to share, but what's the point when I know you won't believe me? I'm gonna go, but before I do, I have to tell you, just once, that I love you. I've been in love with you since the beginning and no matter what happens now, I'll love you for the rest of this life and the next."

His breathing picks up at my words, his hands fisted on his lap, but he doesn't speak, and that's okay. I've said what I needed to.

I stand and move to step past him when, in seconds, he's on his feet with his hands in my hair and his lips on mine in a full out assault on my senses.

I don't fight him, I submit, giving myself over, allowing us to have this one moment that will have to last forever.

He walks me back to the bedroom, tearing off my clothes as we go until we both fall on his bed in a tangle of limbs.

His hot lips tear from mine, but only so he can slide down my body and suck on my nipples briefly before descending farther. There's no lace between him and me, no visible barrier to stop us, and to show him I'm okay with it, I grip his hair in my hands and push his head even lower, directing him exactly where I need him to be. He wastes no time, his talented tongue delving inside me, making me gasp as tiny tremors wrack my body. Dragging his tongue up over my swollen clit, he lashes it over and over until I'm a quivering mess.

Needing more, I yank his head. Thankfully, he takes the

hint and crawls up the bed and slides between my legs, the hard column of his dick pressed between us. His eyes stay fixed on mine as he reaches over and snags a condom from the bedside drawer, rolling it down over his thick cock.

Settling back on top of me, he coats the head with my juices before lining himself up.

"Are you sure?" He breathes the words, his arms trembling with restraint as he holds himself above me.

I lift my hand and curve it around his neck, staring into his lust-filled eyes. "I've never been more sure of anything in my life."

I barely finish getting the words out before he's pushing inside me, breaking through the barrier I guarded feverishly. Instead of feeling a sense of loss, I feel empowered, because I got to give it to someone of my choice, instead of having it taken from me. The sharp bite of pain makes me wince, but the fullness of having him inside me, connected to me in the most primal of ways, has me begging him for more.

"Please." I don't know what it is exactly I'm asking for, but he does, pulling back almost completely before gliding back in again to the hilt. I'm wet, but I know not all of it is from arousal. Even so, the prospect of my blood staining his cock makes me feel a sense of ownership over this man. The world outside our door can fall to wreck and ruin because in here, at this moment, there is no one else in the world but him and me.

"Jesus, Red, so fucking tight, so hot." He speeds up, thrusting into me harder and faster, the tenderness of the moment giving way to passion and lust. Want and need collide in technicolor, making me see stars.

"More," I beg. It hurts a little, and yet, it's not enough. I want to feel branded, knowing that when this is over, neither of us will ever be the same. The thought of losing him should make me stop, beg insanity, and hope that everything goes back to the way it was before, but I can't. Now that I've felt heaven, I'll never be able to go back.

"Fuck, touch yourself, Red," he grunts out.

I obey without hesitation, sliding my fingers down between my slick folds, feeling him disappear inside me. I coat my fingers with my wetness and drag them up over my clit, swirling around the swollen nub, speeding up my movements to mimic his.

"I'm not gonna last much longer, V, get yourself there," he warns, but it's not needed, I've been balanced on the edge, just waiting for him. When he dips his head and snags my earlobe between his teeth and bites, I scream, clenching around him as that tiny hint of pain shoves me over the edge, and I drag him right over with me.

We both stay still for a moment, our breaths rapid, our bodies slick with sweat before he rolls off me and pulls me against him.

"Wow. That was, wow. I can see why people like doing that," I breathe out heavily.

He laughs, "Well, I'm going to take that as a compliment."

"Oh, you should, you definitely should," I agree.

"Let me just get rid of this condom," he murmurs, pulling

away from me, disappearing into the bathroom as my eyes close and I snuggle deeper into the pillow with a contented grin on my face as sleep pulls me under.

The sound of a gun cocking has me blinking my eyes open, suddenly wide awake.

"Well, I guess I thought you'd have better pillow talk than that, but then what did I expect?" I choke out, the light from the hall casting just enough of a glow through the cracked door to illuminate Kai's naked body with his gun in his hand aimed at my head.

He might not have pulled the trigger yet, but my heart's already bleeding out all over the floor.

"Sorry, V, it wasn't really meant to go this far, but you make me lose my mind. Get up," he orders.

I slide from the bed, wincing at the pain between my legs, but I don't show any outward reaction. The dim room offers me just enough cover to shield my facial expressions.

I stand before him as naked as he is, feeling my cooling arousal and blood on my thighs and blink when he flicks the lamp on. He freezes when he catches sight of my blood on the sheets, making me realize that he's not as okay with hurting me as he has convinced himself.

"What's the plan now, Reid, you gonna shoot me? Is that why you insisted on a condom? So you didn't leave all your DNA inside me, or was it because you were worried about fucking a dirty little street rat?"

"Shut up. You have no idea what you've done. What

you've set in motion. I tried to get you to fly under the radar, but it was just impossible."

"Save me your fucking speeches, Reid. If you're going to kill me, do it now. I have better things to do, like dying, for instance, than listening to you justify your actions."

"Shut up," he snaps.

"Why? You're going to kill me anyway, so what does it matter?"

He pulls the gun away and grips his hair with both hands. The gun still in his hand keeps me glued to my spot.

Trying a different tactic, I rein in my temper and try a different approach. "I trusted you. I gave you the only thing I had that was all mine, and you shit all over it. I thought we were more, but I guess I really am the naïve little girl you always painted me as."

"I told you I was a bad man, the fucking worst, but you insisted on seeing something in me that just isn't there."

"Bullshit. I know you care for me, Reid, you're just too chickenshit to admit it and too fucking under Zodiac's thumb to ever be your own man. I guess my mistake was thinking you might one day be king when you'll never be anything more than a foot soldier."

He turns the gun back toward me, aims, and fires.

I fall to the unforgiving stone floor, my head smacking against the ground hard enough for me to see stars. I wait for the pain to hit me before Reid steps around the bed and looks down at me with the gun still in his hand.

"Did you really think he didn't know? That he wouldn't

recognize you? He knew who you were the second you walked into Jimmy's bar. You were the girl he ordered, who disappeared into the night before delivery could be made. He wasn't happy when his name came up in the investigation of Clyde's death, but lucky for you, it kept him away until you landed right back in his lap.

"But once you were back, he decided you needed to be punished for what you did. He wanted to give you the world just so he could rip it away from you before turning you into a broodmare for his next round of heirs. But you didn't want anything he had to offer."

"Except you," I whisper, wondering why I can't feel where the bullet hit even as my body shakes with adrenaline. Gianni. Clyde had called him G. I remember him now from that night so long ago.

"Except me. He's holding a meeting on Saturday, as a reminder to the division heads what happens when he is double-crossed."

"I'm the only thing you really care about, so it seems fitting that I be the one to take you out. Besides, you're my punishment too, you know? He knows how I feel about you, but a sacrifice needs to be made." He looks at me in defeat.

I try to speak, but he continues talking.

"He bought you for me. It's an odd gift for a father to bestow upon his son, I'll admit, but it's the world we live in." He shrugs nonchalantly before he fires the gun again once, twice, three times. Each time the bullets ricochet off the floor beside my head as he stares down at me, his eyes trying to tell me what his mouth can't.

"Goodbye, Viddy." He drops the gun beside me and bends to grab his jeans from the floor.

"Don't move until you hear the door close. Jude is disabling the cameras," he whispers so softly I almost miss it over the thundering of my heart and the ringing in my ears.

I don't answer as his words finally sink in and I realize he staged everything to make it look as if he killed me. He's faked my death and filmed it. The video footage will confirm everything. To Zodiac, I'm gone.

He saved me. He chose me.

Tears track down my face as I listen to the sound of him pulling on the rest of his clothes, not daring to move a muscle in case the camera picks it up.

He bends, one last time, and picks up the gun. Turning to glance at me, he dips his head and whispers, "Whatever happens now, know I regret nothing. You were always too good for this world. I might be about to go out in a blaze of glory, but if it means saving the woman I love, so fucking be it."

He leaves the room as I fight back a sob.

If Zodiac finds out the truth, he will kill Kai, no matter what. Zodiac has no loyalty to anyone but himself.

Except Estelle.

I pause as the name hits me.

I know what I have to do to end this. I just hope it's not too late.

# CHAPTER THIRTY-SEVEN

I make my way around the back of the house, my whole body covered head to toe in black from my biker boots up to the black balaclava hiding my hair and most of my face.

I keep the gun up at my side and send a nod to Danny, who is the only man I can see from this vantage point.

I wait for the thumbs up telling me that he has confirmation of Zodiac's whereabouts, far from here, and make my way inside.

The door is unlocked, which baffles me. I get that she lives in the middle of nowhere, but she knows what her husband does for a living. Have they become that complacent? Nobody is untouchable, and I'm about to prove just how true that is.

I close the door, leaving the men to guard outside, and make my way through the empty kitchen and down the hallway. All the lights are off, which I'd expect for most people at this hour, and head toward the bedrooms.

The first one I come across is empty, so I move to the next and find exactly who I'm looking for. Walking on silent feet to the bed, I slip the syringe from my pocket and pull off the cap with my teeth.

Holding the gun up, pointing right at her, I slide her hair back to confirm identity. I take a relieved breath to see it is indeed Estelle. Clearly, I've watched one too many scary movies. I lean over and stab the needle into her neck and press the plunger, stepping back as she comes awake with a startled gasp.

I keep the gun aimed at her, but I'm not worried. The shit I gave her is fast-acting, and she can thank her husband for that. It's his latest version of the date rape drug, leaving victims completely aware of what's going on, but paralyzed while it's happening. Once the stuff has burned through their system, they don't remember a thing from about an hour before they ingested it, and it won't show up on any toxicology reports. Why sick fucks can come up with this shit and yet can't cure cancer is beyond me.

I signal for the man behind me to approach, and just like we planned, he scoops her up and we make our way out to the kitchen area to get things set up for our little photo shoot.

I stand to the side as Danny arranges Estelle in one of the kitchen chairs, her head lolling from side to side as he ties her to it, and feel nothing but disdain for the woman. I know none of the men here will lay a hand on her, having very strong views about hurting women. I have no such qualms about it, especially when the woman in question is just as much a predator as her husband is.

Once she's secured, we get to work on the second part of our plan, bringing in every piece of incriminating evidence I've been able to grab over the years, plus some added fun stuff that will help hammer home the final nail in Zodiac's coffin—like a dead man's ledger and the gun that killed him.

By the time everything is set up the way I want, Estelle is awake and struggling in her bonds. The guys back out of the kitchen and leave me to it, knowing I'll shout for them if I need a hand.

I grab one of the other chairs from the table, drag it over to Estelle, and sit in front of her.

"Hello, Estelle, it's nice to formally meet you." I greet her with a friendly smile, which freaks her out even more, and she struggles harder.

"I wouldn't bother, the ropes are tight. My man knows what he's doing," I tell her, watching as she carries on until her wrists are bloody and she runs out of steam.

"Well, as fun as this has been, I have places to be. Now I have a few questions and if you answer me truthfully and in a timely fashion, I will get out of your hair before morning."

"Fuck you!" she spits.

"I'll pass, thanks. Tell me, do you know who I am?"

She looks to the left briefly before shaking her head no.

"Liar," I whisper before backhanding her in the face.

She yelps in shock, staring at me with wide eyes. Seriously? Did she think this was going to be a picnic?

"Do you know who I am?" I repeat, daring her to lie again.

"Gemini," she answers quietly.

"And beyond that?"

She hesitates again. "No." The word is barely out of her mouth before I haul back and punch her in the face, making her scream as blood erupts from her nose.

"Fuck! Okay. You're the girl Zodiac bought for Reid. He wanted heirs, a legacy to leave behind when he was gone. He already has Lily."

I slap her again, hard. Once, twice, making her cry out each time.

"He has nothing. He will never get his hands on Lily. You know you disgust me. You're worse than he is. You held down your own sister while she was brutally raped by your husband, you sick fuck. I bet you fucked him in the same bed afterward, rolling around in the sheets stained with your sister's innocence." I seethe, but she doesn't deny it.

She frowns. "How do you know about Joan?" She looks surprised.

I stare at her and realize this woman is as much a psychopath as her husband. I might be fucked up, but I still care about people. Sure, my ability to feel fear and remorse is a little iffy, but my ability to love is surprisingly still intact.

"Your husband decided to kill her in some kind of statement to Lily's father. Seems like a pointless endeavor to me, as he couldn't care less if she lived or died after how she treated her daughter, but me, I can still drum up sympathy for the woman. I mean, fuck, I could have been her," I point out.

She looks at me confused, so I'm guessing Zodiac didn't share that part of his plan with her.

"Tell me, Estelle, was it just Joan you creamed your panties for, or was it all the little girls he brought home and you helped hold down?"

"It wasn't like that. Do you know what it feels like to be told you can't have children? That you can't give babies to the man you love?" she screeches at me.

"No, I don't. Looking at you, I'm guessing God figured out early on you shouldn't be able to procreate." I stand and lean over her, gripping her hair and yanking her head back.

"You made a bunch of traumatized children unwilling surrogates, then once they were pregnant, you brushed them aside. If I had time I would rip you apart and send a piece of you to each of your victims. Only there aren't many left. Suicide, drug overdoses, alcoholism, they all tried to find ways to cope with the horror they had endured at your hands." I glare at her, but there isn't even a flicker of remorse in her eyes.

"I was supposed to be Kai's, but I'm guessing you and Zodiac planned on breaking me in first?"

She doesn't answer but heat flares briefly before she can hide it.

"That's what I thought. You know something, Estelle, I'm

really going to enjoy this," I warn her before I pull back and punch her again. This time I don't stop hitting her until she's out cold and dripping with blood and I'm completely out of breath.

I step back and admire my handiwork for a minute before giving her another dose to keep her out of it for a while.

I walk outside and see my men waiting for me. Knowing the drill, I strip off my clothes and toss them in the bag Baker is holding out for me.

"She still alive?" Danny asks, holding out some baby wipes for my hands and face.

I clean myself up, not bothered that I'm standing outside in nothing more than my underwear, and nod.

"For now. I still need her for leverage. Did I get it all?" I ask, looking up at him.

He takes a fresh wipe and gently runs it over my face before tossing it in the bag. "It's all good. Your spare clothes are in the SUV. Get changed and I'll drop you off. Are you sure about this next part?" he questions softly.

"No. Yes, Maybe." I blow out a harsh breath. "I have to at least try for Kai's sake."

Danny doesn't try to talk me out of it, for that I'm grateful, but I know he thinks this is a bad idea. I can't argue with him though, because he's right, this is a fucking terrible idea.

Seems luck was on my side to find his car parked at the far end of the lot. I sit patiently in the back seat, the tinted rear windows keeping me hidden from prying eyes, and I wait.

I let the quiet soothe me, almost like the starry night sky is a blanket that I wrap around myself for comfort. If I closed my eyes, I'd be asleep in seconds and likely wouldn't wake up for a year.

I spot him approaching out of the corner of my eye. He looks tired as he rubs a hand over his handsome face, but I have little sympathy. I shuffle down until I'm lying flat and bring my gun up, ready.

He opens the door and climbs in, shutting it behind him before he freezes. I don't know how, but I know he senses me somehow, so I sit up and point my gun at the back of his head.

"Hello, Jude."

"Cherry," he answers warily.

"Drive, please, we need to have a chat."

He doesn't say anything, just stares at me in the rearview mirror before sighing and starting the car.

He waits until he pulls out of the lot onto the quiet side street before talking. "I can't believe you did this in front of the station."

"I can't believe you're a cop, but hey ho, life is surprising."

"Cherry," he sighs.

"Oh no, I'm not your Cherry, not anymore. Tell me something, does Kai know you're a cop?"

His shoulders slump. "No."

"Start at the beginning and don't leave anything out. Lie to me, and I will put a pretty little hole in your head."

He grips the steering wheel hard, and for a minute, I think he's going to choose the latter of the two options before he speaks.

"You know that Zodiac is my father?"

When I nod, he continues.

"I always knew. My mom wrote a letter, paranoid that he would hunt us down when she ran. It explained everything that had happened, how he had raped her and she fell pregnant with Kai and me."

"After we were born, she knew she had to get away, but Zodiac always kept one of us with a guard, knowing she wouldn't run and leave the other behind."

"Until she did," I whisper.

He nods, looking sad. "She was twelve. She thought if she could just get away, she could get help, and the police would storm the building, and everything would be okay. Only once she was free, her terror at the thought of somehow ending up back there kept her silent. There was a car crash. I was thrown from the wreckage, my car seat and all, which is what protected me. A cop found me and the letter my mother carried everywhere. He took me home, changed my name from Jude Reid to Jude Daniels, and faked it to look like I died right along with my mother."

"What the fuck? Why would he do that?" My heart races at the thought that Jude escaped one monster only to end up in the hands of another.

"Because his sister was one of Zodiac's first victims. She hung herself when she found out she was pregnant. There was not enough evidence to press charges, hell he wasn't even brought in for questioning."

"And so he raised you, knowing you could be the key to getting the evidence he needed," I answer, feeling sick at the thought of him being a pawn.

"He was a good man. He loved me, but it was no secret that he expected me to join the force and pick up where he left off, to bring Zodiac down."

I sit quietly for a moment as Jude drives aimlessly around the city.

"When did you meet Kai?"

"When we were both nineteen. I had intel that he would be at a club on the outskirts of the city. I accidentally on purpose bumped into him coming out of the bathroom. Anyway, long story short, I convinced him that I wanted to get to know him, but without Zodiac knowing about me. Kai was smart enough to know Zodiac would be a wildcard. In the end, Kai's need to get to know me better won out over his need to spill his guts to his father."

"Fast forward, however many years. How does that lead to you and Kai playing a dangerous version of the parent trap?"

"I claimed I wanted to get to know him, see if I might be welcomed back in the fold. I had to prove myself to Kai first, so we switched places, and I had to..." He pauses for a minute. "...do things that Kai was expected to do," he answers vaguely, but I can fill in the blanks. He had to beat people, torture them, perhaps even kill, all in the name of snagging Zodiac.

"But it's been years, so what changed?"

"Zodiac only became more and more unstable. I think Kai realized that Zodiac would sooner kill me than welcome me back with open arms, but by then, we had fallen into a sort of routine. And, surprisingly, we liked being brothers. Kai was happy for things to stay as they were, and I used my time spent with Zodiac to collect evidence." He shrugs.

"Did you ever stop to think what this would do, *will do* to Kai when he finds out?"

Jude, at least, has the grace to look ashamed. "I love him. He's my brother, but he can't see past his loyalty to Zodiac and I can't let that man keep doing what he's doing."

Well, at least we both agree on that. "I wouldn't be so sure about Kai's loyalty to Zodiac right now. When he messaged you the other day to tell you to switch off the camera in your apartment, did you do it?"

"Yes. We had only had them set up for a few days, so I figured there was an issue. He told me he would explain everything later, but he hasn't called yet." He frowns.

"Zodiac ordered Kai to kill me and that's what the video will show. It's only after you switched it off that I miraculously came alive and left."

"What the fuck, Cherry?" He brakes abruptly before swerving to the side of the road and stopping.

"Seems like he's not the only brother trying to kill me.

Look, I don't have time to fill you in on everything, but here is what you do need to know. At the planetarium on Saturday, Zodiac is going to be responsible for multiple murders. My men and I will be in place to take him down. If you want all the evidence to finally prove his guilt, you'll find it up at his ranch. Estelle was very helpful."

"Jesus fuck, Viddy, he will kill you!"

"I'm already dead, Jude. Now stay away from Kai, and please stay the fuck away from the apartment. You are the only thing left Kai cares about, and Zodiac will take you out to hurt him.

"I saw the footage from the shoot-out at your place," he says softly.

"Yeah, so did Kai. He now knows the truth about his father. Imagine what it's going to do to him to find out his brother is a cop who used him. Just, please, for the love of God, stay away from him, at least until after Saturday. And keep your head down. Zodiac has a hit out on you, after all."

I open the back door and climb out, but before I can close it, he calls my name.

"For what it's worth, I'm sorry about everything."

"Yeah, me too, Jude, but it doesn't change a damn thing now, does it?"

# CHAPTER THIRTY-EIGHT

I walked into the planetarium under a shroud of a black starless sky. It's like the heavens already know there will be bloodshed tonight.

Wearing all black, I wait in the shadows for the players to arrive. Once all the pawns are in place, it will be time for the queen to make her move.

The division heads are looking around confused as each of them has a robed and hooded person sitting on a chair in front of them. None of them say anything because they know better than to question Zodiac, but I can feel the tension in the air even from back here. There is nothing distinguishable about the people in baggy shapeless robes, and with them seated, it's even impossible to tell if they are male or female. The only thing that sets one apart from the other is an emblem stitched into the breast pocket showing the corresponding star sign for the division head behind them.

None of the robed figures struggle or try to break free, which I'm sure is adding to the confusion. If they were here against their will, they would fight, right? Yeah, not with the potent cocktail of drugs running through their systems. I'd be surprised if any of them could stay upright without the ropes strapping them to the chairs, keeping them in place.

The only things out of place are the empty space where Kai's hooded person would sit and the space where I should be standing. Sure, there is a robed and hooded person sitting in the empty spot where I *should* be, apparently sacrificing me isn't enough. Zodiac wants to make an example out of me. Not that it matters. I planned for this too.

"Let's begin," Zodiac starts, climbing to his feet. I watch from behind him as he walks down the empty floor space, surrounded by the division heads.

"I know you all thought you'd be gathered here today to welcome a new Cancer, but it has come to my attention that there is dissension in our ranks. Some of you have been getting too big for your boots and need reminding what will happen if you cross me," he says, his voice filled with glee.

"And so this will serve as your reminder."

He pulls his gun from his jacket and makes his way around the circle, firing one shot into the head of each hooded figure until he casually stops and reloads the gun before continuing.

Jesus. I thought he would make this some kind of

initiation test, but Zodiac has completely gone off the deep end.

He stops when he has only one hooded person left upright.

Gemini's sacrificial offering.

Kai stands frozen as a statue, his hands clenched so tight I can see the white of his knuckles from here.

"Ah, Kai, you are perhaps my favorite son." The voices whisper around the room before Zodiac screams at them, "*Silence!*"

"Your mother sure was a pretty little thing, but she had a defiance in her that was hard to break. Seems we are attracted to the same kind of woman."

"I like them out of training bras, so I guess we differ there." Kai's voice echoes around the room, making my chest tighten.

Shit, keep it together, Kai.

Zodiac, however, just waves him off before continuing, "I'll give her her dues though, she managed to not only produce one heir to the throne, but two. I can't begin to explain how upset I was when she ran with your brother and was killed in an unfortunate car crash—such a waste."

Zodiac steps closer to Kai as all eyes watch them, unable to look away from the scene unfolding.

"I'll admit, I'm happy you managed to take out Gemini like I asked. That video will be one I watch over and over. Such raw passion." He sighs, making my mouth water with the urge to hurl. "But, there is still the need to deal with your deception. Now, I'm a reasonable man, and after what you did to Gemini, well, it's eased my wrath a touch. This sacrifice was going to be about her, but now she's not here, is she?"

He shrugs. "Actually, this one might be better. I believe your beloved Gemini cared deeply about this person, perhaps almost as much as you do. Shoot him," Zodiac orders as I edge a touch closer with my gun in my hand.

Fuck, fuck, fuck. Zodiac is a lying bastard. As far as he knows, Wyatt is under that hood. He's just testing Kai, and Kai will fail because he doesn't know that it's not Jude under there.

"Shoot him now, or I'll shoot you," Zodiac snaps.

"So, shoot me, *Dad*," Kai snaps sarcastically. "I'll welcome the relief of being free from you once and for all."

"Such fucking disloyalty. I have the video of you, I can send it to every police station in the country and have you arrested for first-degree murder. Shall I remind you of the footage?"

He shoves his hand in his pocket and pulls out a remote, flicking a button until the big screen above us is filled with images of Kai and me kissing, tearing off our clothes as we make our way down the hallway to the bedroom.

"Shoot him," Zodiac orders.

"Fuck you," Kai bites out.

"So be it," Zodiac answers before lifting his gun and firing a shot into the robed person's head.

Kai roars and moves toward the body as it slumps forward but freezes when the gun swings to point at him.

"Well, I guess this answers so many of my questions. It's a shame, Kai, you really did have so much potential."

As the image of Kai and me falling onto the bed together plays, a high-pitched noise makes everyone wince before the image changes to a lone figure sitting with a hood over their head and a robe covering their body. You can't see who the figure is, but you can damn well see the kitchen they're in.

"Estelle," Zodiac roars, seeing the image. The person lifts their head and moans as if they can hear him.

"You," Zodiac screams at Kai, which is when I step out of the shadows with my gun pointed at his head.

"Actually, it was me, and if you want your precious Estelle to live through the night, you'll drop the gun."

"Fuck you, you dirty whore. I should have killed you myself." His accent comes out into full force with his anger.

"Yeah, you really should have," I agree. Zodiac's face bleaches white when he sees a masked figure on the screen press a gun to Estelle's temple.

"Drop the fucking gun," I spit out.

Surprisingly, he does. I don't pretend to understand what the deal is with him and Estelle, they are as fucked up as each other, but they do genuinely seem to love each other in their weird and twisted way.

I look to Kai, whose eyes are blazing, and mouth for him to trust me before I turn back to face the rest of the room. I pull off the black beanie I had been wearing and my hair tumbles over my shoulders, showing the rest of the division heads who I am.

"So, fun fact, guys, I'm not dead. Sorry if that pisses a few of you off, but we'll get to that."

I hear Cash snort, but I don't look at him, keeping my eyes firmly on Zodiac.

"Did you all know how big of a pedophile Zodiac was? I mean, I know the man has issues but, Jesus Christ. And he sure likes to spread his seed about too. A Hitler for the new ages as he tries to create his own supergroup. In case you're not picking up what I'm putting down, all of you are brothers, thanks to Zodiac here raping your mothers at one time or another. Anywhoo," I continue as people start to get louder now, whispering angrily, "except me. He wanted me to call him daddy, I'm sure, but perhaps not in the same way. Did you know he bought me off another man when I was still a little girl?"

I shake my head in disgust. "True story. Well, no more. As of today, Zodiac's dictatorship is over."

"I will kill you, you'll never set foot in this city without being hunted down and slaughtered like the bitch you are." Spittle flies from his mouth as he seethes.

"Oh, Gianni—you don't mind if I call you that, do you?" I step closer to him, putting extra sway in my hips. "You're not the boss here now, I am."

He throws his head back and laughs maniacally before turning to look at the people watching in the circle.

"She'll be your downfall. I made you all and I say—"

"Lord, help me with this one," I mutter, cutting him off.

"Leo, if you would be so kind." I look at Cash and he winks, lifting a remote just like Zodiac's from his pocket. He steps out to stand to the right of Zodiac.

The video changes above us to the cargo hold, showing the people collected there.

"What the fuck?" I turn to see Taurus looking at a freeze-frame of his sister on the screen before horror takes over his features, and he looks down at the figure in front of him.

"Hey, Taurus, trust me for a minute, okay?"

He looks up, his eyes filled with despair and hate, but he grits his teeth and holds his ground.

"Each of you has a person in front of you who, I'm sorry to say, is about as dead as they can get, thanks to Zodiac here. Bullet holes to the head are hard to come back from. Zodiac handpicked each of these people because they meant something to you and he wanted to send you all messages. It seems like daddy dearest doesn't like it when his kiddos go off plan."

"This man," I point at Zodiac as I circle closer to him, seeing the rest of my team melt out of the shadows behind the other division heads, "is not the man you want at your back. Why should you be loyal to him when he doesn't return it? You are his puppets. All your pretty penthouses are wired with high-end cameras. He knows everything, sees everything, and uses what he can as a weapon while pointing his fingers at everyone else."

I keep my gun trained on Zodiac even as I lift my head

and take in the rest of the division heads. "But Zodiac is not in power here anymore, I am. If you want to stay, then you should know that things are going to change around here because shit like that," I point at the screen above, "won't fly with me."

"Why would we follow you? You're nothing. I could rule better than you." I turn to look at Virgo just as Zodiac pulls a second gun from behind his back. I shoot him in the shoulder and when he drops the gun, I walk over to him, with mine pointed firmly at his head once more. I kick the other one over to Leo.

"Now that wasn't nice, was it?" I kick him hard in the back of his legs and watch with satisfaction as his knees give out and he crumples to the floor.

"Now, where was I? Oh yes, Virgo, Virgo, Virgo. You are a lot more like your father than most people in this room, but if you take another look at the footage, you'll see your little sister too." He gasps, just spotting her, as she is mostly obscured by the large man standing in front of her.

"Daddy just blew her brains out for you, but in her case, I'm sure it's a relief because you love your sister just a little too much now, don't you?" He moves to yank the hood of the fallen figure in front of him, but Leo cocks his gun and aims it at Virgo's head.

"Ah-ah, no touching. Danny?" I call and watch as my man materializes beside Virgo.

"Oh good, you're here. Let's show these lovely people all the reasons why I should be queen. Well, apart from the obvious fact I would look wicked with a crown," I muse, making Danny snort.

"Let's start with Taurus," I order, knowing he was barely holding himself together, and yet he held back on my word.

"Taurus, if you declare your loyalty to me, I will declare it to you and as an extension, your family. So that this will never happen again." I point at the screen before Baker steps out from the shadows and pulls the hood from the figure in front of Taurus. Seeing the person slumped over, Taurus's legs almost give out, but Baker reaches up and steadies him.

"This is Hector Ramierios. He is the man who snatched your sister from outside her school. She is safe and looking forward to seeing you later," I tell Taurus softly.

He stares at me, a dozen fleeting emotions flit across his face before he crosses one arm over his chest and nods respectfully.

"Next up, Virgo." Danny moves into position and rips the hood from the body. Virgo howls and moves to grab Danny, but Leo shoots a warning shot his way.

"John Peters, your best friend, I believe, Virgo. Or former best friend, I should say. He too liked your sister and figured if you could bang her, so could he. Your sister is safe from him now," I tell him and watch his shoulders relax, so he misses when I lift my gun and aim it, "but she is also safe from you." I fire and watch it hit him in the face, the blood spraying on Danny, making him curse.

I carry on moving around the circle, revealing each hooded person's identity and securing the division head's loyalty until all that remains is the hooded figure sitting in front of my usual spot.

"So, Gianni," I spin and address the man on his knees who has been surprisingly quiet.

"Obviously, you know by now the name of the game is switcharoo. Now, as much as I would like to kill you and I really, really would love nothing more than to choke you with your own entrails, I think that's letting you off too lightly. You have spent years, decades even, destroying lives in the cruelest way possible, so why should I show you any mercy?

"The person you chose as my sacrifice? Well, let's just say if you were successful, I would have burned this city to the ground, including that pretty little ranch style house you and your lovely wife own.

"Say hi to the camera, Estelle," I say as the video feed flips back to Estelle's kitchen, but I keep my eyes on Zodiac.

"Leave her the fuck alone," he roars, trying to get to his feet, but he freezes when the hood comes off to reveal a smiling Wyatt.

"Switch," is the only thing he says as Thomas wheels in an old school wheelchair leftover from when Shadow Falls was still a hospital. I lift my gun and aim it at the hooded figure seated in the wheelchair.

Thomas leaves the wheelchair in the empty space in front of Kai before stepping back into the shadows.

"Bet you wish you were nicer to me now, huh?" I tease.

Zodiac moves to stand again, but Taurus steps out from his spot and places his gun against his temple.

I nod in thanks. I didn't need his help, but I appreciate it's his way of showing his support.

"Say goodbye to your wife, Gianni."

"No, no, stop, what do you want?" he begs.

"I want you to tell everyone here what you did. I want you to admit to them all what a monster you are, and don't you dare miss any of the details, or so help me God, I will shoot first and ask you to repeat yourself after."

Kai makes his way to me and wraps a possessive arm around my chest from behind, holding me close as he nuzzles my temple. We all stand in silence as Zodiac bows his head, and for the next hour, he admits every crime he committed. By the time he's finished, his voice is hoarse, and any loyalty the division heads might have still had is shattered beyond repair.

"There, I've done what you asked, now let her go. I told you everything," he growls.

"You did," I agree with a soothing voice before addressing the hooded figure in the wheelchair. "You get everything you need?"

The figure stands and pulls the hood off, making curses ring out around the room, but no louder than Kai's

"What the fuck?" Kai spits out.

"Yeah, Cherry, I got it," Jude replies quietly, stepping forward and placing a soft kiss against my lips before pulling back.

I fight back the tears and ignore the look of longing in his eyes. There is no going back from this. He stands on one side of the law while I'm firmly on the other.

"No, nooo, where's my wife, you fucking bitch?" Zodiac screams.

Jude walks over to him, pulling off his robe and revealing jeans and a white T-shirt underneath with his badge hanging around his neck. Kai goes rock solid behind me, so I reach my free hand up and rub it soothingly over his arm.

"You're going to arrest me?" Zodiac spits incredulously.

"You bet your sorry fucking ass I am. Gemini bought everyone in this room temporary immunity, and in exchange, we get you."

"You fucking cocksucker. Where is my wife? I want my lawyer," he bellows.

Jude turns to face me and Kai, a look of sad resignation on his face.

"Everyone is free to leave. I only came for Zodiac," he tells me softly.

"I knew you would come. That's why I left Thomas out there waiting for you with the robe and the wheelchair. Everything that happened tonight was recorded. I'll send you the footage—"

Zodiac's screaming cuts me off.

"I want my fucking wife or so help me God," he spits. I pull free from Kai and walk over to Zodiac, nodding at Leo, who moves into position.

"I'm afraid that's not going to be possible at this time and you really have nobody to blame but yourself."

I nod toward Leo, who pulls the hood from the figure sitting in Gemini's spot. The figure he thought was Wyatt. With the hood gone, Estelle's dark brown hair tumbles down over her shoulders. Her eyes are swollen shut and her face is bruised from the beating I gave her, but she looks peaceful, almost as if she's sleeping, or she would if it wasn't for the fact that part of her brain is splattered all over her face.

Zodiac roars, trying to get to her, but Jude pushes him to the floor and pins him down with his knee against his back.

"Viddy?" Jude looks at me with questions in his eyes. Yeah, he would never have given me immunity if he knew about this.

"She was as much a part of this as he was, so don't look at me like that. She held down her kid sister while her husband raped her over and over again. But then she got a taste for it. She got off on the power of being his wife. I might be a monster, but Zodiac and Estelle are as evil as they come. These guys," I swing my arm around to encompass everyone else in the room, "are my family and I'll protect them at all costs, so don't expect me to be sorry because I'm not."

He looks at me, a dozen things running through his eyes.

"He sanctioned my death. Excuse me if I have zero fucks to give. If he hadn't fired his gun, his wife would still be alive and in a fancy prison cell of her own." I shrug callously. He might not like it, but it's not my problem.

"Everyone clear out. Cops will be here soon. Your family members who were in the cargo hold are being returned home as we speak. I'll be in touch," I call out to the room and watch as they all nod and clear out, my men following suit.

Taurus stops as he passes me. "Thank you," he acknowledges.

"You're welcome." I smile, and I mean it. He turns and leaves without a backward glance until the only people remaining with me are Kai, Jude, and a hissing Zodiac.

"Everything else you might need on him to make this case airtight is up at the ranch, including enough drugs to get him for distribution." I look behind me at Kai, who can't take his eyes off Jude's badge.

"Was it all a lie just to get to him?" Kai asks Jude, his voice void of all emotion.

"To start with, but it hasn't been that way for a long time. I wanted my brother in my life, but you refused to see Zodiac for who he really is."

"Maybe if you had told me what you knew—" Kai snaps, but I place my hand on his chest to stop him from lunging.

"You wouldn't have believed him, Kai," I tell him softly. "You had to see what he was truly like, yourself."

"I don't know why you're defending him. He's the one that exposed you to Zodiac," Kai snaps at me.

"I know. Worse still, he did it knowing exactly who I was, didn't you, Jude?" I look over at him as he stands pressing his foot against Zodiac's back.

"He was untouchable. I needed someone who could put a chink in his amour. But you became so much more than I anticipated." He swallows.

"I forgive you. I know you kept your mouth shut about Megan, so for that at least I'll let this all go. But this is over now. It has to be." I step forward, cup his jaw and kiss him like it's the last time my lips will ever touch his, because it is.

I pull back, wipe the stray tear from my face just as the cops start pouring in.

"I love you, Jude, but don't come back."

"And you, where do you stand?" Jude asks Kai.

"At her back, where I was always supposed to be," he replies, making me swallow hard.

"Just like that? After everything he did, you'll take him back?"

"He saved me, and when faced with an impossible choice, he chose me, so yeah, Jude, just like that."

Kai slips his fingers through mine and pulls me toward the door. I feel a dozen pairs of eyes on me, but nobody tries to stop us. I turn one last time and find Jude watching me and his brother; the look of pain on his face is so stark it makes me want to run back to him, but I don't.

I'm not the white picket girl who colors inside the lines.

I'm fire and chaos with a little bit of mayhem thrown in for good measure.

We walk down the twisted path to my waiting SUV. Climbing inside, I pull Kai in behind me.

Ben sits in the driver's seat, waiting for us to close the doors. "Where to, V?" he asks softly, sensing the somber mood.

"Home, please Ben, take us home."

# CHAPTER THIRTY-NINE

"You okay?" I stroke my fingers lazily over Kai's chest as my head rests in the crook of his arm.

"No," he rolls me onto my back and looms down over me, "but I will be." He strokes his hand down the side of my face before dipping his head and taking my mouth in a blistering kiss.

I bend my legs and cradle his hips with my knees, feeling his hard cock press against me.

"I should have said this earlier, but I'm clean. I got tested when I moved out here because, you know, and well, you're the only guy I've been with that way and—" He cuts me off with another kiss, sliding his cock up and down my slick folds, our earlier lovemaking doing nothing to dampen our arousal. It feels like we'll never be sated.

"I'm clean too, and I've never been with someone ungloved. What about birth control?" he asks softly.

"I have the implant—ah fuck," I gasp as he surges inside me.

"Shit," he groans, dipping his head and burying it against the side of my neck.

I cross my ankles behind him and hold on tight as he fucks me in slow lazy strokes, working us both into a frenzy until I can't take it anymore and I rake my nails down his back as I convulse around him. He roars out his own release and spills himself inside me before collapsing on top of me.

"Can't breathe," I mumble, making him laugh. He lifts his weight onto one of his forearms before gently pulling himself free.

I feel his cum run out of me and make a face. "You know they make this seem much sexier in my books," I grumble.

"I don't know," he pulls back and takes the cover with him, scooting down my body, "seeing my cum run out of you, knowing it's marked you where nobody else has been? Fuck, it's making me hard again."

I flush. "Jesus, you're a caveman."

"You might be right there, Red, but I don't hear you complaining. Now let's get cleaned up and eat. As tempting as you look right now, I don't want to fuck you into a wheelchair." He grins.

"No kidding. Your dick should come with a warning label," I agree as he climbs off the bed and picks me up, carrying me to the bathroom.

"A girl could get used to this," I tease as he reaches over and turns on the shower and climbs inside with me still in his arms.

I kiss him softly, before pulling back so he can lower me to my feet.

We don't speak as we get cleaned up and climb out, drying off side by side before dressing.

I watch him as I slip into a pair of short sleep shorts and a tank top before blasting my hair with the hairdryer until it's sleek and shiny.

By the time I'm done, he's on the end of the bed with his head in his hands.

"Hey," I say, sitting next to him. He slides his large hand over my thigh, against my bare skin.

"I don't know where to go from here," he admits without looking at me.

"Then don't go anywhere. Stay here with me."

He lifts his head and stares at me, guilt in his eyes. "I could have killed you. If you had moved, even an inch to the left, you'd have been dead."

"But I didn't, and because of you, I was able to bring him down. I'm not sorry he's going to rot in jail, but I am sorry that you got hurt in the process," I tell him, biting my lip. Zodiac might be a dick of epic proportions, but he was still his father.

"Jesus, is that what you think? He tried to have the woman I love killed. He tried to kill Jude, and as much as I'm pissed at him right now, I don't want him dead. The only reason I didn't lose my shit and kill Zodiac last night was that you asked me to trust you. So I did."

"I'm still sorry it all played out the way it did. I couldn't risk letting you in on the plan though, I'm sorry."

"No, Red, don't you dare fucking apologize. Not for any of it. I'm..." he rubs his hand over his face before looking back at me, "I'm just waiting for you to come to your senses and tell me to go."

"Yeah, that's not gonna happen, sorry to disappoint you. You're stuck with me now, even if I have to tie you to my bed and keep you as my sex slave."

"Well, I can't refuse an offer like that now, can I?" He leans toward me and kisses me, his hand sliding up the inside of my thigh.

"No, down boy. If I don't eat something before we start again, I'm going to die. And I'd kinda like to make it to my birthday tomorrow." I stand and offer him my hand. "Feed me, then fuck me, deal?"

He slips his hand in mine. "Deal, nice doing business with you. And FYI, as a birthday treat, I'm willing to accept the terms of being your sex slave. My gift to you." He winks.

"Best present ever." I grin.

My phone chooses that moment to ring, making me groan.

He laughs. "Ah, the joys of being the boss."

"Yeah about that, are you okay with this?"

"What, being bossed around? As long as when we're in

the bedroom I'm the boss, then yeah, I'm game. I never wanted the crown anyway."

I smile, relieved, and answer the phone.

"Hey, Baker, what's up?"

"There are some people here to see you, V."

I frown and glance at the clock on my bedside table.

"Baker, it's eleven pm," I remind him.

There's a noise on the other end before Wyatt's voice comes over the line. "Viddy, you're going to want to see this," he tells me softly, then hangs up.

Urgh, I hate it when he does that. He's lucky he's going home in a few days, or I would kick his ass.

"Come on, seems someone needs to talk to me, and they have decided that the middle of the night is the best time to do it."

I make my way toward the living area where the voices are coming from, Kai beside me holding my hand as we step into the warmly lit room, and I'm hit by a battering ram. Kai grabs me before I can go flying, thankfully, but I wrap my arms tightly around the person who tried to put me on my ass.

When she pulls back, I see tears in her eyes. "Viddy," she says a touch too softly.

"Megan." I smile, wiping her cheeks.

I hear a scuffle and see two men trying to hold back a third. I take in their leather jackets and quickly realize these guys are bikers, and not just any bikers, but Chaos Demons, the same club that hurt Megan.

I shove her behind me protectively and growl. "What the fuck are you doing here?"

That sets my men on guard. Seeing that I deem them hostile, they draw their weapons and aim.

"Viddy, stop, they aren't hurting me. These are my men," Megan yells, shoving her way to stand protectively in front of the men she arrived with.

"Yeah, you remember that thing I needed to explain?" Wyatt interrupts, but I glare at him, making him shut up.

"I'm happy, Viddy, I swear to you. I've never been happier in my life than I am right now."

I look at her, taking in her flushed face and bright eyes. I can see what she's saying is true, so I step back and relax next to Kai, who remains silent, watching the bikers.

The biker who had been struggling finally pulls free from his friends and tries to move around Megan, but she stops him. "Grim, no."

He's closer now, so I study his large muscular frame covered in denim jeans and a black T-shirt beneath his leather jacket. He has a few days' worth of stubble on his face, and his eyes—

I freeze solid for a moment as recognition dawns.

I slip my hand into the back of Kai's jeans and grab his gun and aim it at *Grim*, flicking the safety off.

"Viddy, no, please," Megan begs as the two other bikers pull their guns, aiming them at me, which makes Megan scream.

"No, stop it, all of you, God fucking damn it," she curses.

Grim takes a step toward me. "Chicken."

"Don't," I choke. He can't be here, not now, not after everything.

"Vida, please, I've been looking for you for so long."

"Yeah? Well, maybe you shouldn't have fucking abandoned me in the first place," I bark.

"Viddy, who is this guy?" Kai grunts.

"Not that it's any of your business, but I'm her brother," Grim growls at him.

"Everything about Viddy is my business. Now, if you don't want me to rip out your spleen and feed it to you, you'll back off."

"I'm her brother," he snaps once more, but I'm done. So fucking done.

"Once upon a time maybe, but that was a lifetime ago for me. Looks like you found a new family, so go back to them, you're not welcome in mine," I spit venomously.

"Viddy!" Megan gasps, shocked.

"No, Megan, I'm sorry. You know I love you, but this was a shitty thing for you to do."

"He just wanted to find you, make things right—"

"Yeah? And what about what I want? You think I like being blindsided by a ghost in my home?" Her face flashes with guilt because she knows I'm right.

I look at the man who now goes by *Grim* and lay it all out, the whole burden I've been carrying that I never even shared with Megan. I don't even care who hears it.

"You left me and you never came back. I wrote to you,

Jesus, I wrote so many letters begging you to come home." My arm wobbles a little under the weight of Kai's gun, so I drop my arm for a minute.

"I didn't get any letters, Vida," he replies softly.

"Bullshit. I wrote you one every single day for four years until Mama told me to give up, you must be dead, and it was time to move on."

He finches and shakes his head. "I didn't get any letters, V, I swear it."

"I suppose you forgot your way home, too," I whisper.

"I have no excuse; I saw things over there that I couldn't handle—"

I cut him off again with a laugh that sounds dark and twisted. "Couldn't handle it? You couldn't handle it?" I repeat, struggling to make sense of his words.

I look him dead in the eye and force my shame out through my lips. "He came to my room every night. He sodomized me until blood ran down my legs, and throat fucked me until I turned blue and passed out. But even then, I prayed for you to come save me. I was twelve years old when it started, and fourteen when I realized I was on my fucking own and if I wanted saving, I had to do it myself."

I suck in a deep breath and see Wyatt holding my brother back, who has tears running down his face. Megan is sobbing quietly into the arms of one of the other bikers and I'm vaguely aware of Kai's hands on my hips and his heat at my back, offering me his silent support.

"The day Mama died, he decided I was too old for him, so

he sold me, but he still wanted his one last night with his favorite doll." I take a deep breath and blow it out.

"I couldn't do it anymore, not one more second, and I certainly wasn't swapping one cage for another, so when he climbed into bed with me, I shot him point blank and killed him."

I take a step close to my brother, Kai following along right behind me.

"I lived on the streets. Days would go by where I would be so hungry, I would rummage through trash for food, not caring it was riddled with maggots and flies. I was so thin my skin was translucent, and you could count each of my ribs. Some days, I so badly just wanted to lay down in the gutter and die, and yet I couldn't. I had to prove to myself, and to the ghost of Mama and the memory of you, that I was worth something. That one day, I would be more than just the throwaway girl. And I did. I survived; I'm loved. And now you want to come back and tie a fucking bow on it? Fuck you. You don't get me now that I might be of use to you." I turn and run out of the room.

It might make me a coward, but if I stayed a second longer, I would have shot him for the audacity of showing up, or myself to stop the vile voices shouting in my head.

I ignore people calling my name and disappear into one of the tunnels. I keep going even when my steps slow, and my breath burns in my lungs.

I end up on the far side of the cemetery and keep walking until I'm in the heart of the city. By now, my bare feet are bleeding, and I have a stitch that feels more like I've been stabbed in the side. I make my way to the penthouse as it is the closest place I can think of that I can get off the streets. I know better than to leave without protection, especially now that I'm the boss.

I make my way there and head for the elevator, hitting the button for the top floor. It isn't until I'm in the hallway that I remember I don't have my bag or the key to get in.

Sighing, I turn to head back and then see the door that leads to the roof and think *fuck it*. It seems as good a place as any to hideout.

I swing the door open and limp out onto the flat top, moving to the edge of the building so I can look down.

The lights of the city make everything look so pretty from up here, hiding the darker underbelly beneath their neon glow. I climb up on the ledge and swing my feet over, sitting down to finally rest.

I'm beyond tired. I'm mentally, emotionally, and physically exhausted. I think if I laid down right here, I would sleep for an eternity, completely oblivious to the world around me.

Come morning, I'm sure I'll be embarrassed. I spewed all that shit out, airing my dirty laundry for all to judge. Now they will see precisely how tainted I am.

The gutter queen.

I'm still reeling from seeing Drake after all this time. I hurt him; I know I did. My words lashed against his skin as if I were flaying him open with a knife and I relished in it. I wanted him to hurt as much as I had been, but now as I sit here alone, I'm angry at myself for losing control.

I don't know how long I sit here, but it's long enough that my body is shaking from the cold and a pink tint has lightened the night sky.

I start when a pair of denim-clad legs climb up and sit on the ledge beside me. I look up and jolt again when I see his face.

"What are you doing here, Jude?" My voice comes out sounding hoarse, as if I've started smoking twenty cigarettes a day.

"Kai called. Everyone was frantically trying to find you until you turned up here and Baker spotted you on the security camera."

"Right, of course, the cameras." Such an idiot.

I look away, but he cups my jaw, turning me to look at him.

"Why are you here? Have you come to see how the mighty have fallen? From queen to trash all in one night because that's who I really am, Jude. Beneath the designer clothes and expensive heels is the same dirty girl you met that day in the alleyway."

"Good, because that's the girl I fell for even when I knew it was wrong. That girl grew up to be the strongest, most formidable woman I have ever met."

I let the tears fall then, as he crushes me to his chest, having zero strength to hold them back. I cry so hard it's like a dam has burst, and I don't know if I'll ever be able to stop.

All the while, Jude just holds me, running his hand up and down my spine in a soothing gesture.

Eventually, the tears stop, even though my body still jerks as my breath hitches in my chest.

"Let's get you home. You're freezing," he coaxes, rubbing his hands up and down my arms. That's when I notice he's only in a T-shirt himself.

I nod and wait for him to stand before twisting and letting him help me up. I wince when I stand, feet feeling raw.

"What is it?"

"My feet are a little sore, but I'll be okay."

He bends to take a look before cursing. "Christ Cherry, these are a mess." He scoops me up before I can protest.

"Wait, Kai's gun."

He dips me so I can grab the gun from the ledge and then stand, tucking me into him as if to shelter me from the cold.

"Why did you come for me?"

"I told you, everyone was worried."

"Yeah, but why you? You're not a part of this world anymore, Jude. You can't just pop in and out. It's not safe."

He doesn't answer. He just stares at the elevator door with his jaw tense.

"Jude," I try again as the door slides open.

He walks us inside and hits the button to close the doors. I wait for him to press the button for the ground floor, but he doesn't. He stands there, his breathing picking up speed as he holds me tighter, then suddenly he stalks forward and pushes me up against the elevator wall.

"My superiors wanted me to bring you in. They wanted me to set you up using any means necessary. It's never fucking ending, and no matter which side I'm on, you are always in the middle," he growls, letting the wall take some of my weight.

I close my eyes in resignation but snap them open again when his hand slides up the inside of my thigh, the baggy shorts offering no resistance as he hooks my panties with his pinky finger and pulls the material away from my pussy.

"What's going on? Is this your final *fuck you* before you bring me in? Huh? Is that what this is?" I shout.

He slides two fingers inside me, making me hiss. The fact that I'm wet makes me want to punch myself as much as I want to punch him.

"Get the fuck off me! You made your choice, now move," I yell, bucking against him but he just yanks my shorts and panties off before hoisting me back up again. I struggle as he undoes his fly and frees his heavy cock and positions it against my pussy.

"Jude," the panic in my voice is clear for both of us to hear. He freezes for a moment, pressing his forehead against mine.

"I told them to fuck off. I quit, Cherry, I choose you," he whispers before surging inside me.

I scream in shock as his words penetrate.

"What?"

"I choose you, today, tomorrow, and every day," he answers, pulling almost all the way out before sliding back in to the hilt.

I sob as he fucks me, unable to stop myself as my body ignites under his touch and with his words. I grip his hair and kiss him hard, holding him tight to me in case he tries to let me go.

He fucks me hard and deep, hitting a spot inside me that makes me clench around him.

When I come, I bury my face in his neck and shout out his name, feeling him jerk inside me. That's when I realize we didn't use a condom.

And I just fucked Kai's brother.

"Oh, God," I groan.

"Hey, it's okay, I'm clean." He lowers me to my feet gently, then tucks himself away as I scramble to slide my clothes back on.

"I need to talk to Kai."

"Hey, it's going to be okay. Kai and I have shit to work out, but we will because that's what brothers do. And as for you, well, the bastard can fight me for you or learn to share. He managed to share a womb for nine months with me. I'm sure we'll figure it out. And, Cherry, he talked about this with me before everything became such a mess. He was the one who proposed the idea of sharing you, so he'll be on board, eventually. After he's thrown a few punches. Now let's get you home."

I nod, speechless, as Jude hits the descend button

because what else can I do? Kai would have every right to be pissed even if they did pass me between them for a year. I still should have talked to him first.

When the doors slide open, I realize I've lost Kai's gun again. *Jesus Christ.*

"Erm...I appear to be missing a gun again." I chew my lip, making him laugh.

He pulls it from behind him and offers it to me.

"I took it. I didn't want you shooting my dick off before I could explain." He reaches to lift me, but I can see his car through the glass doors, so it's not too far for me to walk.

"I'm okay Jude, promise. I can walk. Besides, if anyone is watching, I don't want to look weak," I admit.

He sighs but nods. "Fine, come on. Kai will be losing his mind."

He grabs my free hand and tugs me toward the door, holding it open for me to pass through.

It's starting to get light now. I spot a couple of people on the street and a few cars milling about. Jude closes the door and steps beside me as the couple approaching get closer. One of them calls out, "Hey, Jude, your father says hey."

As soon as he says the word *father,* my body reacts before my mind does. I step in front of Jude and fire at the same time they do. But I don't stop until they're down, shooting round after round into them.

"Fucking hell, Cherry, the one time I'm unarmed. Turn your gun and your badge in," he mocks, imitating what his captain must have said to him, but his voice sounds far away.

"Cherry?" I turn at the sound of his voice, or I try to, but my legs give out, and I fall.

"No, fuck no." Jude catches me before I hit the pavement, lowering me down gently as he checks me over.

"Oh, Jesus, hold on, Cherry." He pulls out his phone and starts yelling, but I can't make out the words, so I focus on the streetlamp above me that blinks on and off.

"Stay with me, sweetheart, an ambulance is on its way." His face is so pale, and I can see tears in his eyes. I don't like that.

"Shh, it's okay." I try to soothe him, but that just makes him suck in a sharp breath.

"Five minutes, Cherry, just five more minutes. You can do that. You're the strongest person I know."

"I'm so c... cold," I admit, my eyes feeling heavy and it's getting harder and harder to breathe.

"I promise, if you hold on, I'll take you home and you can snuggle up between Kai and me okay? We'll keep you warm, just please, hold the fuck on!" He's crying now, I can feel his tears dripping on my face.

"I have loved you since the first time I saw you, Diablo, did you know that?" I whisper, hearing the sirens in the distance.

"Yeah, baby, I always knew," he whispers back when a thought occurs to me.

"It's my birthday today. A year since you gave me my first kiss." I smile sadly.

"Stay with me, Cherry, and I'll mark every birthday with one."

"Kiss me," I whisper, feeling my tears track down the side of my face. I was so close, so close to having it all.

He leans over and presses his lips to mine as everything fades away.

It seems fitting that I gave him my first kiss and my last.

# CHAPTER FORTY

"I did this. This is my fault." I hear an anguish-filled voice.

"Yeah, you did. I'd kill you where you sit if I didn't think it would hurt her when she woke up," a second voice says.

When who wakes up?

"That's enough. If you guys want to have a pissing contest then, by all means, have at it, but fuck off outside before I rip off those dicks you seem so intent on measuring."

All these voices seem so familiar, but I can't put my finger on who they are.

I try to open my eyes, but my body flat out refuses to listen. I panic then, wondering what's wrong with me. I hear loud beeping and people yelling, but nothing is as loud as the roaring in my head. I feel a sharp prick in my arm before a soothing coolness washes over me, and I feel nothing once again.

"YOU NEED SOME SLEEP, Grim, I swear when she wakes up, I'll call you." I know that voice. *Megan.*

"I can't leave her, not again. Never again, Megan. I'm her big brother, I was supposed to protect her, and Christ, I failed at every turn. No wonder she hates me. I hate me too."

"It's gonna be okay, she just needs time."

"No, she doesn't owe me any more time. I mean, hasn't she waited enough? I earned every hateful word when I stayed away. I thought I was protecting her from the man I had turned into, but instead, I left her to fend off a monster."

"Grim," she says softly. Grim, that's right, my Drake is Grim now. But he's not my Drake anymore, he's Megan's.

"You see these? Viper and Zero found them when I sent them back to the trailer."

"What? I don't understand, what trailer?"

"The one where Vida and I grew up. I sent money home and made sure it was paid off so Mama didn't have to worry about it. I kept it all this time, hoping Viddy would know she would always have a safe place there, but she never went back."

"I don't think she knew, Grim. If she had, well I don't know. Maybe it held too many memories for her, but she would have sent me there to get me off the streets, that much I'm sure of."

"Yeah, I figured. I sent them to torch the place. Her guys are destroying the monsters from her life, but I wanted to get rid of the demons from her past. But then Zero found these hidden in a lockbox underneath a broken floorboard. It's the letters Vida wrote. All of them. Mama didn't mail them like she obviously told her she had, but why would she lie?"

"I don't know. Maybe she thought she was protecting her somehow," Megan offers.

"Don't Megs, don't make excuses for her. She cut me out and traded Vida's safety for her own happiness. She was always materialistic, but I just thought it was what trailer life did to people. But it was more than that. She wanted a glamorous lifestyle, and she didn't care who suffered on her way to reach it."

"Have you read them?"

"I'm psyching myself up," he admits while I still try to understand what he's saying. Mama never mailed them. But why?

I know though. It's everything Drake says and more because as I filter back through my memories without the veil of youthful innocence over my eyes, I see moments in time, snapshots my brain took and stored but refused to process.

Her face wincing when I flinched whenever Clyde touched me. The fleeting look of sorrow and guilt when she saw how unhappy I was or the moments I was scared. *She knew.* She knew what her husband was doing, and yet she stayed so she could drink champagne and wear her pretty diamonds. I guess love does have a price tag after all.

I feel numb, but not surprised. I think deep down, I always knew.

"Want me to read them to you?" she asks him softly.

I hear the sound of papers rustling before Megan's soft voice begins reading the words penned so long ago.

*Dear Drake,*

*It's been forever now since I've seen you, when are you coming home? Mom lost her job at the diner when it got burned down last month, but she has a new one at a club in the city. She has to work nights, so she lets me stay up late and watch tv as long as I don't answer the door for anyone. It's kind of boring, and watching SpongeBob just makes me think of you. What's it like where you are? I bet it's hot. Maybe you could send me a picture. I haven't gotten a letter in a while so I think some might be getting lost. Can you be extra careful when you write our address down? I know how messy your writing can be. I have to go now, I have school in the morning, and I have a spelling bee. Stupid David thinks he's going to beat me, but he won't. I've been practicing all week.*

*Anyways, love you.*

*Chicken.*

*Dear Drake,*

*Mom met a man at work, and she seems really happy, but*

*she's not here much anymore. I don't like being on my own all the time. The tv broke last week, and there's nothing to do once all my homework is done. Oh, I have a new book from the library though. It has a dragon in it, which everyone is afraid of, but really he's just sad and lonely. When are you coming home, Drake?*

*I miss you,*
*Chicken*

*Dear Drake,*

*Did I do something wrong? I don't know why you won't write back, but I promise I'm being good. I just miss you so much, Drake.*

*Please write back,*
*Chicken*

"Jesus," Drake's choked voice cuts Megan off for a minute. I want to open my eyes and see him, but my body still refuses to do anything but hold me hostage.

"You want me to stop?" she whispers, sounding choked up herself.

"No, she wrote them, she lived them. The least I can do is hear her now. She deserves that." I feel my heart crack at that. I want to keep it protected behind the walls I built, but hearing his pain is hurting me more than I thought it would.

Megan starts reading again, and I have no choice but to lie there in the dark and listen as she strips me bare.

*Dear Drake,*

*Mama is crying again. Her boyfriend won't leave his wife, and now they are having a baby. She says we'll never get out of here now. I'm not really sure what she means, but it makes her angry. I won't miss him; he smelled kinda weird.*

*I miss you Drake, please come home. Maybe then Mama won't cry so much.*

*Chicken*

*Dear Drake,*

*It's my birthday today. You forgot again, just like last year. I used my birthday wishes and wished for you to come home, but wishes don't come true, do they Drake? Mama is in love again. She says this one is different (she says that every time) she thinks he will get us out of the trailer park and into some big fancy house on the hill. I don't need fancy houses, Drake; I just need you. I've only met Clyde twice. Don't tell Mama, but I don't like him much. He looks at me strangely and makes my tummy feel twisty and not like the time you took me on the rollercoaster at the fair.*

*Please come back, I need you.*

*Chicken*

*Dear Drake,*

*You promised me you would always be here for me, that if the sky ever fell, you would protect me. Well, my sky is falling Drake, so where the hell are you? Mom is sick, real sick Drake. We need you; I need you. Clyde is moving us in with him, but I don't want to go. He freaks me out. Sometimes, I wake up in the night and see him standing in the shadows watching me. He says he's just protecting me, but I don't feel very safe anymore.*

*Please, please, please, come back.*

*Chicken.*

I can hear crying, but I don't know who it belongs to, I'm too caught up in the words I wrote.

*Drake,*

*Nobody knows what's wrong with Mama, but she gets sicker every day, especially if Clyde visits. I think she's allergic to his toxic personality, but I don't tell her that. There's no point, she won't listen. She never does. We move tomorrow, up to a fancy house on the hill, just like she always wanted. She thinks Clyde is her hero, and maybe he is to her, but I see him for who he really is. He's the villain of the story. He might wear fancy suits and drive a nice car, but I know he's a bad man Drake. His touches might be soft in the dark of night, but I can feel the violence and excitement in his trembling hands. I hate him Drake, I hate him so much. Mama said this has to be my last letter to you. A new house means a fresh start, but she only sees what she wants to. She thinks you're dead, but I know you're not. I'd feel it if you were gone. Sometimes I wish you were because then I would know that you didn't come save me because you couldn't, not because you didn't care about me anymore. I don't know what I did to make you stop loving me; I tried to do everything you asked of me. I guess I just wasn't enough.*

    *Bye Drake.*

    *Chicken.*


"Oh God," Grim chokes out when Megan reads the final letter I sent. I can hear them both openly crying, and I can feel my tears running over my cheeks.

Hearing those words read back to me hurts like someone has picked a scab and made the healing wound beneath it start to bleed again. But I'm not that girl anymore. I'm Gemini, God fucking dammit.

I fight, giving it everything I have, and feel my eyelids flutter. The slight movement gives me hope, so I keep pushing until I manage to open them, the bright light making me snap them shut again immediately.

"Vida?" Drake's voice sounds beside me. I feel hands on my face smoothing my hair back, so I blink my eyes open once more and see Drake staring down at me with wet eyes.

"Welcome back, Chicken."

WITH THE TUBE removed from my throat and about a thousand pillows behind me, I feel a little more comfortable and alert. Well, about as comfortable as someone can be when they've been shot in the chest.

I look around the room and see Wyatt, Drake, and

Megan, but no sign of the Reid brothers. I try not to react and give away how much it hurts, but it feels like my chest has been cracked open again, and I'm bleeding out.

I focus on one thing at a time and turn to look at Drake, who is sitting next to my bed, watching me warily.

"I'm sorry, Vida, for everything. I didn't know, it's no excuse but I swear I didn't. When I came back I tried to find you, I followed every lead, investigated every sighting. I never stopped, but you were just—"

"A ghost," I finish, knowing it would have been near impossible to find me. "I heard you reading the letters. I know what Mama did. I can't pretend that I'm okay with what you did, and I'm not sure we'll ever get back what we lost but," I look over at Megan who is standing next to Wyatt, his arm wrapped around her shoulder, "I'm willing to see where things will go."

Drake takes a deep, shuddering breath, his shoulders relaxing a little. He reaches over and slips his hand in mine. I grip it, although I still don't have much strength.

"I forgive you, Drake," I whisper as he presses his head into the mattress beside me.

I feel him shake, but nobody says anything, letting him have his moment. Wyatt turns Megan into his arms and holds her, looking at me, asking me silently if I'm okay.

I nod. I will be.

"Where is everyone else?" I swallow, wincing because that shit hurts, before asking what I really want to know. "Where are Kai and Jude?"

Drake snorts from beside me, lifting his head and wiping a hand over his face.

"Those guys are fucking insane. I'd be kidnapping you away if I didn't know how much they loved you."

"You didn't answer my question," I point out.

This time it's Wyatt who laughs. "Someone hurt their woman, where the fuck do you think they are?"

I think about it, remembering the gun firing, the guy's words.

"The shooter was after Jude. Zodiac sent a hitman—" I pause, looking at Drake. "They went after Zodiac."

"Yeah, you could say that. Zodiac is dead. He supposedly killed himself, but I've never heard of anyone cutting open their stomach and hanging themselves with their own intestines before."

I shake my head, yeah, that's not likely.

"Then any business or contact Zodiac had was either signed over to you or burned to the ground. Kristoff Libernesh is dead, his trafficking business shut down. Cash and William are working on relocating people now. All the division heads are making sure business runs smoothly. It's a sight to be seen for sure. The streets are running with blood, but it seems, sister dearest, your empire is stronger than ever."

"Where are they?" I ask for what feels like the tenth time. If they don't tell me, I'm going to climb off this fucking bed and find them myself.

"We're right here."

I look up sharply at the sound of Kai's voice and sob, seeing him standing side by side with Jude.

Drake stands and places a kiss on my forehead before walking over and taking Megan from Wyatt. She looks over at me and waves, and Wyatt offers me a chin lift as everyone leaves except Jude and Kai.

"You came back. I thought—" I whisper as they stalk toward me, one on each side of the bed.

"We're not going anywhere, Red," Kai tells me, kissing me softly. I feel my tears start up again, can taste them as he continues to kiss me for a moment before pulling away.

I turn to Jude, who swipes his thumb over the apple of my cheek. "If you ever pull a stunt like that again, I will blister your ass," he growls before his lips are on mine, harder than Kai's, a touch of anger still riding him.

He pulls back and glares at me, but I just offer him a smile. I promise nothing. I'd take a thousand bullets for this man, for both of them.

They each sit beside me, their moves looking almost synchronized as they take one of my hands in each of theirs.

"I heard you both. I think you were arguing." I look at Jude and shake my head. "This isn't your fault. I stepped in front of that bullet."

"I was the one who took you to him in the first place—" he argues, but I cut him off.

"He would have found me anyway if he hadn't already. Looking back, that whole situation just seems too convenient. He sure as shit didn't seem surprised to see me."

Jude considers my words, but he doesn't say anything. It will take time to convince the stubborn ass.

"And Kai," I turn to look at him, "you should really know better than to throw stones when you live in a glasshouse. It wasn't that long ago you were shooting at me, and let's not forget the whole taser thing. Actually, now that I think about it, you both might be more trouble than you're worth," I tease.

"Tough shit, Cherry, because you're stuck with us now."

"Am I? Both of you? Because I love you both too much to choose."

"Both of us," Kai nods, "but that means Cash and Will need to keep their fucking lips to themselves or I'll cut them off. I'll share with Jude, but you are off fucking limits to everyone else," he warns.

"I don't want anyone else. How greedy do you think I am?"

"You know your girl Megan has three men, right?" Jude points out.

"Yeah, but her men seem slightly more sane than mine. You'll keep me busy. Now all I need is for you to bust me out of here."

"Whoa, no can do, Red. You need to stay at least for a little longer." Kai shakes his head.

"Oh, come on, I'm fine."

"No," Jude snaps, "you almost died in my arms. You crashed in the ambulance twice and coded again when they got you here. You will stay here and get better if I have to strap you to the damn bed myself!" His chest heaves.

"Hey, I'm sorry. I'm okay, I'll stay," I soothe, looking to Kai for help.

"We can't lose you, Red. I'm with Jude. Rest up and heal. We have the rest of our lives to figure everything else out."

"I didn't mean to snap, but that night will haunt me for the rest of my days," Jude admits, lifting his hand and rubbing it against his face. "You should be dead, it's a fucking miracle you're awake and talking at all. That bullet should have gone straight through your heart, only it ricocheted and grazed it instead, puncturing your lung and nicking an artery. You're down to your last life now, Cherry, so for fuck's sake, take care of yourself."

"I will, and with you guys by my side, I have a feeling nothing will touch me again. I'm gonna nap now." I smile, unable to fight the exhaustion any longer. It takes a lot of energy to heal, and right now, I'm as weak as a newborn kitten.

I'm not worried though, it won't last forever, and with my guys at my side, I'll eventually be stronger than I ever was.

After all, we have a city to run.

And a mother fucking empire to rule.


The End

# ALSO BY CANDICE WRIGHT

## THE UNDERESTIMATED SERIES

The Queen of Carnage: An Underestimated Novel Book One

https://books2read.com/u/47EMrj

The Princess of Chaos: An Underestimated Novel Book Two

https://books2read.com/u/mBOX9Z

The Reign of Kings: An Underestimated Novel Book Three

https://books2read.com/u/b55AL7

## THE PHOENIX PROJECT DUET

From the Ashes: Book one

https://books2read.com/u/bO65pN

From the Fire: Book Two

https://books2read.com/u/38ZQ9w

## THE INHERITANCE SERIES

Rewriting yesterday

https://books2read.com/u/3JVj6v

In this moment

https://books2read.com/u/bxvnJd

The Promise of tomorrow

https://books2read.com/u/bowEy1

The Complete Inheritance Series Box Set

https://books2read.com/u/mBO7ev

THE FOUR HORSEWOMEN OF THE APOCALYPSE
SERIES

The Pures

https://books2read.com/u/mdGl1y

CAUTIOUS: An Everyday Heroes World Novel

https://amzn.to/2XPn2Oa

# ACKNOWLEDGMENTS

Nichole Witholder – Cover Magician.

Tanya Oemig – My incredible editor - AKA miracle worker, who goes above and beyond.

Missy Stewart - Proofreader and lifesaver.

Gina Wynn - Formatting Queen.

My girl squad. I'm blessed to have such amazing, strong and talented women in my life.

My Beta Angels – Rachel, Sue, Julie and Jessica. You ladies are the bee's knees. I will never be able to tell you how much I love and appreciate everything you do for me.

Thais, Aspen & Catherine – My mighty Alpha's. There isn't enough words in the dictionary to express my gratitude for you.

My readers – You guys are everything to me. I am in awe

of the love and support I have received. Thanks for taking a chance on me and on each of the books that I write.

Remember, If you enjoy it, please leave a review.

# ABOUT THE AUTHOR

Candice is a romance writer who lives in the UK with her long-suffering partner and her three slightly unhinged children. As an avid reader herself, you will often find her curled up with a book from one of her favourite authors, drinking her body weight in coffee. If you would like to find out more, here are her stalker links:

FB Group https://www.facebook.com/groups/949889858546168/

Amazon http://amazon.com/author/candicewrightauthor

Instagram https://www.instagram.com/authorcandicewright/

FB Page https://www.facebook.com/candicewrightauthor/

Twitter https://twitter.com/Candice47749980

BookBub https://www.bookbub.com/profile/candice-wright

Goodreads https://www.goodreads.com/author/show/
18582893.Candice_M_Wright

Printed by Amazon Italia Logistica S.r.l.
Torrazza Piemonte (TO), Italy

17188019R00237